Moscow USA

Gordon Stevens is the author of eight novels, including the bestselling *Provo* and *Kara's Game*. He lives with his family in the New Forest.

D0892631

GORDON STEVENS

MOSCOW USA

HarperCollins*Publishers*

HarperCollins*Publishers*
77–85 Fulham Palace Road,
Hammersmith, London W6 8JB

This paperback slightly revised edition 1998
1 3 5 7 9 8 6 4 2

First published in Great Britain by
HarperCollins*Publishers* 1997

ISBN 0 00 649782 9

Set in Aldus

Printed and bound in Great Britain by
Caledonian International Book Manufacturing Ltd, Glasgow

A great many people in London, Washington, New York and Moscow helped with this book. Because of their pasts, and in some cases their futures, few of them would wish to be identified. They know who they are.

The company Omega is based on an actual organization. Its name and certain of its details have been changed to protect it, its founders and its personnel.

Gordon Stevens
Moscow

Moscow USA

ALPHA

The beginning. The first letter of the Greek alphabet.
Until the dissolution of the Soviet Union in December 1991, the Special Forces unit of the KGB.

OMEGA

The ending. The last letter of the Greek alphabet.
An investigation/security firm comprising mainly ex-Alpha members in the new Moscow.

ALPHA/OMEGA

The first and the last.
The basic reason for being, the most important part.

ALPHA
the beginning

The weather that morning was hot, which was one of the things those questioned later would remember. In addition to the personal things, and the fact that Hurricane Bob was beating a circle off Florida and threatening to wreak havoc up the East Coast. Items of no consequence to the Dark Suits. And even then the woman with the child and the salesman and the Mormon preacher would never know the real reason for the visit. There were others, of course, a total of 184 passengers on the two flights, plus air crew and staff at the relevant airports, but the woman and the salesman and the preacher were those in whom the investigators had a special interest, because they had not only caught flight 2171 but had made phone calls at the same places and the same times as the man called Joshua.

The airport, four miles west of town, was modern but small. Rolling Idaho wheatfields around it, the occasional poplar tree, and two low hangars. The terminal itself was single-storey and glass-fronted, one room serving both arrivals and departures. The check-in desk was to the left, the baggage X-ray machine was in the centre, opposite the entrance, and the coffee and candy machines, the pay phones and the mail box, were against the wall to the right. Flights in and out every hour, but only to a handful of destinations; the parking lot never full and the drop-offs and pick-ups quick and easy.

The Shermans arrived fifty minutes before departure, the three of them crammed into the front seat of the Chevy pick-up. Annie Sherman was thirty-two years old, her face and hands tanned with the seasons, though the first tell-tale crow's-feet of worry were wrinkled at the sides of her eyes. Her husband Ted was two years older, tall, with cornflower-blue eyes. The suit he wore uncomfortably that morning was dark navy, and the neck of the shirt was slightly too tight. Ted and Annie Sherman had been married eight years and struggled against the odds, plus the occasional flood and the interest on a bank loan, to run 300 acres east of town, on the road to Genesee. Their daughter Mary was six, the Chevy was second-hand, and a year from today the bank would foreclose and the three would stand silent as their home and their worldly goods, for which they had fought and sweated and bled, were auctioned in front of them. Today, however, the mood was lighter: Annie taking Mary to visit the girl's grandmother on the occasion of her seventieth birthday.

As they arrived a Toyota Landcruiser pulled away.

Ted hauled their bags from the back, waited as they stood in the queue and glanced at his watch. The meeting with the bank was at nine thirty.

'You go,' Annie told him. 'We're okay.'

'Better call Mom.' The concern furrowed his brow. 'Let her know that the flight's on time.'

. . . What did she do then? the Dark Suits would ask. FBI, the Dark Suits had said. Investigating someone running a scam and the person might have been on the flight.

Ted left, she would tell them; she and Mary checked in, then they went for a coffee. From the machines by the far wall, she would explain, even though they hadn't asked, because that was the way they were, expecting the detail and wanting you to give them more than you thought you knew.

Anything she'd missed, they would come back at Annie; how about any phone calls? Because she was on the airport security video as making one, though they wouldn't tell her. Called Mom, she would remember, told her that she and Mary would be arriving on time and confirming the pick-up. Who else was around? they would ask; anyone else making a call at that time, anything she remembered about the other people making calls?

A salesman – she would screw up her eyes in concentration. And a bible-puncher, short hair and beaming faith. No one else. And they would wait, because they knew she was wrong. One other person, she would suddenly remember. Somewhere in his late forties or early fifties, well-cut suit, good-looking but without being obvious. Couldn't get through to the number he was calling, because he hung up without speaking then tried again.

Anything else about the man in the suit? they would ask. Because you can't really see much on the security video. Even though, as far as we can tell, there's nobody else we know at the airport at that time. But if there had been, Joshua wouldn't have made the call . . .

Good-looking woman, Joshua thought; nice-looking girl; life taking its toll on the woman even though she was fighting to mask it. The woman and the girl left the phones and carried their bags to the X-ray machine. He dialled again. Not the same number, because the first he had tried had been unavailable rather than busy. The tone he heard was high-pitched and whining. Both direct lines closed down, he understood; one might be unfortunate, two wouldn't be a coincidence. Therefore it was already under way, the man to whom he wished to speak cut off and isolated, even though he probably still thought he was surrounded by his friends. Even though he was one of the two most important men in the world.

It was still thirty minutes to the flight. Joshua crossed to the seats and wrote the letter. No name because that would be a security risk . . . *When you receive this*, he began, *it will be over. If I have been able to achieve what I am about to do, then I will tell you; if not, then others might not* . . . He finished it, read it but did not sign it, folded it once and slid it into the envelope, sealed the envelope but left it blank, folded it, slid it into a second envelope, and addressed and stamped the second. Then he rose and walked to the mail box, hesitated for a second, slid it in, waited till he heard it drop, walked to the pay phones, and called the number in New York.

Jack Kincaid ignored the file on the coffee table in front of him and looked at the man opposite him. The safe house was on the outskirts of Miami's Little Havana. Outside the temperature was closing on 95, inside it was almost chilly, the drapes drawn and the air conditioning humming slightly.

Kincaid was late thirties and deceptively big build. The man three metres away was slim and urbane, smart suit, hair greased back and thin moustache. Cuban diplomat, the Miami office had said: access to secret police records and knowledge of Russian intelligence activities in Central America, both past and present. Anti-Fidel, despite his background and position, and wanting to trade.

Call for you, Kincaid was informed. Perfect timing, he thought. He nodded at the Cuban and went to the next room.

'Jack, this is Bram.' O'Bramsky was deputy head of division. 'You're needed in New York. Briefing here first. My assistant will pick you up at National.'

'When?' Kincaid asked.

'It's an immediate.' Immediate was a message prefix. Immediate meant NOW. PRIORITY. DROP EVERYTHING. Only one prefix ranked above immediate. Flash. And flash meant the bombs were about to fall. 'The DCI has been notified. At this moment he's briefing the President.'

DCI – the Director of Central Intelligence, the head of CIA.

'On my way,' Kincaid told O'Bramsky.

Kincaid's flight from Miami to Washington National was on a commercial 737. An Agency plane would not have covered the distance any quicker. At National he was third off. He strode quickly through the terminal, picked up O'Bramsky's assistant, followed him to the unmarked Chevy in the satellite parking area, and slid into the back seat without asking what was running. The driver left National, turned right along George Washington Parkway, the Potomac glistening on the right, and began to climb through the trees. Fifteen minutes later the car stopped by the elevators in the underground parking lot beneath the large off-white building tucked amongst the woodlands of Virginia. The first elevator was engaged. Kincaid pressed the other button, rode the executive elevator to the division, and was escorted immediately to the bubble.

Each division had its own secure room – no walls on the outside of the building, no windows, even internally; electronic grids, white noise and lead-lined drapes. Regular sweeps just to make sure. Conference table in the centre and communications facilities along one wall.

Jameson, O'Bramsky and Miller were waiting. Others as well: the heads of operations and security, plus counter-intelligence. But Jameson, O'Bramsky and Miller were the ones that mattered.

Grere Jameson, forty-five years old, tall, with the first grey playing in his hair. Chief of Soviet and Eastern Europe Division for the past three years.

O'Bramsky, two years older and Jameson's deputy, white hair, hands like the lumberjack's his father had been, and brain like an IBM mainframe.

Ed Miller, early forties and Russia desk chief.

Kincaid sat down, was given a coffee, and the briefing began. No other formalities, because there was no time.

O'Bramsky faced him across the table. 'Three hours ago someone calling himself Hemmings contacted the New York office and asked to speak with Leo Panelli.' Kincaid had worked with Panelli, starting in Berlin. 'Hemmings, it transpires, is KGB. He and Leo know each other because they both worked the United Nations. Leo is in Paris on leave. Hemmings said it was an immediate. Because of this we arranged for Hemmings to speak with Leo. Before they spoke, Leo sent us this cable.'

O'Bramsky passed the de-crypt across the table. Kincaid read it once.

The Director – on the first line.

The security classification – SECRET – on the second. Only FLASH messages warranted TOP SECRET.

The slug, the routing indicator for the computers which would receive the cable at Langley, on the next. Slugs related cables to specific projects, operators, agents or geographic areas.

The slug on the de-crypt in front of Kincaid was AMSNOW. The first two letters, AM, were a prefix for Soviet Division, and the next four, SNOW, indicated a general message within that division.

I have been notified by New York office that a contact identifying himself as Hemmings has been in communication. Hemmings stated he wished to speak with me and said it was an immediate. NY station will give him a direct number into Paris station. Hemmings is a private code between the individual and myself.

Kincaid passed the de-crypt back.

O'Bramsky took it and slid him another. 'Leo then sent this follow-up.'

Never refer to someone and give their identity in the same cable, Kincaid thought. Perhaps Panelli was old school, despite encryption; perhaps it was the game; perhaps Panelli was aware he was about to send Langley ballistic. Because send them ballistic he had – DCI, the President, briefings in the Sit Room, now the eagles locked in the bubble and the whole show running like there was no tomorrow.

Kincaid read the single line.

Hemmings is Joshua.

He handed the cable back and waited for O'Bramsky to continue.

'Joshua wants a face-to-face, but Leo can't make it back till tomorrow and Joshua says tomorrow will be too late. Leo suggested you and Joshua agreed. At this point we don't know whether Joshua's buying or selling, though we assume it's the latter. Until Leo gets back, you're holding Joshua's hand.'

'You're saying there's a chance that Joshua's defecting?'

'Possibly, but we're still not sure.'

At the other end of the conference table the eagles still threw the arguments between themselves. Reasons for the Joshua contact. Implications. Anything it might spin into or rebound off. Joshua's personality. Was Joshua under stress or had Joshua been drinking? How had he conducted himself in the past and how was he conducting himself now? Had he shown any previous signs of such an approach? What might Joshua know? How much did he know about the other side and what might he know or want to know about theirs? Was the contact genuine or the first stage of a sting?

O'Bramsky took a mouthful of coffee. 'Nothing's happening that might indicate why else Joshua's been in touch. The DCI's seen the President; according to the White House and the State Department there's nothing in the pipeline which would impact on a defection, or which might be affected by it. Moscow station also reports that everything's quiet. The Kremlin's closed down

6

for the summer and Gorbachev is on holiday in the Crimea.'

Gorbachev the architect and champion of the new Russia.

'Except . . . ?' Kincaid asked.

'Except when Joshua made contact with New York station he said it was an immediate, and when he spoke to Leo he upgraded it to flash.' The bombs were about to fall. 'When Leo said he could be state-side tomorrow, Joshua said that tomorrow would be too late.'

'Who's Joshua?' Kincaid asked.

Bram looked at him across the table, then the IBM mainframe switched on. 'Mikhail Sergeyevich Buskov. Born Leningrad. Married with one daughter. Former KGB *rezident* at the United Nations, also KGB *rezident* in Washington DC.'

A *rezident* was the Soviet equivalent of chief of station.

Christ, Kincaid thought. 'What's Buskov's present status?'

'Mikhail Buskov is now a major-general in the First Chief Directorate at KGB headquarters in Yasenevo, Moscow. We believe he's behind some of the financial scams the Directorate is running to finance its overseas operations.' O'Bramsky paused. 'He's the biggest one we'll ever get, Jack. Make sure you bring him home.'

Kincaid nodded. 'How did he get in touch?'

'As I say, he phoned the New York station.'

'Where from?'

O'Bramsky half-smiled. 'You're not going to believe this.'

'Try me.'

'Joshua was calling from Moscow.' He saw the disbelief in Kincaid's eyes. 'Not Moscow as in USSR. Moscow as in Idaho, Moscow USA.'

Served by the airport four miles out of town.

'Arrangements and timetable?' Kincaid asked.

'Joshua's inbound to New York from Seattle. He's due to arrive at Newark at 1800. We've already spoken to him and will speak again when he lands. He'll be directed through a number of cut-outs. After that he'll be on his way to you. The contact is at the Famiglia restaurant on East 54th. You'll be waiting. The security boys will be there as well, in case the opposition finds out or beats the surveillance and tries a heist.'

'Who's riding shotgun?'
'Langley's bringing in the best.'

Erickson received the call fourteen minutes and thirty seconds after the hour. Daniel Michael Erickson was thirty-nine years old, tall, eyes shading between blue and slate-grey, and a body strength concealed beneath the loose sweater and slacks he habitually wore.

'You're needed in New York,' his controller told him on his cellphone. 'Usual communications.'

Erickson closed the call and returned to the North End area of the city. Boston was warm but quiet, already tightening slightly in anticipation of Hurricane Bob which was forecast to hit the city sometime the following afternoon.

He changed into a suit, collar and tie, checked the credentials he was carrying, left the safe house, walked three blocks, took a cab to the airport, and caught the next shuttle to La Guardia. The nerves were already eating him. No fear, no edge – he remembered what his instructor had told him.

At La Guardia he left the plane, cleared the arrivals gate, and automatically scoured the sea of faces for the one that was out of place or the eyes that turned away from his. Perhaps he was getting too old for this, Erickson sometimes thought; perhaps the image of his wife and daughter played on his mind too much nowadays.

He made his way to the pay phones, called the contact number, switched phones, and waited for the next instructions.

Kincaid told the driver to drop him two blocks from La Famiglia and walked down the street. Joshua's flight would be landing in ten minutes; between an hour and ninety minutes after that Joshua would be stepping out of a cab in front of where Kincaid now stood, and entering the restaurant. He checked up and down the street, checked the houses in front and behind. The parked cars were a problem, because the cab dropping Joshua would have to stop in the middle of the street. But it would only be a problem if the Langley tails decided that someone else was sitting on Joshua, and if they did, then the meet would already have been

8

aborted at one of the cut-outs, and Joshua would call the contact number the next day for fresh instructions. Except Joshua had been specific that tomorrow was too late.

He concentrated on La Famiglia. The front was white and double-fronted, blue woodwork round the windows, and dining areas either side of the door. There was a bar in the middle, according to the briefing, men's room at the rear with a back door on to the alleyway behind. When the meet went down, the security section would be sitting in the restaurant, with more in a car at the rear in case the opposition tried to come in the back, or in case they had to take Joshua out that way in a hurry. Plus the faceless ones, who would oversee everything.

Kincaid left the street, checked the rear, walked back to the pick-up vehicle, and returned to the safe house.

'Code name Caesar,' Daniel Erickson was informed. He switched phones. 'La Famiglia restaurant, on East 54th,' he was informed. He switched phones again. Typical organization – he cursed quietly; typical concern with security. He was carrying a cellphone, but cellphones were notoriously insecure.

'What does Caesar look like?' he asked.

'Tall, early fifties, dark hair, wearing a dark-blue suit and carrying a brown leather attaché case. He'll be arriving by cab.'

'Any opposition?' Erickson was always careful.

'Shouldn't be.'

Erickson took a cab to the World Trade Center then another to East 52nd and walked the rest. East 54th was nondescript. He checked up and down the street, checked the streets and alleys behind it and running off it. Walked past the entrance to La Famiglia and imagined the moment Caesar stepped from the cab. The parked cars might have been a problem, because he might have lost line of vision as Caesar stepped through them, on to the pavement, and into the restaurant. Except the position he had already selected was high above, from where he could view all around him.

Joshua has arrived at Newark, Kincaid was informed. Joshua has been code-named Caesar for the tails. The tails in place at each

9

of the cut-outs, the boys from security ready to move into position inside and outside La Famiglia, and the game running. Joshua has made contact with Langley, O'Bramsky updated him. Joshua has taken a cab from Newark and is inbound for the first cut-out. Joshua is approaching the first cut-out.

Kincaid left the safe house and was driven to East 54th.

Caesar is approaching the first cut-out, the tails reported back. Caesar is looking clean. Caesar is leaving the first cut-out and is still looking clean.

Kincaid walked down 54th and into the restaurant. The dining area was in two sections, a bar in the middle, and a corridor to the bathrooms at the rear. The tables were covered with gingham cloths and the waiters wore black waistcoats. Half the tables were occupied. He sat at the bar, in a position from which he could see the door, and ordered a Jack Daniels. Caesar is approaching the second cut-out, the shadows reported back. Caesar is at the second cut-out. Caesar is looking clean. Kincaid left the bar and checked the bathroom, checked the corridor and the door at the rear, and made sure the door would open.

In his position above 54th Erickson swept the street for any sign of the opposition.

Kincaid's cellphone rang. 'Mac. It's Dennis. Managed to get those tickets for the Yankees game. The tenth be okay for you?' Joshua through the last cut-out and with him in ten minutes. 'Sounds good. I'll see you.'

Erickson scanned the streets and pavements below for the first indication that something might be wrong. The cellphone rang. In the silence of his concentration the noise was like thunder. He pressed the button and held the set close to his left ear. 'Caesar is clean. He'll be with you in ten.' The nerves washed away and the calm and the cold took their place.

The cab stopped outside the restaurant. Middle of the street, because of the cars parked either side. Too soon, Kincaid knew, and looked away from the window. Thank God for the security boys – those he could see but especially those he couldn't.

Erickson saw the couple step out. Man and woman, mid-twenties, the man paying the driver and the woman walking between the parked cars and waiting on the pavement for him, then the two of them going into the restaurant. His line of vision had remained unimpaired as the woman stepped between the parked cars. Significant, or just chance that a couple arrived just before Caesar was due?

Six minutes now, five, and counting down. Another cab slowed then moved away without stopping. A man walked up 54th and entered the restaurant. Wrong age, wrong description.

One minute. Kincaid ran the Jack Daniels around the glass and told himself to relax.

The cab stopped and Joshua stepped out.

On time, Kincaid thought.

Right age, Daniel Erickson thought, right description. Dark-blue suit, early fifties, brown leather attaché case.

Joshua paid the driver, stepped between the parked cars and stood on the pavement.

Kincaid placed the glass on the table and moved slightly so that he could view the door without appearing to do so.

In the building opposite Erickson reached to his right.

Daniel Michael Erickson did not exist. As a driving licence and a social security number, as a name on a credit card and an entry on the passenger list from Boston to La Guardia. As a cover.

But not as a person.

Nikolai Alexandrovich Sherenko did.

The target's more important than you could ever imagine, Vorkov his controller had told him; make sure you take him out.

Sherenko held his breath gently, so that his body and mind were still and controlled, and squeezed the trigger.

The last shuttle of the evening touched down at Boston thirty seconds early. Sherenko hurried through the emptying terminal, took a cab to the city centre, then a second to the North End. By midnight he was in the two-room safe house between the wine bar and the boutique.

The Black Label was in the drinks cabinet. Sherenko would have preferred Stolichnaya, but vodka might have threatened his cover. He threw a handful of ice into a glass, topped it up, and switched on the television. Perhaps he was right, perhaps he really was too old for this game; perhaps he was thinking of his family too much. At least Vorkov had talked about going home soon.

The local stations were all running news reports on the progress of Hurricane Bob up the eastern seaboard and the threat to Boston and the surrounding area the following day. He flicked to CNN, went through to the bathroom, began to strip, and heard the sudden change in tone of the newscaster.

'This is a news flash. We are just getting reports from Moscow that there has been a coup in Russia. President Gorbachev has been placed under house arrest in his holiday dacha in the Crimea. First reports say that hard-liners from the KGB and the Red Army have taken over.'

The morgue was white-tiled and silent, an echo somewhere down a corridor and the smell of disinfectant in his nostrils. There were no staff present, no pathologists or attendants, no clerks to note down the details and ask for a signature against release of a corpse. Kincaid stood alone and stared at the body bag on the slab in the centre of the floor.

I was point man for you – for the past hours he had tried to push the confessional from his mind. I was babysitting you, Joshua; I was the one who was supposed to bring you through. I was the one in whose hands you put your faith and your trust and your life. And I let you down.

He ran his fingers along the body bag.

So what game *were* you playing, Joshua? Was whatever you were doing connected to the events in the Soviet Union? Langley was going ape-shit, of course: Langley and State and the White House and Christ only knew who else. Tanks on the streets of Moscow. Swan Lake being run non-stop on Soviet television, and the new order, the new Russia, which Gorbachev was promising, suddenly under threat and the image of a return to the bad old days looming large.

He unzipped the body bag and looked at the face.

The Agency had covered itself, of course. Pulled everything and everybody out of East 54th, so that even in the handful of seconds before the first blue and whites of the NYPD arrived there was no link. Just a businessman with an attaché case shot through the back. No ID, no name or plastic or driving licence.

Plus Langley had made certain arrangements. The Club took care of its own, even though they were from different sides. So not even Langley, in a way especially not Soviet Division, wanted Joshua to spend the statutory two weeks in a freezer in the county morgue at Belle Vue, then be consigned to a city burial along with the other John Does. Therefore Langley had made the call – discreet, person to person, the same way that Joshua had sought to contact Leo Panelli.

No autopsy, though, no incision in the chest, no rib cage cut open. Partly because Joshua had only been of use alive, partly to say to the opposition: he's yours, we had nothing to do with it, so take him home and lay him to rest where his wife and his daughter can mourn over him. Whatever lies you tell them about where and how he died, because lie you will. As we would.

In forty seconds the footsteps would come down the corridor.

'Sorry, my friend . . .'

He zipped up the bag and left.

Sherenko stood at the window and looked across the street at the first winds and the first black rain.

The epicentre of Hurricane Bob was scheduled to hit Boston shortly after four. Now it was 3.45 and the sky was black. Down the coast torrential rain and winds were whipping off roofs and throwing trees in the air as if they were the devil's playthings. In Boston the streets were deserted and the city waited, emergency services on full alert.

On the television set in the corner of the room CNN was running updates from Moscow, retired military and intelligence specialists being wheeled in to comment, and politicians renting their opinions about what might or might not happen.

Sherenko turned from the window and flicked back to one of the local channels.

'The epicentre of Hurricane Bob is five minutes from Boston.' The newscaster was tense. 'Do not go outside. Repeat, do not go outside.'

Sherenko went to the bedroom, stripped, and put on shorts and Nikes.

'The epicentre of Hurricane Bob is one minute from Boston.' The newscaster's voice was almost shrill. The rain outside was horizontal and the trees bent in the wind.

'Hurricane Bob is one minute, repeat, one minute, from Boston city centre.'

Sherenko stepped outside, locked the door behind him, and began to run.

Kincaid left Langley and drove to the bar on the edge of McLean which the old-timers used as one of their watering holes. O'Bramsky was waiting for him. The evening was closing in and the bottle of Black Label was on the table. Kincaid settled in a chair and nodded as O'Bramsky filled his glass. 'So what's new from Moscow station?'

'A handful of politicians are standing up and being counted.' O'Bramsky ran his fingers through his white hair. 'Yeltsin's in Moscow and on his way to the White House. The first crowds are gathering outside to defend the building against the army and the KGB, but there are reports that KGB Alpha teams are already in the building with orders to assassinate him.'

'What about Joshua? How does he relate to what's going down in Moscow?'

'At this stage nobody's sure. One theory is that he knew of the plans for the putsch but didn't know who was behind it, therefore didn't know who to alert in order to stop it, so he contacted us.'

They both knew what Kincaid was going to say.

'And we let him down.'

Bram refilled their glasses. 'Don't take it personally, Jack.'

'Difficult not to, Bram.'

Difficult to stand in the morgue at Belle Vue and not think that you betrayed the man in the bag. Difficult not to try and work out what little thing you might have done that would have made the difference.

He swilled the Black Label around the glass, downed it in one, reached across the table and poured them each another. 'Funny,

14

isn't it? In five years nobody will remember what happened in August '91. Nobody will remember the attempt to depose Gorbachev.'

'What are you getting at, Jack?'

'I guess that some things you remember for the fact that they were a crossroads for the world. Some things you forget, even though at the time the world thought they were cataclysmic. Some things you remember for what they meant to you as an individual.'

O'Bramsky looked across the table at him. 'Like I said, Jack, don't take it personally.'

At eleven the next morning Kincaid took his seat before the panel investigating the Joshua affair. No Jameson or O'Bramsky, he noted. Miller was present, so Ed had covered his ass, and thank Christ for that. Some faces from the seventh floor, plus a woman he didn't know. Early forties, good-looking, ash-blond hair and cut-glass English accent. So London had been cut in on the deal somewhere along the line and were now demanding their pound of flesh.

In Moscow the crowd defending the White House had grown to a hundred thousand, the KGB Alpha teams which had been sent to assassinate Yeltsin had changed sides and were now protecting him, key units of the army were also going over, and the coup showed every sign of collapsing.

Where were you when you were first informed of Joshua . . . ? the questioning began. When did you first hear the code-name Joshua . . . ? Who told you and who did you speak to after that point . . . ?

The Leningrad sun was hot on her back, and the sweat ran in streams down the faces of the men carrying the coffin. Anna Buskova stood at her mother's side and held her mother's arm. An hour earlier, before they had screwed down the lid, she had kissed her father goodbye for the last time.

Love you, she told him again now. Remember so many things, remember the toys you made me when I was young and before you and Mamma had any money, remember how you were away so much later. Remember the porcelain horseman you gave me.

Remember not just the gifts you brought back when you returned, but how you brought them back. As if they were no more or no less precious than the dolls you made for me at the kitchen table.

And now, my father, you are dead. Now you lie in your KGB uniform, and the other generals have come to say goodbye, though the times are strange and the conversation before the service was muted and conspiratorial, as it will be after.

The coup has ended, probably Communism as well. All of which is irrelevant to me because the only thing I will remember about August 1991 is the fact that my father, whom I loved dearly, was taken from me.

The KGB still takes care of its own, though. So that when your body was returned to us, after you had suffered the heart attack, you were already in dress uniform, your eyes closed and your hands folded in peace across your chest.

A heron flew overhead. She heard the ruffle of its wings and looked up. The guard of honour snapped to attention and the first volley echoed into the sky.

The December snow was on the ground and the sky was a dark threatening grey. Anna Buskova picked her way between the headstones, the white of the snow like mantles on them, till she came to the mound in the corner. In the spring, when the earth had settled, they would erect a proper headstone, now the grave was marked by a simple cross.

The snow fell from the sky again, and her hands and feet were cold. She removed her gloves and took the envelope from the pocket of her greatcoat. The envelope was thick, as if something was folded inside it. She took the second envelope from it, then the letter from inside it. The envelopes had been delivered by an American friend ten days earlier, when she was in Moscow. The snow was falling more heavily now. She brushed the flakes from her eyelids and opened the single sheet of the letter. There was a date on it, a date in August, but no names, neither hers at the top nor her father's at the bottom.

She wiped the snowflakes from her cheeks, except they were not snowflakes and began to read.

When you receive this it will be over. If I have been able to

*achieve what I am about to do, then I will tell you; if not, then
others might not. If others tell you, judge them, not me, by what
they say. What I do, I do because I remember the day you were
born and wish that others might know such happiness. What I
do, I do because even now I know I have a smile on my face at
the memories of our family together, and wish that others might
also smile. But that they may smile in freedom and in joy. What
I do now, I do because I am a patriot. What I do now I do for
Mother Russia. Always be strong, always smile.*

She wiped her cheeks again, then she folded the sheet of paper
and placed it inside the first envelope. The envelope had no name
or address on it. Then she folded it and tucked it inside the second
envelope. The second bore the name and address of the friend in
Boston who had hand-delivered it to her, the stamp in the top
right corner was a United States 32 cents issue, and the postmark
indicated Moscow, though the date and the state were blurred
and barely legible.

Tomorrow she would bring flowers, she decided. Tomorrow,
even though the snow would be deep and the ice would be packed
hard, she would place the flowers on the grave of her father.
Anna Buskova turned, placed the envelope in her coat pocket,
and retraced the line of her footsteps.

The snow was turning to ice on the pavements outside and the
windows of the bar were steamed with condensation. Sad night,
Kincaid thought, sad faces: Jameson and Panelli, himself and
O'Bramsky. Ed Miller there with them, even though he'd survived the night of the knives.

Miller rose, pulled on his coat, and patted each of them on
the shoulder. Sorry, the gesture said. Can't find the words, but
you know how I feel. He turned and left, Jameson and Panelli
followed him into the snow ten minutes later.

Kincaid called the waiter and asked for two more Black Labels.
'Ironic, isn't it?'

'Why ironic?'

'If Joshua had been aware of his death, then he would have
thought he had failed. But he didn't need to try anyway, because
the putsch collapsed and the old days are over for ever.'

That morning the Soviet Union had ceased to exist.

O'Bramsky nodded. O'Bramsky hadn't spoken much all evening.

'So what did the enquiry report say, Bram? Because you've seen a draft and I haven't.'

'That Joshua was trying to make contact with us to prevent the Gorbachev putsch, and that his own people suspected what he was about to do, tailed him, and took him out.'

'No other reason why he should contact us?'

'Not according to the draft report.'

'But we carry the blame.'

O'Bramsky laughed.

'What about Moscow, Idaho?' Kincaid asked. 'What about the fact that Joshua made the first call from there?'

'The enquiry will decide that Moscow USA was irrelevant, that Joshua was covering his tracks and trying to confuse us.'

Kincaid drained his glass. 'So what you going to do now, Bram?'

'What I should've done long time back; do up the house on the Chesapeake, paint the Hobie, and tell myself the last twenty-five years didn't end like this.'

And what about you, Jack? – it was in O'Bramsky's stare. I know that there's something on your mind, but I can't tell what.

'I had a dream last night, Bram. I dreamt I met up with the bastard who took out Joshua. Actually I've had the dream every night.'

'Why?' O'Bramsky asked.

'Because I feel guilty about Joshua, I guess. Almost as if I'd betrayed him.'

'And it's eating you up?'

'Yeah, Bram, it's eating me up.'

They stood to leave.

'You got to shake it off, Jack.' O'Bramsky pulled on his coat. 'What happened was business, not personal. You can't carry Joshua's ghost with you for the rest of your life or it will devour you, every day you live and every second you breathe.'

They stepped outside. The snow was falling thicker now; as they walked down the street it was a mantle on their shoulders.

'I know, Bram. But I'd still like to get whoever pulled the trigger.'

'Forget it, Jack.'

'Because it was business not personal?'

'No.' O'Bramsky sunk his hands deeper into his coat.

'So why?'

The snow was falling even heavier; the sounds around them were muffled and the street lamps hung like halos in the white.

'You know the game, Jack. You're part of the Club. You know there's no way the two of you will ever meet.'

Five Years Later . . .
August 1996

1

Kazakhstan that August morning was like Kazakhstan every August morning: hot, the land flat and featureless and stretching for ever, and the ground below it running with wealth. ConTex had signed up three years before, and now operated an oilfield on the north-east coast of the Caspian Sea. ConTex was also hustling contracts elsewhere, which was why its head office was in Moscow.

Maddox rose at five.

Arnold Maddox, Arnie to both friends and colleagues, had been with the Consolidated Oil Company of Texas six years and had switched from Angola to Moscow nine months earlier. Maddox was late thirties, tall and lean build, hailed from Austin, Texas, and had been in exploration and production since graduation. He was married with two teenage boys, though his wife and family never accompanied him on his overseas postings. In the political chaos of Angola he had brought order and efficiency; in the frontier atmosphere which was the new Russia he brought an instinct for the local way of doing things which singled him out from many of the foreign businessmen now streaming east. Thus the night before he had spent four hours over black bread, local black caviar and Absolut vodka with the general introduced to him as head of the republic's KGB, even though the KGB had been renamed and reorganized after the dissolution of the Soviet Union five years ago.

By seven he had tied up the remnants of paperwork left over from the previous day; at seven-fifteen, over breakfast of cheese, cold meats and black coffee, he held a final meeting with the local manager and security chief. By early afternoon he was back in Moscow.

23

The suites which ConTex occupied were on the eighth floor of a modern block off Tverskaya. Red Square and the Kremlin were 200 metres away, on the other side of the inner ring road, and the red and yellow of McDonald's occupied the ground floor.

After Kazakhstan the office seemed the height of civilization: prints of ConTex's various operations on the walls, cocktail cabinet, conference table at the end nearest the door, and Maddox's mahogany desk in front of the window. PC to the right, a bank of telephone monitors, including a Stu-iii, to the left, mandatory family photograph in the middle and executive chair behind.

He checked with his secretary, asked her to get him a coffee, and called Dwyer on an internal line. 'I'm back. Do we need to talk?'

Ten days earlier, and two months before they would even unofficially be known to exist, Maddox had acquired the preliminary details of a new exploration area, plus names and backgrounds of relevant officials and politicians, and ConTex had sent in Dwyer.

Dwyer came through, sat down and shook his head when Maddox's secretary offered him coffee. 'Looks like we'll get what we want.' Dwyer was Vice President responsible for New Business Development and on the main board. 'I'll need five million.' At this moment in time, and at this stage of the process. Because five million dollars was small beer. When it got really heavy you could put a zero on the end of that, and ConTex wouldn't think it was out of place.

So five million, plus the one million Maddox needed for Kazakhstan to cover local wages, expenses and other payments. Delivery tomorrow and everything straightforward and routine. Three minutes later the request had been sent to Houston on the secure fax.

When Maddox and Dwyer left the office the early evening was warm. Maddox's driver dropped Dwyer at the Balltschug-Kempinski, across the Moskva river from the Kremlin and next to the British embassy residence, then took Maddox to the former sanatorium, now a country club, where he leased a luxury chalet. At eight-thirty, having showered and changed, Maddox joined Dwyer for dinner.

The Kempinski was expensive, but the Kempinski was safe – relatively speaking, but everything was relative in the new Moscow. Black-windowed Mercedes and BMWs were parked outside, but black-windowed Mercedes and BMWs were parked outside everywhere nowadays. Guards on the doors, but it was only when there were no guards that you began to worry.

At nine-thirty they left the hotel, crossed the river, and walked past St Basil's into Red Square. The evening was still warm and the sky was an almost transparent shade of blue.

'You want a drink?' Dwyer asked.

'Where?'

'How about Nite Flite?'

They crossed Red Square then dropped between the Arsenal Tower of the Kremlin and the sterner red brick of the Historical Museum into the tarmac area beyond. Even though it was late evening the area still milled with people: along the pavement to Ploshchad Revolyutsii the booths selling cigarettes and alcohol were crowded with shoppers. Opposite, on the pavement under the grey featureless mass of the Moskva Hotel, was a single stall selling drinks, a handful of wooden tables around it and cars parked in front of it. At the entrance to the subway under the inner ring road to Tverskaya and the Okhatniy Ryad metro station, there was another cluster of vendors – mainly men but two women.

The first woman was selling cigarettes. She looked mid-sixties, small and thin and stooped. She was wearing a cardigan, skirt, torn basketball boots, and a Michael Jordan cap which had long lost its shape and colour.

The second was taller and early fifties. On a tray in front of her, balanced on makeshift legs, were sets of audio tapes. Her hair was tied back, her back was straight and her dress was blue and clean and neatly pressed. A light coat was thrown over her shoulders and on the left side of her bodice she wore a row of medals.

They walked past her and down the steps into the underpass. The passageway was the familiar grey concrete, beggars and vendors lining the walls: a blind war veteran holding out his hands and a couple selling matryoshka dolls, a woman selling lottery tickets and more stalls selling military badges and fake icons. From the end nearest the metro came the sound of a string quartet.

They passed the musicians and took the steps to Tverskaya. The National Hotel was on the corner, Maxim's nightclub on the ground floor below it and a fashion boutique next to it. Food stalls were spaced to the left, people eating at tables and a gypsy girl, thin and pretty, begging near them, her parents watching from twenty yards away. Beyond the shops the Intourist Hotel towered into the sky, Mercedes and BMWs were parked three deep on the road and along the pavement outside, a stretch limousine was pulled against the steps to the canopy over the entrance, and heavily-built young men in suits stood like phalanxes at the doors.

Ten minutes later they came to Nite Flite. Two well-dressed young women smiled at the thick-set man on the door and went in. Behind him a queue of tourists waited patiently. Maddox ignored the queue and went to the man on the door. Two more big men hovered in the shadows inside.

'Full,' the man told him.

Maddox reached inside his jacket for his wallet and snapped out two $50 bills. The minder took them, stepped aside and allowed them in.

The following morning Maddox spent ninety minutes in the office then took the 9.55 flight to St Petersburg. In London it was seven in the morning. Forty minutes earlier American Airlines flight AA106 had touched down from New York. Amongst the items unloaded and placed in bond were the six million dollars Maddox had ordered the previous afternoon. By the time they were secured in the bond area near Terminal 4 Zak Whyte had done his five miles, returned to the Holiday Inn at the edge of the airport, showered and changed, and taken the lift to the restaurant on the ground floor.

Zak Whyte was thirty-one years old: he stood six-three, weighed in at 190 pounds, and had been out of the United States Marine Corps two years. The security/courier company for which he worked, like others in related fields, had a propensity to recruit men of similar backgrounds. Pearce, the courier who would double up with Whyte on the Moscow run, had served nine years with the British Royal Marine Commandos, making corporal and ending his service with the elite Mountain and Arctic Warfare cadre.

When Whyte entered the restaurant Pearce was already at a table in the corner furthest from the door. Whyte helped himself to orange juice and full English breakfast, and sat down.

'You all right?'

Pearce's coffee was untouched. 'No.' The belt of pain tightened across his abdomen.

'What is it?'

'No idea. Been up since three this morning.' He forced down some coffee. 'What time we due out?'

'They're collecting us at eight-thirty, pick-up at eight forty-five; the flight's confirmed as leaving at nine-fifty.'

They always cut it tight. Nobody liked hanging around with what they would be carrying, even in London.

'Should be okay by then.' Pearce excused himself and returned to his room.

When Whyte checked him at seven-thirty he was motionless on his bed; at seven forty-five he had not moved. At eight Whyte checked with the office that the pick-up car was en route, notified them of Pearce's condition, suggested a doctor, and was informed that no other couriers with the relevant visas were available at such notice. He would therefore have to carry the two bags himself, even though they normally doubled up if they were carrying over a million, especially going into Moscow. But one man could carry the two bags, and the boys would meet him the moment he stepped off the plane at Sheremetyevo.

He briefed Pearce, collected the small overnight bag, stuffed it inside the canvas holdall, checked out, and waited in the foyer for the pick-up. Pity about Mick, because Moscow could be fun, especially if you knew where to go. And old sweats like Mick and himself had it worked out, as they had most things worked out.

The Vauxhall Senator stopped outside, the two men in it. Twenty minutes later they had collected the six million from bond, transferred it to the two holdalls (reinforced bottoms, locks and shoulder straps) and driven to Terminal 4.

The drop-off area outside was busy. Whyte went first, pushing the baggage cart, the minder behind so that Whyte and the money were always in his vision. The interior was large and echoing. Whyte pushed the cart to one of the club class check-ins, smiled at the woman and handed over his passport and two tickets.

'Moscow flight. A Mr Pearce and I have three confirmed seats. Mr Pearce has had to cancel. I'd still like the two bulkhead window seats.'

The entrance to the departure lounge was to the left. The minder watched as Whyte pushed the cart through, handed over his boarding pass for inspection, and cleared passport control. Airside was more secure, but even airside you didn't hang around. He lifted the bags on to the screening belt, no indication of their weight or contents, parked the trolley to the side, and stepped through the magnetometer frame. To his left the X-ray operator stopped the belt and scanned the image on the screen. Paperwork, Whyte would say if asked. Check with the American embassy, my company and the airline security he would tell them if they pulled him on suspicion of carrying laundered money.

Gate 5 was at the far end of the departure area, flight BA872 already boarding and the last passengers going through. Whyte found the seats, stowed the bags as tightly as he could on the floor, and strapped himself into the seat nearest the aisle. Routine procedure: the bags on the seat or the floor next to the window, the courier in the aisle seat, and the other courier – if they were doubling up – in the nearest seat on the other side of the aisle. No one allowed to get anywhere near the holdalls.

Five minutes later the 767 pushed back; three minutes after that, at 10.02 GMT, it lifted off, climbed over north London, and turned east on the standard route to Moscow over Amsterdam and Berlin. Two hours and sixteen minutes later it crossed the border of what had once been the Soviet Union. An hour and sixteen minutes after that it dropped on to the pockmarked runway of Moscow's Sheremetyevo airport, trundled to Gate 9, the air bridge was connected, the engines died, and the seatbelt signs flicked off. Whyte lifted the bags and joined the queue to leave the plane.

The boys were waiting at the top of the jetbridge. There were two of them, thirties, big build and disciplined, automatics concealed in waist holsters. A tall woman in the dark green of the Border Guards stood beside them.

'Good flight?' The bodyguard's English was precise without being perfect.

'Fine.'

Arnie Maddox was halfway to the airport when the cellphone rang. It was six-fifty in the evening; fifteen minutes to the airport and another forty after that till his flight took off for Moscow. The seven hours he had spent in St Petersburg that day had gone well and the paperwork from the last meeting was balanced on his lap.

'Arnie?'

'Yep.' He held the cellphone with his left hand and used his right to turn over the page of the document he was reading.

'Arnie, it's Phil. There's a problem. The money that was coming in this afternoon . . .' Dwyer's voice trailed off.

'What about it?'

'It's gone missing.'

Maddox's flight landed at Sheremetyevo just over three hours later. Arriving now, Maddox told his driver on the cellphone the moment he stepped off the plane. Even late evening the militia moved cars on outside the airport, so drivers waited at the Novotel, 200 metres away. Maddox pushed his way through the freelance drivers offering cab rides into the city and went outside. The Cherokee Grand Jeep pulled in. Maddox grunted a greeting, slid into the rear seat, and phoned Dwyer that he was on his way in. Thirty-five minutes later he was in his office off Tverskaya.

Dwyer sat opposite him and slightly left, his facial muscles twitching occasionally with nerves, and the American manager liaising with the Russian security company contracted by ConTex sat to the right, trying not to show anything. Maddox thanked his secretary for working late and asked her to bring him coffee.

'Tell me.' He looked at the security liaison manager.

'The courier company confirm that one of their people, Whyte, left London as scheduled. Whyte was travelling alone. The courier scheduled to accompany him was taken ill this morning and there wasn't time to bring in a replacement. British Airways have confirmed that Whyte was on the flight; the last time they saw him was walking up the jetbridge from the aircraft. Immigration confirm that Whyte was met by two security people. Problem is, they weren't ours. The security team who were supposed to meet him were held up and arrived late.'

'Jeez . . .' Heads and jobs and reputations on the line, Maddox was aware; not just the man opposite him. He swung in the chair, sipped the coffee and gave himself time to think. 'Houston's been informed?' It was to the security liaison.

'Yes.'

'And you've spoken to McIntyre?' This time to Dwyer.

Cal McIntyre was President of ConTex, Cal McIntyre was ConTex. Cal McIntyre would already have been informed, but McIntyre would be waiting for Maddox to call him, because that was the way McIntyre operated.

'Not personally.'

'Better do it, then.' Maddox put the mug back on the table. 'Anything else before I talk to Cal?'

'I still need the five million,' Dwyer told him.

Thanks, Maddox almost said. He punched one of the direct numbers to McIntyre's office in Houston on the Stu-iii, flicked the telephone on conference so they could all hear, then left his desk and stood with his back to the window, because that was what McIntyre would do when he took the call.

'Cal McIntyre's office.' The secretary was honey-toned. Blond hair and good-looking, Maddox remembered. And efficient, because that was the only way you survived with McIntyre.

'Hi, Shirl, it's Arnie Maddox in Moscow. Is Cal there?' He waited for the connection. In Moscow it was late evening, the sky purpling. In Houston it was early afternoon, the sky blue and the sun blazing. 'Cal. Arnie Maddox in Moscow.'

'Arnie.' McIntyre was tall, big-boned but gaunt, early sixties

30

and hide skin. He pushed the chair back from the desk, stood up, and leaned with his back against the window, the city spread seventeen storeys below.

'Cal, I'm going secure.' Maddox put the call on hold and turned the key of the Stu-iii. In Houston McIntyre did the same. 'You've been informed.' Maddox resumed the conversation.

'Yep.'

Time to do it, Maddox understood; time to play it as Cal McIntyre would have played it.

'Okay, Cal. This is the score. As you're aware, this morning's shipment went missing. I've begun running checks this end, first indication is that the security contractor screwed up.' He made a point of taking a mouthful of coffee. 'The insurance people will obviously want to run their own checks on this. I'm happy with that as long as they don't get their noses up the wrong asses. Phil's deal is looking good, Kazakhstan's on schedule. In view of the latter two points we need a replacement shipment ASAP.'

'Big shipment, Arnie,' McIntyre told him, just to let Maddox know, then turned his attention to Dwyer. 'Phil how close are you?'

'Close as we can be at this stage.'

'Anybody else sniffing?'

'Nobody yet, but it's only a matter of time.'

McIntyre switched his attention back to Maddox. 'Okay, Arnie, you got another shipment coming in tomorrow.' But don't fuck up again. Because you've covered your ass on this one, but next time . . . 'What about security?'

'You want me to sort out someone else?'

'I will. Speak to you in an hour.' The ConTex president hung up, returned to his desk, consulted the confidential list of telephone numbers he had drawn up over the years, drew out two, and called the first.

'Drew, this is Cal McIntyre at ConTex. Got a little problem in Moscow and would appreciate some advice on it.'

'Shoot,' the man in the lush forested green of the Virginia countryside told him.

'Shipment of money's gone missing. The security company ConTex has been employing are either involved or haven't got their asses in the ball game. I need another company, able to provide security plus investigation.'

'Give me an hour,' the man from Langley told him.

McIntyre thanked him, called the second number, and waited while the secretary connected him.

'Jon, this is Cal McIntyre at ConTex.'

'Cal, good to hear. How's it going?' A year ago the Deputy Assistant Secretary had been one of the smartest counsels on Capitol Hill; now he was amongst the brightest of the bright at State.

'Got me a problem in Moscow, Jon. Hear you just got back from there and wondered whether you might be able to help me . . .'

'Plenty of security companies in Russia at the moment,' the former lawyer told him after McIntyre had explained. 'Give me an hour.'

Forty-three minutes later the Langley desk chief phoned back.

'Cal, this is Drew. I know it sounds like jobs for the brothers, but the guy you want is Grere Jameson. Used to be with the Agency. One of the best. Should've stayed but left to set up his own company. Now runs an outfit called ISS, one of the Beltway Bandits.' One of the myriad of companies set up by ex-government employees and located within the Washington Beltway. 'Jameson has a joint venture going with the Russians, goes by the name Omega.'

'Why do you say he should have stayed?'

'Because he's the sort the Agency should have fought like hell to keep instead of allowing him to get pissed off with internal fuck-ups and cost-cuttings.'

He gave McIntyre the number in Bethesda.

'Thanks, Drew. I owe you.'

Three minutes later the former Capitol Hill counsel phoned back.

'For what you want, there's only one.'

'Who?'

'Omega.'

He gave McIntyre the details.

'Thanks, Jon. It's appreciated.'

The area code was 301. McIntyre called it and asked to speak to Grere Jameson. Mr Jameson was not available, the receptionist informed him and connected him to Jameson's secretary. Mr Jameson was out of town, the secretary told him, could someone else help or could she get Mr Jameson to phone him back?

'How long will it take for him to get back to me?'

'How urgent is it?'

'Very.'

'Ten minutes. If he can't, I'll let you know.'

COPEX, the Covert and Operational Procurement Exhibition, occupied one entire floor of the Javits Center in the middle of Manhattan. The exhibits themselves were as the name suggested: state-of-the-art covert, security, surveillance, assault and operational gadgetry. Entrance was by invitation only, and requests for invites were carefully vetted. Most of those present were from national or international agencies, governmental or private, and many were from overseas.

Grere Jameson left the intelligence briefing on economic espionage and returned to the main exhibition area.

Five years ago this week someone calling himself Hemmings was phoning the Agency office in New York and asking to speak to Leon Panelli ... Four years ago he was out in the cold and setting up his own company ... Three years ago a London contact had introduced him to a Russian called Gerasimov who was in town looking for partners for a joint venture project in Moscow ...

He stopped to check out a computer encryption programme, then hurried to the bar. Leo Panelli was waiting. Today Leo was senior partner in a Washington think tank providing high level intelligence analysis and risk assessment to US companies contemplating investment overseas.

'Leo, good to see you.'

'You too, Grere old friend.'

They shook hands, asked about business, and avoided talking about five years ago. Jameson's cellphone rang. He excused himself and moved to a corner.

'Grere, it's Jenny. A Cal McIntyre from ConTex just phoned. Said it was urgent and asked if you could phone him back. ConTex is an E and P operator with contracts in Russia and Kazakhstan. I've had a check run in D and B. Cal McIntyre is president.'

Dun and Bradstreet was a subscriber database providing in-depth information on business issues such as company structures, stock-holders and corporate personnel.

Plus ConTex was a big player getting bigger, Jameson thought. Which D and B wouldn't know. And their Russian security contract expired in four months, because he and Gerasimov had discussed it the previous week.

'Did he say what he wanted?'

'No. He just said it was urgent. I told him you'd phone back in ten minutes.'

'How long ago was that?'

'Two minutes fifteen.'

'Get me the times of flights from New York to Houston later this afternoon. Just in case.'

'I've held a seat for you on the 17.25 Continental out of Newark.'

Jameson took down the number in Houston, hooked the encryptor unit on to the cellphone, and called the Moscow number. In Moscow it was twelve midnight. Gerasimov answered on the sixth ring.

'Mikhail, it's Grere.' The conversation was in Russian. 'I'm going secure.' Jameson activated the encryptor and resumed the conversation. 'Cal McIntyre from ConTex just called; he wants me to phone him back urgently. I'm checking in case you know what's running.'

They discussed the options. Three and a half minutes gone since the office had phoned – Jameson checked the time. He ended the call and keyed the number in Houston.

Grere Jameson on two, McIntyre's secretary informed the ConTex president. McIntyre glanced up at the clocks on the wall. Eight minutes down, two still to go.

'Mr Jameson, good afternoon. This is Cal McIntyre. Thanks for calling back so promptly.'

'My pleasure.'

'Got a little problem in Moscow.' Perhaps the Texan drawl was exaggerated, perhaps it was the way McIntyre opened every business discussion. 'Like to chew it over with you.'

'I'm in New York. I could be on the five twenty-five Continental flight, be with you eight twenty-one your time. A car at the airport would speed things up.'

'You got it.'

The sign which the driver held up said simply ConTex. Jameson declined the man's offer of assistance with his travel bag and followed him outside. In the sky to the west the sun was setting in a ball of fire. Twenty minutes later he shook hands with McIntyre in the ConTex president's office.

McIntyre was wearing a dinner jacket, red bow tie and cummerbund, as if he had just come from, or was on his way to, an engagement. He poured them each a Black Label and took his place behind his desk.

'Tell me about ISS and Omega.'

Jameson settled in a large wing-back leather chair in front of McIntyre's desk but slightly to the right so that he wasn't facing into the window.

'ISS is an international security and investigation company staffed by former members of the security and intelligence services, mainly American but sometimes others. We have main offices in Washington and London, and subsidiary offices in other cities. Where necessary we form specific companies for separate projects or countries. In Russia this has taken the form of a joint venture. Omega is the company name of that joint venture.'

'And who are your Russian partners?'

The sun had set now, and the sky was a gentle layer of blue and purple.

'Omega is headed by a former KGB general. Most of the staff are former KGB, specialists in their fields.'

'Why Omega?' McIntyre asked.

Jameson hadn't touched the Black Label. 'Alpha-Omega, the beginning and the end, we provide it all. We would have

35

liked to call the company Alpha, but that would have been confusing.'

'Why?'

'Alpha was the KGB's anti-terrorist and special forces unit. Each republic had its Alpha unit. The head of our company in Moscow is the former head of state Alpha, the man who oversaw it all. A large number of the men we employ are also former members.'

McIntyre leaned forward. 'Ten years ago they were the enemy, now you're working with them?'

Jameson smiled. 'The Berlin Wall came down in '89, so in fact it's seven years ago that they were the enemy, not ten.' He placed the Black Label on McIntyre's desk. 'It also depends how you define the enemy. Militarily and politically the Russians may no longer be the enemy, commercially they still are, but so are all our former friends. Britain, Germany, France, Japan. It's something my Russian partner and I are totally aware of.' He leaned forward and picked up the glass again. 'You said you had a problem.'

'This morning we shipped a consignment of dollars into Moscow. It went missing. We want it investigated.'

'How much went missing?'

McIntyre took off his jacket, draped it across the back of his chair, and loosened his bow tie. 'Six million dollars.' He studied Jameson's face for a reaction to the amount. Six million was small change, he understood. When the big shipments were going through there were armoured trucks waiting on the runway to load the dollars direct off the plane, and armed guards keeping everyone, but everyone, away. But six million of *his* money was six million of *his* money.

'Hand-carried through Sheremetyevo?' Jameson asked.

'Yes.'

'How many couriers?'

'There should have been two but one got sick.'

'You had a secure collection?'

'We were supposed to have.'

'What went wrong?'

McIntyre took a file from a drawer on the right side of his

36

desk and passed it to Jameson. Jameson opened it, speed-read the five sheets of report inside, then laid it on the desk. Most people in his business guaranteed the world, but sometimes it was better to be straight. 'I have to tell you that the chances of recovering that money are less than remote.'

'The Russian mafia,' McIntyre suggested.

'Define Russian mafia.'

'That's why I contract people like you, for you to define it for me.'

'One thing before I do. Are you sending another shipment over to replace the missing money?'

'En route from New York to London at this moment.'

'When do you want it in Moscow?'

'Tomorrow.'

Today in London and Moscow, because of the time difference.

'I assume you want Omega to provide the secure collection at Sheremetyevo?'

'Yes.'

'In that case, would you excuse me while I make the arrangements?'

Jameson telephoned Bethesda and ran the normal security routine. 'Jim, it's Grere. I'm with Cal McIntyre at ConTex. We have an immediate escort assignment, London–Moscow, leaving London on the next Moscow flight. I assume that's the 9.50 AM British Airways. The shipment is six million, so we'll need two couriers. There's also an investigation, I'll send you the background, but the first priority is the escort. Check with London who's available, and put Moscow on standby for a secure collection at Sheremetyevo. Tell Moscow I want a guardian angel in addition to the pick-up boys. I'll also speak to Gerasimov.'

On the other side of the desk Cal McIntyre leaned to his right, picked up a phone and spoke to his personal assistant. 'My appointment tonight. Send my apologies that I can't attend. Then dinner for two in my office.'

Jameson ended the call, punched Gerasimov's number, and repeated the security procedure. 'Mikhail, I'm with Cal McIntyre at ConTex.' The conversation, in Russian, paralleled the one he had held thirty seconds earlier. 'Jim's phoning you from DC. I've told him I want an *angel-khzanitel* at Sheremetyevo as well as the pick-up team.'

He finished the call and sipped the Black Label. The cellphone rang. London and Moscow were running, he was informed. 'Who's London sending?' he asked.

'The lead man is Brady.'

'Where's Kincaid?' Jameson was already thinking ahead.

'Amsterdam.'

'Bring him in. Brady makes the run with him, but Kincaid is number one. Tell Kincaid he might be in Moscow for a while, and get someone to Amsterdam in his place.'

McIntyre left his position behind his desk and settled in a chair opposite Jameson. 'Define mafia,' he said when Jameson had finished the calls.

'You want the long or the short lecture?'

'Somewhere in the middle.'

Jameson laughed. 'The Russian mafia is not like the Sicilian variety, not la Cosa Nostra. In a simplistic way, mafia in present-day Russia, and I'm using Russia as shorthand for the whole set-up east of what was the Iron Curtain, simply means crime. Everyone's running scams, or exposed to scams, in Russia at the moment. Each factory or business or office is offered *kreshna*, a roof; each street trader is requested to align himself or herself with a group who say they will protect him.

'However, it's actually more multi-dimensional than that. Mafia isn't just about market traders offering vegetables at high prices or hoods shooting each other or blowing each other's Mercs up over territorial disputes. It isn't just about hitting bankers and industrialists and judges. Mafia isn't even about US or UK or other foreign firms taking on Russian partners and discovering after ten, fifteen years, that they're in bed with the baddies. In a way it's how society, from top to bottom, operates; it's a recognized way of doing things. Many of the people at the top of the old economy are the new leaders of the new capitalism. Some things don't change. The old connections, the old agreements, have simply been updated.'

McIntyre leaned forward. 'So those are the bad guys. Tell me about the good. Tell me about Omega. Actually, tell me about Alpha.'

Jameson sipped the Black Label again. 'In addition to its intelligence role, both inside and outside the Soviet Union, the KGB had a number of secret armed units. One of them was Alpha. Alpha itself was created in the 1970s; its first major operation was a dirty job in Afghanistan: assist in the storming of the presidential palace in Kabul and the assassination of the then president Amin. This was before the Soviet Union occupied Afghanistan and Afghanistan became its Vietnam. In the eighties Alpha became the KGB's anti-terrorist and Special Forces arm. Everyone knows about them now; then they were top secret.'

McIntyre leaned back and considered. 'If everyone in Russia is on the make, how can you be sure your guys aren't?'

'Because of where their loyalty lies.'

'Explain.'

The clock on the wall ticked past midnight.

'What happened five years ago this week?'

McIntyre shook his head.

'The Gorbachev putsch,' Jameson reminded him. 'Gorbachev, the architect of the new Russia, on vacation in the Crimea, senior KGB and Red Army officers ordering his arrest, the crowds gathering in the streets, and Yeltsin about to make a last stand in the White House. The KGB sent an Alpha unit into the White House to assassinate Yeltsin. Instead they protected him. If they hadn't, perhaps the coup would have succeeded. In the event, it failed.'

'Why did Alpha do that?'

Jameson shrugged.

'So they're the guys providing the security.'

'Yes.'

The ConTex president returned to his desk, opened a drawer, pulled out a cigar box, offered it to Jameson – Jameson declining – selected a Havana for himself, and sat down again. 'And who'll be doing the investigation?'

'One of the Moscow office.'

'A former member of the KGB.'

'Correct.'

39

McIntyre lit the Havana. 'I'd like an American on board as well.'

'One of the two couriers will stay on as joint investigator.'

'Kincaid from Amsterdam?'

'Correct again.'

'What's Kincaid's background?'

'Ex-Agency. Soviet Division.'

The cigar smoke circled McIntyre like a halo. 'What about the Russian?'

'That's Gerasimov's business, not mine.'

'So Gerasimov will be running the show?'

'Gerasimov and myself. I'm flying to Moscow the day after tomorrow.'

Which was what he knew McIntyre wanted to hear.

The cumulus was white against the grey-green of the North Sea. Kincaid declined coffee, eased the business class seat back, and drifted into a light sleep. Thirty-three minutes later the stewardess shook him awake, asked him to fasten his seatbelt, and offered him a hot towel. He thanked her and massaged his face. The Thames was suddenly below him, London in front, then Heathrow, the lights coming fast at them. The 737 touched down, gently but firmly, and taxied to Terminal 4. Behind them a 747 lifted into the morning sky. The seatbelt signs flicked off. He pulled his bag from the overhead locker and made sure he was among the first off. Nine minutes later he was in the public area of Terminal 4. The queues were already clustered round the economy check-ins, and the boys were waiting at the coffee bar at the far end.

Brady rose and shook his hand. 'You want a coffee?'

'No time.'

'Pick us up,' the escort told the driver on the cellphone.

Twenty minutes later they had collected the shipment from bond, Kincaid and Brady dividing the load between them, and returned to the terminal. Fifty minutes after that BA872 climbed into the sky and carved a graceful bank east. An hour and seventeen minutes after that it crossed into what President Reagan had called the Evil Empire.

His first time back in Russia since the death on East 54th – the ghost crept up on him ... His first time in Moscow since he'd betrayed Joshua ...

The man who collected the BMW and began the twenty-minute drive to the airport wore an inconspicuous grey suit. The first gun he carried, in a shoulder holster on his left side was a Sig Sauer P226, 15-round magazine, and the second was a shortened AKSU47, 5.45mm 30-round mag, which he would hang on a pull strap under his jacket.

Central Moscow was hot and busy; the usual BMWs and Mercedes parked outside the usual places, and the usual minders with the usual padded jackets. Last year the fashion had been shell-suits and tennis-ball haircuts.

The traffic lights next to the Moscow Dynamo stadium weren't working, and there was an army tank at the crossroads outside the red-brick complex built for Catherine the Great to change her clothes before entering Moscow on her visits from St Petersburg, so there might be a road block later.

He had bought the 320 in Berlin, driven through Poland, crossed the border at Brest, and waited patiently while the police to the west checked his sales and purchase documents and those in the east his travel visas. And when he had arrived in Moscow he had customized it to his own specification. Rear window apparently cracked, no hub caps and front left wing slightly dented. Paintwork off-colour and seat covers, though not the leather beneath them, worn and ripped. Everyone in Moscow wanted a BMW, but with any luck nobody would want his.

The M10 to St Petersburg stretched in front of him, and the white and glass façade of the Novotel Hotel loomed to his right. He jerked round a pot-hole and pulled off the road and into the airport complex. The road in front divided, one section looping to the departures area on the upper floor, and the other passing underneath the canopy to arrivals. He drove through, parked near the Novotel, hung the Kalashnikov under his jacket, and walked back to the terminal.

The interior of the arrivals area was dirty and poorly-lit, the usual group of freelance cab drivers clustered around the exit from customs, and more drivers circling the floor near the bank and the shop. A few guards, not many and even those not paying attention. He returned outside and stood on the pavement.

Two minutes later the convoy swept in – two Saab 9000s, the Volvo between them. Pick-up time, he thought. The drivers remained in the cars, plus one passenger in each of the Saabs. The four men who left them – two from the first, one each from the second and third – moved inside. All were young – late twenties, early thirties – big build but athletic movement. The men went inside and the convoy pulled toward the Novotel.

In the sky to the west he saw the sun glint on the incoming plane.

Kincaid felt the bump as the 767 touched down. The Boeing swung right, followed the taxiway and stopped, and the seatbelt signs flicked off. Kincaid pulled one bag on to the seat, stood in the aisle, and allowed Brady to stand in front of him and pull the other bag from the floor. Whyte came this way yesterday, he was aware; Whyte thought everything was going smoothly. He took the weight of the bag, thanked the cabin crew and walked up the tunnel of the jetbridge. The woman in the Border Guard uniform was at the top, two men with her.

'Kincaid?' One of the two pick-ups greeted him in Russian.

'Yes.'

'How's the weather in London?' The first line of the code, still in Russian.

'Fine, how about Moscow?'

'Sunnier than Washington.'

Right pick-up team today.

He and Brady gave the woman their passports and visas; she ticked them off a list, waited till one other passenger joined them, the others going right to the normal immigration area, then she led them left, along the corridor, through the duty free area, and up the stairs to the VIP lounge. The room was small, a bar to the left, a Daewoo television set in one corner, an arrivals/departures monitor hanging from the ceiling, and two girls in an immigration booth to the right. The walls were covered with dark grey hessian and the seats were vinyl.

Two more pick-ups were waiting for them. Ten minutes later one of the pick-ups collected the passports from the window of the immigration booth. 'Bring the cars in,' the *komandir*, the team leader, told the drivers on the Motorola.

They left the lounge, went down the stairs, and cut through the crowds in the arrivals area. Sheremetyevo smelt wrong – it hit Kincaid: dark terminal and darker corners; so who was waiting for him, who was going to try to take him and Brady and the Omega guys around them? They sliced through the waiting drivers. So where the hell's the *angel-khzanitel*, because that was what the briefing in London had said: security pick-up plus guardian angel. Hope to Christ the Omega boys had spotted whoever might be waiting for them, hope to hell the *angel-khzanitel* had him covered. Christ, why wasn't he carrying?

The convoy came in – Saab 9000 in front, Volvo, second Saab 9000 behind – and stopped immediately opposite the main doors, the drivers remaining in place, engines running, and two men getting out of the lead and tail cars, neither of them looking at the cars, Uzis held discreetly beneath their coats and eyes scanning the crowd and the pavement and the doors.

Kincaid came through the door and saw the convoy: Saab, Volvo, Saab; saw the two men by the cars still scanning the crowd. Knew he was being taken care of but looked round anyway. They were five metres from the Volvo. The man beside it opened the rear door. Kincaid threw the bag on to the floor, crossed over to the other side of the car, one of the pick-ups already in the roadway on that side, and slid in. Brady threw his bag on the seat and tumbled in beside it. One of the pick-ups eased into the front passenger seat and clicked on the thief locks. The other pick-ups were already getting into the Saabs, two remaining on the pavement and still checking, even as the convoy began to pull off, then dropping through the doors as the drivers accelerated away.

The man with the Sig Sauer and the AKSU47 under his coat collected the BMW, left Sheremetyevo and pulled left toward Moscow.

Five years ago this week Vorkov had contacted him in Boston

– the *teni proshlovo* came back at him again ... Five years ago he had been in the air to La Guardia – the ghost reminded him ... Five years ago Vorkov had directed him to the restaurant on East 54th ...

In front of him Nikolai Sherenko saw the convoy.

2

The convoy cut across the river, passed the outer ring road, dropped toward the city centre and turned right down Gertsena Ulica. The street was lined with shops, three- or four-storey apartments and offices above them, and an occasional white-painted church or garden, railed off and set back from the road. The lead Saab stopped and the pick-ups stepped on to the pavement.

The door was wood and painted a dark heavy brown, no number on it. On one side was an electrical shop and on the other a small supermarket, both filled with shoppers. One of the pick-ups crossed the pavement and checked inside. The Volvo slid in behind the lead Saab, no doors opening, and the Volvo itself pointing out with enough space in front to scream away. The tail Saab slid in behind the Volvo and the other pick-ups got out, hands inside their jackets. The pick-up at the door checked inside and nodded.

Still a chance for someone to take them out – Kincaid glanced down and across the street. On the opposite side of the road the BMW pulled into position.

Clear, the *komandir* told Kincaid. Kincaid slid out, pulled the bag after him, Brady behind him and the pick-ups tight around them, crossed the pavement, up the single worn step to the door, and entered the building.

The floor inside was stone, there were stone stairs to the left, the walls were painted a faded off-cream, and an ancient elevator with a metal grille rattled up the front. The Omega team ignored the elevator and took the stairs, turned a corner, came to a landing, two doors off it, and continued up, came to another landing then another. The door on the left was wood but the one on the

45

right was padded leather, the usual indication that the door itself was steel. The keyboard for the security lock was on the left. The team leader punched in the combination, pushed open the door and went in, Kincaid and Brady behind him and the pick-ups behind them.

The walls and ceiling of the outer office were lined with wood and the linoleum on the floor was worn. There were two desks, the men lounging against them standing to greet them as they came in. A door on the left ran back down a corridor, no indication what was there, and another corridor ran off the outer room, directly in front of them, two doors off it on the left and one on the right. A shaft of sun struggled through the bars on the single window in the room, the dust playing in its light.

'Welcome to Omega,' the team leader said in Russian.

Sure, Kincaid thought.

The man who entered from one of the rooms in the corridor in front of them was mid-thirties, just under six feet tall and wiry build. 'Glad you made it safely.' The accent was English. 'Pat Riley.' ISS's manager in Moscow, Kincaid understood; service with the Parachute Regiment, ending his career as a major in the Third Battalion, plenty of time at the sharp end, including Northern Ireland, and fluent in Russian.

They shook hands then Riley led Kincaid and Brady along the corridor.

'ConTex have been notified that you've arrived. They want five million delivered right away, the boys will see to that. They want the other million escorted to Kazakhstan tomorrow morning. Tom, you take that down with an escort. Mikhail's on his way in.' Mikhail Gerasimov, Grere Jameson's partner in Moscow. 'Conference as soon as he arrives. You needn't attend, Tom.'

He led them into the office on the right of the corridor, overlooking the street. The room was functional but sparse: cream-painted walls, desks with computers, a good-looking woman at one, late twenties and well-dressed, and men at the others. Riley introduced them in Russian, translating for Brady:

'Tatyana, our office manager . . .

'Oleg and Josef, a couple of the boys . . .

'Igor Lukyanov . . .' Former KGB intelligence, their access

point to the present FSB. Lukyanov was five-six and squat; his blond hair was short, and the suit jacket which hung on the back of his chair was expensive and well-cut.

'Igor, this is Jack Kincaid and Tom Brady from DC. Jack's working on the ConTex investigation. You probably had a file on him in the old days.'

Gerasimov's room was on the opposite side of the corridor, and furthest from the outer office. It was wood-lined and small, functional desk and computer, grey carpet on the floor, one print on the wall, and a single window to the courtyard at the rear. The conference room next to it was also small: oval table with hard-backed chairs round it, window on to the courtyard, and the walls were papered, the design like the onion domes of St Basil's in Red Square.

'Not like ISS's offices in London or DC,' Riley suggested to Brady.

'Not quite,' the ex-FBI man conceded.

Riley perched himself on the edge of the table. 'One thing you have to realize, Tom. Moscow is the third most expensive city in the world. Office space is at a premium; so you pay through the nose or you do a deal with someone you know for somewhere like this. Another thing you have to understand is how the system works here. The owner's an old friend of Mikhail's. He runs an import-export business from an office down the corridor, to the left as you come in. We get cheap rates for Omega, and he gets protection from the government and the mafia.'

He led them back to the main office and poured them each a coffee from the percolator in the corner. On one of the phones someone was speaking to Kazakhstan, on another to Kiev, the secure fax humming in the background.

'While you're in Moscow, for this trip at least, you'll be staying in the company apartment which I use. Tom, you'll be collected at five tomorrow morning, then fly to Kazakhstan with an escort and an interpreter. You return to London via Budapest. It's an eye-opener. You may even enjoy it.' He finished the coffee and poured himself another. 'I've asked one of the boys to show you both around this evening.'

47

He turned to Brady. 'Give us five, Tom.' The order was polite and friendly. Brady nodded. Riley settled behind the desk in the left corner of the room and Kincaid pulled a chair in front of it and took the file Riley gave him.

'Background on the ConTex investigation. You'll be working with one of Mikhail's people. We know this is a team job, but remember this is Moscow. New Moscow maybe, but some things never change. If you want anything, do it through them.'

Mikhail Gerasimov was on his way in, the office manager told them.

'Any questions?' Riley asked Kincaid.

'Not yet.'

Kincaid went through to the conference room, sat at the table and read through the file. It was eleven hours since he had first been woken in Amsterdam and told to get to London, and the tiredness was seeping into him. Perhaps because he had been woken in the middle of the night, perhaps because he'd been carrying six million dollars and the previous day six million dollars had gone missing. Perhaps because he was in Moscow again.

The door opened and Gerasimov and Riley came in. Gerasimov was forty-eight, tall and powerfully built.

'Mikhail Sergeyevich Gerasimov.' Riley did the introductions. 'Jack Kincaid.'

'Good to meet you, Jack.'

'You too, Mikhail.'

They sat at the conference table, Gerasimov at the head, his back to the window and facing the door, Riley at the other end, and Kincaid between them. The door to the boardroom opened again and the fourth man came in. *I know you* – it was a flash in Kincaid's subconscious. *I've seen you before.*

'Jack Kincaid, Nikolai Sherenko.' Gerasimov did the introductions this time. 'I think you've already met.'

'Sort of.' Kincaid spoke in Russian. The *angel-khzanitel*, at the airport. 'Good to meet you.'

'You too.' Sherenko's reply was in English. Traces of East Coast, almost Boston, Kincaid thought.

Sherenko hung his jacket on the back of the chair opposite

48

Kincaid and sat down. The Sig Sauer still hung in the shoulder holster, but he had left the Kalashnikov in the secure cupboard in the other office.

'Anyone interested in what was happening today?' Gerasimov asked him.

Sherenko shook his head. 'Not after yesterday.'

Gerasimov nodded and opened the briefing. 'The pick-up went smoothly, which it should have done anyway, but ConTex is pleased. ConTex has now confirmed the contract to investigate the six million that went missing yesterday. Grere Jameson flies in from DC tomorrow to head up that investigation.'

'Why?' Sherenko asked.

'Why what?'

'Why is it necessary for someone to come in from DC to head an investigation in Moscow?'

Arrogant bastard – it was a flicker in Kincaid's subconscious.

Gerasimov was unruffled. 'Politics. ConTex is an American company, therefore wants to see an American running the show. We want the main ConTex security contract, they call the tune, we dance.' He switched his attention to Kincaid. 'You've read the reports?'

'Yes.'

They ran through the various lines of enquiry. Whether the theft came from a conspiracy or a leak of information. ConTex itself, and the Americans and Russians who worked for the company. Whether the plan for the robbery began in Kazakhstan or Moscow, and who knew or might have known of the shipment. The security and courier companies contracted to ConTex and the couriers themselves, including the significance of Pearce's sudden illness.

'No sign of Whyte yet?' Kincaid asked.

'We haven't had time to make enquiries. The primary objective today was the safe pick-up of the second shipment.' Gerasimov spread his hands on the table. The hands were large and the fingers were thick and muscular. 'We have his personal details and description, but we're still waiting for a photograph.'

They finished the preliminaries and moved to the short and medium term stages of the investigation.

'Background checks on the key players, both American and Russian. Whether any of them are in financial trouble or show indications in the past of sudden jumps in wealth.' Gerasimov spoke in shorthand, Kincaid thought; the delivery clear-cut but staccato. Or perhaps it was the way he himself heard it, the combination of tiredness and the fact that he hadn't listened to someone speaking Russian for five years. 'Whether any of them are screwing, or being screwed by, anyone who might be a security leak. Jack, you run one set of checks through ISS's offices in London and Washington. Nik, you run a second set through Igor Lukyanov, see if the computers at the FSB have anything to offer. You also check the morgues. Start this evening, show ConTex in Houston that we're already moving.'

Five years ago this week he stood in the morgue at Belle Vue . . . it was a wisp in Kincaid's subconscious.

'Jack, you arrange interviews with ConTex personnel. Nik, you do the same with the security company personnel. Electronic sweep of ConTex offices and examination of their communication systems. Questions to airline and airport staff, plus interviews with VIP lounge staff and Border Guard personnel for a description of the bogus team which met Whyte.'

Gerasimov looked round the table. 'Questions?'

Sherenko raised his hand. 'How much time do we have and how long and how far do we go?'

'I'll tell you after Grere and I have talked.'

'But what's the bottom line?'

'We want the main security contract for ConTex, therefore we'll pursue this enquiry as far as we can, but the bottom line is that we don't stand a snowball's chance in hell of getting the money back.'

'And ConTex know that?'

'Grere has already warned them that the chances of getting the money back are zero. ConTex aren't virgins. If we come up with anything more than a detailed report, they'll be happy.'

He closed the meeting and they returned to the main offices, Sherenko to his desk in one corner of the main office, and Kincaid to one opposite which had been cleared for him. Brady was waiting patiently. Couple of things to set up, then they'd be gone, Kincaid told him.

Igor Lukyanov crossed the room and slipped the photograph on to Sherenko's desk. 'Zak Whyte. Just come through from London.'

Sherenko studied it and passed it to Kincaid. Better get it out the way, his expression said. He lifted the telephone and punched the number. 'This is Nikolai Sherenko at Omega. We're looking for someone who went missing yesterday. Okay if we come now?' He put the phone down. 'You ready?'

My first time in Moscow since Joshua, Kincaid thought, and the first thing we do is go to a morgue. 'Yeah, I'm ready.' He turned to Brady. 'Get Riley to arrange transport for you back to the apartment. We'll pick you up when we're through.'

They ran off copies of the photograph, took the stone stairs to the ground floor and collected Sherenko's BMW from the courtyard at the rear. The evening was busy, the pavements crowded.

Kincaid settled in the passenger seat. 'So where are we going?'

'The central criminal morgue. Anybody goes missing, that's where they turn up.'

'If they turn up,' Kincaid suggested.

Sherenko laughed.

They crossed the river, drove along Leninski Prospekt, and turned left down Profsojuznaja Ulica. It was early evening, warm and pleasant, Sherenko driving with the window open and children playing on the green areas between the apartment blocks. They approached the junction with Krasikova Ulica and the entrances to Profsojuznaja metro station. The buildings here were more grey and featureless, arcades of shops along the street and brightly painted kiosks selling liquor, food, vegetables and bread along the pavements on each of the roads leading into the junction, men and women milling around them. Sherenko turned left at the lights, stopped in a pull-in for buses and trams in front of a line of kiosks, and got out, Kincaid behind him.

Most of the kiosks on this stretch of road were selling alcohol or cigarettes; the doors were locked and the vendors were seated inside behind a small window. Sherenko checked along the line, stopped at the third, crouched slightly because the windows were low, examined the bottles on display, and pointed.

Stolichnaya.

Small bottle.

The woman inside took a bottle from a shelf, and placed it on the wooden ledge inside the window. Sherenko counted out nine 1000-rouble notes, passed them through, and the woman passed him the bottle. Sherenko checked that the seal on the top was intact, checked the writing on the label, checked the number stamp on the back of the label, turned the bottle over and checked that the glue on the back of the label ran in wide even lines, shook the bottle and watched for the vortex of bubbles. When he was satisfied the vodka wasn't counterfeit he turned back to the car and put the bottle in the glove compartment. The evening was still warm, still sunny. They drove up the hill and turned into C'urupy Ulica.

Kincaid left the subway and crossed to Belle Vue hospital. Manhattan was noisy around him, a helicopter in the sky above and the wail of police sirens from the other side of the block.

Washing hung from the balconies of apartment blocks on the right and children played on the grass in front. A woman pushed a pram and a young couple walked together, holding hands. They passed a tennis court, also on the right, two thin girls playing with one ball and broken rackets. Silver birches lay on the ground where they had been cut down during the winter but not sawn up or hauled away, foliage still clinging to them and children playing in them. A dog crossed the road in front of them.

Kincaid stepped through the reception area. Time running out already, he knew. And he shouldn't be here anyway.

The building to the left was new and low. Beyond it was another, set back from the road and grey, seven storeys high. Sherenko passed the modern building, passed the grey building, and turned left down the rough earth track along its far side. The link metal fencing on either side was torn, grass and weeds growing up through it, and the security gate at the bottom was hanging off its hinges. Beyond it was a second grey-brick building, two storeys high though the height and shape of the wide doors in front suggested there was only one level. Two policemen lounged in the doorway and a rubbish skip lay in the weeds to the right. A young man with blond hair, blood splashed over his surgical greens and white boots, fetched something from one of the three cars parked on a dust patch in front.

Sherenko parked, got out, nodded at the policemen and shook hands with the attendant. A bird was singing in a tree behind the grey-brick building. Kincaid left the car and glanced inside. The building was dark and cavernous, high ceiling, no upper levels, and a large concrete floor with a tarpaulin over something in the centre. No bodies, though. The attendant went into an office on the right and returned with two pairs of surgical gloves. 'I'll see you down there.'

The corridors smelt of antiseptic and the hospital bustled around him. Kincaid picked up the signs, turned left, then right. Checked his watch and hurried on.

Sherenko took one pair of gloves, gave Kincaid the other, and walked past the building. The area was rough and overgrown, grass and weeds growing on mounds and through a tangle of metal to the right. In front of them and to their left a ramp dropped underground towards the block on the road at an angle of around twenty degrees. The surface had been tarmacked at some stage but now it was torn and rough, and the sides were red brick, washed over with concrete. It was some fifty metres long, the last ten under the overhang of the ground above.

They walked down. No birds any more, Kincaid realized. The sides now were tarred black as protection against wet and damp, though the black and the concrete were peeling off and the brick-work underneath was decayed and crumbling. They stepped out of the sunlight. There were two doors in the semi-darkness at the bottom. The one to the right was metal and painted black, a padlock on it, and the one to the left was rusted red, no locks visible on it, therefore apparently no way of accessing it. They stood and waited, not speaking. There was a grating sound from inside the door to the left, as if someone was turning a handle, then the door was pushed open and they stepped through.

The corridors were silent around him now, though the smell of antiseptic was stronger. He turned right and stood in front of

*the door, punched the combination into the security lock, pushed
the door open, and stepped inside.*

The corridor was long; its floor, ceiling and walls were tiled
white, but the tiles were discoloured and chipped, and eerie in
the low-power overhead lighting. Left, Kincaid assumed, was back
to the building at the rear. The attendant turned right. They
followed him fifteen metres, turned half right then half left. The
door was to the right. It was large and metalled, rusting at the
edges and the bottom, a large metal handle in the centre also
rusted slightly. The attendant looked at them. 'You ready?' He
grasped the handle and turned it anti-clockwise, the sound the
same as when he opened the main door to the outside, then
pulled open the door. The light inside was already on. The attendant moved aside and Kincaid stepped through.

*The morgue was empty, but that was the way it had been
arranged. No attendants to ask questions and no pen-pushers to
request signatures when the footsteps came down the corridor
in two minutes' time. The gleaming white examination slab was
in the centre of the floor and the plastic body bag lay upon it.
I was point man for you. I was baby-sitting you, Joshua; I was
the one who was supposed to bring you through. I was the one
Leo Panelli recommended to you, the one in whose hands you
put your faith and your trust and your life. And I let you down.
He walked round the slab, unzipped the bag, and looked at the
face.*

Oh Christ, Kincaid thought.

The bodies were naked and stacked on top of each other to
the ceiling. Some blue, some white, some a garish tinted orange.
Four or five deep, shoulders and heads hanging over one edge of
the two tables which ran from the door to the far end, and legs
and feet over the other. More on the floor underneath – again
stacked on each other – as well as on the trolleys between. Eyes
staring at him and mouths open to him. The lighting was in
grilles overhead and the refrigeration bars which ran round the
walls halfway up were rusting.

Oh Christ, he thought again.

The body nearest him had once been a man. The hair was
long and matted, the eyes and mouth were open and twisted so

the corpse seemed to be looking at him, the front of the torso was stitched following an autopsy, and the skin was orange. The body on which it lay was white, the one below that tinged a pale blue. The woman on the nearest trolley to him had a scarf tied round her head. A dirty sheet covered her nakedness – the only body covered – but her mouth was still open, her eyes were twisted up so that no matter where he stood they seemed to be staring at him, and the smell drifted out at him. Perhaps her smell, perhaps the smell of them all.

He looked for Joshua and saw the girl.

What had once been a beautiful face. Body still beautiful, breasts still full and nipples still dark on them. Blond hair splayed like corn over her shoulders and long slender legs slightly open as if the male body below was penetrating her.

Sherenko showed the attendant Whyte's photograph and pulled on the surgical gloves. 'He went missing yesterday, so where might he be?'

'Should be at the front, but I've been away, and in this place you never know.

Sherenko nodded. *'Vpered.'* Let's do it.

Sherenko picked his way between the two tables and Kincaid squeezed along the narrow space along the wall to the right.

Male, stiff and old, yellow skin and gunshot wound in lower abdomen. Woman, mid-forties, so don't bother to look. Another male, too young – hell, no more than a kid. Another woman. Kincaid tried not to breathe, tried to look only at the faces, tried to stop the faces looking back at him.

'Take the feet,' Sherenko told him.

Business not personal, O'Bramsky had said five years ago. Business not personal, Sherenko's attitude and eyes said now. Bastard, Kincaid thought. He grabbed the woman's feet, Sherenko the shoulders, and moved her so they could see the face of the male underneath. Kincaid straightened and glanced at the girl even though he did not want to. Beautiful girl, beautiful body. So what the hell is someone like her doing here? Why the hell is Sherenko staring at her as if he'd paid his money at a peepshow?

The smell crept over them, consumed them; the eyes and the

limbs and the hair. They came to the end, made their way back, and began to check the bodies on the table along the left wall. Male, white flesh almost translucent, the arm broken at a grotesque angle, either before death or after. Female, needle marks up the arms and face half missing. They finished checking the bodies on the tables, bent down, and checked underneath. An arm brushed against Kincaid's face.

They came to the trolleys in the middle, came closer to the girl. Female, so no need to check, but the body beneath her was male, so they had to touch her, handle her. Move her so they could see the face of the man across whose body her legs were spread.

They came to the end.

In forty seconds the footsteps would come down the corridor. 'Sorry, my friend . . .' Kincaid zipped up the bag and left.

The attendant swung the door back in place and sealed the dead back in their own world, then they went back down the white-tiled passageway and out through the metalled rusting door to the gloom at the bottom of the incline down.

'Thanks.' Sherenko pulled off the gloves, shook the attendant's hand, handed him a business card and slid him a folded hundred-dollar bill. 'Keep the photo. If he shows, let me know.'

The man disappeared back inside and pulled the door shut. Kincaid and Sherenko walked back up the slope, into the sun at the top, and drove away.

The thin girls were still playing tennis and the children were still climbing amongst the felled trees, the washing was still hanging on the balconies and the couple were sitting on the grass holding hands. Kincaid rolled down his side window and allowed the little wind there was to brush against his face. At the top Sherenko turned left and dropped toward the Profsojuznaja metro station, past the kiosk where he had bought the Stolichnaya, then turned right at the lights toward Leninski Prospekt. Five minutes later Red Square was on their left, on the other side of the river, the domes of St Basil's sparkling in the evening sun and the walls and towers of the Kremlin behind it. They crossed the river and turned right, up one street and down another. The buildings were suddenly changing, a set of kiosks on a corner – better built kiosks, better-dressed people round them – music coming from somewhere, and shops on either side.

Sherenko pulled in, switched off the engine, got out, and sat against the bonnet, breathing deeply. A well-dressed couple passed them, passed the armed guard on the door to the club behind them. A black Mercedes pulled in and two men – smart haircuts and padded suits – got out and went inside. Kincaid stepped out of the BMW and drew the air into his lungs, ran his fingers through his hair again as if that would dispel the odour. Sherenko fetched the Stolichnaya from the glove compartment and leaned again against the bonnet, cracked open the top and took a long *stogram*.

Chert vozmi, Kincaid thought. Screw you. You didn't stand in the morgue at Belle Vue, you had no idea what it means to go into a place like the morgue on C'urupy Ulica. He leaned across, wrenched the bottle from Sherenko's grasp, and took a long pull.

Sherenko took the bottle back, emptied it, threw it in a bin at the side of a kiosk with tables in front, jerked into the driver's seat and started the engine in one movement, and pulled away, barely waiting for Kincaid to get in.

'Riley said you and Brady were showing me Moscow tonight.' Sherenko's eyes were fixed on the road in front.

Screw you, Sherenko, Kincaid thought again. Screw you, Joshua. 'Yeah. Show you Moscow.'

When the two of them plus Brady arrived at the Santa Fe it was almost nine-thirty. The restaurant, in one of Moscow's residential suburbs, was protected by tall white walls, BMWs and Mercedes were pulled in to the dust strip between the road and the wall, and the South Western American style double gates were slightly ajar, one guard outside and a second inside. Sherenko nodded at the guards and led Kincaid and Brady through. The restaurant was to the left, white-washed and Spanish style, with steps up to it.

The first bar was spacious, high ceilings and tables and chairs around the edge. All of those present were well-dressed, a mix of expats and Russians. They looked round, chose a table near the door, and smiled at the waitress who asked for their drink orders. Didn't expect to find tequila and Tex-Mex in Moscow, Brady joked, and ordered a margarita. Same, Kincaid told the waitress. Three – Sherenko held up three fingers. Two minutes later the waitress brought the margaritas and took their orders: salsa dip, ribs and French fries, and San Miguels in the bottle.

'*Vashe zdorovye*.' Kincaid held up the glass.

The woman came in the door behind them, looked at Kincaid and Brady, allowed her eyes to settle on Sherenko, and walked through to the restaurant at the far end. She was mid-twenties, tall, dark hair immaculately groomed, high-heeled shoes and expensive dress.

Brady turned as she went past.

'Don't even think about it,' Sherenko told him.

'Why not?'

'You couldn't afford it.'

Brady was still watching the woman. 'Why couldn't I?'

The waitress cleared the cocktails and brought the San Miguels.

Sherenko rubbed the lime round the rim of the bottle. 'To understand, you have to understand the new Russian women, some of whom you see here tonight.' He waved his hand towards the rest of the bar, the movement controlled and economic. 'Okay, some of them are working girls. Some of them are young, probably late teens, dressing up and trying to look good. Others are high-class, good lookers, good dressers. Probably born into the party. By which I mean the Communist Party.'

He took a pull of San Miguel and smiled as the waitress served them the tortilla chips and salsa.

'There is, however, a third type. Probably slightly older. Late twenties, early thirties. Similar background, university educated and multi-lingual, but now running their own businesses, or at least successful in their chosen careers. High-earners and high-players, but not on the game.' He played with the bottle. 'A woman like this might be single or might still be married but is running the show, might have got fed up with her husband. Perhaps he drinks too much Stoli so she's kicked him out.'

He looked at Kincaid. Too close to home – Kincaid felt the

unease, though for Stolichnaya read Jack Daniels. Screw you, Sherenko.

Sherenko looked back at Brady. 'So she works hard during the daytime and plays hard at night. Comes to a place like this – hell, you can see them, see the way they do it. They could make the catwalks in Milan without problems, but the fashion world doesn't appeal because it's not as much fun as here.' Sherenko looked round the bar again and Kincaid realized the woman who had come in earlier was glancing at him. 'So she comes in, looks round, decides who she likes the look of. Makes eye contact and they'll eat, possibly dance. She might pay, he might pay, it doesn't matter. Might take in a club, might do some dope. And if she fancies him then she'll go to bed with him; if she doesn't, she'll say ciao.' He paused slightly. '*Takova zhizn.*' He threw back his head and hands in a slightly exaggerated manner. 'I'm me and nobody else. Take me or leave me.'

Arrogant son-of-a-bitch, Kincaid thought again.

'So why couldn't I afford one?' Brady asked.

'You could still afford some of them, but not the high class girls, not the ones you're really talking about.'

And you're saying you could, Kincaid thought. More than that. You're saying you wouldn't have to.

'Why not?' Brady asked.

'A year ago the men they went for, the ones with the dollars, were the expats, the foreign businessmen. Now the ones with the real money in Moscow are the mafia.'

When Sherenko dropped them at the block containing the company apartment it was past eleven. The apartment was on the fourth floor, the furniture and decor functional rather than attractive. Two bedrooms, sitting-room, kitchen at the rear, and small bathroom. No bath, but an electric power shower bought in London.

Riley was at a computer in the sitting-room. 'Coffee?' He logged off the Internet.

'Anything stronger?' Kincaid asked.

'Glenmorangie?'

'Sounds fine.'

Brady claimed an early start the next morning and went to the second bedroom – two single beds, not much space between.

Riley fetched two glasses and a bottle. 'Where'd Nik take you?'

'The Santa Fe. Playing it safe, I guess.'

Riley laughed, poured them each a measure, and settled in the armchair. 'How was it?' he asked.

'Take it or leave it,' Kincaid told him. 'Tell me about Sherenko,' he asked.

'Why?'

Kincaid shrugged.

Riley sipped the malt. 'You have problems with Nik, Jack?'

'He's not the easiest man to work with.'

'Which is why Tom's pissed off and gone to bed?'

Kincaid shrugged again but said nothing.

Riley stared at him above the glass. 'Can I ask you something, Jack?'

'Sure.'

'You got problems with Moscow?'

'No. Why'd you ask?'

'No reason.'

'So tell me about Sherenko.'

'Not much to say really. Ex-Alpha, like a lot of the boys. Apparently he served with Alpha for a while, then left. Surfaced two, three years back and Mikhail signed him up. Good operator, probably the best. Bit of a loner, keeps himself to himself. Divorced, couple of kids.'

Riley poured himself another Glenmorangie and passed the bottle across.

'There's one other thing I don't understand.' Kincaid splashed the clear brown liquid into the glass. 'Sherenko was a member of Alpha.'

'Yes.'

'Alpha was Special Forces, including anti-terrorism, but primarily within the Soviet Union.'

'For most of its history. Why?'

'Nothing.'

Except if Alpha was internal, there was no reason for members of Alpha to speak English. The Omega guys are all Alpha, and they don't. A few words perhaps, but nothing more. So why does Sherenko speak it fluently?

For the past hour he had lain on the bed and tried not to sleep; now he felt himself taking the first inevitable steps. The sunlight gave way to the shadow, the rusted door to the left opened, and the morgue attendant beckoned him in. He stepped into the cold; the white tiles of the corridor were almost blurred and the sounds of his footsteps were muffled yet echoing. You knew you would come this way, the sliver of rationality told him. He fought it anyway, tried to escape from it even though he knew it was to no avail. Moved slowly – all such moments were in slow motion – and followed the attendant. Stepped forward as the attendant moved aside, saw that it was his own hands which gripped the wheel at the centre of the door and ground it anti-clockwise. The sweat poured off his body. The lock gave way and the door swung open. He glanced to his left and saw the attendant grinning at him, the smile not on the face but on the gash of red which had once been his throat. Saw that the face was not the attendant's, but his own. Saw his own hand, dismembered from his arm, beckoning him inside. The bodies were stacked to the ceiling. Red and blue and orange, the colours exaggerated and unreal, as if they had never been real, as if they were dummies from the set of a horror movie. He pulled the rubber gloves on. His fingers slid through the rips in the rubber, and he began the search. Saw the man: yellow skin and gunshot wound in the lower abdomen. Except there were two wounds, not one: the entry point of the 8.58x71mm round neat in the centre of his shoulders, and the front and chest of the body torn where the round had exited. He saw the girl. Naked body still beautiful, breasts still full and nipples dark on them, long legs slightly open as if the male body below her was penetrating her, blonde hair splayed like corn over her shoulders. Except the hair was black and the girl he now saw wore Levis.

Nikolai Sherenko pulled himself from the nightmare and stared at the ceiling. The apartment was quiet around him and the first light shone cold through the windows. He checked the time, rose, pulled on a dressing-gown, and made himself coffee. When he left it was six-thirty. Three minutes before seven he was at the office. Kincaid arrived at seven-fifteen. By seven-thirty they had updated the case log and Gerasimov and Riley had joined them.

The first backgrounds on Maddox and Dwyer at ConTex, and the couriers Whyte and Pearce, had come in overnight. They called for fresh coffee and flicked through them, then Kincaid and Sherenko were driven to the ConTex offices off the Tverskaya.

Maddox and Dwyer were waiting for them in Maddox's office; both were in shirtsleeves and Maddox wore cowboy boots. They shook hands and sat down, Maddox leaning back in his chair with his feet on the desk, Dwyer in a high-backed leather chair to the right, and Kincaid and Sherenko facing them.

'I'd like to make two things clear right away.' Kincaid took the lead. US company, US money goes missing after all. 'First, we're all on the same side. Second, I brought in six million yesterday, and only one million of that went to Kazakhstan, so you've obviously got something else going which you might not want to talk about.'

'Appreciated.' Dwyer looked nervous.

Maddox changed position slightly. 'Shoot.'

'I'd like to do the interviews separately.'

'No problems.'

Because we're all on the same side, Kincaid understood; because us American boys have to stick together. He opened the briefcase he carried and took out a Sony cassette recorder. 'I'd also like to tape the interviews. That way there's no misunderstanding.'

'Fine,' Maddox told him. 'Who'd you want to speak to first?'

'Guess we'll start with you.'

Dwyer began to leave. Got a meeting over lunch, but other than that he'd made the day free, he informed them. Kincaid thanked him, watched him go, accepted a coffee and clicked on the cassette recorder. 'Arnie, I've read the reports. Can you take me through them, give us the general overall picture of what happened.' His ballgame, his demeanour said; him calling the plays.

Maddox led them through his return from Kazakhstan, which was routine; the need for the dollars there, which was also routine, plus the need for additional dollars to finance something Phil Dwyer was working on.

'Can you tell me what that is?'

Difficult, Maddox's grimace said.

Commercial confidentiality – Kincaid nodded his understanding, no problems. Take me on, he told Maddox: how'd you communicate with Houston over this? When Kazakhstan wants money, how do your people there tell you? How did this shipment differ from any others? How many staff would have known about it and how much did the company providing the security pick-up know?

They broke for ten minutes while Maddox took a call from Kazakhstan.

Take me through your personal timetable, Kincaid asked Maddox when they reconvened; who you met and who you talked to. Take me through that day. What about the waiter who served him and Phil Dwyer at dinner, what about when he and Phil went for a walk after? What about Nite Flite; anyone pick them out more than the usual way, anyone target them? What about when they left, when Maddox's driver picked them up?

They moved next door to the office Dwyer was using and ran the same routine, Kincaid asking the questions because the show was his.

Anybody Dwyer had met who'd asked him about what he was doing, anybody ask about the dollar shipments? The shipment was in two sections, they didn't want the details of course, but what about the people he was dealing with? Were they from a company or a government department or were they individuals? How and when did the subject of payment come up? Did the guys he was dealing with specify a date and did they therefore know the money was coming in? Anyone asked him anything, but anything, which in retrospect struck him as unusual? What about his staff? Anyone at the hotel or Nite Flite?

Dwyer glanced at his watch.

'Time to leave?' Kincaid asked.

'Afraid so.' Dwyer stood up. 'Like I said, I have to meet some-one over lunch. Feel free to come back this afternoon.'

'Not necessary, Phil. I think we have everything we want.' Kincaid returned the cassette recorder to the briefcase and allowed Dwyer to show them out of his office and down the corridor. The atmosphere was relaxed and friendly. They shook hands. Dwyer half-turned from them to return to his office.

'Hope you used some protection, Phil.' It was Sherenko, casual, boys amongst boys, beer at the bar and your round next. 'You know about the girls in Moscow.'

''Course I used some protection.' Dwyer was still on the half-turn, the laugh on his face and the conspiracy in his eyes. ''Course we all know about the girls in . . .' His face froze.

The fog descended on Kincaid: deep and cold and freezing. Screw you, Sherenko, he thought, because all morning you sat and listened and didn't intervene. Okay, so I didn't give you the chance, but screw you anyway. Screw you Dwyer and Maddox, because you played the American card with me and I fell for it. Thought you were telling me the truth therefore went easy on you. Okay, so I believed you because the ConTex enquiry is as good as wrapped up and the report's as good as written. Okay, so I went into the goddam interview believing you before you'd even said a word, because I detest and loathe this city just as I detest and loathe people like Sherenko. So screw you, Dwyer and Maddox, for taking me to the cleaners. Screw you, Sherenko, for knowing what they were doing all along, even screw you for getting me out of it. Screw you, Joshua, because you're still sitting on my shoulder as Bram said you would.

He stared at Dwyer. 'Thought you said Arnie's driver collected you and him from Nite Flite, Phil.' There was just enough threat in his voice. 'Thought you said you didn't score that night?'

'Yeah, well . . .' Dwyer hesitated.

'Think you'd better cancel lunch, Phil.' Kincaid walked past Dwyer and back into the office, held the door while Dwyer then Sherenko came in, and closed it. 'You want to sit down, Phil?'

Dwyer sat at his desk, the desk itself no longer a barrier between them, no protection for him. 'Okay.' He pulled the handkerchief from his pocket and wiped his face. 'I scored at Nite Flite.' He looked at his watch again. 'Look guys, I really got to make this lunch.'

'No problems, Phil,' Sherenko told him. 'Do lunch and speak to us after.' He rose and opened the door for Dwyer. 'Hell, Phil. Look on the positive side. At least you did wear some protection.'

The relief flooded over Dwyer. 'Yeah, at least I did.'

They watched him leave, made sure he didn't speak with Maddox, told Maddox's secretary they needed ten minutes with the boss, and waited till they were shown in again.

'Got a problem, Arnie.' Kincaid looked straight at Maddox. No preamble. 'You said that you and Phil left Night Flite together, that your driver picked you both up and drove you both home.' We got it on tape, Arnie – it was in Kincaid's stare; so time to come clean, time to drop the bullshit. 'Phil tells us he scored that night. Phil says he picked up someone at Nite Flite.'

Okay, guys – Maddox was always bullish when he was on the defensive. Phil pulled someone. Good-looking chick, but they all were. He'd made sure Phil was covered, though, because although Phil was a man of the world, Moscow was something else. So he'd called his driver, made sure he was waiting outside Nite Flite with strict orders to take Phil and Phil's piece of ass to Phil's hotel and nowhere else. Then he had made his own way home. Except Phil was married – hell, they all were. So when Phil had asked him to cover it, he'd agreed.

Bastards – the anger boiled inside Kincaid. You set me up, laughed at me all the way to the bank. No problems, he told Maddox; they'd have to run a couple of things past Phil, but it was Phil who'd suggested he'd scored that night in the first place, so Arnie was covered. And no sweat anyway, because we all like a bit of spare occasionally, especially when we're away from home.

'Nite Flite . . .' Kincaid picked up with Dwyer when he returned. 'No problems, and everything's confidential. The chick you picked up, though. Did you pick her up, or did she pick you up? Good idea taking her to your own hotel, of course, because you have to be careful.'

'Lucky it wasn't the Intourist.' Sherenko's voice was like winter.

'Why?' Dwyer looked at him.

'Because there you have to buy in-house.' Kincaid came at him like a wind out of Siberia. 'Try to take your own in and they beat the shit out of you both.'

Dwyer was theirs, Dwyer would do anything for them. Dwyer would tell them nothing but the purest, most absolute truth.

'Okay, Phil,' Kincaid told him. 'Take us through that evening.'

At four-thirty they left ConTex and the technical team moved in to sweep the premises. Freelance team, by which Sherenko meant FSB boys on a moonlight. Good at their job – installing or detecting – and American gear they'd bought personally from the shop at Frankfurt airport.

By the time Sherenko and Kincaid reached the Omega office Grere Jameson had arrived from Washington via an overnight in London. Kincaid did the introductions, then updated the case log and Sherenko phoned the morgue.

'No Whyte.' He put the phone down.

'You don't think we should check for ourselves?'

'You want to?'

'No point if we've left a photo.'

Riley came in, Gerasimov and Jameson behind him. They went through to the conference room, Jameson looking slightly tired and allowing Gerasimov to lead. Gerasimov checked his watch, brought the session to order and asked Sherenko for an update.

'Looks leaky,' Sherenko told him.

'Explain.'

'The organizational front at ConTex to begin with. The internal security is bad. Knowledge of a money shipment is not restricted. The chain of command and communication is such that too many people know when and how much is coming in, and we haven't even started on the Russian staff or the office in Kazakhstan.'

Gerasimov turned to Kincaid.

'There are also potential security problems on the personal front,' Kincaid told them. 'Five million of the missing money was requested by a ConTex vice president, Dwyer, who is doing some deal in Moscow. Probably getting ahead of the game in oil or gas leases. Unless it's a scam, which is not our business at the moment, though I guess it might be sometime. On the night the money was ordered he and Maddox went to Nite Flite. Although they tried to brush it over, Dwyer picked someone up and spent the night with her.'

Gerasimov nodded. 'Next?'

'The motor the security pick-up used,' Sherenko told him. 'We should get the fingerprint people to take a look at it.'

'Why?'

'If it was involved in an accident, and the accident was one reason they didn't make the airport for the pick-up, there's an outside chance someone might have left a print.'

'I'll get someone in tomorrow.'

'What about the courier who fell sick in London?' Jameson spoke for the first time.

'Tomorrow Nik does the security pick-up team and starts on the ConTex staff, and Jack flies to London to interview the courier. You carrying, Jack?'

'No.'

'Might be an idea. Fix him up, Nik.' Gerasimov looked around the table. 'What else?'

'Might be good to know who runs the mafia at the airport.' It was Sherenko again.

'Why?'

'Because if we don't get anywhere within ConTex, whoever runs the airport mafia might not be too happy that someone else is doing something on his patch. Assuming he had nothing to do with it, of course.'

'I'll check it out,' Gerasimov told him.

They left the conference room and returned to their offices. Gerasimov checked that his driver was waiting, then he and Jameson left.

'Where are they going?' Kincaid asked Riley.

'Get changed, I guess.'

'What for?'

'Some sort of party.'

Kincaid waited for an explanation.

Riley sat forward slightly in his chair. 'You remember what happened five years ago this week?'

'Yeah. I remember what happened five years ago.' Kincaid picked up his coat. 'So why are Gerasimov and Jameson going to a party?'

'Five years ago today it was Gerasimov's men who were sent to assassinate Yeltsin in the White House. Five years ago tomorrow Gerasimov's men protected Yeltsin instead of assassinating him, and probably changed the course of history.' And that's why he and Jameson are going to a party. 'Drink?' he asked.

'Thanks anyway, but not tonight.' Kincaid dusted his jacket. 'See you tomorrow,' he told Sherenko.

'Yeah, see you in the morning.'

Kincaid left the office, walked down Gertsena Ulica and crossed to the Tverskaya. The evening was warm, there were strands of thin cloud across the sky, and the pavements were busy, cars parked along them and vehicles passing. So what's this about, Jack my friend? What are you doing and why are you doing it? He stepped between the parked cars and held his hand in the air. The first Lada passed him and the second pulled in.

'*Leningradski vokzal.*' The Russian was too much like the language school rather than the pavements of Moscow.

'Twenty thousand roubles.'

'Too much.'

'It's out of my way.'

Kincaid stood back, watched the Lada jerk away, and held his hand in the air again. Another Lada swerved in.

'*Leningradski voksal.*' Better, he told himself.

'Eighteen thousand roubles.'

'Ten thousand.'

'Fifteen.'

'Okay.'

He opened the door and slipped into the rear seat. The windscreen was cracked, a fresh air filter was stuck to the dashboard and the back of the driver's seat was ripped. 'What time is it?' he asked. The driver pulled out into the line of traffic without bothering to look and glanced at his watch. 'Five to eight.'

'Nice watch, what sort is it?'

'Tag Heuer.'

'Christ, you must earn a fortune.'

'Counterfeit. Twenty dollars.'

They talked about prices in Moscow, where you could get what. You heard the joke about the new Russian, he told the driver. Goes to London and buys a watch for twenty thousand dollars. That evening he shows it to a friend. You've been done, the friend tells him: I know where I can get the same watch for thirty thousand.

The driver laughed and swerved, either to avoid a pothole or another cab, possibly both. New Russian wipes out his Merc, he told Kincaid. Why the hell you crying, a friend says; the car's nothing; look, you've lost an arm. The man looks down. Christ, he says, my Cartier.

So what are you playing at, Jack, what are you up to?

The driver pulled in to the station. The building was brown and single-storey, steps going up to its three doors and people packed around it. Kincaid paid the driver and went inside. The hall was small and dark, connecting stairs and passages running off it, a kiosk selling drinks and a man who hadn't shaved selling *pirozhki*, small pastries, from a wooden tray. People pushing past and the evening sun breaking through the dust on the windows at the far end. He felt in his pocket and pulled out a handful of notes. Counted them carefully and handed them over, moved to a corner and ate the *pirozhki* and drank the Coke, and sidled on. Passengers were already gathering for the mid-evening trains, a policewoman clearing a drunk from amongst them. Kincaid left the main station and crossed to the metro.

So what's tonight all about, Jack old friend? What game are you playing and why?

Not Jack – he corrected himself. Jack Mikhailovich Kincaid, because in Russian everyone used the first name of their father as their own middle name.

Okay, Jack Mikhailovich, so what's running?

He stepped on to the escalator, the descent reminding him of the metro stations at Dupont Circle or Bethesda, except in Washington the walls and ceilings were grey and concrete. He came to the bottom and stepped into a different world. Walked through the hallway connecting the various platforms and could have been walking through the Louvre or the Smithsonian or the Hermitage. The floor and walls and ceilings were marbled, marbled busts on plinths and marbled garlands in alcoves.

At the end of the platform a digital clock indicated how long ago the previous train had left and therefore, by deduction, how long the next would be. Even in mid-evening the platform was crowded. The train pulled in and the doors opened. Those waiting on the platform stood to each side, and those arriving poured off. The moment the last left the train those waiting streamed on. He found a seat and looked up and down the carriage at his fellow travellers.

So what's this about, Jack Mikhailovich? Why take a cab, then the metro, and end up less than a thousand metres from where you started?

His observations over the next hour were footnotes to what had gone before. When he returned to the flat shortly before eleven the message from Riley was on a notepad.

Nik will pick you up at six. Session at range for six-thirty. You're on the nine o'clock flight to London.

Gerasimov's driver collected Jameson from his hotel at eight. Gerasimov was in the rear seat. He wore a dark blue suit and matching tie. In his left lapel he wore an Alpha pin. The driver cut across the inner ring road, skirted Red Square, and eased down the narrow tree-lined street three hundred yards from the Kremlin.

'Brief me on who'll be there tonight,' Jameson requested.

Gerasimov briefed him.

'Who's important?' Jameson asked.

'They're all important, but the man for the future is Malenkov. He was First Chief Directorate, now he's a major-general in the SVR.'

The Omega driver eased to a halt on the right side of the street. They left the car and crossed to the building on the left. The house was three-storey, grey and anonymous, black door and no obvious security. As Gerasimov and Jameson crossed the road another car pulled in behind theirs.

The doorbell was on the left; before they had pressed it the black door opened and they stepped inside. The reception area was marbled, marbled stairs on the right leading to the floors above and a desk on the left, the monitors of the security cameras above it, one man at the console and another standing. They were escorted up the stairs, past the next floor, to the next. The double doors were wood and highly varnished, another set of stairs leading to the floor above. They went through the doors and into the flat.

The hallway was long, the walls a pleasant pastel, and the lounge was on the left. It was large, windows on to the street, and the furniture and decoration were art nouveau. The library was through a door in the far corner, the dining-room was on the other side of the hall – exquisite oval table, finest tableware, elegant chandelier above it and priceless Lalique glassware behind it. The first bedroom – as Jameson would be shown later – was on the same side as the dining-room: again art nouveau and twin beds. The bathroom, large and luxurious, was next to it, and the double bedroom – king-size art nouveau bed – was opposite the bathroom, on the same side as the lounge.

Half a dozen men were already in the room. Most were in their forties or early fifties, though two were older, all were wearing suits, and all were former or present generals in the KGB or its successors, the FSB, the internal security service, and the SVR, the Foreign Intelligence Service.

Jameson looked around. 'Nice place.'

'Marcus Wolfe used to use it when he was in town,' Gerasimov told him.

Marcus Wolfe was the legendary East German spymaster.

'What I would have given to have been here ten years ago,' Jameson joked.

'What we would have given to have had you here,' Gerasimov joked back.

They accepted a Lagavulin and caviar and Gerasimov began the introductions, the conversations switching easily between English and Russian, and the handshakes and welcomes as if Jameson was a new friend rather than an old enemy.

There was a movement at the door from the corridor and

Malenkov came in. He was six feet tall, late forties and slim; hair beginning to turn silver and hand-cut suit that made him look like a high-flyer in an American or European bank or blue-chip investment house. His eyes were sharp and blue, the antithesis of the West's image of a KGB general.

'General Sergei Malenkov, Grere Jameson . . .' Gerasimov did the introductions.

'Recognize you from your file,' Jameson joked in perfect Russian.

'And I recognize you from yours.' Malenkov's face was locked in a smile and his reply was in flawless English.

3

Sherenko rose at six.

The apartment was almost too big for him now. It had been small when Natasha and the girls had been there; the girls had had the bedroom, and he and his wife (when he was at home) a pull-down in the sitting-room. Their photos were still on the sideboard and the documents which chronicled their lives together lay in a folder in a drawer.

He made coffee, ate a small breakfast, then cleared the table, washed up, slipped on the shoulder holster and Sig Sauer, locked the flat and collected the BMW, checking underneath it before he opened it. Fifteen minutes later he turned into the street where the company apartment was situated. The street was almost empty: half a dozen slightly battered cars were parked along the sides, the pavements were dusty, and a dog was relieving itself against a tree. The only man in the street, leaning with his back against the wall as if he was waiting for a tram or trolleybus, was as grey and inconspicuous as the street itself. Sherenko stopped and Kincaid got in.

'*Nu, chto vchera delal?*' So what did you do last night?

'*Nichevo osolennovo.*' Nothing in particular.

The building, when they reached it, was faded red brick and looked like a factory. Sherenko turned through an unlit archway, showed an ID at the security barrier, then drove into the court-yard beyond. Despite the hour there were other cars already there, plus two transits. The morning was quiet, as if the walls around them deadened any noise. Sherenko locked the BMW and led Kincaid through a door in the wall opposite the archway, then down a set of stone stairs to the range.

There were ten plywood targets, paper facing on them; seven

were Figure 11s, half-body and head, and three Figure 12s, head
and shoulders. Six of them were being used: the men shooting
at them were dressed in battle fatigues, no insignia or identification, and all were in their early twenties. Their instructor nodded
at Sherenko, his students glancing across.

'What did you train on?' Sherenko seemed at ease in the place.

'Normal stuff,' Kincaid told him. 'Walther, Beretta, Uzi.'

'What do you feel comfortable with?'

'They're mostly the same, I guess.'

Sherenko took the automatic from his shoulder holster and
gave it to Kincaid. 'Sig Sauer P226. Swiss manufacture. The
British SAS put it through two years of testing before they
decided to adopt it in preference to the Browning. Fifteen-round
mag, which is why the SAS also likes it.'

Kincaid checked that the safety was on, settled in front of one
of the targets, dropped into a combat crouch and brought the Sig
Sauer up. Felt for the safety with his right and fired six rounds.
Sherenko wound back the target. One round had hit the right
shoulder, three the chest and abdomen area, and two more were
slightly to the left.

'When did you last use a gun?'

The residue of antagonism flashed in Kincaid's brain. 'A few
years back.'

'You were a desk or a field man?'

Kincaid hesitated. 'Field man.' He hesitated again. 'But we had
gorillas to take care of the dirty stuff.'

Sherenko looked at him. 'In Moscow you don't have time to
call the gorillas.'

Kincaid fired six more rounds.

'I suggest you come in each morning.' Sherenko took the gun,
slid in a fresh magazine, put the automatic back in his shoulder
holster and turned away from the target.

Screw you, you arrogant bastard, Kincaid thought as he had
thought the previous evening.

Sherenko turned, hand taking the Sig Sauer as he did so, body
dropping fluidly into a combat crouch, the automatic on target
as if it was an extension of himself and the right thumb flicking
off the safety smoothly and naturally. Three rounds, change

position, second three rounds. Drop and roll to left, always present a moving target. Three more rounds.

Flash bastard – the other men on the range glanced across. Except he's an old flash bastard. They themselves had been firing much quicker, getting off more rounds than Sherenko and were still on target, their rounds, like his, in a tight cluster.

Sherenko suddenly looks his age, Kincaid thought; Sherenko suddenly looks like me. The real flash bastards, the ones who really were on the ball, were the guys twenty metres away.

Sherenko stood, slipped on the safety, handed Kincaid the Sig Sauer, and wound back the target. The rounds were positioned in a tight cluster round the centre of the chest, none outside. 'So that was my job and yours was running people. But this is Moscow, and in Moscow, if a street trader doesn't pay up his pittance of roubles for protection, or a banker calls in a loan, he ends up in a place like C'urupy Ulica.'

'And . . .' Kincaid asked.

'And we're working together. If they come for you I might be there. So I'm looking after my ass as well as yours.'

'Fuck you, Nik,' Kincaid said.

'Fuck you too, my friend.'

They left forty minutes later. In the last quarter-hour Kincaid's groupings had begun to improve, and in the final five minutes the rate of improvement had accelerated.

'What time's the flight?' Sherenko cut past a line of cars. The traffic was heavy now, but most of it was coming the other way, into Moscow.

'Nine.'

'I thought the first BA flight is this afternoon.'

'I'm flying Aeroflot.'

So lucky you, Sherenko's eyes said. 'What time you seeing Pearce?'

'As soon as I get in.'

'What about the flight back?'

'The first one as soon as I've wrapped up with Pearce. I'll let the office know.'

Sherenko slowed for a set of lights. 'Don't get a cab into town. Most of the drivers are cowboys and the road is bad. Cross to the Novotel, there's a shuttle for hotel guests every fifteen minutes.' He turned into Sheremetyevo. 'Riley told you about the party tonight?'

'Yeah, he gave me the name of the restaurant. I'll make it if I can.'

Sherenko pulled up the slope and stopped in front of the departures area on the upper level of the airport building. Kincaid hurried inside, checked on the monitors that his flight was on time, then stood in line for the currency, customs, ticket and passport formalities. Most of those checking in were businessmen, some of them Russian, the expats wearing the standard suits and the Russians wearing Versaces and looking as if they were going to a nightclub. Kincaid bought a black coffee in the Irish Bar and waited for the flight to be called.

So what was that about last night? Why the hell had he gone walkabout?

Because Sherenko and Riley had been right, even though they hadn't told him directly. Because he, Jack Kincaid, God knows how many years in the game, had come into Moscow like all the other expats. Believing that he owned the world. Believing that because Moscow had lost the Cold War the Russians had everything to learn from him, and he had nothing to learn from them. And gently – actually not so gently – but in their different ways, Sherenko and Riley had let him know.

Riley to start with, when Kincaid had shown his reaction to the Omega offices on Gertsena Ulica, even though Riley had done it indirectly through Brady. Then Sherenko at the Santa Fe, indirectly again, via Brady; and Riley in the company apartment that night. You got a problem with Moscow, Riley had asked. And Riley after he had failed to show Gerasimov the proper respect at their first meeting. Good to meet you, Mikhail, Kincaid had said. Mikhail Sergeyevich – Riley had referred to Gerasimov in the conversation he had had with Kincaid the evening after. Had thrown in Gerasimov's patronymic, his second name, because in Russian that was a sign of respect. Especially formally, or at a first meeting.

And Sherenko had pulled him out of the proverbial at the ConTex meeting. Kincaid had assumed that because the guys at

ConTex, by whom he meant Maddox and Dwyer, were American like himself, they were telling him the truth. And all the time the bastards had been lying.

So screw Jack Kincaid, not Riley and Sherenko. Which was what last night had been about.

He looked up at the monitor, saw that flight SU247 was delayed an hour, and bought another coffee.

By the time he landed at Heathrow the delay had extended to an hour and a half. He cleared immigration and took the walkway from Terminal 4 to the Hilton.

So you went into Moscow like the proverbial virgin, Jack old friend. But why? Why did you screw up even though you knew what you were doing? Because you did know, right from the beginning.

Because five years ago this week I was supposed to hold Joshua's hand and I didn't, and therefore, and however indirectly it might have been, I betrayed him as surely as if it had been me who pulled the trigger on him. And all I could do instead was apologize to him and say goodbye to him in the morgue at Belle Vue before the hoods came to take him back to Moscow. And ever since then, Joshua has been sitting on my shoulder like a ghost. So that was what last night was about. Laying Joshua's ghost. Getting him off my back. And last night I did it.

He checked with reception and telephoned the suite ISS had rented for the day.

'Rich, it's Jack Kincaid. I'm downstairs. I wonder if you and I should talk before I come up.'

Matthews joined him two minutes later.

'Any problems?' Kincaid asked.

'They're fidgety.'

'So would you be if one of your people went missing with six million dollars.'

They ordered coffee, then Kincaid read through the range of reports collated by the London office: the second courier's statement, the doctor's report on his condition, and the background searches on both couriers, including financial details. Plus a security report on both.

'The doctor said Pearce had a viral problem and that he's still suffering from it?'

'Yes.'

'Could we arrange a lab test, see if anything could be used to produce or simulate the condition? A forensic analysis might also be useful – try the toxicology people at Aldermaston. They've experience of how the Soviets used to work, so they'll know what to look for. We might need a polygraph if Pearce doesn't play ball, or if we suspect he's not telling us the truth.'

Matthews signed for the coffee and they went upstairs. The courier Pearce was in an armchair and two other men, a representative of the company and a lawyer, sat on a sofa. Matthews introduced them and they shook hands.

'Before we begin there are certain guidelines.' The lawyer was mid-thirties, public school accent, and dressed in a pinstripe suit.

Of course, the ISS man Matthews began to agree.

Kincaid smiled at the lawyer. 'Before you say anything else, may I remind you that your clients lost six million dollars of my clients' money.' He smiled again. 'I view this meeting as amicable. I also view your presence at this meeting as being at my discretion. If you have any problems with that you can leave now.'

The lawyer began to suggest to the company representative that they withdraw for a discussion.

'I'm on the three o'clock flight back to Moscow,' Kincaid told him. 'Any costs incurred by any delay will be charged to you.'

The lawyer sat down.

Okay, Mike – Kincaid looked at Pearce and switched on the cassette recorder. Take me back to that morning; take me back to the night before. This viral problem, when were you first aware of it, when did you first tell Zak? How did the routine that morning differ from any other? Did you and Zak always know how much you were carrying? Who else knew . . .

Got to ask you this, Mike. Any chance Zak set you up, doctored your food or something so you couldn't make the trip . . . He watched carefully for Pearce's reaction. Got to ask you this as well, Mike. Any chance that you set up your own sickness, so that when Zak went into Sheremetyevo he didn't have you by

78

his side. Yeah, Mike, I know what I'm asking. What I'm asking is: were you part of the set-up? How do you feel about a polygraph, make sure you're telling the truth when you deny what I've just said . . .

How about a break for refreshments, the lawyer suggested. Get something sent in, Kincaid told him.

So where do you and Zak stay in Moscow, Mike? You use a hotel or a company pad? Know anybody in Moscow? Outside the company, I mean . . . The stylus on a polygraph would have flickered, he was aware. What about girls, Mike? I mean, Moscow's full of them? No girls, at all? So what the hell do you do in the evenings, because you don't remind me of a Bolshoi man, if you know what I mean . . .

'Okay,' Pearce told him. 'Zak and I have a couple of girls we see regularly when we're in Moscow.'

Oh shit – Kincaid heard the slight drawing in of breath as the company representative tried not to react.

'Couple of girls you see regularly in Paris and Rome and New York as well, I guess.'

Pearce laughed. 'Actually not Paris or Rome because we don't overnight there.'

This is like Dwyer at Nite Flite, Kincaid thought, this is one big honeypot.

The interview ended an hour later. It was fifty minutes to the last Moscow flight of the day. Kincaid hand-wrote a summary report on the interview, plus a request for Ivor Lukyanov to run checks on the two girls named by Pearce, and instructed Matthews to send them to Moscow on the secure fax.

The sky was laced with purple and the runway lights of Sheremetyevo were bright against the grey. The Ilyushin touched down and taxied toward the terminal. Walk to the Novotel and get the courtesy coach into town, Sherenko had said. Hope to hell immigration is quick tonight, Kincaid thought. The aircraft stopped and the seat belt sign flicked off. He stood, joined the line, and hurried off the plane. Sherenko was waiting at the top of the jetbridge. Ten minutes later they turned left out of the airport towards Moscow.

Kincaid settled in the passenger seat. 'The pick-up's appreciated.'

Sherenko waved the thanks aside. 'So what about Pearce? You think the girlfriends might be involved?'

'Pearce is straight. It could be he or Whyte let something slip, but if it was I don't think it was Pearce.'

'Why not?'

'Pearce was Mountain and Arctic Warfare Cadre, therefore he'd have done the interrogation course.'

Sherenko changed down to beat a set of traffic lights. 'Except the interrogation course doesn't tell you what to say when somebody's unzipping your flies. Or perhaps yours did.'

'So what about Moscow?' Kincaid asked.

'You mean the interrogation course or the Contex money?'

'Whichever.'

'The ConTex interviews were routine though a couple of people were missing, including Maddox's secretary. The financial backgrounds on Maddox and Dwyer are still coming in, but we might have a problem with Maddox. He's married, but according to sources he's having an affair with a First Secretary at the US embassy.'

'Any indication she's screwing with someone else as well?'

'Not yet, but we're checking. We're also checking on the girl-friends of the two couriers.'

'What about the security company who were supposed to make the pick-up?' Kincaid asked.

'Leaks like a sieve. The boys making the pick-up cocked up all the way down the line but seemed straightforward.'

'You believe them?'

'Probably.'

'Why?'

'The same reason you would. If I'd lifted six million, even if I had a cut of six million, I wouldn't be in Moscow now.'

'What about whoever runs the mafia at Sheremetyevo?'

'Mikhail came up with a name. Alexei Kosygin. Igor's running a check on him.' Sherenko leaned back and handed Kincaid a box from the rear seat. 'Present. You're booked in at the range at six in the morning.'

They crossed the ring road and dropped toward the city centre, the traffic suddenly busy around them. Sherenko turned off the main road and into a side street, trees along the pavement and cars parked on either side.

'So what was Moscow like five years ago today?' Kincaid asked.

Sherenko reversed into a space and switched off the engine. 'No idea. I wasn't here.'

Vorkov left the glass-fronted building at Yasenevo, on the outskirts of Moscow, and was driven towards the city. It was shortly after ten.

Felix Andreyevich Vorkov was forty-three years old, tall, with dark hair swept back, well-built but even better dressed. In the old KGB Vorkov had attained the rank of major. In the new order, with the KGB disbanded and its functions divided, Vorkov had made full colonel in the SVR, the Russian Foreign Intelligence Service, formerly the First Chief Directorate.

Five years ago there had been chaos in Moscow . . . Five years ago today in New York Nikolai Sherenko had done the job on East 54th – the ghost came at him . . . Not that Vorkov knew all the details, because then, as now, Malenkov didn't tell him everything. Thank God Malenkov had known about the bastard, though; thank God Sherenko had taken him out.

The cellphone rang.

'Yes.'

'The shipment's on the way,' he was informed. No other details, because the line wasn't secure.

'Good.'

Thirteen minutes later Vorkov's unmarked car stopped outside the Up and Down Club. Vorkov told his driver he would call him when he needed collection and went inside.

Alexei Kosygin was seated at a table in the corner. Kosygin was early thirties, squat build, and dressed in a designer suit. He had two bodyguards on the next table, and two girls at his own. He greeted Vorkov, poured him a glass of champagne, and nodded that the girls should leave for a moment.

'Za nas.' Vorkov emptied the glass in one and allowed Kosygin to pour him another. 'Thought you ought to know . . .' It was

81

said casually, as if it was interesting rather than important. 'Somebody pulled your FSB file this evening.'

Kosygin poured them each another glass. 'Which somebody?'

'Omega, the security company. I'm not sure who in the company is looking at you. No doubt we'll find out.'

4

The headlights bumped through the night behind him and the half moon arced like a shepherd's crook over him. Another thirty minutes and he'd take a break. Karpov changed up and checked in the wing mirrors. Karpov was ex-military, so did things like checking rear mirrors. The man in the passenger seat unscrewed the flask and poured him a mug. Karpov swung round the bend and saw the car pulled into the roadside, saw the woman – mid-twenties and short skirt – waving to him. Christ, he laughed: must think he'd been born yesterday. He changed down and eased his foot on the accelerator. The trees on either side were like ghosts. They overtook a series of slower-moving trucks and purred on, the trees flashing by as if they, not him, were moving. The night was a brighter silver now and the man to his right was slumped in the seat, apparently asleep. Karpov rounded the bend. The Volvo was slewed at an angle, totally blocking the road.

'We're on,' the man in the passenger seat whispered in the Motorola and wound down his window.

Karpov changed down and stopped thirty metres away from the Volvo. The men came out from the trees, five of them, all armed – in the dark he couldn't make out the details. The first man reached him. His face was blackened and the gun he pointed at Karpov was a Kalashnikov. Another man joined him on the driver's side of the cab, two others on the passenger side and one in front. What're you carrying, they would ask; behave and you're okay, they would tell him. Would kill him anyway.

'Get down,' the first man ordered him. The moon was more three-quarters than half, Karpov thought; funny how you noticed the insignificant things. 'Get down,' the man told him again.

The night erupted, sub-machine fire pouring in from the murk of the woods on either side, the first rounds tearing down the man giving the orders, plus the man at his side, and more slamming into the man in front of the cab. To Karpov's right the man in the passenger seat raised his AK so that it cleared the window and squeezed the trigger.

The silence descended again. The figures came out of the trees, kicked the bodies round the cab, and made sure they were dead. *'Bezdelniki luybiteli.'* Fucking amateurs. The turbo-charged Mitsubishi Shogun emerged from the black behind them and stopped behind the Scania. Karpov lit a Marlboro, left the cab and stepped through the carnage to the Volvo. The keys were in place. He started the engine, pulled the Volvo clear, returned to the Scania, and drove on.

Behind him the headlights of the back-up fell into position.

Kincaid's brain was beginning to swim. He declined another vodka, knew he couldn't win, shrugged, held up the glass in a toast, and downed another *stogram*. A waiter brought the next round of food, and a second the next bottle. Joshua dead and buried, so what the hell.

The party was in a private room off the main dining area; the table was circular, the centre section revolving so they could help themselves to the food piled high on the plates. Sherenko was on the other side of the table, drinking beer and an occasional malt. Grere Jameson was to his right, at Gerasimov's side.

Mikhail Gerasimov rose and raised his glass. 'To Alpha.'

They downed the vodka, the glasses were refilled, and someone else stood up and proposed another toast. 'To Russia.'

Another round was poured, another toast. 'To the job at the White House.'

'To Afghanistan.'

'To the bastards at the Kremlin.'

There was an uneasy silence.

Gerasimov stood again. 'To Friends.' He raised his glass. 'That they, like we, never forget.'

The mood changed back again. 'To Friends.'

When the Omega driver delivered him to the building which concealed the firing range five hours later, Kincaid's head was surprisingly clear. There is a God, he decided, and this morning God was on his side. The range was busy. He ignored those around him, worked carefully and methodically for forty minutes, then was driven to the Omega offices. Sherenko was at his desk. They briefed Riley on their arrangements for that day, checked that Igor Lukyanov had not received any intelligence on the mafia boss Alex Kosygin or the Moscow girlfriends of the couriers Whyte and Pearce, confirmed that no body resembling Whyte's had been brought in to the morgue on C'urupy Ulica, and drove to the ConTex offices for the interviews with non-American staff members absent the previous day. By midday they were back.

'So?' Sherenko settled behind his desk.

'So last night is beginning to wreak its revenge.'

Kincaid fetched two black coffees.

'Update on the financial backgrounds of Maddox and Dwyer.' Riley gave them the reports. 'All the bank accounts credited to each appear to be in order. How was ConTex?'

'Two of the three who weren't at work yesterday are back,' Sherenko told him. 'Maddox's secretary wasn't there again. There was a message at the switchboard that she was sick.'

Riley perched on the front of the desk. 'What do you think?'

'No problems with the two we interviewed.'

'But?'

'Money goes missing, next day Maddox's secretary doesn't show for work. We investigate, she goes sick.'

'So what do you suggest?'

'Leave it till tomorrow. If she doesn't show, we go see her.'

The Kosygin material began to come through. Sherenko copied it and Kincaid tried the telephone numbers of the girls Pearce had given him in London the day before.

'No answer,' he told Sherenko.

They settled down to the material:

Alexei Ivanevich Kosygin. Born 1964. Education: School Number 20 and Moscow State Institute of International Relations. Occupation: businessman. Frequent trips to Europe and the Middle and Far East. Home and office address and telephone numbers.

'Not much.' Kincaid tossed his copy on to the desk. 'Either we have the wrong man or the file's been filleted.' His head thumped and his mouth and throat were dry. 'What's the conventional wisdom from Moscow?'

Sherenko shrugged. 'Either he's clean, which nobody is. Or he's bent, which everyone is. Or he has connections and somebody's protecting him.'

Kincaid read the report again. 'If he's mafia, what sort of things is he running as well as the airport?'

'Could be anything. He was educated at School Number 20, one of the top schools in Moscow, which suggests his parents were high up in the Party. He was also educated at the Institute of International Relations, which is the best there is, so his classmates will already be going places in government or business. He'll speak at least one foreign language, certainly English, and he's sophisticated, with good connections.' Sherenko leaned back in his chair. 'He's doing the airport because that's a nice little earner, but which probably also keeps him cosy with the FSB. He lets them know what's going on, and they give him some protection. Probably the SVR, the foreign intelligence people as well.

'He probably has interests in some clubs, runs one or two floors of a couple of hotels. Almost certainly he has some deals going with foreign businessmen.' Sherenko stood up and paced the room. 'Hell, he's just what the Americans and the English and the French and the Germans and everybody else is screaming for. So he goes into partnership with them, fronts them. Plus he's probably doing some share scams, might be into property, including overseas. Next time you go home you'll probably find he owns half of New England. I mean, this guy is what the Protestant ethic and the American dream are all about. And in twenty, thirty years time he'll be a pillar of the community.

'Oh yeah, he's probably having some run-ins with the banks. He'll have taken out some loans, I mean big loans, but now some of the banks will be calling them in. So a banker goes missing, or goes dead. Gets blown up, gets shot, gets dead because someone's put some sort of poison in his telephone, so every time he uses it he's killing himself.

'And each evening friend Alexei does the clubs, and picks up the girls, and has a great time.' He looked at Kincaid. 'Remind you of anyone?'

'Yeah. He reminds me of the way some of America's own great and good got started.'

'You said it, not me.'

Something about the night before, Kincaid remembered. 'Last night at the party.'

'Yeah?'

'One of the toasts was the bastards at the Kremlin, another was to Friends. What was that about?'

'Betrayal.' Sherenko was sharp, almost aggressive. He swung in his chair, checked the details on the report, lifted the telephone, and punched the number.

'This is Nikolai Sherenko, from Omega. I'd like to speak with Mr Kosygin.' He flicked the phone on to mute. 'Kosygin also loves being called Mister.' He flicked the mute off. 'Sure, I'll wait.' He stared at the ceiling. 'Mr Kosygin. Good afternoon. This is Nikolai Sherenko from Omega. There's something we should talk about . . .' He listened. 'Yeah, the Tokyo at eight would be fine.'

He put the phone down.

'So . . .' Kincaid asked.

'That was too easy. The bastard didn't even ask who or what Omega was, or what it was about.'

'Therefore he knows about the money?'

'Either that or someone tipped him off.'

Gerasimov and Jameson were still out. They had a meeting with Kosygin this evening, they told Riley; like to put it on record in case there were any comebacks; like to get the company's and ConTex's go-ahead. Decision by six, Riley told them.

Alexei Kosygin replaced the phone and sat back in the leather executive chair he had had flown in from Berlin. The office was situated on an upper floor of the Intourist Hotel, at the end looking toward Red Square and the Kremlin. It was modern –

computer, fax, shredder, three telephones, plus concealed drinks cabinet. It was also relatively secure, minders in the outer office, where his two secretaries sat, and reinforced doors.

He swung in the chair and punched Vorkov's direct number at Yasenevo. There was no answer. He pressed the button for another line and punched the number of the cellphone. Felix Vorkov answered three seconds later.

'It's Alexei. The thing you mentioned last night. They've been in touch. I'm meeting them tonight.'

Vorkov was relaxed, as if it didn't matter. Plus the fact that cellphones were still notoriously insecure. 'Fine. I'll be in touch tomorrow.'

Kosygin pressed the button for another line and called the second cellphone.

'Yuri, it's Alexei. Slight change of plan for tonight . . . Yeah, the Tokyo . . .'

He called the next number.

'Olga. It's Alexei. Change of plan for this evening. We'll go to the Tokyo first.' Olga knew the score and did what she was told. 'Tell Tanya.'

So what else, who else? Because tonight was a game, and Kosygin liked games. He called the next number, spoke to the secretary, and was put through.

'It's Alexei. Wondered what you were doing this evening. It's Yuri's last night in town for a couple of weeks.'

'Alexei, *last* night was Yuri's last in town.'

'Apparently he was delayed; he phoned me this morning.'

'Who else is coming?'

'Couple of girls, Olga and Tanya.'

'You playing one of your games, Alexei?'

'What makes you think I'm playing a game?'

'Because I know you.'

'So you want in?'

'Sure.'

At five Kincaid made contact with the first of the girls named by Pearce in London. They can't make tonight – he flicked the phone to mute and told Sherenko; she suggests tomorrow evening.

Sherenko looked across the desk. 'Where?'

'The Up and Down.'

'Just make sure you clear the expenses first.'

They filed into the conference room and ran through the investigation so far. Most of the day Gerasimov had been at the Kremlin and Jameson at the American embassy.

'Bottom line,' Jameson told them. 'I've spoken direct with Cal McIntyre in Houston. He always understood that he wouldn't get his money back, but he's more than happy with the way things have gone. What's outstanding?'

'Alexei Kosygin, the couriers' girlfriends and Maddox's secretary.'

'You think you'll get anywhere?'

'Who knows?'

'Give it another couple of days, then we'll review.'

'What about Maddox's woman at the embassy?' Kincaid asked.

'Leave it. Dwyer's little escapade at Nite Flite as well. When you write the case up, leave them off it. I'll report it to McIntyre personally.'

'What about this evening's meeting with Kosygin?'

Jameson shuffled his papers uneasily. 'I've spoken to London and Washington, as well as ConTex here and in Houston. The decision, which I agree with, is to go on it.' He shuffled the papers again. 'There's a second decision, which both Michael and I oppose totally but on which we have been overruled by our clients. Only Nik is to go.'

'Because if there's trouble, and a Russian is killed or gets up to his neck in hassle, that's one thing,' Kincaid suggested. 'But an American . . .'

Fact of life, Jameson's silence said.

'So who looks after Nik's back?'

'I think Nik can look after his own,' Gerasimov told him dryly.

At six-thirty Sherenko and Kincaid updated the case log, then Sherenko picked up the BMW and drove back to the apartment, showered and changed, and drove to the Tokyo.

The restaurant was on a ground floor corner of the Rossiya Hotel, facing across the Moskva river and close to Red Square and the Kremlin. The hotel was square and massive, and built around a central grass area. Originally it had been designed to accommodate the thousands of delegates attending Party functions, now parts of it had been sold or leased to private individuals or companies. Black-windowed Mercedes and BMWs were parked along the pavement outside, plus the occasional four-wheel drive, their drivers sitting with the windows open, some of them looking at miniature television sets.

Sherenko parked facing out, locked the BMW and went in, past the minder inside the door. The reception desk was round the corner, two women seated behind it. Sherenko nodded at the man, smiled at the women, and informed them he was meeting Mr Kosygin.

'Your name, please?'

'Sherenko.'

'If you wouldn't mind waiting a moment.'

Because with guests like Mr Kosygin we have to check that he really is expecting you.

Kosygin would be sitting on the left, Sherenko understood. On the right and he would be sitting next to the window on to the pavement against which some of the Mercs and BMs were parked, which would constitute a security risk. Therefore Kosygin would be sitting next to the window facing the enclosed square round which the hotel was built.

'This way, Mr Sherenko.'

He thanked the receptionist and followed the waiter left, up a small set of carpeted steps.

The cocktail bar was first right, two private dining areas to the left, and the main body of the restaurant further on. The walls were a pale golden yellow and lanterns hung from the ceilings. The cooking, like the decor, was traditional Japanese: guests seated along one side of a bar, high-backed chairs along the length and at either end, and chefs cooking the food on stainless steel hotplates on the inner side of the bar. The restaurant proper was sectioned into areas, each containing two bars facing each other, the chef at one working with his back to the other, and partitions between the areas.

Kosygin and his entourage occupied both bars of the first area on the right: Kosygin and friends sitting with their backs to him and Kosygin's minders – thickset with powerful shoulders and heads sunk in so they apparently had no necks – at the bar opposite so they could observe everyone entering from the concierge's desk.

Kosygin himself was seated in the centre chair along the length of the bar. Another man was to his right and a woman to his left, a second woman on the right of the other male, and a third in the chair at the end of the bar to Kosygin's left.

Sherenko held out his hand. 'Alexei Kosygin ... Nikolai Sherenko.'

Kosygin's suit was Armani, Sherenko guessed; silk shirt and tie probably the same. Kosygin looked anywhere between twenty-eight and thirty-five, squat but not obviously powerfully built.

'Good to meet you, Nik.'

They shook hands.

'You too, Alex.'

Kosygin snapped his fingers at a waitress. 'A place for my guest.' He indicated the seat at the right end, back to the window and facing the woman at the other end.

This is a game, Sherenko's instinct told him. This is a set-up.

'Nik, meet my friends.'

Kosygin introduced them:

Olga, to his left: mid-twenties, tall and brunette, soft silky dress and long hair swept back. Tanya, on the right of the second male, therefore to Sherenko's immediate left: younger, slightly shorter and blonde, exquisite figure and low-cut one-piece. Yuri Dushkin, the other male: early thirties and tall, hair slightly long, colourful tie and suit.

He came to the third woman.

To understand Russia you have to understand the new Russian woman, Sherenko had told Brady at the Santa Fe. There's a third type, he'd also told Brady. Born into the Party, university-educated, probably speaks a couple of languages. Late twenties, early thirties; runs her own business or is successful in her own career. Works hard and plays harder.

The woman at the far end stood and introduced herself. 'Anna

91

Mikhailovna.' Her use of the patronymic was a challenge rather than a formality.

Leave it, Sherenko told himself; don't pick up on it. Christ, the woman was beautiful, Christ she was stunning. Tall with dark hair and black eyes. Dress simple but expensive. Hell, the woman wasn't just beautiful, though, was more than that. 'Nikolai Alexandrovich,' he said.

'Hello, Nikolai Alexandrovich.' Beautiful man – she felt the shiver. Tall, ten years older than herself. Casual suit but smart, shirt unbuttoned at the top and no tie; eyes that pierced you. More than that, though, more than just Alexei's little game.

Break it, Sherenko told himself; stop the game now. 'Hello, Anna Mikhailovna.'

'What are you drinking?' Kosygin asked. He and Dushkin were drinking vodka, the women champagne.

'Champagne,' Sherenko told him.

A waitress poured him a glass and another placed the leather-bound menu in front of him. Same as the others, Sherenko told her.

'Yuri, Anna and I were at university together.' Kosygin flicked his fingers for another bottle, then flicked moods equally easily. 'What are you carrying, Nik?'

The no-necks opposite tensed.

Sherenko held his coat open with his left hand, the movement deliberately slow and obvious, and took out the handgun with the thumb and forefinger of his right, the movement even slower. 'Sig Sauer.' Everything was a game, sometimes you won and sometimes you lost. 'You?'

'Beretta.' Kosygin took it from the chamois shoulder holster. The gunmetal had been blued and the handgrip was mother of pearl.

'Nice.' Sherenko told him. He slipped the P226 back and raised his glass. '*Vashe zdorovye.*' To your health.

The no-necks were still tense.

'*Na pososhok.*' Kosygin clinked his glass against Sherenko's and the no-necks relaxed.

So this is the game is it, Alexei – Anna glanced at Kosygin then at Sherenko. More correctly, this is part of the game, but what's the rest? Look at me, Nikolai Alexandrovich. How long before you break your concentration and turn to me? How long before I make you?

Kosygin and the, others were already eating. A waitress brought Sherenko a hot towel and a bar on which to lay his chopsticks, and another brought him sushi.

This is a game – Sherenko glanced at Anna. This is several games. But is this also a set-up?

Kosygin sat back and drew his napkin across his lips. 'So, Nik. You said we should talk.'

Sherenko nodded. 'It's business.' Therefore it's up to you whether we discuss it in front of the others.

'Of course.' Kosygin smiled and waited.

Sherenko put down the chopsticks. 'As you're aware, I work for a security company called Omega.' It was the first mention of security. 'We have been contracted by a client who has lost a certain amount of money.' Perhaps the temperature dropped slightly.

So that's the game – Anna fixed her eyes on him. At least that's the game between you and Alexei, and as part of that game Alexei wants his audience. And Alexei, devious bastard that he is, set up another game. Because life is a game. Sometimes you want in, and sometimes you simply say *ciao* and walk away. Except this one I don't walk out on, this one I have no control over.

Sherenko shrugged, as if to say: what the hell. 'Actually my clients lost six million dollars.' He sat back on his chair and sipped the champagne. Anna Mikhailovna was looking at him. Okay, they were all looking at him, but Anna he could smell and breathe. What if Kosygin organized the heist, Jack had asked. Kosygin hadn't – Sherenko could tell by the look on his face. Kosygin had pulled God knows how many scams but not this one.

Kosygin made a point of glancing at the others before he spoke. 'So why should we be talking?'

'The money went missing at the airport. I understand you have business interests there.'

Except Sherenko didn't say it quite like that, Anna was aware.

What he said was: 'I understand that you have . . .' Then there was a pause and a shrug and another pause, the second pause saying I understand that you have *what we might call* '. . . business interests there.'

'What sort of business do you understand I have at the airport?' Kosygin asked.

'What sort of business does one normally have?'

Anna's eyes were still fixed on Sherenko.

'You said that your client's money went missing,' Kosygin re-routed the conversation. 'How exactly?'

'A courier was bringing it in in dollars. Usual thing. Hundred-dollar bills fresh out of the Bureau of Engraving and Printing. Security pick-up at the airport, except the right security people had an accident on the way out to Sheremetyevo, and the wrong ones met the courier.' He made a point of laughing. 'Hasn't been seen since.'

So somebody's shitting on your doorstep, my friend. Somebody lifted six million from your patch, and you haven't seen a cent of it. So even though somebody's laughing at my client's expense, they're also laughing at yours. Which I won't say here, because that would be outside the rules of the game, but it's what we both know.

Kosygin also laughed, more a snort than a laugh, though it was a laugh on his face. He turned to Olga and Tanya. 'Would you excuse us for a moment?' They left and went to the powder-room near the concierge's desk. You as well – Kosygin's look to the chef said. So why were Yuri Dushkin and Anna Mikhailovna allowed to remain, Sherenko wondered. Because Kosygin still needed his audience, he supposed; but only an audience he trusted.

'When did the money go missing?' Kosygin was different, more direct. Eyes dangerous.

'British Airways flight BA872, four days ago. The courier was met off the plane by two men and taken through VIP clearance, presumably with a car waiting outside. He thought it was the normal security pick-up and fell for it.'

'Where was the normal security team?'

'Delayed.'

94

'And the courier was alone?' Kosygin was slightly incredulous.

'He was supposed to be accompanied, but the other courier got sick at the last moment. We've checked that out; it was genuine.'

A waiter offered more vodka and champagne. Kosygin began to wave him away, then made himself smile at the man and nod that he should bring two more bottles. 'So what do you want from me?'

'Your help.'

'To do what?'

'To recover the money.'

'And what's in it for me?'

'The insurance reward, say ten per cent.'

'Doesn't sound much.'

'I imagine it's negotiable.'

'As I said, not a lot compared to six million.' Kosygin waited while the waiter brought the bottles and refilled their glasses. 'There's an alternative, of course. I could find the six million and you could take the cut the insurance people would have paid.' You could take the six hundred thousand dollars.

'I could . . .' But spoken in a way which said, *Thanks, but I won't.*

'So where do we go from here?'

'I'm sure your organization and mine could still do business together on this one.'

Kosygin downed the vodka. 'How can I contact you?'

They exchanged business cards.

'Nice doing business with you, Nik.'

'And with you, Alex.'

'You'll finish the meal with us?'

'If the ladies don't mind.'

For the next hour they talked small talk, sometimes serious, most of the time joking and laughing. When they were finished Kosygin snapped his fingers, asked for the bill, and made a show of paying. 'We're going to Maxim's,' he told Sherenko. 'Join us if you want.'

'Thanks anyway,' Sherenko told him.

'How about you?' Kosygin asked Anna.

'I'll pass tonight.'

Kosygin prepared to leave, the no-necks already rising. 'One thing, Alex.' Sherenko told him.

'What, Nik?'

'Great meal, great company, Alex. Wrong table.'

Anna saw the first anger in Kosygin's face. What the hell are you doing, Nik? What the hell are you playing at? Nobody says that to someone like Alexei, because the one thing people like him don't like losing, apart from their money, is face.

Sherenko's voice was quiet. 'You're next to the outside window, Alex, and the glass isn't plated. Anybody outside could take you with a submachine or a bomb. Next time take a table by the inside windows.'

Quit now Nik – Anna stared at him. Quit while you've still got your tongue in your mouth and your balls between your legs, because the way you're going you want them changed round.

Sherenko stared at Kosygin's face. 'Hell, Alex. I might be the guy sitting next to you.'

The mask on Kosygin's face broke into a smile. This man I love – Kosygin said it in the way he raised his arms. You got that – he glared at the no-necks then turned back again to Sherenko. 'I'm in London for a few days. Let's speak when I get back.'

The no-necks closed round him and he swept away.

'So . . .' Sherenko looked at Anna.

'So . . .' She returned the look.

'Another champagne?' he asked.

'I've had enough. China tea would be good though.'

A waitress cleared the rest of the bar and stood hovering. Two teas, Sherenko requested. Why didn't you go with them? He asked. Why didn't you go? Anna asked him back.

'So who are you, Nikolai Alexandrovich?' Her eyes fixed on his.

'You know who I am.'

'I know you work for a security company called Omega, but I don't know who you are.' She changed chairs so she was sitting beside him. 'I also know you're a crazy man.'

'Why?'

'For turning down six hundred thousand dollars.'

'Perhaps I'd be crazy if I accepted.'

'Because of what Alexei does?' Anna threw the challenge at him. 'Because of the way he makes his money, you mean.'

'What does Alexei do?' Sherenko came back at her. 'How does Alexei make his money?'

The waitress poured the tea and withdrew. Around them the restaurant was still full. Anna held the cup with the fingers of two hands and sipped from it. 'So you don't like Alexei?'

'Did I say that?'

'But you disapprove of him?'

Sherenko shrugged.

'And if you disapprove of Alexei you disapprove of his friends.'

Sherenko shrugged again.

'Therefore you disapprove of me.'

Sherenko shrugged a third time.

'Hell,' Anna said. 'Why not another bottle.'

'Another champagne,' Sherenko told the waitress.

'You don't drink vodka?' Anna asked.

'No.'

'Why not?'

'Do you always ask so many questions, Anna Mikhailovna?'

She laughed. 'The gun. Have you ever used it?'

'I practise with it, yes.'

'You know that's not what I meant. Have you ever used it in anger?'

'Never in anger.'

She thought through his answer. 'I'll re-phrase it. Have you ever used that gun, or any other gun, for real?'

Perhaps – it was the shrug.

'But not like Alexei's apes?'

'I hope not.'

She leaned back and allowed the waiter to pour her a fresh glass.

'Beautiful outfit,' Sherenko told her.

'Thank you.'

'So tell me about Alexei and Yuri. How do you know them?'

'Is this business . . .' she came back at him like a winter wind off the Baltic. 'You interrogating me about Alexei and Yuri, trying to find out something about them through me. Is this what this drink is about? So we stop now or what?'

He looked at her. 'You mind if I ask you something?'

'Depends what it is.'

'Is this a honey trap? Is this all part of a set-up?'

The anger flared in her eyes. 'You think I'm a honey trap, Nik?'

'If you were Olga or Tanya, yes.'

'If I was, what would you think?'

'You know what I'd think,' Sherenko told her.

She looked at him for ten, twenty seconds, not speaking. 'Actually Yuri and I met at university,' she said at last. 'Yuri had been at school with Alexei. Alexei was at the International Affairs Institute and Yuri introduced us. Alexei's into whatever Alexei's into. Yuri left a few years back and now lives in Berlin. He's into art and antiques.' She had leant forward slightly, so their faces were close. 'Yes, we screwed each other. A long time ago. Now we're friends.' She refilled their glasses. 'So what about you?'

'What about me?'

'Whatever you want to tell me.'

Whose game are you playing now, Anna – Sherenko looked at her. What do you want to know about me?'

'Okay,' Anna told him. 'You work for a security company.'

'Yes.'

'You live in Moscow?'

Sherenko nodded.

'You married, you have a family?' Not that it matters, because such things don't matter. Especially in Moscow.

'I was. I have two girls. My wife and I are now separated; she lives in St Petersburg.'

'Why?'

'Work, the fact that I was away too much. Actually it was more than that. Something happened, I quit my job, hit the vodka. My wife couldn't take it and left.' He stared at her. And what about you, Anna Mikhailovna . . .

'I kicked my husband out four years go. Now I run my own business.'

'Doing what?'

'Computers. I have a degree in it. Actually I have two. One from Moscow, plus a Masters from MIT.'

'Nice place, Boston.'

'You know it?'

'I've passed through.'

So where do we go from here, Anna Mikhailovna? What do we do tonight, because we should be going to bed together tonight. Except don't ask me why, but we both know we're not going to.

'Dinner tomorrow?' he asked.

'I can't. The day after tomorrow is a special anniversary. I spend it with my mother. I fly up tomorrow evening.'

'Where?'

'St Petersburg.'

'What about the day after?'

'I'm in London for a few days.'

'With Alexei?' Wrong question, Sherenko knew.

'That worry you?' Anna held him with her eyes.

'Perhaps.'

'I might see Alexei, but I was going anyway. It's business.'

'I'll call you.'

She wrote her private number on the back of a business card, gave it him, and took the card he gave her with his private number on the back, then they went outside and he walked her to her car. BMW 3-series, latest model. The minders at the other cars were looking at them. He waited while she unlocked the door then opened it for her.

Anna looked up at him. 'You're smiling.'

'So are you.'

He held the door open. 'Take care in London.'

She slid in. 'You take care in Moscow.'

He watched her drive off. The business card she had given him was in his jacket pocket. He took it out and read her name: Anna Mikhailovna Buskova.

Yuri Dushkin – he wrote the name of the male present that

evening on one side of the card, then he placed the card in his wallet and drove away.

Yuri Dushkin left Maxim's shortly before two. Most nights Dushkin would have stayed, most nights Dushkin would not have left alone. But tomorrow – by which he meant today – was important, therefore he excused himself and left. Which left Alexei with the two girls, but that was no problem, because Alexei was doing coke like the whole of Bolivia and Peru had been visited by the hand of God and it was the last white powder he would ever get.

By seven Dushkin was at the warehouse.

The building was in a dock area on the Moskva river, north of the city. The exterior walls were of brick, no windows, and the working area, where items for export or those imported by the company were stored, was separated from the loading bay by a partition. The office, in the far corner, was modern with the usual range of furniture and floor-to-ceiling metal shelving along the wall opposite the door. The vault – the reason for the warehouse and its elaborate cover – was concealed behind this shelving.

Dushkin fetched another coffee, checked the time, and walked to the loading bay.

The false floor and sides of the Scania had been removed and the cargo it had brought from St Petersburg unloaded and catalogued, then re-wrapped ready for the next stage of its journey. When the loads were in, the premises were minded twenty-four hours a day by armed guards. Not patrolling the grounds, though, no show of anything unusual. Just the men who had escorted it from St Petersburg, sitting quietly and patiently inside.

He sniffed – okay, so perhaps he had snorted a little last night – and returned to the store-room.

The car drew up at the heavy mesh gate and a guard in overalls unlocked the gate, allowed the car through, and locked the gate again. The car slid into the loading bay. There were no passengers. Vorkov got out, nodded a greeting, and walked through to the office.

'How's it going?' Vorkov drew a Marlboro from a silver case and lit it.

'Fine.' Dushkin offered him coffee and poured them each a cup. 'Slight problem on the trip down.' Which Vorkov would have heard of, because Vorkov heard of everything. Besides, that was Vorkov's domain anyway. Dushkin was in charge of acquisition and sale, not the minutiae of how they moved the pieces round Russia.

Vorkov spooned sugar into the coffee. 'Schedule?'

'Karpov and the back-up leave at midday, they'll cross the border tonight.' The timing was crucial because the right shift had to be on duty. 'I fly out today, and meet them in Berlin.'

Then Zurich and Amsterdam, to set things up, and London for the auction. Dinner with Alexei Kosygin and Anna Buskova, who'd also be in town. Which wasn't Vorkov's business. And after that Los Angeles and New York via Moscow, then back to Berlin and Russia.

'Good.'

Vorkov left the warehouse and drove to Tverskaya. Twenty minutes later he was in Alexei Kosygin's office at the Intourist. Not that the secretary or the minders in the outer office knew his identity or connection with Kosygin, not that they even knew his name.

'So how did the meeting with Omega go?' Vorkov settled easily in an armchair.

'No problems.' Kosygin lit a cigar. 'Some money went missing at Sheremetyevo, Omega's investigating it and wanted my help.'

Vorkov smiled thinly. 'I wonder why?'

Kosygin laughed. 'Coffee? Something in it?'

Cognac, he would suggest, and then only the best.

Vorkov declined. 'How much money went missing?'

'Six million dollars.'

Not a lot, Vorkov thought. 'Who was it for?'

'An American company, ConTex.'

Interesting – Vorkov filed the name with the other details in his brain. Interesting because ConTex wasn't one of the big operators. ConTex was E and P, therefore wouldn't normally be bringing in more than half a million to a million per shipment. Which meant that ConTex was up to something. Early days, of course, because five million was little more than a down payment. But a down payment on something.

Perhaps he would take a coffee, he suggested. 'What were they offering in return for your help?'

Kosygin pressed the intercom and asked his secretary to bring in two fresh coffees. 'Ten per cent.'

'Who was representing Omega?' It was a detail. Nothing more. A fact to file with the others. No problems with Omega and Kosygin, the reassurance had already seeped in; no reason why anyone should be seeking to disrupt the system.

'Someone called Sherenko.'

The doors clanged down. Vorkov smiled as the secretary brought them each a coffee and nodded as Kosygin poured a stiff measure of cognac into each. 'Igor Sherenko?' he asked, and covered his tracks.

'Nikolai.' Kosygin pulled out his wallet and passed Vorkov the business card.

Vorkov examined it and handed it back.

'You know Sherenko?' Kosygin asked.

'Thought I did.' But not this one – it was in the intonation. 'So where'd you meet?' He threw the question in casually.

'The Tokyo.'

'Good dinner?'

'Always is.'

So what about Sherenko?

Felix Vorkov hunched over his desk and stared into the past. Five years ago this week ... the ghosts came at him ...

Vorkov's room was on the third floor of the seven-storey block at the heart of the place named Yasenevo, which others – especially in times past – called the Centre. More recent additions were taller and more modern, but the block in which Vorkov's office was situated remained the hub. In the trees nearby, up three sets of steps, was the white stone memorial, the emblem of the sword and the shield upon it, to those members of the former First Chief Directorate, now called the Foreign Intelligence Service, who had died whilst serving their organization, their country, their Party, or a combination of the three.

The meeting was at eleven. At five minutes to the hour he checked with the general's secretary, then took the stairs to the fifth floor.

Malenkov's office was functional, with no personal items and few decorations other than photographs of Malenkov with the president, as well as with other heads of state, replaceable if politics required, and a bust of Iron Felix. Even though his statue had been torn from its pedestal outside the Lubyanka, Felix Dzerzhinsky remained a hero to those who had followed.

Malenkov was on a secure line to the embassy in Washington. He waved for Vorkov to sit and concluded the conversation.

'How's Dushkin?' He leaned forward, elbows on the desk. Malenkov was in shirtsleeves, the jacket of his immaculately-cut suit on a hanger on the back of the door.

'Everything's fine. The shipment goes out today on schedule. Dushkin flies to Berlin this afternoon.'

'After that?'

'The usual routine.'

So what about Sherenko, Vorkov wondered again; what about the Omega connection? Malenkov was going to be out of town for a few days. The politicians had decided that an intelligence mini-summit would be a fitting way to mark the new era of co-operation and friendship which was supposed to be sweeping the world, the civil servants had set up a conference in London, and Malenkov and an entourage of aides were attending. Therefore mention Sherenko and the Omega connection, Vorkov decided.

'Anything else?' Malenkov asked.

'Sherenko's surfaced.'

Malenkov's face did not change. 'How?' he asked.

'Five days ago an American oil company, ConTex, was bringing in six million dollars by courier. The courier and the money disappeared at Sheremetyevo. Omega's been called in and Sherenko's the investigator.'

No problems, Malenkov's body language said, nothing to worry about. 'How do we know this?'

'Omega ran a check on who controlled the mafia at Shereme-tyevo and had Kosygin's file pulled. The file was flagged, which was when we first learned of Omega's interest, though not at this stage of Sherenko's involvement. I warned Kosygin, and he reported back to me that the investigator who made contact was Sherenko.'

A *teni proshlovo*, Malenkov thought, though he continued to disguise it. A ghost coming back to haunt him. This week of all weeks. But anniversaries were when ghosts usually appeared. If you believed in such things.

'Any links with anything else?' he asked.

'No,' Vorkov told him.

'Keep close to it.'

Malenkov watched as Vorkov left.

A *teni proshlovo* – it was like a whisper in the night; a ghost called Joshua returning to haunt him. He spent twenty minutes being briefed on the forthcoming intelligence conference in London, then he was driven to the Metropole Hotel, told his driver to wait, went to the telephones off the foyer, made the call, and crossed to the Moskva Hotel. Exactly thirty minutes after he had made the call, the telephone in the booth in which he was waiting rang.

'How's the weather in Moscow this morning?' The first line of the code.

'Predictable. And with you?'

'Raining as it always is at this time of year.'

Going secure, Malenkov told the caller and clipped on the encryptor.

Secure, the caller confirmed.

Malenkov swept the hallway around him. 'The shipment's fine,' he told the caller. 'But we might have a problem with something else.'

'What?'

'Sherenko's re-surfaced.'

'Why might that be a problem?'

'He's working as an investigator for Omega. He's currently

looking into the theft of six million dollars being couriered in for an American company called ConTex.'

'And?'

'Grere Jameson's also in town. I met him at a reception a couple of nights ago.'

'Any reason either of them might put two and two together?'

'No.'

'But you think I should check it out?'

'I think you should.'

Sherenko had risen early, arrived at the office early.

Anna Mikhailovna . . .

What about Anna Mikhailovna, Nik?

Kincaid arrived at eight. That morning he had spent an hour in the range in the anonymous building in the northern suburbs of Moscow.

'How was it?' Sherenko asked.

Kincaid helped himself to the habitual coffee. 'Getting better. How was Kosygin?'

'I offered him ten per cent of the missing money if he helped us recover it, and he offered me ten per cent if I helped him find it.'

'So you don't think he was involved?'

'No, but he wishes to hell he had been.'

At nine they went to the conference room for the first briefing of the day.

The boys who'd done the electronic sweep of the ConTex offices had found a listening device, Riley informed the meeting; but the battery was dead and the device was a model in production before ConTex had moved in, so the chances were that it was the company occupying the offices before ConTex which had been the target. Either way it looked good that Omega had found the device. The technical people had had no joy with fingerprints or forensics on the car the security company had used for what should have been the Whyte pick-up, he also informed them.

'Nothing on Whyte,' Sherenko told them.

'What about Maddox's secretary?' Jameson asked.

'She's still off sick.'

'What about Kosygin?' Gerasimov leaned forward, elbows on the table.

'I met him at the Tokyo. Every indication was that he wasn't aware of the heist.' He detailed the discussion. 'He asked what was in it for him. I told him ten per cent insurance. He said six hundred thousand was nothing.'

'Bottom line?' Gerasimov asked.

'Bottom line is I doubt we'll get any of the money back through Kosygin.'

'So what do we do now?' Jameson asked.

'Check out Maddox's secretary.'

'One other thing.' Gerasimov indicated that Jameson wished to add something.

Jameson nodded. 'I said yesterday I thought we might be wrapping this one up soon. As I also said, ConTex are more than happy with us. We now have their main security contract.'

'Where does that leave the investigation?'

'Give it another couple of days, then ConTex can decide if it wants to continue. There are so many loose ends we could spend six months chasing them and getting nowhere. My feeling is that ConTex will want to get shot of it. Which also means that the only reason for my being here is no longer valid.' Hell – he shrugged; you guys never needed me here anyway. 'Therefore I'll give it another forty-eight hours then pull out.'

Fifteen minutes later Sherenko and Kincaid left the office in one of the company's Quick Reaction Force cars, Sherenko and the driver in the front, Kincaid and the *chernomeshochnik*, the black bag man, in the rear.

The address was fifteen minutes' drive, on the fourth floor of an apartment block overlooking a park in the university area of the city. At ten on a weekday morning the neighbourhood was quiet. The driver parked, then Sherenko and Kincaid walked the area looking for stake-outs, for anything unusual. The weather was hot and the scent of flowers mixed with the pollution of the city.

'You mind if I ask you something, Nik?'

'Depends what it is.'

The entrance to the apartment block was fifty metres in front of them and the stake-out car was a hundred metres to the right.

'At the party the other night you drank beer and malt, never vodka.'

'Correct.'

'So if you don't drink vodka, why did you buy a bottle when we went to the morgue on C'urupy Ulica?'

Sherenko stared at the front door of the apartment block. 'You're an American, Jack,' he said at last. 'You believe every boy can make a million and every man can become president.'

'What the hell you going on about, Nik?'

'You been to the Pentagon, Jack?'

'Sure I've been to the Pentagon.'

'You know what they've got at the Pentagon? In the middle of Pentagon City, I mean.'

'I don't know, Nik. Tell me what they've got in the middle of Pentagon City.'

'They've got shops and fast food bars and a shopping mall. You know what I thought for the forty years of the Cold War? That our missiles were targeting the heart of evil, that our ICBMs were aimed at the Pentagon. But you know what they were really targeting, Jack? All that time what they were really targeting was a fucking McDonald's. And what was the first restaurant we allow to open in Moscow when the Cold War ends?'

'A fucking McDonald's. So what are you telling me, Nik? What the hell has this to do with the morgue on C'urupy Ulica?'

Sherenko turned and walked back to the car. '*Vpered.*' Let's do it. They collected the *chernomeshochnik* and entered the block, Sherenko and the *chernomeshochnik* first, Kincaid thirty seconds behind them and from the other direction. The *chernomeshochnik* cleared the combination lock on the front door and they went inside, ignored the lift and took the stairs. A woman coming down scuttled past, not looking at them. Three men in suits taking the stairs were normally mafia, and accommodation in Moscow was at a premium. Therefore find a pensioner, pay him or her a few thousand dollars plus a contract guaranteeing that he or she could live there for the rest of his or her life. Two weeks later the pensioner's dead and more than likely the dollars are stuffed in the mattress.

Sherenko unwrapped two sticks of gum, gave one to Kincaid, and began chewing the other. They came to the fourth floor. 'Clear?' He checked on the Motorola.

'Clear.'

There were three doors off the landing: one to the right, one to the left, and one facing them in the centre. Each had a spy hole. Sherenko took some of the gum from his mouth and plugged the holes. A Russian might like to know what the mafia was doing, but would never open the door to find out.

The *chernomeshochnik* unlocked the door in the wall facing them. Inside was a small dark passageway, a door at either end. Kincaid plugged the spy hole in the door on the left and pressed the bell on the door on the right – one short ring, then one long, as if he knew the person inside. There was no reply. Do it – he nodded and pulled on the thin black leather gloves. The *chernomeshochnik* swung the door open and stood back. Sherenko slid past him, Kincaid close behind, Sig Sauers in combat position and safeties off.

The hallway was two metres long and led into a sitting-room at the far end, the door open, one door to the right and one to the left, both closed. Cover these, Sherenko's look said. Kincaid nodded and Sherenko moved forward into the sitting-room. Nobody – he shook his head and moved right, out of Kincaid's vision, into the kitchen. Came back, shook his head again, and covered Kincaid while Kincaid opened the door to the right. The bedroom was empty. He checked the door to the left. The bathroom was clean and tidy, and also empty. They put the Sig Sauers back in the holsters and began the search.

We don't know anything about Lyza Kulikova, Kincaid thought; we don't knew her age, whether or not she's married, whether she has a partner, male or female. No children, though, because the apartment didn't have that feel to it. He picked up a set of photographs. The one person in each of them, other than the one of an old couple, was a woman in her mid-twenties.

Sherenko began to examine the drawers and bookshelf, and Kincaid went to the bedroom. The bed was made and there were dresses hanging in a wardrobe, women's shoes on the floor of the wardrobe and a silk bathrobe on the back of the door.

Sherenko finished the sitting-room and went through to the bathroom. It was just big enough for a toilet and shower. Kincaid finished the bedroom and went to the kitchen. It was clean and tidy, and the crockery and cutlery had been put away. He checked the refrigerator. There was a can of meat on one shelf and mayonnaise on another. No milk, he noted.

Sherenko came through from the bedroom. 'Only a few personal items. Sort of thing a woman living by herself might have. No indication whether she's gone or not.'

Kincaid began searching methodically through the drawers. The plastic rubbish bag was under the sink, tied at the top. Sherenko placed it on the table and untied it.

'Interesting . . . Everything else is clean and neat, not even any milk left in the fridge, so why didn't she throw away the trash as well?'

He began to go through the items: two empty cans, some tissue paper, stale bread. Empty coffee pot, broken cup, clear heavy-duty plastic shrink wrapping, strip of paper approximately six inches long and an inch wide.

'I think Lyza Kulikova has a problem,' Kincaid told him.

An hour later they returned to the office. Gerasimov was at the Kremlin and Jameson was on the phone in his office. They might have a development, they informed Riley. They led him through to the conference room, closed the door and showed him the items Sherenko had found in the trash bag.

'What are they?'

'The paper is called a band,' Kincaid told him. 'It's what the US Bureau of Engraving and Printing use to bundle dollar notes together. In this case hundred-dollar bills.'

'What about the plastic?'

'US bills are banded together in what the Bureau of Engraving and Printing calls straps. Each strap contains a hundred notes. Straps are then shrink-wrapped in bundles, each containing ten straps, and so on. My guess is that the plastic is shrink wrapping.'

Jameson returned to the office and they updated him.

'So Maddox's secretary appears to be involved?' he asked.

'Possibly.' There was a hesitation in Sherenko's voice.

'Why only possibly?'

'A number of reasons. Jack and I discussed them on the way back.'

'Tell me.'

'It might seem a coincidence that Lyza Kulikova goes missing and we find a band and wrapping in a trash bag in her kitchen. Everything else in the apartment was neat and clean, so why didn't she throw the trash bag away? If she *was* involved it would have been incredibly careless of her to leave the band and the wrapping. Looking at the apartment, she's not the sort to make that sort of mistake. We therefore have to consider the possibility that she or we have been set up.'

'So what do you suggest?'

'Run a check on her and talk to Maddox at ConTex.'

Call from Washington for you, the officer manager informed Jameson. Someone called Miller.

Put him through to Mikhail's office, Jameson told her and left.

'Who's Miller?' Riley asked Kincaid.

Ed Miller had been Russia desk chief the day Joshua called Leon Panelli – the ghost came back at Kincaid even though he thought he had laid it. Ed Miller had been one of the eagles Jameson gathered round him in the bubble as Joshua came in from Moscow USA. Ed Miller had been one of the few to survive after Joshua was taken out, but thank Christ someone from Division survived, thank Christ Ed was now chief of Division, because most of those whom the seventh floor brought in after the Joshua inquisition were new brooms who didn't know their ass from their elbow.

'Colleague from the old days,' he said simply.

Jameson hurried through, sat at Gerasimov's desk, and took the call. 'Ed, good to speak with you. So how you doing?'

'Fine,' Miller told him. 'Someone mentioned that Cal McIntyre at ConTex had phoned asking about security companies, said they'd recommended you, so I thought I'd check how it was going. Your Bethesda office said you were in Moscow. So what's new?'

Kincaid tapped lightly on the door and glanced in. Come on

through, Jameson told him. 'Yeah, Ed, we got the contract, the investigation's going well, I'm pulling out tomorrow or the day after . . .'

I'm in London for a conference, Miller told him; any chance of you passing through and the two of us meeting up, because we always say we'll see each other in DC, but we never do.

'Yeah, let's meet up. Great idea. You can fill me in on what's happening to the old place . . . Hey, Ed, got someone here who wants to say hello . . . Sure thing, see you in London.'

He passed the phone to Kincaid.

'Ed, long time no see. How the hell are you doing . . .'

Sherenko left the conference room and returned to the main office. 'File check on Lyza Kulikova.' He gave Igor Lukyanov the details.

'Anyone else while I'm about it?'

'No.'

'You're sure?'

'Actually . . .' Sherenko opened his wallet, pulled out the business card Anna had given him, and gave it to Lukyanov. 'Yuri Dushkin.'

'Just getting through to Maddox,' Riley told him from the other side of the office. 'You want to speak to him or shall I?'

'Where's Jack?'

'Still on the line to Washington.'

'I'll speak to Maddox then.' Sherenko turned away from Igor Lukyanov, took the phone and left the business card on Lukyanov's desk. 'Arnie, it's Nik Sherenko. Arnie, something's come up and we need to meet. Yeah, like yesterday.'

Jameson and Kincaid came into the office. Sherenko cupped his hand over the mouthpiece. 'Seeing Maddox right away.'

Kincaid nodded.

Sherenko took his hand away from the mouthpiece. 'Thanks, Arnie, it's appreciated. See you in ten.'

Anna played with the business card. Turned it over and read the name in Russian and English. Laid it on the desk and picked it up again.

So what about you, Nikolai Alexandrovich?

The office was in two rooms on the twentieth floor of the Sovin Centre, overlooking the Moskva river. The Mezhdunarodnaya hotels and long-term apartments, which everyone called Mezhd 1 and Mezhd 2 were on either side and half its height.

A reception area had been created inside the door, with comfortable sofa and palms, and the rest of the outer and larger room was taken by programmers and managers. Anna's own room was off it and smaller, decorated personally, two Sverchkov prints and a Gorbatov oil on the walls. Her desk was leather-topped mahogany, clear of decoration or adornment except for a porcelain horse and rider. A Pentium computer was on a swing table to her right, and an oval conference table occupied the section of the office closest to the door.

Phone me, Nikolai Alexandrovich; speak to me. Or should I phone you?

She lifted the phone and called the number in St Petersburg.

'Mama, it's me. Just confirming I'm coming up this evening . . . Of course I'm looking forward to seeing you, Mama . . . Of course I'm not too busy . . . Why am I sounding happy? Am I sounding happy? See you tonight, Mama.'

She rang off and checked the time. The lunch appointment was at one. She checked her diary for that afternoon and confirmed the table reservation at the Metropol Zal. It was twelve-fifteen. She made sure she had the relevant papers, put the cellphone in the briefcase, and left the office. The car her secretary had booked was waiting.

'The Intourist,' she told the driver.

The two men were seated in a 5-series BMW. One was mid-thirties, big build with a suit which fitted tightly over his shoulders and arms, and the other was slightly younger, not such a large build, hair greased back and colourful tie. A ten-dollar bill to the gatekeeper near the river had overcome the fact that parking in the area outside the Sovin Centre was restricted to business people with offices in the block or hotel guests. They watched as Anna left, then sank back in their seats and waited for her to return.

Fifteen minutes later the cab dropped her at the Intourist Hotel, at the bottom of Tverskaya, ten minutes' walk from the Metropol. Anna checked the window of the fashion house next to the National, then walked down the steps to the metro station and the passageway towards Red Square. The underpass was lined with the usual vendors selling the usual items: mock fur hats, matryoshka dolls and Red Army memorabilia. Someone was playing a guitar and someone else was singing, the sounds echoing against each other down the concrete.

Thirty seconds later she stepped back into the sunlight.

There were more vendors at the exit, the usual guides trying to sell the usual tours, and a woman in her fifties, though she might be any age, torn basketball boots and a Michael Jordan cap which had long lost its shape and colour, trying to sell cigarettes. Another woman stood slightly away from her, straight back, clean clothes and a row of medals, something like a lapel badge above the medals, selling audio cassettes.

Anna rehearsed the conversation she would have over lunch, barely registering their presence, and crossed to the Metropol.

The foyer was busy. She went to the bar at the corner of the main reception area, settled in a large leather wing-back chair, and asked for tonic water. Hopkins arrived five minutes later. He was late thirties and already showing the strain of working in Moscow. Anna shook his hand, waited for him to order a drink, and told the waiter to put it on her bill. They talked about business in general for fifteen minutes, then she settled the bill and they moved to the restaurant. Been here before? she asked as they crossed to the double doors. No, Hopkins admitted.

They stepped inside.

The walls were tall, pillars rising up them and full-length mirrors reflecting back into the room. Along each wall except the one where they now stood ran a marbled terrace. A fountain flowed gently in the centre of the floor, a pianist played on a raised dais next to the door, and the ceiling was vaulted glass and exquisitely decorated, the sun shining through it.

'Lenin made one of his greatest speeches from the terrace overlooking this room,' she told Hopkins. 'Ribbentrop and Molotov signed the 1938 non-aggression pact between Germany and Russia in the Red Room.'

A waiter escorted them to their table and held Anna's chair for her, and another offered them the menu.

A Chablis, she suggested. Hopkins nodded, still looking round the room. They ordered the business lunch and she gave him the proposal documents. Hopkins allowed the waiter to pour him a glass of wine, sat back slightly, and read through them.

'Prices look reasonable.' It was half to her, half to himself, and deliberately so. 'Had better prices from a couple of your competitors, though.'

Anna looked at him across the table. 'The first company you're talking about isn't up and running yet and you need your system in fast. The second may be offering a good deal on the hardware, but they don't have any bilingual specialists. They have some interpreters, but interpreters in Moscow are two to a penny, and what I'm talking about is bilingual computer specialists to set up your systems and train your staff. Plus bilingual back-up, training and call-out.'

When Anna returned to her office it was shortly after three. She asked her secretary for fresh coffee and called the contracts and training managers in that order. 'Looks like we have the Hopkins contract,' she told them both. 'Anyone phone while I was out?' Anyone called Nikolai Alexandrovich Sherenko.

She checked her watch, made sure she was leaving plenty of time to get to Sheremetyevo, and asked the secretary to confirm the car.

Why the hell do you have to go to St Petersburg tonight, Anna? Why the hell do you have to go to London immediately after? Why the hell didn't you sleep with him last night, because that's the game. So if you didn't sleep with him, what game are you both playing?

The intercom rang. 'Someone to see you.' Her secretary sounded different.

'Who?' Twenty minutes, she thought, then she would explain she had to leave.

The door opened and the two men came in. One was mid-thirties, big build with a suit which fitted tightly over his shoulders and arms. The other was slightly younger, not such a large build, hair greased back and colourful tie.

Oh God – she understood the fear in her secretary's voice.

The man with the tie chose a chair by her desk, undid the buttons of his coat so that the front parted slightly, and revealed the gun he carried in a shoulder holster. Behind him the no-neck man closed the door, stared round the room, and selected a chair at the conference table.

The man with the tie took a cigar from his breast pocket and bit off the end. 'You don't mind if I smoke.' He rolled the cigar between the thumb and first finger of his left hand and took his time lighting it.

Her muscles tightened in involuntary spasms and the nails of her fingers dug into the soft flesh of her palms. In front of her the no-neck rose and examined the paintings on the wall.

'Lot of nice equipment outside.' The man with the tie drew on the cigar and placed it deliberately on the leather of the desk. 'Computers must be expensive.' The cigar smoke drifted in a curl and the red made the first burn in the leather. Behind him the no-neck took one of the Sverchkovs off the wall. 'Wouldn't want anything to happen, would we?' The man with the tie picked up the cigar and dusted the ash from the desk, drew on the cigar again and replaced it on the leather. 'Dangerous area this.' He swept his right hand across the desk, knocked the cigar to the carpet and ground it in. Selected another and lit it. Leaned forward and placed it on the desk near the porcelain horse.

Control it, Anna tried to tell herself. Work out what you have to do and what you have to say.

'What is it?' he asked.

'What's what?' It was the first time she had spoken.

'The picture.'

'A Sverchkov.'

'Nice.' The man with the tie reached for the cigar and drew on it.

Behind him the no-neck let the print slip from his grasp. She saw the movement and recoiled with shock at the sound of the glass smashing on the floor. Sorry, the no-neck said. He moved a pace to the right, took the next Sverchkov from the wall, and began to examine it as he had examined the first. On the desk in front of her the cigar burnt its way through the leather.

Bastard – she felt the first anger.

Without warning the man with the tie rose and walked behind her.

Don't turn, she told herself, tensed with fear anyway.

His right hand slid inside his jacket and came out again, gun in it. The hand swept down and she jolted sideways, heard the smash as he drove the butt of the gun through the monitor.

Okay, you bastards, you want to play a game, but you don't play games with me. You don't know what game you're playing or who you're playing with. Because Alexei plays games like this, but Alexei and his boys are so far above your class that you wouldn't even begin to understand.

The man with the tie put the gun back in the shoulder holster, returned to the chair, sat down and drew again on the cigar. 'What you need is a *kresha*.' A roof. 'What you need is someone to look after your business interests, make sure nobody tries to hustle in on you.' The no-neck dropped the second Sverchkov and stepped on it as he moved toward the Gorbatov. The man with the tie drew on the cigar again, leaned forward and ground it into the leather of the desk.

Okay, you bastards – her mind was clear now. You're small fry, you're scum of scum. Alexei will have your balls when I tell him. When Alexei starts on you then you'll know fear, and when Alexei's finished with you you'll curse your own mothers for even bringing you into this world. So stall now, she told herself, get them to come back, then Alexei and his boys will cut them into little pieces.

The man with the tie selected a third cigar, rolled it deliberately slowly between his finger and thumb, and lit it. Behind him the no-neck peered at the Gorbatov and took out a pen.

Oh Christ – she felt the new fear and tried to understand what it was.

'What's the painting?' The no-neck leaned closer to read the signature in the bottom right corner.

A Gorbatov. Cost fifteen thousand dollars. 'I'm not sure.' Anna could barely speak. Christ, why was she feeling frightened again? Because even if she had to pay up now, they'd be back. Therefore she could do what she had to do today and still unleash Alexei and his gorillas on the bastards. So why the panic, Anna? Why the sudden terrifying fear that outstrips everything else?

Oh Christ – she remembered. Alexei's not in town, Alexei's flying to London to do some sort of business there. No problem. Alexei carried a cellphone and she knew his hotel in London, because Alexei always stayed at the same hotel.

Except that wasn't it, that wasn't the new fear which was nailing her to the cross.

Her face and her body were shaking again and the blood trickled from her palms. Oh Christ, I know what it is . . . Don't think it – she struggled to warn herself. Because if you do the bastard in the tie will understand. And if he does there's only one thing he'll do. Therefore do what you have to do, Anna, do anything.

The no-neck was still staring at the signature on the painting.

'Actually it's a Gorbatov.' Her voice was stronger.

'How much is it worth?'

Couple of grand, she almost said. Don't think of what you must protect, because once you do the bastards will know – she knew she was losing the battle against herself. Sacrifice the Sverchkovs, assign the Gorbatov to the flames of hell, but save what you have to save.

'Actually, it's worth fifteen thousand dollars.'

She rose, walked round the desk, and took the pen from the no-neck. I know what you were going to do, the action said, because you made it so goddam obvious. But this is mine, so don't touch it.

And please God may it work.

She sat down again.

The no-neck took the painting from the wall and dropped it on the floor.

'How much a week do you make?' the man with the tie asked.

'Enough.'

'Must be a lot to afford this.'

She shrugged. Like Nikolai Alexandrovich shrugged, she

thought. Crazy thought to have and crazy time to have it.

'A roof will cost the usual twenty-five per cent of profit.' The man with the tie leaned back. 'US hundred-dollar bills. Which I'm sure you'll have no trouble getting.'

'I'll have to clear it with my partners.' She felt the fear rising in her again and fought to control it. 'You don't think I could put this together without backing.'

'Tomorrow.'

Not tomorrow, because tomorrow I have to be with my mother. 'What time?' Because then Alexei and the boys could be waiting. I'm confused, Nik. Help me, Nik.

'Some time.' the man with the tie told her.

'Okay.' She tried to keep the control in her voice. 'Tomorrow.'

The no-neck reached down, picked up the Gorbatov and hung it back on the wall. The glass was embedded in it, and the image was scarred.

Made it, Anna felt the flood of relief; saved what she had to save.

The cigar was still burning the leather. 'Nice to do business with you.' The man with the tie stood and turned, looked at her and smiled, and she knew what he was going to do.

The movement was slow, almost delicate. The fingers ran across the desk, touched the mane of the horse and knocked it over. The horse rolled gently to the edge of the desk, hung as if for a lifetime, then tumbled slowly to the floor and shattered into what seemed a thousand pieces.

Malenkov took the call in one of the booths in the foyer of the Intourist. At the reception desk twenty metres away a group of American tourists checked in.

'Going secure.'

'Secure.'

'Sergei, we might have ourselves a problem . . .'

Malenkov waited.

'Jameson's in town to oversee the investigation you said Sherenko was working on, but Sherenko isn't the only investigator.'

'Who else is there?'

'You're not going to believe this, my friend. The other investigator is Kincaid.'

Malenkov felt the ghost pass over his grave. 'But neither Jameson nor Kincaid know about Sherenko's involvement with Joshua, and he knows nothing about theirs.'

'Sherenko's your business. At present, however, we're clear on Jameson and Kincaid.' The caller hesitated. 'There's no way Sherenko and Kincaid can trace anything back through the Con-Tex investigation?'

'What exactly do you mean?' Malenkov asked.

'No way they can get to Moscow USA?'

Malenkov thought it through. 'Only via Yuri Dushkin, and they don't know him.'

'Thank Christ for that.'

Sherenko and Kincaid sat to the right of Maddox's desk, Maddox facing them and Jameson to the left.

'You want some coffee?' Maddox asked.

Jameson shook his head. 'Later perhaps.'

'We might have a development.' Kincaid spoke quietly.

'So I understood from your phone call. Which is why I've cancelled two meetings.' Maddox was impatient, almost aggressive.

'Lyza Kulikova. She's been missing from the office since the shipment went missing.'

'Yes.'

'We went to her apartment this morning. She wasn't there. There was no sign of her having been there for several days.' Kincaid handed Maddox a plastic bag containing the band and shrink wrapping. 'We found these in the apartment.'

'What are they?' Maddox began to unzip the bag.

'Don't,' Kincaid told him.

'Why not?'

'You don't want your fingerprints on them.'

'Why not?' Maddox asked again.

'The paper strip is what the US Bureau of Engraving and Printing calls a band. A band is what the Bureau uses to bind a strap of bills together. A strap is a hundred bills. This band is for a strap for hundred-dollar bills. The denomination is on it. Straps are shrink-wrapped into bundles, each containing ten straps. We calculate this wrapping was for a bundle. We tried it with paper.'

The colour drained from Maddox's face. 'That's a hundred thousand dollars?'

'Yes.'

'From the missing shipment?'

'Could be.'

'So Lyza was the leak?' Maddox face was death white. 'You want some coffee now?' he asked.

'I think coffee at this point would be a good idea.'

Maddox ordered coffee. 'So what next?' His face had frozen into a death mask.

'We're already checking whether Lyza has a visa, whether she's left the country under her own name. We're also running checks on possible acquaintances.'

'But?'

'We're suspicious that we found the band and wrapping in her apartment. To work here she must have been smart, and those weren't smart things to leave for someone to find.'

Maddox nodded.

'Plus we only found one of each.' Sherenko spoke for the first time.

'Why is that significant?'

'A hundred grand seems a lot, but not compared with six million.'

'You're saying the flat was a set-up?' The first colour seeped back into the death mask.

'It's one possibility.'

'But if it was?'

'Then she's dead. Even if she was involved as the leak she might be dead.'

Kincaid passed the photograph across the desk. 'We removed this from the apartment. Is this her?'

Twenty minutes later Sherenko and Kincaid dropped Jameson at the Omega offices. The afternoon seemed hotter. They stopped for the Stolichnaya at the kiosks by Profsojuznaja metro and drove up Krasikov Ulica, turned right into C'urupy Ulica and passed the apartment blocks and the tennis court and the felled trees.

'Remember we're seeing the couriers' girlfriends tonight.' Kincaid spoke as if his mind was elsewhere.

'Haven't forgotten,' Sherenko told him.

They turned left and bumped down the track, passed the broken gate and stopped in front of the grey brick building. No Whyte yet, the attendant told them; he would have phoned if anyone answering the American's description had turned up.

'Not Whyte this time.' They showed him the photograph.

'You're not healthy people to know.' He laughed at them and disappeared.

They walked away from the brick building and down the ramp to the left, waited in the black at the bottom and heard the grinding sound as the attendant opened the door. Followed him along the white-tiled corridor and stood with him as he turned the lever on the rusted door to the refrigeration room. Pulled on the rubber gloves, stepped inside and began checking.

Ten minutes later they left. A group of boys were playing in the trees and music drifted from the apartments. They drove to the river and stood leaning against the stone balustrade. Sherenko cracked the seal and raised the bottle. Always the Russian way of holding it, Kincaid thought, always Sherenko's fingers grasped tight round like it was his salvation.

'*Do svidanya.*' Even though it wasn't a toast in Russian. He drank *iz gorla*, a neck of vodka each time; held it for Kincaid to take it without looking at him.

Kincaid took the bottle, fingers wrapped round it as if he would never let it go. 'Last time I asked you about the morgue on C'urupy Ulica you told me some bullshit story about the Pentagon.'

Sherenko still stared across the river. 'You a father, Jack?' he asked at last.

'Yeah, Nik, I'm a father. Close to home though, because the job screwed me. So I see my kids once every six months and have missed the most important years of their lives.'

'So perhaps you'll understand.' Sherenko watched as a barge

passed them. 'Say you're not American, Jack. Say you're a Russian, say you're in the Party, say you're KGB.' The shrug again, the expression on the face which said that it didn't matter what you were, but we're actually talking KGB now.

'You get married, you have kids. You watch your kids grow up, guide them, protect them. Do everything you can to help them get on. When they come home from school and tell you what they've been taught, and ask you if it's right, you say of course it's right. Because the Party has said it's right even though you might know it's wrong.

'Then one day the system changes and your kids come home and say: you remember all these things we asked you, and you said they were correct. Well they're not, and you knew they weren't. So why didn't you tell us?'

Kincaid waited. I can see what this has to do with what you said last time, Nik. I can see what this has to do with the fall of the Soviet Union and the new capitalism. But what has it to do with the morgue on C'urupy Ulica?

Sherenko's eyes were still locked in a stare. 'Then your kids stop going to school, or college. And when you ask why, they tell you to look at what's going on. A teacher earns a hundred and fifty dollars a month, if he or she gets paid that is, and a black marketeer a few thousand. They ask you for a pair of Levis, but you can't afford it. You say: go and work, so you can buy a pair. And your daughter says that's crazy, because to buy a pair you'd have to work months at the sort of job you're talking about. And you know what else she's thinking, but she doesn't say. That for the price of one fuck with a foreigner she can buy as many as she wants.'

'So one day she comes home wearing Levis,' Kincaid suggested. He took another *stogram* and passed the Stolichnaya across.

'Yeah, Jack. One day she comes home wearing a pair of Levis.' Sherenko held the bottle up as if in a toast. '*Do svidanya.*' he said again.

Felix Vorkov sat back in his chair and considered the documents in front of him. The report didn't specify Sherenko because it

122

wouldn't, but the request had come from Omega. It might be someone else within Omega, of course, but if it was someone else then it was an almighty coincidence.

So how the hell had Sherenko made the connection? Why the hell had Nikolai Sherenko pulled the FSB file on Yuri Dushkin?

He leaned forward and called Dushkin's cellphone. Dushkin was probably in his apartment in Berlin, but with Dushkin you could never tell.

'Yuri, it's Felix.'

'Good evening, Felix.' Dushkin balanced the flute of champagne on the arm of the chair.

The Lufthansa flight had arrived at Berlin on schedule. Dushkin had taken a yellow cab to the apartment in one of the side streets off the Kurfürstendamm and spent the last three hours at the computer. Yuri Dushkin was of the generation which recorded everything on computer. In Dushkin's case either direct, when he was working from Berlin, or via the TravelMate 5000 when he was away. Total security, of course, firewalls and everything coded.

'Everything in order?' Vorkov asked.

'Everything's in order.'

'Two nights ago. Were you and Alexei Kosygin in the Tokyo?'

Dushkin thought back. 'Early on. We went to Maxim's later.'

'Who else was there?'

'At the Tokyo or at Maxim's?'

'The Tokyo.'

'Couple of girls. Plus some business contact Alexei had invited.'

'What was his name?'

'Sherenko, I think. Why?'

'You're sure that was his name?' It was said as if Sherenko wasn't the name Vorkov wanted to hear.

'Positive. Nikolai Sherenko.'

'Okay, Yuri. Sorry to have troubled you.'

Vorkov hung up and sat forward, shoulders hunched. After ten minutes he reached to his right and moved the note pad to the centre of the desk. When he was satisfied he shredded the notes, telephoned Malenkov's secretary, and asked for an urgent meeting. Fifteen minutes later he sat in the chair he always sat in in Malenkov's office.

'There may be a problem.' Vorkov came immediately to the point.

'With the shipment?'

'No, with Sherenko. Sherenko pulled Kosygin's file . . .'

Malenkov felt the unease. 'Yes.'

'Sherenko has now pulled the FSB file on Yuri Dushkin.'

A *teni proshlovo*, Malenkov felt the chill. The bells tolled in his head. No sound, though, as if the bells were swinging in the wind and their clappers were striking, yet no sound was coming from them even though he was aware of the warning they were sending him.

'We're sure it was Sherenko?' Malenkov asked.

'The request came from Omega. It would be a coincidence if it wasn't Sherenko.'

'Why would it be?'

'Because Dushkin was present the night Sherenko met Kosygin at the Tokyo.'

The ghost drifted past Malenkov again. He heard its rustle and felt its chill, as if he was standing alone in the iron grey of the Cathedral of the Archangel, inside the Kremlin walls, the stone tombs of the Tsars cold upon cold floor, and the past beckoning him.

'You've confirmed this?' he asked.

'I spoke to Dushkin fifteen minutes ago.'

'So what do you suggest?'

'Sherenko disappears. If it becomes necessary, of course. The problem, however, is that if an investigator like Sherenko merely disappears, or is seen to merely disappear, suspicion will obviously be aroused that he has *been* disappeared. Omega would connect it to whatever he had been working on, and would send in more investigators.'

'Therefore?'

'We set Sherenko up. We make it seem as though he's accessed at least part of the money but is concealing the fact from Omega, and deal with him then.'

'And Omega closes down the enquiry and tries to forget Sherenko as fast as they can.'

'Precisely.'

'How?' Malenkov asked.

Vorkov went into detail.

'One question,' Malenkov said when Vorkov had finished. 'Is Sherenko the only investigator working on the ConTex case?'

Vorkov stiffened slightly. 'You think there might be another?'

Malenkov sat back and spread his hands on the desk top. 'I don't know. I only ask.'

5

The wall where the Sverchkovs and the Gorbatov had hung was bare and the porcelain horse lay in pieces in front of her. The shards of glass had been vacuumed from the carpet and Anna had positioned place mats over the burn marks in the leather of the desk, but still she could smell the burning and hear the sound of the horse smashing on the floor.

It was early evening, the sun slanting through the window.

Anna sat at her desk and stared into the void in front of her. Her make-up had run and she had wiped it off, but there was still a smudge around her eyes, her cheeks were stained with wet, and she clutched a piece of porcelain tight in her right hand.

Alexei had checked into his hotel in London but Alexei wasn't there. Alexei's cellphone wasn't working, and when she'd phoned his Moscow numbers his people had merely agreed to tell him to contact her urgently if he phoned.

Her body shook again and her fingernails dug deeper into the soft palms of her hands. She fought to control herself and called St Petersburg.

'Mama, it's Anna. I'm sorry, but something came up at work and I missed the flight . . . No, Mama. I can't catch the first flight up in the morning . . . No, Mama. Everything's all right . . . Perhaps tomorrow evening or the day after . . . I know I was supposed to be going to London, but that doesn't matter . . .'

She hung up and stared again into the void. Sorry to let you down, my mother; sorry not to be at your side on the day you need me to be there. Sorry that I allowed them to break the present you gave me, my father. Sorry that I cannot pay my respects to you this year; sorry that I cannot stand at your grave and read the letter you wrote me, as I do every year.

The letter was in her handbag. Most weeks and months of the year she kept it in the wall safe in her apartment; this time of year – this month and this day – she carried it with her. Would have taken it with her to St Petersburg so she could stand and read it as she had stood and read it in the snow and the cold of the winter after her father's death.

She reached down, opened her bag and took it out. The hand-writing on the envelope was firm and strong and the stamp in the top right corner was for thirty-two cents. She opened it and took out the second envelope. There was no name on it. She opened it, took out the single sheet of paper inside and unfolded it. There were no names on it, no clue to whom or by whom it was written. For one moment she was standing in the heat of a St Petersburg summer the day they had laid her father to rest; for one moment she was standing alone in the cold of a St Petersburg winter the day she had visited her father's grave and read the letter over it.

If you were still alive I could turn to you, my father; so who can I turn to now?

Vorkov made contact with the anonymous red brick building in the north of Moscow at seven.

'Gennadi, this is Felix . . . Does Nik Sherenko use the range much nowadays?'

'Once, twice a week.'

'Next time he comes in I wouldn't mind some of his spent rounds.'

'I'll see what I can do,' the range warden told him.

In the old days ranges used sandbags behind the targets; now-adays they used rubber baffles to slow the rounds down, with steel sheeting behind to flatten the rounds and drop them into a trough at the bottom. Therefore all he could hope was that Sherenko might fire some rounds from the extreme end of the range and that one might lodge in the rubber.

'Thanks,' Vorkov told him.

'No problems.'

And no questions. Once on the payroll, always on the payroll.

* * *

Sherenko left his apartment twenty minutes after the hour and began the drive to the meeting with the Moscow girlfriends of Whyte and Pearce. Tonight would be interesting, but would probably get them no closer to the ConTex money; so tomorrow or the next day, or the day after that, Jameson would report back to ConTex and ConTex would wind up the investigation.

The cellphone rang. Kincaid, he assumed. He had offered to pick Kincaid up, but the company apartment was on the other side of the city and they had agreed it would be easier for Jack to pick up a Lada and negotiate a price to the Up and Down. Or the morgue on C'urupy Ulica – Sherenko felt the wrench in his stomach.

'Yes,' he said, without identifying himself.

'Nik?'

'Yes.'

'It's Anna.'

'How's St Petersburg?'

'I'm still in Moscow. I need to see you.'

He picked up the panic in her voice. 'When?'

'Now.'

'I'm working.'

'How long are you working for?'

It wasn't panic, he realized, it was fear. 'You all right?'

'No.'

He checked the rear mirror and pulled in to the kerb. 'Where are you?'

'At my office.'

'I'll phone in five minutes. Give me the number.'

He clicked the stop button and called Kincaid's cellphone. 'Jack, it's Nik. Something's come up. Nothing to do with ConTex. Can you cover for me?'

'Sure. Anything I can do?'

'It's okay. Call me if you get anywhere and need me.'

'Likewise.'

'Thanks, Jack. I owe.'

Even though Anna was expecting the call the sudden ringing startled her. 'Yes.' She realized she was playing with the piece of the horse again.

'It's Nik. I'll be with you in fifteen minutes.'

He checked behind him, cut in front of a line of cars, and swung the BMW in a tight circle. Ten minutes later he parked at the side of the road running along the river, close to the security barrier into the hotel/business tower complex. He ignored the entrance to the business tower, went through the foyer of Mezhd-1, up the stairs to the arcade of boutiques connecting the two hotels, then through the service corridor to the business section. Only then did he take the lift.

The corridor was empty and featureless. He checked the numbers, came to Anna's office, and knocked. The door opened and he saw Anna's face. The skin was white and drawn tight, her eyes were tinted with a mix of anger and fear, and there was something clutched tightly in her right hand.

'Thanks for coming.'

She held his arm, led him through the outer office and into her own. There were squares on the walls, a lighter shade than the rest, where he assumed paintings had hung, burn holes in the leather top of the desk, though Anna had tried to cover them, and pieces of broken porcelain close to them. He looked round the office for somewhere that hadn't been involved in whatever had taken place, moved two of the conference table chairs away from the wall so they were facing each other, made Anna sit down, and sat opposite but close to her.

'You want a drink?' she asked.

'Tell me what's wrong first.'

'I had a visit. Someone wanting to sell me protection.' She played with the pieces of porcelain in her hand, began to shake, and fought to control it. 'They're coming back tomorrow.'

'Did they hurt you?'

'No. They broke up a few things, but they didn't touch me.' She was still shaking. 'Wasn't shaking before,' she almost apologized.

Sherenko slipped his arm round her shoulders. 'It's okay. Everything's okay now.' He gave her time to settle. 'You know them?'

'No.'

'How many?'

129

'Two.'

'And you're sure they didn't hurt you?'

'Positive.' She nodded to emphasize the point.

'But they did something else?'

She nodded again and clutched the porcelain.

'How much do they want?' Sherenko asked.

'The usual, twenty-five per cent.'

'What about Alexei?'

'I tried to contact him.' Her eyes looked at him through the veil of wet. 'He's out of town. He's supposed to be in London but isn't. At least he's not in his hotel.' She tried to pull her shoulders straight, rose and walked to the drinks cabinet. 'Drink now.' She poured two whiskys, ice with each.

'So what do you want me to do?'

She gave him the glass. 'I don't know.'

She was shaking again. He stood and lifted her, put his arms round her shoulders and wrapped her into him. She slid her arms round his back and buried her face in his chest. 'It's okay,' he told her. Held her with his left hand, held the back of her neck with his right hand and stroked her hair. 'You should have phoned me as soon as it happened.'

'I know.'

They sat down again, finished the whisky and he poured them each another. The fingers of her right hand were clamped tight. He held the hand and stroked it, told her again that everything would be all right, and eased the fingers open. The head of the horse lay in her palm, the jagged edge of the porcelain had cut into her palm. He went to the bathroom, wet his handkerchief, and wiped the blood away.

'Why was the horse the most important thing?' he asked.

'It was a present from my father.'

Tell me what happened this afternoon, Sherenko said; tell me from the beginning; tell me everything.

She told him. I'm feeling better, Nikolai Alexandrovich; thank you for being here, thank you for coming. I feel safe with you, secure with you. Okay, I know that you excite me, but you're also a wall around me behind which I can find peace. Sorry I didn't call you first, Nikolai Alexandrovich. Christ she looked a mess, she told Sherenko; laughed about it, went to the bathroom, washed and dried her face, and put on more make-up.

'You were supposed to be in St Petersburg,' he asked when Anna came back.

'Yes.'

'Catch the first flight up in the morning. I'll handle everything tomorrow.'

'I'll stay.' She lifted the phone and dialled the number in St Petersburg. 'Mama, it's me. I know you were worried after my last call. It's okay now . . . Yes, mama, I'll enjoy London.'

She put the phone down.

'You want to eat?' Sherenko asked.

'I prefer to walk.'

'Where?'

'Red Square.'

They locked the offices, went downstairs and drove to Revol'ucii Ploscad. It was mid-evening, the sky a thinning turquoise. They parked near the Metropol and walked south. The Moskva Hotel was to their right, cars in front of it, then a barrier across the road preventing vehicles parking closer to Red Square, a cluster of kiosks and people to the left, and a single kiosk to the right, under the grey of the hotel. People, mainly young and not well dressed, sitting and eating at a handful of tables.

'You all right now?' he asked.

'Getting all right,' she told him.

They passed the entrance to Dkhotniy Ryad metro station, passed the usual things: the street traders, a gypsy girl looking thin and beautiful, a legless Afghan veteran, the sound of a violin. A woman – aged anywhere between fifty and whatever happened after – Michael Jordan cap and torn trainers, selling cigarettes. Another woman – clean blue dress and cardigan over her shoulders, straight back and the hint of pride still clinging to her face, selling audio cassettes from a tray she held in front of her. A row of medals on the left breast of her dress, and what seemed like a lapel badge above them.

Sherenko stopped. 'The woman with the blue dress.'

'What about her?'

He took two ten-dollar notes from his wallet. 'Buy some cassettes from her. Say you don't have any change and give her this.'

Anna's eyes widened slightly. 'You know her?'

'No.'

'She knows you?'

'No.'

'Then why can't you buy the cassettes yourself?'

He shrugged. Anna crossed back to the subway entrance and approached the woman, talked to her and laughed with her. Sherenko watched her choose a handful of cassettes and shrug as she handed the woman the notes. Watched the woman's face, then Anna's as she came back.

'Thanks,' he told her.

'For doing what you asked me to do?'

'For doing it in a way which left her with her dignity.'

They walked up the slope and into Red Square. The sky was cloudless, almost glowing. The GUM department store was to their left, and the walls of the Kremlin to their right, St Basil's in front. They walked across the cobbles, past the small squat building which constituted Lenin's mausoleum.

'Why did you want to walk in Red Square tonight?' Sherenko asked.

'Because it was in Red Square that my father gave me the porcelain horse.'

'You're close to your father?'

'I was. He's dead.'

Anna slipped her left hand through Sherenko's right arm. He took it away and crossed to her right. Sorry, he said; habit. Sword hand, Anna joked. You're carrying, she asked. Of course – it was in the way he looked at her.

She slid her right hand through his left arm. 'Why do you dislike Alexei so much?'

'It's not Alexei. It's nothing personal.'

'So what is it?'

'The times, I guess. What we've done to ourselves or allowed others to do to us. The new capitalism, the new Russia.'

'But I'm the new Russia, Nik. You're the new Russia.' Saviour

Gate was gaunt to their right now. 'Something about the woman with the cassettes,' Anna suggested.

'Partly.'

'And partly something else?'

'Yes.'

They reached St Basil's, sat side-by-side on the steps and looked back across Red Square. 'Tell me,' Anna said simply.

Sherenko shook his head.

'Tell me,' Anna insisted.

The light in Red Square was soft and the world seemed quiet around them. 'You're a father,' Sherenko said at last. 'You watch your kids grow up. Do everything you can to help them get on. Within the system, of course. Then one day the system changes . . .

'Your kids ask for a pair of Levis, but you can't afford it. You say: go and work, so you can buy a pair. And your daughter says that's crazy, because to buy a pair you'd have to work a month at the sort of job you're talking about. And you know what else she's thinking, but she doesn't say. That for the price of one fuck with a foreigner she can buy as many as she wants. So one day she comes home wearing Levis . . .'

Anna held his arm tighter.

'Then one day she doesn't come home. And you start looking for her. You go to your best friend and you sit down and finally you explain. So your best friend tells you what to do and where to look: the bars and the clubs and the discos. And when you can't find her, your best friend tells you the last resort. Which is actually the morgue on C'urupy Ulica . . .'

And that's where you find her – Sherenko spoke now as if he was somewhere else. You drive down the road, past the Institute of Morphology, and turn left down a track that looks as if it's leading nowhere. Stop at the end and park by the grey brick building that looks like a garage or a warehouse. Slip someone a few dollars and walk down the ramp as if you're descending into Hell, which is what you are doing. Wait in the dark at the bottom and hear the sound as the rusted door is forced open; turn right along the cracked tiles of the corridor and wait at the other rusted door. Then you see them: naked and torn and bereft

133

of any dignity, stacked almost to the ceiling. The colours and the shapes, the mouths open and the eyes all staring at you. Which is where you find her. And all because she wanted a pair of Levis and the new ethic said: go out and get.

Anna held his arm tight with her right hand and slipped her left hand round his arm so they were locked together. 'Your daughter?' she asked at last.

Sherenko shook his head. 'Thank God no.'

'Whose?'

'A friend's.'

'But it was you who went to the morgue on C'urupy Ulica.'

'I couldn't let her father find her like that.'

She sat tight against him, looked across the cobbles and allowed him his moment of silence.

'Funny.' Sherenko's voice was so low she could barely hear it, and his eyes seemed locked into the distance.

'What's funny?'

'I've never told anyone that story. Now I've told two people, both of whom I've just met.'

'Who was the other person?'

'Someone I'm working with.'

'A Russian?'

'No, an American.' Sherenko looked at Anna. 'Actually I didn't tell him about the morgue.'

'Why not?'

'I'm not sure.'

They walked back over the cobbles and turned left into Alexander Gardens. The red brick of the Kremlin wall still towered above them, couples walked along the path through the trees or sat on the wooden benches beneath them, and children played on the grass. They passed under the bridge leading to Trinity Tower and into the lower section of the garden, bought two *pirozhki* from a stall and two beers from another. To their left a grassy slope ran up against the Kremlin wall, children tumbling down it.

'I used to slide down there in the snow.' Sherenko smiled at the memory.

'You're from Moscow?'

'Alpha only recruited from Moscow originally.'

'So you were with Alpha?'

In front of them a ZIL slid out of Borovitskiy Gate.

Sherenko changed the subject. 'Where are you from?'

'St Petersburg, my parents came to Moscow when I was five.'

'Work?'

'Yes.'

'What did your father do?'

'He worked for the government.'

'And now your parents live in St Petersburg?'

'My mother, yes. As I said, my father's dead. That's why I was supposed to go to St Petersburg. He died five years ago. Tomorrow is the anniversary of his funeral.'

'I'm sorry.'

They walked back through the gardens to Red Square. The sun had gone now and the sky above St Basil's had the awesome clarity of late evening.

'What are you thinking, Anna Mikhailovna?'

'I'm thinking of some words.'

'What words?'

'The words of a letter my father wrote me.'

'You want to tell me?'

'Some other time.'

They stood for another five minutes then returned to the car. Anna gave him directions and Sherenko drove to the apartment block. The main door had a security lock. He parked the BMW then they went inside and took the lift to the twelfth floor. Anna unlocked the door and they stepped inside.

'You want a drink?' she asked.

'No.'

Anna's hair lay across the pillow and the silk sheet was contoured with her shape. Sherenko rolled from the bed and went to the bathroom. His body was marked where she had bitten him and his entire being felt as if she was still around him. He showered, dried himself, dressed, went to the kitchen, and poured himself an orange juice. Took it to the lounge and stood staring at the sky of the new day. Pulled on the shoulder holster and Sig Sauer, and heard the sound of bare feet on the carpet behind him.

'You're leaving.' Anna was wearing a dressing-gown, a Chinese dragon across it.

'There are some things I have to do.'

'You want some coffee, something to eat?'

'No.'

She watched him put on his coat, her eyes picking up every movement. Still feel you in me, Nikolai Alexandrovich, still riding the wind with you, still experiencing places and sounds neither of us knew existed. I feel afraid like I've never felt afraid, Nikolai Alexandrovich. I wish to God today wasn't going to happen.

'You okay?' he asked.

'Yeah, I'm okay.'

'So what is it?'

'You remember I told you last evening about a letter my father wrote me.'

'Yes.'

'My father died after he wrote it.'

So . . .

'Don't die for me today, Nikolai Alexandrovich.'

He kissed her goodbye, went to the car, drove to his own apartment, shaved and changed clothes, and collected the Beretta and ankle holster. By the time he reached the red brick building in the north of the city it was six-fifteen.

'Okay to use the CQB?' he asked the range warden.

'Some of the boys are already in there but it should be all right.'

Sherenko went through to the close quarter battle room. The team were locked into their training, one man tensed and waiting for the targets to flash in front of him. The others glanced across as Sherenko entered. Come to see how it's done – it was in their eyes, in the arrogance of their age and their training. Used to be like you once, Sherenko thought; in some ways I wish I was still like you.

The first image flicked from behind the street corner. Gunman, automatic in hand. The marksman in the centre of the floor reacted fast, three rounds, gunman down. The marksman

crouched again and checked, left and right, swung left as the
next target appeared. Kids, no rounds. Swung left as he detected
another movement. Gunman from right. He saw it in time,
swung right, three more rounds. Woman, scarf round neck. He
checked her, saw the gun in the first millisecond, three rounds.
Told you we're good, the eyes of the others would have suggested
to Sherenko. React like this, old timer, take them before, theoreti-
cally, they have a chance to take you? The man in the centre of
the range was fast. Man with gun on left, three rounds and change
mag. Man seeming to have gun on right. Gun a carpenter's tool.
Don't shoot. Woman with scarf, no gun. Woman with scarf, gun
in hand. Three rounds. They were coming at him faster now.
Woman with pram around corner, baby in pram. Don't shoot.
Another man, couple of kids, and another woman, pushing pram
and bending down for gun. Three rounds. Oh Christ, no gun,
woman bending down for kid. Another kid – he was suddenly
disoriented, reactions faster, reactions still split second. Three
rounds, three more rounds. Christ, kid that time. Hell, kid with
gun. He squeezed the trigger. Out of rounds, Sherenko would
have told him.

'You want it?' the instructor asked Sherenko.

'If that's okay.'

The young bloods looked at him.

He ignored them and went through the routine: P226 in shoulder holster; 15-round 9mm and spare mags in left coat pocket,
emptied then reloaded by hand. Beretta P060 in ankle holster;
7-round mag, 0.22 hollow point, spare clips in left trouser pocket.
More difficult to get to than coat pocket, but the Beretta was
back-up and he didn't want to waste time feeling for the different
rounds.

He took his position and walked left, walked right, turned and
faced away from the targets, turned back again. In the side door
to the right Kincaid slipped in unseen and stood watching. Turn
again, walk again, get used to feeling the tension, get ready to
react.

'Go . . .'

Sherenko turned, engaged the target, right hand already inside
left lapel, fingers round the butt of the Sig Sauer and targets

coming into his lateral vision from the left. Three targets. Gunman, gunman, gunman.

Sherenko reacted automatically, bringing the weapon up and flicking off the safety with his right thumb. One tap on One – the opposition on the left. Swing slightly, one tap on Two – opposition in centre. Swing again, two taps on Three. Counting the rounds because unless you knew how many you'd fired you didn't know how many you had left, and then you were dead. Move to right, seek whatever cover anything could give you, and move back along line. Triple tap on Two in the middle. Triple tap on One. Move position again and assess situation. Woman coming from right. Not the reaction of the trainee who had just left the range, the young bloods watching noted. Not the merest milli-second before the finger squeezed the trigger. Not many milli-seconds, of course, but the slightest pause as the man in the arena assessed the target, looked for what he needed to look for and made his decision. Woman, no gun, Sherenko saw. Looked for the next target. Kid, no gun, Man behind him. Automatic rifle. Three rounds. Woman, pram and kid. No gun. Mag out of Sig Sauer and second in from left pocket even though he had rounds left in the first, because you never left yourself with a mag that was almost empty. Older woman, grey hair, no gun. Woman with pram, no gun. Woman with gun. Three rounds. Roll left, disorientate himself because this *was* training. Woman with kid. The trainees picked up the heartbeats in which he assessed. Not kid, doll. Christ, gun. Their fingers came down on their triggers. Why hadn't he taken her? Oh Christ, no gun. Woman beside her, apparently smiling at her. They were still in shock. Christ why was he firing? Oh Christ, no. The woman with the doll a come-on, the second woman with a gun. Two gunmen, obvious. Down the line again, triple tap, triple tap. Sig Sauer jams, although Sig Sauers don't jam, which was why people like the SAS and himself used them. But this is practice, so Sig Sauer jams. Roll to left, partly to seek cover, partly to disorientate himself again. Right hand to right ankle, Beretta coming up and thumb flicking off safety in one fluid movement as he acquired the target. Triple tap on woman from crouch position.

Endex, the instructor told him. End of exercise.

Christ, Kincaid thought.

Sherenko straightened and saw him. 'Your turn?'

'What's running, Nik?'

They went to the range in the adjoining area.

'How'd you mean?'

'That was for real.'

Sherenko shrugged. 'You want a lift after?'

'Wouldn't mind.'

Half an hour later they left the range and began the drive to the office.

'Thanks for last night.' Sherenko accelerated past a line of Ladas. 'How'd it go with the girls?'

'Good company, no obvious leads.' Kincaid went into detail.

'So nothing we can use?' Sherenko asked.

'No.'

They reached Gertsena Ulica. Sherenko pulled in but left the engine running. 'There's something I have to do. Cover for me again, will you?'

'Don't make a habit of it.'

'Last time.'

'You'll be carrying your phone?'

'Of course.'

Vorkov took the call at eight. I have what you want, the range warden from the red-brick building in the north of the city told him. Vorkov ended the call and punched the number for Omega.

'Nik Sherenko,' he told the man who answered and prepared to cut the call off if he was connected.

'Sherenko's not in at the moment. You want to speak with Kincaid?'

There *was* a God, Vorkov thought. 'Kincaid's working with Nik on the ConTex case?'

'*Da.*'

'What's his first name?'

'Jack.'

'He's American?'

'Yes.'

'Actually, I need to speak with Nik. I'll call later.'

He hung up and confirmed the arrangements for Sherenko: the counterfoil from the bank in Austria; the airline ticket and the computer records in Moscow and Vienna; the entry into Sherenko's apartment and the teams for the following morning.

Anna had been at work an hour. When she arrived she had checked her diary for the day, then remembered that there would be no appointments because she was supposed to be in St Petersburg. So what are you thinking, Anna? What do the rules of the game say now? Because some time today Nik will face the bastards who destroyed your office and broke your father's present to you. So how do you feel about the fact that you've asked so much of him?

The staff came in at eight, nervous and white-faced. Everything will be all right, she told them, last night she'd spoken to a friend. Sherenko arrived at five minutes to nine, carrying an airline navigation bag.

'You want some coffee now?' she asked.

'Coffee would be good.'

She waited till her secretary brought them the coffee, then shut the door. Six hours ago they were making love, now they had not even kissed.

'The staff know you expect another visit?' Sherenko sat at the conference table.

'I told them yesterday.'

'And they all came in this morning?'

'Yes.'

'Have you told them about me?'

'I said you were a friend who was going to negotiate for me.'

'I'd like to explain certain things to them, but before that I need to talk to you.'

'Talk to me.'

'Point one. I need to set some things up here.

'Point two. I don't want to be here when they arrive. That would give them a psychological advantage. I'll therefore be waiting outside. I have my cellphone but I need a second in case mine goes down or someone phones at a crucial moment. I'm also going to bug this room and will be listening outside, so I'll have a second way of knowing when I have to move. I'm also going to video the faces of the men who visit.

'Point three. When they arrive your secretary shows them in, shuts the door, and phones me. Firstly on my cell phone, then on yours if necessary. I won't answer any calls whatever on either. Your secretary phones me, lets it ring twice, then hangs up. She does this once more, that's a total of two calls, two rings each time.

'Point four. When they arrive, everyone leaves. When I enter your office, you leave. You don't say anything. You not only leave your office, you leave with the others. I'll collect you when I'm ready.'

He looked at Anna. 'Questions?'

'You're going to be okay?'

'I hope so.'

'Is anyone else helping you?'

'No.'

'Why not?' She knew how he was about to react. 'Don't shrug at me,' she told him. 'Okay,' she conceded. 'Don't answer.'

'Anything else?' He glanced at his watch.

'The others can leave. I'll leave this room, but I'm not leaving the outer office.'

'You have some things you can hang on the walls?'

'Yes.'

'Put them up then, something nice on the desk.'

He clicked open the security lock of the navigation bag and took out four solid glass ashtrays and four miniature fighter aircraft, made of metal and mounted on metal bases, then he placed one of each on the desk at the side of the burn mark, the second set on the conference table, and the last two on the cabinet along the wall where Anna was hanging the prints.

'Don't ask,' he told her, and took a clock/radio from the navigation bag.

The radio was small and modern, in keeping with the office. The lens was fitted behind the speaker grille, the transistor was in the body of the radio transmitting to a receiver which Sherenko would place in the secretary's desk outside, the receiver connected to a VCR. The transmitter ran from the radio's own power source, therefore no wiring was visible, and a separate microphone was also concealed within the clock/radio, the frequency of the audio surveillance already set and the ICOM scanner which Sherenko would carry also pre-set to that frequency.

'Does the window open?' he asked.

'Yes, but it's locked.'

'Unlock it.'

They returned to the outer office and he briefed the staff, slowly and methodically till he was sure they understood. 'Questions,' he asked at the end.

There was one.

'How do we know they won't come back again, or do something to Anna or one of us after?'

'They won't.'

He left the office and took his position in the BMW.

Where's Nik, Jameson asked at the briefing fifteen minutes later. Nik had something to sort out, Kincaid told him. He left the conference room, updated the case log, began what he hoped would be the final report, and called Sherenko's cellphone.

It was ten o'clock. Sherenko sat in the BMW with the window open and the phones on the passenger seat, and listened in to Anna's office on the earpiece of the ICOM, the battery in his coat pocket. His cellphone rang and he began to count. Two sets of two each, he had told Anna and her secretary. Thirty seconds later the ringing stopped.

Eleven o'clock. When are you going to show – the nerves coiled tighter in Anna's stomach. Suddenly don't want you to do it, Nik. Suddenly want to pay up rather than make you go on the line for me.

Twelve noon. Life was about waiting, Sherenko reminded himself. The cellphone rang again. Nobody resembling the targets had gone in, he was certain. Except they could have gone in through one of the hotels, but they wouldn't, because that wasn't in their mind frame. The cellphone was still ringing. He ignored it and watched the door.

Where are you, Nik, Kincaid wondered. Why aren't you answering your phone?

* * *

Vorkov's meeting with Malenko was at twelve-thirty.

'You were right. Sherenko does have a partner on the ConTex investigation.'

'Anyone we know?' Malenkov asked.

'No,' Vorkov told him.

'Name?'

'Jack Kincaid.'

'You've run a check on him?'

Vorkov shook his head. 'I thought it best not to suggest we had any interest in him. He's American working for Omega, therefore I assume he's ex-CIA.'

Malenkov nodded. The Cathedral of the Archangel was dark around him, Resurrection Bell tolling midnight and the stone coffins cold and silent around him. Finish it and finish it fast, the entire structure of his logic told him. Finish it before the last coffin was prised open and the last ghost released.

Lucky Malenkov had suggested checking whether Sherenko had a partner, Vorkov thought. Because take out Sherenko the way he was planning, and Sherenko was working alone, and everything would be fine. But take out Sherenko and Sherenko had a partner, then the partner would continue the investigation.

'So what do you suggest we do?' Malenkov asked.

'We take them both out,' Vorkov said, as if the solution had been his.

It was one o'clock; Anna was too nervous to eat. Two o'clock; perhaps they weren't coming today. Three, the tension winding and no one in the office able to concentrate. Four, the bastards were playing a game, Sherenko thought; the bastards were putting Anna on the rack. Five o'clock. The 5-series BMW pulled up and the two men got out. Funny how he knew it was them. Partly Anna's description of them, partly instinct. Interesting motor, not the latest model, so they weren't big league, because big league always had the best. Therefore the hoods getting out were second division playing at being hard men. Careful though, my friend, because when the opposition isn't top division you relax, and that's when the bastards get you.

He gave them thirty seconds, left the car and followed them

inside. The lifts were around a corner on the left. Chance in a million, but lifts sometimes jammed. He took the stairs, walking quickly but controlling his breathing. His cellphone rang. Two rings, stop. Two rings . . .

Don't give it away, Anna told herself. Nik was right in not being here, because if he had been then the bastards opposite her would have had the psychological advantage. Don't play the game too long though, Nik. The men settled as they had settled the day before, the man with the red tie in the chair by the desk and the no-neck at the conference table.

'You've spoken to your partners?' The man in the red tie reached in his pocket, selected a cigar, and began to light it.

'Yes.'

He drew on the cigar, ignored the ashtray, and laid it on the leather of the table. Behind him the no-neck stood as he had done the day before and examined the paintings on the wall.

'What did they say?'

'They weren't happy.' Where are you, Nik? Come on, Nik.

'They could be less happy.' The first wave of the hand toward the model fighter plane on the desk.

The outer office was empty. Sherenko removed the ear unit, switched off the ICOM, and walked softly across the floor.

'Perhaps we could come to some arrangement.' The man with the red tie drew on the cigar again. 'A share of the partnership, for example.'

The door opened and Sherenko came in. Anna flicked on the intercom, the movement unnoticed, left her desk, walked past him, not speaking, and closed the door behind her. Leave the office entirely, Nik had insisted. She sat at her secretary's desk, switched on the intercom and turned down the volume.

'Who the hell are you?' It was the man with the tie. Behind him the no-neck changed position slightly.

Sherenko settled in Anna's chair. 'I'm the lady's business partner.'

She didn't say you were coming – it was in their eyes and their body language. The man with the tie eased open the left lapel of his coat with his left hand and drew it back, no need for the no-neck behind him to do the same.

'Drink,' Sherenko suggested. He rose, poured three scotches and raised his glass. '*Na pososhok.*' He downed it in one and placed it on the desk, the others doing the same. 'If we're to do business perhaps I should know your name?' He returned to the chair and swung easily in it.

'Leonid Basayev.'

Basayev was a Chechan name.

Sherenko nodded. 'My partner explained that you were offering a *kresha*.' Offering a roof, offering insurance.

'Yes.' Basayev drew on the cigar and leaned forward slightly.

'There's an ashtray,' Sherenko told him.

Basayev smiled at him and ground the cigar into the fine green of the leather.

'I gather that you are now also suggesting a share in the partnership of the business.'

'Yes.'

How do you know that – it should have been a flicker in Basayev's subconscious. Because that's only just been discussed and you weren't here.

Sherenko rocked back in Anna's chair. 'I have to tell you that we already have a *kresha*.'

Basayev selected another cigar. 'Cancel it.' Behind him the no-neck peered at the Gorbatov back in its place on the wall.

'That would be difficult.' Sherenko stood, walked to the window, checked it was still unlocked, and sat down again.

'As I say: cancel it.' Basayev moved the ashtray slightly and lit the cigar.

'Given the structure of our company, an extra partner would also be difficult.'

'You don't understand.' Basayev held his left lapel with his left hand and revealed the Walther for the second time.

Sherenko looked at him across the desk.

Cigar in the stupid bastard's right hand and the no-neck holding the Gorbatov with both hands, therefore in the wrong position to move quickly. The no-neck going to drop the painting, but that wasn't the problem. The problem was that the no-neck was a thug. Basayev had the Walther for show, but the no-neck

145

was carrying for real, probably an SU, the reduced version of the AK47.

He left the chair, walked behind Basayev – Basayev turning slightly and grinning – and faced the no-neck. Two paces from him, so the no-neck couldn't surprise him, and at a slight angle, so that his side rather than his front was to the no-neck.

The no-neck let the painting slip, tightened his grip again just before it slid from his fingers, then looked at Sherenko and smiled.

'Put it back.' The tips of the fingers of Sherenko's right hand touched the metal body of the fighter model.

The no-neck dropped the Gorbatov, began to laugh, and relaxed fractionally, the menace still glinting in his eyes but his body momentarily exposed as the painting fell. The man who confronted him, the woman's business partner, with his hands at his side and nothing near him that could conceivably be a weapon or a threat.

Sherenko shifted his balance lightly and closed his fingers around the body of the fighter model, the nose of the plane sharp and lethal; he changed balance again and drove it forward, all the power of his body and mind behind it. The six inches of metal pierced the no-neck's shirt, just above his trousers, and penetrated into the flesh and organs inside. The no-neck gasped in pain and suprise and doubled up, head coming forward. Sherenko smashed the solid glass ashtray into his face. The no-neck jerked back, Sherenko pulled him forward and crunched the ashtray down on the bones at the rear of the skull. Basayev turned. Basayev not trained, so not going for the Walther. Sherenko took one pace towards him, Basayev still turning, and smashed the ashtray against the bridge of his nose.

What's happening – Anna heard the noises, could hear nothing else. No voices. No indication that Nik was alive or uninjured. She left the desk and ran to the door.

Sherenko dropped the ashtray, spun Basayev round and removed the Walther. Rolled the no-neck over, made sure he was still unconscious, and removed the Kalashnikov.

Basayev was moaning, holding the remains of his face.

'Light a cigar,' Sherenko told him.

You're joking – Basayev's eyes were clouded with agony.

'Light a cigar,' Sherenko told him again.

Anna froze in the doorway. Thank God you're okay, Nikolai Alexandrovich. What are you saying, Nik? What are you telling him to do?

Basayev took his hands from his face and picked a cigar from his pocket. His fingers were covered with blood and mucus, and his hands were trembling.

'Light it.'

Basayev could barely hold the lighter.

'Light it.'

Basayev tried to hold the cigar between his teeth, tried to steady his right hand with his left, tried to light the cigar.

'We don't smoke in this office. Put it out.'

Basayev leaned forward to the ashtray.

Anna was still frozen in the doorway. Thank God you're alive, Nikolai Alexandrovich – the relief flooded through her. Christ, Nik, what the hell's happened though? What in God's name have you done to them?

'Put it out where you normally put it out,' Sherenko told Basayev.

The model fighter was on the corner of the desk. I know what you're going to do – Basayev's body shook with fear. You're going to pin my hand to the desk with the plane. He was too terrified to do it, too terrified not to. Oh Christ no. The bastard wasn't going to pin his hand to the desk, the bastard was going to smash the ashtray down on his fingers.

Anna's eyes narrowed in fear. Watch the other one, Nikolai Alexandrovich. Oh God, Nik, what have you done. What are you going to do now?

Sherenko half-turned away and sat on the edge of the desk. 'As I said, we already carry insurance.'

Basayev laid the cigar in the ashtray. Thank you for not smashing my hand – the relief splintered through the fear. Thank you for not hurting me any more.

Sherenko looked at him. 'There is, however, the minor problem of what happens next.' He looked at Anna. This you shouldn't see – the anger was in his eyes. This is why I told you to stay away till everything was over. Because you think you've seen everything, but it's only the beginning.

Anna looked back at him, face ashen and lips tight together. I know I asked you, Nik, I know you're doing this for me. But Christ, I didn't expect this: Christ, I had no idea.

Sherenko checked the no-neck was still unconscious and turned back to Basayev. 'Specifically, Leonid, we have to look at what you might do after today's little discussion, and what I might have to do to prevent that.'

The pain racked Basayev's face and the fear tore at his mind and his soul. 'There's no problem. I won't come back, I won't touch the woman.'

'Trouble is, how can I believe you?' Sherenko walked round the desk and opened the window.

Oh God – Basayev froze. Oh Jesus Christ Almighty, I know what he's going to do. 'Please. *Klianus.* I give you my word.'

Oh God, no – Anna froze again.

Sherenko walked back from the window, sat on the edge of the desk again, and leaned forward so that his face was close to Basayev's. 'The problem, my friend, is that I might believe you, but how can I trust No-Neck? You're intelligent, you know what I'll do to you if you renege on the deal. I've got your name and your car number, I've got you on surveillance video. I've got your fingerprints, so I can trace you through the files. As I say, the problem is No-Neck because No-Neck won't understand.'

'So?'

'So do it.'

You can't – the fear was as Basayev had never experienced. You can't tell *me* to do it. Because you doing it is one thing, but me . . .

Do what – Anna looked at Sherenko. Oh Christ – she realized. 'Do it.'

I can't, Basayev thought. 'Okay . . .' He felt the strength which comes with self-preservation. 'Okay.' He stood, wiped the blood from his eyes with a handkerchief and flinched with the pain. Held No-Neck by the legs and dragged him round the desk and across the floor.

You can't – Anna tried to move, tried to say something.

The no-neck was beginning to come round. His eyes blinked and his muscles fought to regain some semblance of control. Basayev lifted him, not sure where the strength came to do it. Oh Christ – he glanced at Sherenko: you're going to let me throw him out, then you're going to make me jump. So I won't throw him out. Except if I don't you'll throw us both out, and if I do there's a chance you'll stick by your word and let me go.

Nik was going to stop it, Anna knew. Nik wasn't going to allow it to happen.

Basayev tilted No-Neck through the window space and let go.

'Okay,' Sherenko told him. 'You can go.'

Basayev collapsed on the chair, his shoulders shuddering and his eyes rolling uncontrollably, deep gasps jerking from his lungs. Sherenko took the clip from the Walther, opened Basayev's coat, and put the Walther back in the shoulder holster, then half-led half-carried him past Anna to the washroom in the corner of the outer area and bathed his face.

'Listen, my friend. I'll take you to the rear stairs. Go out that way, through the hotel. The police will be arriving soon; leave your car now and collect it in a couple of hours. You understand?'

'I understand.'

They turned to go.

Anna blocked their way. Explain to me what you've just done, Nikolai Alexandrovich – her eyes riveted on his. Explain to me why you did it in front of me. Okay, so they were bastards, okay, so they were mafia, but I cannot believe what I have just seen, cannot ever forget what I have just seen you do. Her body shook and the bile rose in her throat. I thought I knew you, but I don't know you at all. You were my Alpha and my Omega; in the short time I have known you, you have become my beginning and my end, and everything between. But now you have destroyed me, because you have destroyed what I believed was you.

Sherenko gave Basayev a towel to staunch the blood. 'Tell her.'

Tell me what, Anna thought.

Basayev held the towel tenderly against his face. 'He's right. Shamil wouldn't have forgotten, Shamil would have come back

149

even if I told him not to. Shamil was an animal. He'd have waited, then he would have torn you to pieces.'

Sherenko checked the landing outside and led him to the door of the emergency stairs at the rear.

'Thank you.' Basayev's face was white under the lines of dried blood.

'Go,' Sherenko told him. He returned to the office, collected the no-neck's gun, wiped his fingerprints from it, took the stairs to the top floor, let himself on to the roof area, scuffled the gravel near the edge, placed the gun on the gravel, and returned to the office. Anna had closed the window and was scrubbing the desk, the movements hard, as if she was trying to exorcize what she had just witnessed. Her face was white and she was trembling.

She looked up at him. 'Why, Nik?'

'Why what?'

'Why did you kill him? Why did you kill him that way?' She stood, crossed the floor, and poured herself a Stolichnaya.

'Don't I get one?'

'Sorry.' She poured him one and gave it to him. Broke into tears. Sat in her chair, breathed deeply, and tried to compose herself. 'I don't believe what I just saw, Nik. I can't believe that the man who made love with me last night just did what I saw him do.'

'You believe what Basayev said?'

'About the no-neck coming back?' She reached down into her own morality, because she knew what Sherenko would say to her when she told him what she believed. 'Yes. I believe what he said. I believe that the other one would have come back for me.' She poured them each another Stolichnaya. 'Tell me what you're going to tell, Nik.'

'You're sure you want to hear it?'

'Yes.'

'This is the other side of your life, Anna. So you work hard, but you at least have the opportunity to work hard. You don't have to stand outside a metro station and sell cigarettes or cassettes. You live in an expensive apartment, you wear expensive clothes. You drink expensive champagne and eat expensive meals. But this is the other side of the new world, Anna, this is the price some people have to pay for that world. This is what your friend Alexei does to people every day of every week. Except he doesn't do it to people like Basayev and his gorilla.'

He wrapped the ashtrays and model planes in polythene bags, placed them in the nav bag, and took the clock/radio down. 'You want to know something else, Anna?'

'Yeah, I want to know something else.'

'You think Alexei would have let Basayev off? You think that Alexei wouldn't have killed them both? Not Alexei, of course. Alexei wouldn't have done it personally, one or two of Alexei's apes would have done it. Except they wouldn't have done it with you standing in the doorway. Alexei would have told you he'd taken care of everything, and you could have closed your eyes, had another bottle of champagne with him, and carried on living as if nothing had happened.'

She glared at him, her body still shaking and her eyes blazing through the shock. 'Okay, Nik, that's me. But you're also part of the new Russia. You yourself said that last night. You enjoy it. You enjoy the champagne and the caviar and screwing someone like me. So let's talk about you, Nik; let's talk about what sort of man you really are.'

Sherenko left her office and went to her secretary's desk. 'You want to know something about me, Anna? You really want to know something about me? How what I've just done means to me?' He reached under the secretary's desk.

'Yes, Nik, I really want to know.'

He disconnected the receiver and the VCR. 'Five years ago I did something I've never forgotten. After, I swore there were certain things I'd never do again. To protect me or mine, okay. But never again would I do what I had sometimes done in the past. Today I did it.'

He wrapped the receiver and VCR in polythene and packed them in the nav bag.

'What did you do five years ago?'

'I killed someone.'

'So you were Alpha, you told me that last night. So Alpha kills people: terrorists and gunmen and hijackers. So what's new, Nik?' She stared at him. 'What are you doing?'

He spun the combination on the security lock. 'Leaving.'

She stood in front of him. 'What did you say?'

'I said I'm leaving.'

'Because you've done what I paid you to do? Because you had your payment last night, and now you've done the job?'

'Perhaps.'

She stood close to him, eyes screaming at him. Drew her right hand back and struck him hard across the face. 'Fuck you, Nikolai Alexandrovich. You really think that was what last night was about. You really think that was why I almost agreed to pay them, because I was afraid of what they might do to you. Why I didn't leave the offices like you told me, why I came in because I thought they'd done something to you, even though there would have been nothing I could have done.'

The tears streamed down her face.

'Maybe you're right, maybe I lead my life and ignore the price other people have to pay. Maybe I would have been happier to have closed my eyes. Okay up to that point, okay to accuse me of those things. But after that . . . So fuck you, Nikolai Alexandrovich. Fuck off now if that's all you think you and I are worth.' She wiped the tears and stared at him, stood out of his way so there was no one between him and the door.

Sherenko put the bag on the floor. 'You're a crazy woman, Anna Mikhailovna.'

'You're a crazy man, Nikolai Alexandrovich.' The flood swept over her. She kissed him; held his face in her hands and kissed him again. 'So what are we going to do, Nik?'

'Get this place cleaned up. The police will be some time, but they'll get here eventually. They'll find a gun on the roof, plus signs of a scuffle. Someone will mention mafia and the police will say good riddance.'

He went back into the office and began to clean the floor.

Vorkov briefed Malenkov at eight, in the general's office at Yasenevo.

Yuri Dushkin had been in contact from Berlin, the road shipment had arrived safely, Dushkin was making the usual arrangements and would fly to Zurich and Amsterdam tomorrow or the next day, then to London for the auction.

Malenkov poured them each a malt. 'And Sherenko and Kincaid?'

'Set up and ready to be dealt with.'

'In a way which ties Sherenko to the missing ConTex money?'

'Of course.'

'Tell me.'

Vorkov went into detail.

'When do the boys go into Sherenko's apartment?' Malenkov asked when Vorkov had finished.

'When you give the green light.'

'They're standing by?'

'Yes.'

'Where's Sherenko now?'

'At a restaurant.'

'Who's he with?'

'A woman. The tails weren't sure who.'

'Do it,' Malenkov ordered.

The Moscow sky was streaked with red. A good evening for his last night in town, Jameson thought. The Omega office was quiet around him, Riley at a computer and Gerasimov in his room on the other side of the corridor.

'You're pulling out tomorrow?' Riley logged off and poured them each a malt.

'London for a couple of days, touch base in DC, then Brazil.' ISS spreading its wings and Jameson doing the hard sell. He sat back in the chair, swirled the liquid round the glass and called the number in Virginia. In Washington it would be hot and humid, in the lush green across the Potomac there would be a cool breeze in the air.

'Hi, this is Grere Jameson. Is Ed there?'

He waited while the secretary checked, then heard Miller's voice.

'Grere, how you doing, old buddy?'

'Just confirming we got a meet in London tomorrow.'

'Sure thing. What time you due in?'

'Early evening. The BA flight. I'm staying at the usual place.'

'Okay, I'm taking this evening's flight. Got a few things to catch up on, but I'll be clear by tomorrow evening. How say I pick you up at nine?'

'Sounds good to me.'

Thirty minutes later Jameson and Gerasimov left the Omega office and were driven to a restaurant off Tverskaya. Gerasimov's cellphone rang as they settled.

'Gerasimov, this is Arnie Maddox.'

Maddox sounded bullish, Gerasimov thought; Maddox was deliberately calling him by his last name only and enjoying doing so.

'Gerasimov, you got us a problem.'

6

Sherenko's face was silhouetted against the lamp. Anna trailed her fingers through his hair and across the contours of his face. It was one in the morning, going on two. She lay on her side, her head resting on her left hand, and played the fingers of her right across his lips.

'What was so important about the person you killed five years ago?' she asked him. 'Why did you swear never to do that sort of thing again? Why did you tell me?'

Sherenko smiled at her in the half-light. 'Lots of questions, Anna Mikhailovna.' The smile faded and his face and voice were serious. 'The last first, because it's easiest to answer. I told you because it was important for you to know how far down the line I went for you today. Five years ago I swore I would never kill again because I disapproved of what I came to assume was the reason. Okay, you never knew the reason, but on this occasion there might have been a connection with something.'

'What connection?'

'The next day was the day of the Gorbachev putsch. Other than that I don't know.'

'And you disapproved of the putsch?'

'Yes.'

'Why?'

'Because I thought it was intended to bring back the old system, and I believed in the new Russia.'

Anna lay beside him, looked at him. 'What happened after?'

'I got out.'

'Which was when you hit the vodka, when your wife and family left you?'

'Yes.'

'How does that tie in with the girl you found in the morgue?'

'Because it was the new Russia, the Russia I believed in, that betrayed her.'

The Mercedes left the safe house, two men in the front and the *chernomeshochnik*, the black bag man, one of the two in the rear. Going down, Vorkov informed Malenkov; everything looks good.

The night was warm around them. They made love again, fast and sometimes bordering on violent, then lay back in the peace which followed.

'What are you thinking, Nikolai Alexandrovich?' Anna asked.

'I'm thinking the words of a poem. "Black eyes, how I love you. Black eyes, how I fear you." ' Sherenko laughed, a low, gentle laugh. 'And you, Anna Mikhailovna,' he asked. 'What are you thinking?'

'I'm thinking of the words of the last letter my father wrote to me.' She sat up and pulled on the dressing-gown. 'You want to hear them?'

'If you want me to.'

'I do.'

She fetched her bag from the sitting-room, took out the letter, and knelt on the bed. Opened the first envelope and took out the second; opened the second and took out the letter. Unfolded it and began to read:

'When you receive this it will be over. If I have been able to achieve what I am about to do, then I will tell you; if not, then others might not. If others tell you, judge them, not me, by what they say. What I do, I do because I remember the day you were born and wish that others might know such happiness . . .'

Her voice was almost lost in the night. Sherenko saw the silver of the first tear and stroked it away.

'What I do, I do because even now I know I have a smile on my face at the memories of our family together, and wish that others might also smile. But that they may smile in freedom and in joy. What I do now, I do because I am a patriot. What I do now I do for

Mother Russia. Always be strong, always smile. Never forget me.'

Anna looked up, smiled at Sherenko, then folded the letter into the first envelope and the first envelope into the second.

'What did he mean when he wrote the words?' Sherenko asked. 'What was it that he was about to do?'

'I don't know.'

The Mercedes stopped one street from Sherenko's apartment; the three men entered the block and took the stairs to the fifth floor. The target was still with the woman, they confirmed, therefore the target's flat was unoccupied. The *chernomeshochnik* eased Sherenko's door open and they went in. When they left six minutes later a counterfoil for two hundred and fifty thousand United States dollars, paid into the Schillerhaus bank in Vienna, lay with the family photographs in the folder in the sideboard beside the television, and a used airline ticket Moscow–Vienna return was scrabbled in a ball in the waste bin.

'Tell me about the woman at the metro station,' Anna asked.

'Which woman?'

'The woman with the medals.'

'It wasn't the medals, it was the tie-pin. I have one like it.'

'Alpha?'

'Yes.'

'But they don't have women in Alpha.'

'It was her husband's.'

The night drew on.

'Alpha was formed in the seventies,' Sherenko said at last. 'Originally it was created to do one specific job.' Before the Soviet Union occupied Afghanistan, he explained, before Afghanistan became the Soviet Union's Vietnam. 'The job was to assassinate the then president. Liaise with local opposition in storming the presidential palace, do the job, then pull back to the hills and be airlifted out. Alpha went in, did the job, took a lot of casualties, withdrew to the hills and radioed for the planes to evacuate them, asked for medics for the wounded.'

He fell silent.

'Then?' Anna asked softly.

157

'Then Moscow denied the operation had ever happened or that Alpha even existed. Moscow refused to send the planes to get Alpha out.'

His voice was lost in the dark, as if he did not exist.

'You were there . . .' Anna was almost too afraid to ask.

'No. I joined later.'

'But that was the first betrayal? Even before 1991 and the new Russia.'

'Yes,' Sherenko told her.

'So what happened?'

'Friends defied the Kremlin. Friends sent in medics and planes to get the boys out. Moscow had its revenge, of course. None of the men wounded or injured received compensation, and none of the widows of the men killed were given a pension.'

'Which is why, today, there is a woman wearing an Alpha tie-pin selling audio cassettes outside the metro station at Dkhotniy Ryad,' Anna asked.

'Yes.'

It was five in the morning, the black of night fading into grey, then the grey fading into the crystal light of a new day. The Volvo slid away from the Omega offices and turned west. Sixteen minutes later it stopped one street from the block which housed Sherenko's apartment. The four men left it, the driver remaining as back-up, and made their way into the block, entering easily and using the rear stairs.

In the shadows of the alleyway on the opposite side of the road the team which had entered the apartment two and a half hours earlier watched. Search team entering the target apartment, the leader of the stake-out team informed Vorkov.

Four minutes later the Omega team found the Moscow–Vienna airline ticket in the waste bin, three minutes after that the counterfoil from the Schillerhaus bank of Vienna.

Anna and Sherenko woke at seven. A different wakening this time, from a different sleep. They showered languidly and dressed slowly. Sherenko squeezed fresh orange juice while Anna ground fresh coffee.

'What time's your flight to London?' He loosened the silk of the dressing-gown and kissed her neck.

'I'm not going.'

'Why not?'

'Why do you think?'

'London's business, even though you might also see Alexei Kosygin?' he asked.

'Yes.'

'Then you must go. I'll run you to the airport.'

Searchers have now exited target's apartment but left a stake-out car in position in an adjoining street, the *komandir* informed Vorkov. We have seen them, but they have not seen us. Everything going smoothly, Vorkov informed Malenkov, everything going to plan. Gerasimov has taken the bait and Omega is moving on it.

Kincaid rose at seven. The night before he had decided not to go to the range that morning. The ConTex job showed every sign of winding down, and once it did he would be out of Moscow. And once he was out there would be no need to carry the Sig Sauer, therefore there was no need to practise any more with it. In any case, he was up to whatever standard he would achieve without an intensive course. Plus he had Nik Sherenko to look after him.

So what had Riley been playing at last night . . . The phone call just before midnight and the rush from the company apartment without a word of explanation . . .

He showered, dressed, ate a quick breakfast, and left. The cellphone rang as he crossed the pavement.

'Jack?'

He recognized Jameson's voice. 'Yes.'

'Briefing in fifteen minutes.'

There was something about Jameson's tone. 'On my way in anyway. What's up?'

'Just get here. You've spoken to Sherenko this morning?'

'No.'

'Don't speak to him. Don't phone him. If he phones you be

noncommittal and say you'll see him as usual. Don't mention I've called you in.'

'Understood.'

What's running, Grere; why the hell the panic? What's going down, Nik, where the hell have you been for the last thirty-six hours? Why haven't you been answering your phone?

He tried to wave down a Lada, cursed when the driver didn't stop, and paid over the odds to the next.

Vorkov briefed Malenkov over breakfast. Malenkov had been in since six. That morning he would fly to London for the security conference. Top secret, of course, except not in the way top-secret meant in the old days. Old enemies, new friends – at least that was the official line. Expedient, he supposed, but also amusing, especially as they were all still spying on each other in other areas. But that was the game nowadays, so that was the way you played it. Even the cocktail parties and the official receptions. Which was probably the real reason anyway.

'Everything's in place.' Vorkov poured himself a second coffee. 'The boys planted the stuff in Sherenko's flat last night. Gerasimov was alerted via ConTex. His people went in at five.'

'Where's Sherenko now?'

'Still with the woman.'

'What about Kincaid?'

'Kincaid left his apartment six minutes ago; presumably he's en route to the office.'

'And the teams are set up?'

'Simultaneous hits if possible. If not, Sherenko first, then Kincaid.'

Malenkov nodded in approval. 'What else is there?' he asked Vorkov.

'The woman Sherenko spent the night with. We checked out the address. It's Anna Buskova.'

Kincaid reached the Omega offices fourteen minutes after Jameson's call. Igor Lukyanov was already at his desk. He was tight-faced and merely nodded as Kincaid entered. Gerasimov, Jameson and Riley were locked in Gerasimov's office, and a group of Omega men were hunched around two desks at the far end, drinking coffee and smoking. As he came in they glanced at him then closed back in amongst themselves.

He crossed the corridor, tapped on Gerasimov's door, and went in. Conference room in five minutes, Jameson told him curtly. Kincaid closed the door, returned to the main office, and poured himself a coffee. One of the telephones rang. Igor Lukyanov answered it then cupped his hand over the mouthpiece. 'Call for Nik.' The team at the end of the room tightened. 'The morgue on C'urupy Ulica.'

'I'll take it,' Kincaid told him.

'Viktor. Nik's not in at the moment. This is Jack.'

Gerasimov, Jameson and Riley left Gerasimov's office. Conference room now, Jameson's nod said.

'Viktor, I'll phone you back.'

He picked up the coffee and followed them through. Riley was positioned at the end of the conference table furthest from the door, and Gerasimov and Jameson were seated together on one side of the table, a single chair opposite them and the other chairs against the walls.

'Where's Sherenko?' Gerasimov came straight to the point.

'No idea.'

'When did you last see him?' Jameson this time.

What is this, Kincaid wondered; what's going down. 'Yesterday morning at the range. He gave me a lift in after.'

'I didn't see him.' It was Riley.

'He didn't come in.'

He waited.

'What did he do after?' Gerasimov again.

Kincaid almost shrugged. 'No idea.'

Jameson stared across the table. 'You *are* working with Nik on the ConTex job.'

'Correct.'

'So why don't you know where he is and what he's doing?'

Good question, Kincaid felt like saying. 'Perhaps you should explain what this is about,' he suggested.

Jameson played with his pen. 'We have a problem on the ConTex case, Jack. Maddox phoned last night. He said he'd had a tip-off that Nik Sherenko was involved in the missing money.' He waited for Kincaid's response.

'That's illogical. Omega, you, me, Nik, only knew about the shipment after it disappeared.'

'The suggestion is that Sherenko became involved *after* the money went missing.'

'You mean after we began the investigation?'

'Yes.'

'If Nik's the centre of the allegation, why aren't you asking him?'

'We can't.'

'Why not?'

'We don't know where he is.'

Kincaid finished his coffee. So tell me, his silence said.

Tell him, Gerasimov's nod agreed.

Jameson spread his hands on the table. 'Arnie Maddox contacted us last night. He said he had been tipped off that Sherenko was involved with ConTex's missing money.'

'You've already said that. He give you any evidence?'

'No.'

'But you have to act on it, because Maddox represents the client, and because it's one more avenue to investigate.'

'Precisely.'

'You've tried to contact Nik?'

'At his apartment, plus the office last night in case he was working late. No go on either.'

'His cellphone?'

'He wasn't answering.'

'You don't have any evidence, though.'

Jameson suddenly looked weary or angry or both. 'The evidence is the problem. A team went into Sherenko's apartment early this morning. Sherenko wasn't there. They found a slip for two hundred and fifty thousand dollars cash paid into a bank in Vienna, plus air tickets in Sherenko's name. Moscow—Vienna return.'

Chert, Kincaid thought. 'When were they dated?'

'Everything was yesterday.'

Gerasimov stared across the table. 'Reactions?'

Kincaid thought it through. 'It sounds like a set-up. Just like the band we found in Maddox's secretary's apartment. Nik's smart, he wouldn't leave that sort of evidence hanging round.'

Jameson shook his head. 'It's not just the items we found in his apartment. 'Sherenko's on the airline computer as having used the tickets yesterday, and on the immigration computers at Sheremetyevo and Vienna as having made the trip.'

'Come on, Grere. That's the sort of scam we used to pull every day of the week.'

'In the old days, Jack. Setting up a background for someone, establishing a legend. But that was Big Boys' Games and this isn't. Okay, I might accept your point about the slip and airline ticket, but not the flight lists. Not the immigration records, Moscow and Vienna.'

'So what's happening at the moment?'

'We have a stake-out on his apartment in case he shows, we also have the airport and stations covered. Plus we have people looking for his car.' Jameson looked over the table at Kincaid. 'What are you thinking, Jack?'

'I'm thinking that two hundred and fifty thousand isn't a lot.'

Gerasimov grunted. 'He could have had more and split it. A quarter of a million in different banks.'

'Except why put small amounts in different banks when it's easier to put the lot into one, then transfer out of that bank to wherever you chose to hide it.'

'Perhaps he didn't have the time.'

'All the more reason to go to one bank.'

Fresh coffee, Gerasimov requested his secretary. Take us through any relevant parts of the investigation, he told Kincaid; take us through the last couple of days, since you last saw Sherenko.

'The only relevant thing which comes immediately to mind is the meeting with Alexei Kosygin. Except the meeting was inconsequential, nothing promised and nothing agreed, which was what one would expect with someone like Kosygin, especially at an early stage.'

'Sherenko offered Kosygin ten per cent?'

'Yes. Kosygin laughed at it.'

'Anything else?'

'Kosygin turned it round, as you know. Offered Nik ten per cent if Kosygin got the money.'

'We didn't know that, Jack.' It was Gerasimov. 'Sherenko didn't tell us that.'

'He must have done, otherwise how would I know?'

He didn't, Jack – it was in Jameson's stare. 'I assume it's in the case log.'

'Of course.'

'Mind getting it for us?'

Kincaid left the conference room and went to the main office. The case log was in the lower right drawer. He opened it and found the relevant date and entry. Oh shit – the blackness gathered. He closed the office door and returned to the boardroom. 'It's not entered.' He passed Jameson the log.

Gerasimov's face was bleak. 'Anything else?'

Time to tell it, Kincaid knew. 'You said you haven't been able to contact Nik.'

'Correct.'

'Neither have I.'

'Wondered when you'd get round to that, Jack.'

'Two evenings ago, he and I were supposed to meet the girl-friends of Whyte and the other courier. I was actually on my way when Nik phoned, said something had come up, and asked me to cover him unless there was a major development. There wasn't, so I didn't speak to him again that night. The following morning, yesterday morning, after I saw him at the range, he gave me a lift back, dropped me off and asked me to cover him again. I haven't seen him or spoken to him since.'

'You tried to speak to him?'

'Several times yesterday on his cellphone. There was no answer.'

'Going secure.' Malenkov was using a payphone in the Metropol Hotel.

'Secure.'

'The problem is now compounded. We already know that Sherenko and Kincaid are working together, though they don't know of their past relationship. We also already know that Sherenko had pulled Yuri Dushkin's file, and that was a way for Sherenko to go back to Moscow USA, though he wouldn't know it.'

'Yes . . .' There was trepidation in the voice.

'Sherenko now has another connection into Joshua.'

'What?'

'He's screwing Joshua's daughter.'

Oh Christ – it was in the silence. 'But the daughter has nothing which links her to Moscow USA?'

'Not as far as we know,' Malenkov said cautiously.

Sheremetyevo airport was busy. Sherenko parked as close as he could to the terminal and carried Anna's bag inside. She looked at him, ignored everyone and everything around them. 'You know where I'm staying.' She kissed him on the lips, eyes closed. As he left the airport road Malenkov's convoy pulled in. Target's car might just have left Sheremetyevo, Gerasimov and Jameson were informed thirty seconds later; not confirmed, and stake-out was too far away to follow.

So what the hell have you got running, Nik? Kincaid poured a fresh coffee, remembered he had a call to make, and phoned the morgue on C'urupy Ulica. 'Viktor, it's Jack. Sorry about earlier. You got something for me?'

'Your Mr Whyte. I might have him.'

Christ, Kincaid thought. Gerasimov and Jameson were in Gerasimov's office. Kincaid knocked on the door and went in.

'Might have a development. The morgue just phoned, they might have Whyte. I'm checking it out.'

'Tie in with Sherenko, you think?'

'No idea at this stage.'

'You want a driver?'

'Be better than waving down a Lada.'

He pulled the Whyte photograph and details from the file, even though the morgue attendant had a copy, and waited for one of the QRF drivers.

Eagle leaving offices, the tails informed Vorkov, Eagle and driver in green Saab 9000 travelling down Gertsena Ulica. Any sign of Bear, Vorkov asked the shadows outside Sherenko's apartment. No sign of Bear, they told him. Confirm the opposition stake-out is still in position, Vorkov requested them; confirm they are not aware of your presence. Confirmed, the *komandir* informed him.

The Omega driver drove down Profsojuznaja Ulica and turned left at the lights into Krasikova Ulica. What about the morgue – Kincaid was aware of the tremor in his mind. With any luck Viktor would have pulled the corpse out, so he wouldn't have to dig through a mound of dead flesh, but the morgue on C'urupy Ulica was still the morgue on C'urupy Ulica. Pull over, he told the driver. The man swerved right and stopped. Be right back, Kincaid told him. He left the car and walked to the kiosks.

Eagle out of car at Profsojuznaja metro, the tail informed Vorkov. Eagle buying something,

The cellphone rang.

'Jack, this is Nik. I'm back in business. What's running?'

Thank Christ you've phoned, my friend. You tell me what's running, though. Nik was okay, Nik had an explanation for everything. Therefore there was no harm in letting him know, but he would inform Jameson and Gerasimov anyway.

'The morgue rang. They might have Whyte. I'm on my way there now.'

'I'm stopping off to change clothes. Be with you in fifteen minutes. You got the Stolichnaya?'

'Just getting it.'

Sherenko turned into the street on which his apartment was situated.

We have target, the Omega stake-out informed Gerasimov. Target's car is stopping and target getting out.

Bear's car in sight, the tails outside Sherenko's flat informed Vorkov; Bear's car stopping.

'Confirm Bear,' Vorkov requested.

'Confirmed.'

'Confirm Eagle.'

'Confirmed.'

'Bear go, Eagle go,' Vorkov ordered.

Pick Sherenko up, Gerasimov told the stake-outs.

Sherenko locked the BMW and began to cross the pavement. Why hadn't Jack phoned to say the morgue might have Whyte's body – the wisp of a warning crossed his mind. He stopped at the front door and began to punch the number of the security combination. The Volvo stopped at the kerb behind him and someone walked along the pavement towards him from the right. He was aware of the noise and movement, then the men were suddenly around him.

He tensed, then recognized them. 'Hello, Ivan.' Said with a tone which meant: what are you and the boys doing here?

'Better have your gun, Nik.'

'What's up, Ivan?' What's this about; what the hell are you guys playing at? He held his left lapel with his left hand and opened it, his right hand clear, and revealed the Sig Sauer.

'You should know.' Dimitrov removed the Sig Sauer from the holster, stepped back, and allowed another man to frisk Sherenko.

'He's clean.'

'In the car, back seat.'

Christ – the fear twitched in Sherenko. You've changed sides; Alexei Kosygin got to you and set me up. One man was beside him, a Makharov in his hand, a second holding the rear door of the Volvo open, Makharov also in his hand, Dimitrov on the far side of the car, nearest the road, and getting in, and the driver running the engine and looking back at him. Only one reason why somebody from Kosygin should be picking him up, only one thing they were going to do with him.

Sherenko began to get in and felt the moment the man behind him relaxed and the Makharov went down slightly. Saw that Dimitrov was not only getting in the car, but calling someone on the cellphone. The man he had seen on the pavement was still walking toward them and a Mercedes was coming up the street – Sherenko saw it at the extreme point of his lateral vision. Something about the Merc – it was in his subconscious, something about the man on the pavement.

'Pick-up made,' Dimitrov told Gerasimov. 'Coming in.'

The man on pavement to his left was pulling something from his coat, Sherenko saw. Merc's windows open and men in the back, Merc almost level and sub-machine gun appearing from rear window closest to them. Christ, the man on the pavement had a mini Uzi.

'Down,' he shouted. 'Mafia.'

He dropped and heard the first rounds, felt instinctively for the Sig Sauer but the Sig Sauer wasn't there. The noise was sudden and all-consuming, the crash of sub-machines from the Mercedes and the chatter of the Uzi from the left. Dimitrov took the full force from the Mercedes in his back, his face jerked and his body slid down and into the car. The Omega driver was tilting forward, still half-turned, part of his head missing, and both the man behind him and the one holding the door were crumpling and twisting. Dimitrov was still falling into the car toward him. A set-up, part of Sherenko's mind was thinking; gunmen in car and on pavement still firing, but Dimitrov and the others inadvertently shielding him. Dimitrov has my Sig Sauer, he was also thinking; can't get to it, but man behind me had a Makharov. Prioritize, he told himself. Hit car will pull away soon, back-up in to make sure the job was done and whisk the gunman on the pavement away before anyone woke up to what had happened. The submachine fire was still spraying the car. Any moment now they'll see me, any moment now they'll know I'm not dead, therefore time to move. Get gun from minder behind and check position of gunman on pavement. Check whether hit car is staying or leaving, because that will determine what I do after I have a gun. Doorway to apartment block five metres away across pavement: door is normally locked, but is it now? No time to unlock door, therefore will my body weight carry me through?

The body was falling on him, blood on the shirt, coat and hands. The thunder from hit car continuing, but not from pavement, the gunman on pavement reloading.

Sherenko turned, around and up slightly, felt the slime of blood on the minder's hand, and pulled the gun from his fingers. Rolled back and right slightly, Makharov coming up, finger on trigger and thumb flicking off the safety. Christ the gunman on the pavement was no more than four metres from him. Double tap, cluster in centre of gunman's chest. Two rounds used therefore six left; hell, he could have done with the fifteen rounds of his P226. Double tap again. Would have preferred triple, but that might use too many rounds. The hit car was pulling away. Double tap again, two rounds left. Man on pavement stumbling and Uzi tumbling from his hands. *Chert* – hit car stopping and more rounds pouring in because they knew someone had survived, but the hit car was five metres further on, so the pick-up Volvo was between him and it. He slid across the pavement and snatched the Uzi, more rounds coming in from the Merc but the men in the Merc were firing too high. The new mag was in the Uzi; he pulled the gunman over, felt in his coat pockets, found another mag and slid back to the cover of the Volvo. Another Mercedes screamed up the road and the door to the apartment block opened. Christ, did they have a shooter in the block? The face which looked out at him from the door was old and grey beneath a shock of white hair. Must be deaf, because why the hell else would they open the door? Back-up Merc closer, so more problems soon. The door closed. That option ruled out, Sherenko thought. Time to do it, only one way to do it. The way they won't expect. He moved to the front wing of the car, the rounds still screaming into the main body. 25-round mag on the Uzi, pity the bastard hadn't been using a 32. He changed position slightly, tensed himself, slid from the protection of the wing and poured two streams across the Mercedes. The firing from the car stopped then started again. He poured two more bursts in, this time at the rear section of the Mercedes. Change mags and do it.

He was clear of the Volvo. Go, he shouted at himself, screamed at the Mercedes. Finger on trigger and taking them completely and utterly by surprise. Nobody in their right mind would run at a car pouring bullets at them. Go . . . he was still shouting. Go . . . he was screaming, the fire power from the Uzi smashing into where the opposition gunmen should be. The driver of the Mercedes slammed his foot on the accelerator and pulled away.

The back-up car was thirty metres away.

Sherenko cleared the street and disappeared into the dark of the alley between the anonymous grey of the apartment blocks on the other side. The second Mercedes accelerated past and the street was suddenly quiet. He ran back across the road to the BMW and pulled away.

ConTex money, set-up – his brain functioned automatically. Oh hell. Jack . . .

Kincaid crouched at the window of the kiosk, pointed to a small bottle of Stolichnaya, and pushed his money through. So what the hell *was* Nik playing at? The woman sniffed and slid him the bottle. He checked the seal and the label, checked the vortex of bubbles when he shook the bottle, and walked back across the pavement toward the Saab. The cellphone rang. He stuffed the Stolichnaya in his coat pocket and took out the phone. The Omega driver was still looking at him, there was a drunk on the corner, and a Mercedes was coming up behind the Saab. Rear window open – the image flickered across his subconscious but barely registered.

'Kincaid.'

'Jack, this is N . . .'

Kincaid saw the gun and heard the first rounds simultaneously. 'Mafia,' he screamed the warning to the driver.

He dropped, drew the Sig Sauer in one movement, and rolled to his left. The Mercedes stopped opposite and two metres from the Saab, the sub-machine fire pouring from the rear window. The Omega driver was caught in his seat, the rounds thudding into him. Kincaid rolled left again, round the rear of the Saab. They still think I'm where they first saw me – his mind was cold and clinical. They don't know I'm here. The gunman in the rear right of the Mercedes was still shooting, another sliding out the rear left door and coming round the back. Kincaid kept the boot of the Saab in front of him and dropped into position. Double tap on the gunman rounding the rear of the Merc, swing right, double tap on the gunman in the rear seat. Double tap on rear seat gunman again and swing back, double tap. His driver was screaming in agony but the fire from the Merc was suddenly stopping. Gunman behind Merc trying to raise the sub-machine gun but sliding down the boot, his hands and body leaving a trail of slime and blood. Double tap, double tap, double tap. Kincaid changed position slightly. Eject empty mag and spare in. Up again. Double tap on man hanging out rear window of the Merc. The Mercedes driver crashed the car into gear and slammed his foot on the accelerator, missed the gears and reversed over the body of the gunman behind him. Crashed into forward gear, bounced over the body again, and accelerated away. Kincaid remained crouched behind the Saab and checked the street. No one else coming at him. His driver was still screaming, fainter now though. Patch up the holes in the driver's chest – Kincaid's mind flicked through the options. Stop the bleeding or get the hell out of here. He opened the door, pulled the driver into the passenger seat, ran to the other side, took the driver's position, and screeched away. Which way do I get out of here, he thought; where the hell do I go? At least he was clear of the area, at least the opposition no longer knew where he was. He pulled into a side street, changed mags again so he had a full one in the Sig Sauer, and called Jameson.

'Grere, it's Jack.' He was calm, detached. 'We've been hit. Repeat, we've been hit. Probably mafia. The driver is badly wounded. I'm at ...' he looked up at the street name. 'I'm on Lomonosovskij Prospekt, junction with Leninskij Prospekt.'

'Stay there,' Jameson told him. 'Keep this line open.'

Kincaid's been hit, he shouted to Gerasimov above the office noise. Driver wounded. Lomonosovskij Prospekt, junction with Leninskij Prospekt. The men in the corner of the office were already running. What the hell's going on, Gerasimov wondered; why the hell weren't the team making the Sherenko pick-up answering their mobiles.

'QRF on way,' Jameson told Kincaid.

'What are they driving? Because somebody stops and I don't know them, and I'll blow them to hell.'

'What are the QRF boys driving?' Jameson asked Gerasimov.

'White Saab 9000 series. They'll make contact as they approach him. The team leader is Gregori.'

Jameson passed the details to Kincaid.

'Understood.' Kincaid pulled off his jacket and shirt, and used the shirt to staunch the flow of blood from the driver's chest and side.

One of Gerasimov's cellphones rang.

'Mikhail, this is Nik. I don't know what's running, but I've just been hit. A team from the office tried to lift me, then another team hit us. Get Kincaid off the streets in case it's connected with ConTex and they go for him as well.'

'Where are you, Nik?' Gerasimov asked.

Wrong reaction, Sherenko thought, wrong tone of voice. Gerasimov should have asked what he meant and what had happened.

'Listen, Mikhail. Something's wrong. Get a team to my apartment, there are bodies all over the street. Our people as well as theirs. Kincaid's on his way to the morgue on C'urupy Ulica. If they came for me, they might be going for him as well. I tried to warn him but was cut off. It could be that someone in the office is involved.'

'Where the fuck are you, Nik? Get into the office fast.'

'Pull Kincaid out. I'll phone you back.'

Thanks for the warning, Gerasimov thought; pity it was too late, pity it was after Kincaid himself had already told us he'd been hit. The line went dead and he turned to Jameson. 'Anything from the team picking up Sherenko?'

'None. Who was that?'

'Sherenko saying he'd been hit.'

QRF to the Sherenko location, they agreed. Except they should keep a minimum reserve in case something else went down. Gerasimov to remain in charge and Jameson and a driver would check out the Sherenko pick-up location, they decided.

Kincaid felt the driver's pulse, tightened the shirt round the bleeding, and laid the Sig Sauer on the seat. There was one spare magazine in his coat pocket. He took it out, unloaded the rounds from it and reloaded them, snapping them in with his fingers. Then he checked the street, took the mag out of the Sig Sauer, loaded the full one, and confirmed the number of rounds he had left in the one he had just removed. The driver was coughing blood, the pink frothing lightly at his mouth. Make it fast, he told Jameson on the cellphone. With you in sixty seconds he was informed. Terminate this call. Gregori will identify himself and speak to you as they come in.

Kincaid pulled his coat on and checked the driver again. The cellphone rang.

'Jack, this is Gregori.'

'Good to hear you, Gregori.'

172

'We're coming down Leninskij Prospekt now. One block from you. We can see you.'

Kincaid saw the Saab in the rearview mirror; the headlights flashed once and he stabbed the brake lights in acknowledgement. The Saab pulled in behind him and the men streamed out, two covering them, looking outwards and scanning the street, and two going to the injured man, their own driver staying in the car.

'You okay?' the team leader asked Kincaid.

'Fine.'

'Get in the other car.'

The team leader slipped into the driving seat of the first Saab, someone else moving the injured driver into the rear seat, sitting with him and applying dressings to the wounds, and the car screamed away. Kincaid sat in the rear seat of the second, the rest of the team in front and beside him, and the car pulled away.

'What happened?' the man to his right asked.

'Christ knows. We stopped at Profsojuznaja metro, I went to the kiosks, then a Merc turned up and the turkey shoot began.'

The bottle in his coat pocket was unbroken. What about Whyte, he thought. Whyte was the last of his worries, he decided.

They were at the river.

'Pull in here,' he told the driver.

'The boss said to take you straight back.'

'Fuck the boss.'

He got out, walked across the pavement, leaned against the balustrade, and looked down at the water. The river was grey and running fast, a barge butting its way against the flow. He looked at it and pulled out the bottle.

Jameson's driver jumped the lights and approached the street on which Sherenko's apartment was situated. 'Any news from Jack?' Jameson asked Gerasimov.

'The boys just picked him up.'

'What about the team at Sherenko's?'

'Still no response.'

They turned into the street.

The Omega Volvo was parked on the right side of the road,

against the kerb and facing away from them. Militia cars were slewed round it, lights flashing, an ambulance was parked beyond it, its doors open and its lights also flashing, and a TV crew van was parked on the opposite side of the road, the cameraman and reporter shooting the Volvo, clusters of spectators looking on, and uniformed police and plain clothes detectives swarming the area.

No sign of Sherenko's BMW, Jameson noted. They left the car, locked the doors, and walked up the street. A militiaman tried to stop them; the Omega driver flashed his ID and they walked past. Oh Christ, Jameson thought.

The bodywork of the Volvo was riddled with bullet holes, the windows and windscreen were smashed, and glass was sheeted across the ground. The driver was slumped over the wheel, blood pouring from his face and upper body. The two rear doors were open, Dimitrov's shattered body was half-in the left door, his coat and shirt torn away by bullets and half his back missing. In the centre of the road was a carpet of glass which appeared to have come from another car.

They crossed behind the Volvo, nodded at the plain clothes man who appeared to be in charge, and looked at the bodies on the pavement. Interesting, Jameson thought: the first body four metres behind the car, no weapon but chest shot away as if by a pro. Not one of ours – he picked up the shake of the driver's head. Two more bodies close to the car, one by the rear door – again no gun; one the front side of the door as if the man had been holding it open, a Makharov on the ground by his hand. Ours, the Omega driver nodded to him.

The cameraman turned toward them. 'Not us,' the Omega driver told him. Screw you – the cameraman swung the lens toward Jameson. The driver dropped his shoulder slightly, brought his hand up, gripped the cameraman's testicles and squeezed like iron, the smile still on his face. 'Anybody else, but not me or the guy I'm with. Understand?'

The cameraman nodded through the tears.

The driver squeezed one last time. 'Fuck with me and next time you won't have any left.' He let go and the cameraman turned away.

The militia began to seal off the area. Jameson and the driver left the scene and returned to the QRF car, the militia barely glancing at them as they walked past. The driver pulled out a packet of cigarettes, lit one for himself, and offered the packet. Jameson shook his head, sat in the passenger's seat and phoned Gerasimov.

'All our people are dead, plus one other.' He was careful not to identify anything or anybody. 'There are indications that another vehicle was involved. There is no sign of our man.'

'*Chert*,' Gerasimov swore to himself.

'How's Jack?'

'He's fine, his driver didn't make it.'

The battery of the cellphone was dead. Sherenko pulled the BMW on to the area of rough ground, concealed the Uzi, and slid the Makharov into the shoulder holster. The metro station was to his left, a crowded market – vendors selling from old railroad cars – to his right. He stepped round a pool of dank water, a film of oil glimmering on it, and went to the phones in the hallway of the metro station. People pushed by him, nobody noticing him. So why hadn't he gone straight back to the Omega office, what the hell was running if an Omega team had tried to pick him up? Gerasimov's line was engaged. He tried another and heard Gerasimov's voice.

'Mikhail, this is Nik again.'

'Where are you, Nik? Get into the office fast.'

Gerasimov had cupped his hand over the mouthpiece – Sherenko picked up the change in background noise. Gerasimov was telling someone that he, Sherenko, was on the line, and was issuing orders about it.

'What's happening, Mikhail?'

Gerasimov's control broke. Wrong move, wrong time to lose it, but they were *his* people lying in shreds, *his* boys the militia were laying sheets over. 'What's happening, you bastard? What about the ConTex money, what about the account in Vienna? What about the air trip and the immigration records? What about the attack on Jack?' He fought against the rage. 'Thanks for the warning about Jack, Nik. Pity it came too late. So why not just

175

come in. Nice and quietly. No fuss, no problems. Either that or I'll meet you somewhere, talk it through.'

'What the hell are you talking about, Mikhail?'

'You don't know about the money in Vienna? You don't know about Dimitrov and the boys?'

'Of course I know about Dimitrov and the boys.'

'So you do know what I'm talking about.'

Time to close it – Sherenko checked round him. Time to change location, in case Gerasimov was trying to trace the call.

'Dimitrov and the boys picked me up as I was going into my apartment. As we were getting in their car a second car hit us.' Time to go – the alarm bells were ringing; time to bug out. 'Look, Mikhail; I don't know what's happening but I'll speak to you later.'

He left the metro station, collected the BMW, and cleared the area.

Kincaid's debriefing with Gerasimov, Jameson and Riley began at eleven, starting with the shooting of the team staking out Sherenko's apartment, the involvement of a second car, and Sherenko's escape, plus hypotheses about who the second car contained and whether Sherenko had used them as back-up.

Something was wrong, something wasn't adding up. Kincaid's mind still spun from the events at Profsojuznaja metro. 'You say that none of our people got off any rounds,' he asked.

'Not according to the first police reports,' Jameson told him.

'So who shot the man on the pavement?'

'Try this.' Gerasimov's face was like winter. 'Sherenko turns up and our people move in, but Sherenko's back-up pulls him out. They get away, Sherenko gets away in his own car.'

'Which still doesn't answer the question of who shot the man on the pavement.'

'Perhaps he was there by accident, wrong time wrong place. It happens.'

Kincaid turned to Jameson. 'How was he shot?'

'Tight cluster in the centre of the chest.'

No accident – Kincaid's look said, no wrong time wrong place. 'Who shot at the hit car?'

'How do we know someone shot at the hit car?' Gerasimov came back at him.

'Grere said there was glass on the road.'

They moved to the attack on Kincaid himself.

'Sherenko knew where you were going?' Gerasimov asked.

'Yes.'

'How?'

'I told him.'

'Why do you think he phoned?'

'He said he was back in business, asked what I was doing, and said he'd meet me at the morgue.'

'Why did you stop at that particular place?'

'Because that's where Sherenko and I stopped before.'

'To buy some vodka?'

Kincaid understood where Gerasimov was leading him. 'Yes.'

'Was anything said in the conversation that might relate to that?'

'Yes. When I said I was on the way to the morgue Sherenko asked about the vodka and I said I was just getting it.'

'So Sherenko knew where you were.'

'Yes.'

7

Flight SU241 touched down at Heathrow one minute early. Anna was the fifth passenger off. She passed through immigration, waited at the baggage carousel, then took a cab to Brown's Hotel in central London. The cellphone she had requested was at the concierge's desk and the salesman who was her first appointment was already waiting.

Sergei Malenkov waited till she left the plane, collected his briefcase from the overhead locker and his travel bag from the hanging area next to the galley, thanked the purser and followed her into the air bridge. The First Secretary stepped forward and shook his hand. Twelve minutes after he left the aircraft Malenkov slid into the rear seat of the 7-series BMW, and the car left Heathrow and turned east along the M4 motorway. Thirty minutes later he arrived at the Russian embassy. He took a coffee with the *rezident* and began his first briefings of the day.

When Kincaid arrived at the morgue on C'urupy Ulica, Viktor was taking the sun outside the entrance of the grey brick building, eating a *pirozhki* and drinking a Coke.

'You want to finish?' Kincaid asked.

'No.' Viktor wrapped the pastry in paper, placed it in a tin, put the lid on tight, and disappeared into the brick building. Kincaid walked past it, the driver remaining with the car but the minder Gerasimov had insisted upon accompanying him, turned left, and descended the ramp. Halfway down the cold set in and he could no longer hear the birds. The rusted door ground open and he stepped inside, the minder immediately behind him. The tiles of the corridor seemed dirtier than before. He waited while Viktor pulled the lever on the second door, then the mouths gaped at him and the eyes stared at him, the smell rose up and diffused into every pore of his body and every cell of his soul, and the oranges and the whites and the blues of the cadavers riveted themselves to his memory.

Chert, the minder swore and stepped back into the corridor.

Viktor gave Kincaid the surgical gloves. 'This one,' he said.

At least Viktor had laid it on a trolley and covered it with a sheet, Kincaid thought. He hadn't stopped for the Stolichnaya, he remembered.

Viktor pulled back the sheet.

The body was well-built. The hair was matted with blood, the flesh of the body was an unreal white, and the entry point of the bullet wound to the head was at the rear, the round exiting at the front just above the bridge of the nose and tearing away part of the face as it did so, so that the features were not identifiable.

Could be Whyte – Kincaid clenched his teeth. 'You have a tape measure?'

'I'll get one.'

Viktor left him and Kincaid stood by the body.

So today the bastards came for me like they came for you five years ago – it was as if he was standing in the morgue at Belle Vue, as if he was standing by the body of Joshua. Only difference, old friend, is that the bastards got you but missed me. Everything personal now, though, just as it was personal five years ago, even though Bram kept telling me it was business. So screw Omega and the FSB and whoever else is chasing you, Sherenko, because now it's between you and me. Because I couldn't do anything about whoever took out Joshua five years ago, but I can do something about you.

The footsteps echoed down the corridor. Time to be out of here, his subconscious told him: the hoods coming to take Joshua home. Viktor came back, gave him one end of the tape and held the other at the top of the head. Kincaid moved to the feet and ran the measure down the body.

'Not Whyte. Might have been, though.' He wound in the tape and slipped the attendant a hundred-dollar bill. 'Thanks anyway.'

The debrief with Gerasimov, Jameson and Riley began thirty

minutes later. 'The body at the morgue wasn't Whyte,' Kincaid told them. The atmosphere in the conference room was grim, and the odour and images of the morgue on C'urupy Ulica still clung to him. 'There was a resemblance, but it wasn't tall enough. I suggest fingerprint tests as confirmation.'

They moved to the next item.

'The police covering the shooting this morning have played ball, due to pressure from on high.' Gerasimov was in his usual place at the head of the table. 'Even though Omega is bound to be named Sherenko won't be, and the reason for Omega's presence will be covered. Omega is co-operating with the police, and contacts in the FSB are looking for Sherenko.'

He moved on.

'The police unit dealing with organized crime picked up two bodies this afternoon. Mafia types. They'd been shot. Apparently it was more like an execution.'

'How does that tie in with us?' Kincaid asked.

'The rounds found in the bodies match those in a Sig Sauer found on Dimitrov's body. The Sig Sauer wasn't Dimitrov's, he was carrying his own Makharov. The Sig Sauer was stuck in his belt as if he'd just removed it from someone.'

'And Sherenko uses a Sig Sauer.' It was Kincaid.

'Yes.'

'So the assumption is that the Sig Sauer Dimitrov was carrying was Sherenko's, and that they'd taken it from him when they picked him up.'

'Yes.'

'But we can't tie what we assume is Sherenko's Sig Sauer to the mafia execution until the police have done some forensics and seen whether bullets fired from the Sig Sauer match those found in the bodies.'

Gerasimov's face was frozen. 'They already have. They match. The bullets found in the bodies were fired from Sherenko's gun.'

Kincaid's mind was as bleak as Gerasimov's face. 'What are you saying?' he asked.

Gerasimov looked at him. 'That Sherenko found who was responsible for the ConTex heist, dealt with them, and took the ConTex money, or that part of the money he could access.'

'So where do we go from here?'

'We wait. Sherenko has to show some time. Everybody's looking for him.'

They left the conference room.

'Thought you were supposed to be in London this afternoon,' Kincaid asked Jameson.

With this running . . . Jameson almost laughed. 'Shit . . .' He went to one of the desks in the main office, called the number in London, identified himself and asked for Ed Miller.

'Ed, it's Grere, how you doing . . .' He covered the blackness in his mind. 'Few problems at this end, Ed. I have to stay in Moscow. Actually, Ed, somebody tried to take out Jack Kincaid this morning . . .'

'Oh Christ . . .'

'He's okay.'

'What happened?'

'He was on his way to ID a body. Stopped en route and a hit team tried to take him out. He made it, his driver didn't.'

'But he's okay?'

'Yeah, he got lucky. Not even a flesh wound.'

'Thank Christ for that.'

There was a silence. 'Any idea why?' Miller asked.

'Probably the investigation he was working on.'

'Anything I can do? Any strings I can pull with our people in Moscow?'

'Not at the moment, but it's appreciated.'

The street had appeared empty, but someone was probably watching. Sherenko pulled off the street, through the gates and into the courtyard. The factory was in the outer ring of the city. Once it had made machine parts, now its iron gate swung open on broken hinges, the roof had begun to split open, and grass sprouted between the cobbles. A dog limped across the yard to his left; somewhere Sherenko heard a child crying. He prised open the wooden doors in the building to the right, drove the BMW inside and closed them again. The bricks of the walls were discoloured, remnants of machines were strewn across the floor, sheets of metal rusted in stacks, and dust glinted in shafts of light from broken windows set high in the outer walls. He manoeuvred the BMW into the furthest corner, removed the number plates, checked he had left nothing in the car, and covered it with a tarpaulin. Then he rolled some empty oil barrels against the car and stacked some of the metal sheets around and over it, placed some of the broken plant on top, as if the pile was no more than a dump, brushed dust over the foot and tyre marks, and left. The yard was still silent. He locked the doors as best as he could, turned away from the main gates, exited the factory through a small door on the other side, cleared the area, concealed the number plates and made his way to the nearest metro station.

The station was in the centre of a small park: it was round, steps up to it, and its glass swing doors were slightly dirty. The kiosks were clustered around it, most selling alcohol, food and some clothes, but mainly alcohol, more kiosks along either side of the path leading through the park. Two drunks were arguing near one of the kiosks, people skirting round them, and a line of men sat on the lower of two rails fencing off some shrubs, bottles in their hands or on the ground in front of them. A boy – six, seven years old, with a torn shirt and ripped shoes – collected the bottles the men left or gave to him, and checked whether he could get any deposit money on them. The smell of food hung in the air, kebabs and burgers, fresh bread from one of the kiosks along the path to the park, and the sound of pop music echoed tinnily from a kiosk selling cassettes.

Sherenko bought a beer and a kebab and sat with the men on the lower rail.

So why are you here, Nik old friend. You're from Moscow, therefore you have contacts; friends from the old days, school-friends before that; therefore places to seek help and places to hide. Except the first place Gerasimov and whoever Gerasimov has enlisted will look for you is where your past suggested you'll run to.

A young woman with a red headscarf pushed a pram through the crowd of people around the kiosks. One of the wheels was buckled, but the woman didn't seem to notice. So he had been set up for the ConTex job. So who had set him up, how and why? Forget Gerasimov, Gerasimov was straight. And forget the

Omega team Gerasimov had sent to pick him up that morning. If they had been involved they would have taken him as he crossed the pavement, just as the hit team had taken them. Con-Tex? Maddox and Dwyer? Possible, but neither of them had the contacts to set up the hit in the way the job had been carried out that morning. So Alexei Kosygin. Does spring follow winter? So he should get to Kosygin. Except Kosygin wasn't in Moscow, Kosygin was in London, because Anna was meeting him there.

Malenkov took Vorkov's call shortly before three in the after-noon, London time. Even though he was alone and in the apparent security of the embassy, the conversation was veiled. Both men had listened in to so many other conversations, including the conversations of those whom they called their friends, that there was an inbuilt assumption that others, including their friends, would eavesdrop on theirs.

'The report you were expecting this morning,' Vorkov told him. . . . Sherenko. 'I've afraid it hasn't arrived.' . . . Sherenko not dealt with.

'And the second report?'

'It's also still outstanding.'

Malenkov was surprisingly calm, Vorkov thought.

'Anything else?' Malenkov asked.

'Some bad news about Mikhail Gerasimov.' Vorkov spoke openly now, because it would be in the overnights, and everybody who was anybody in the old KGB knew Gerasimov anyway. 'Some of his Omega people were blown away this morning. One team were hit in a residential area of the city, there were signs of a major gun battle there. One other Omega man was shot dead near the Profsojuznaja metro almost at the same time.'

'Any indication who was responsible?'

'No, but apparently Gerasimov's looking for one of his own people. Ex-Alpha, Nikolai Sherenko.'

Sherenko bought himself another beer and settled back on the rail. Kosygin was his only way out. Kosygin was in London, so how to get to London? The first stage of which was how to exit Russia.

He could get a false ID and try to leave through a place like Sheremetyevo, but Gerasimov and whoever else was looking for him would have exit points like the airport covered. He could go north, get out via the dealers running guns and everything else through the Baltic states, and into Finland, which was his preferred option. He could head south, get a car and pay the usual couple of bottles of vodka to a border guard, except to get that far south he would have to fly, and the airports would be covered. Or he could simply head west, bluff or bribe his way through the border to Belarus and head for Poland. And once he was at the border with Poland getting west was no problem.

Except how far had Gerasimov extended the search for him?

He gave the empty bottle to the boy with ripped shoes, and went to the phones in the metro entrance hall. 'Is Gino there? Hi, Gino. It's Nik Sherenko. I need a BM or Merc. Good motor, no crap. Clean plates.' Gino dealt with cars stolen from Western Europe. Gino could also acquire a set of wheels in Moscow. 'How much? Christ, Gino, go fuck your mother, my friend. Yeah, tomorrow morning.' And payment in dollars. Which we don't even need to ask. Crisp and clean, and which I still have to get.

Malenkov's last meeting of the day was with the team who would attend the security conference the following morning. He sat patiently while an aide to the London *rezident* detailed the agenda, and listed the other nationalities who would be present: senior civil servants, high-ranking police and law enforcement officers from participating countries, and representatives of the relevant intelligence and security services.

It wasn't the normal way of doing things. There *was* liaison, but one-to-one, agency to agency and on something specific. Not committee meetings, not champagne and canapés. But perhaps that was the way things were going. Or, more correctly, the way some people thought things were going.

The meeting broke shortly after six. Malenkov left fifteen minutes later. Officially he was staying at an embassy residence; unofficially he would spend his free hours in an apartment overlooking the canal off Regent's Park in north London, which some might term a private safe house, but which Nikolai Sherenko would refer to as a *lyubovnoye gnezdo* and Jack Kincaid would call a honey pad.

Vorkov phoned at seven, both men using clip-on encryptors therefore the conversation secure.

'What happened this morning?' Malenkov came straight to the point.

Vorkov went into details.

'Where's Sherenko now?'

'Nobody knows but everybody's looking for him.'

Malenkov poured himself a malt. 'What about the shipment?'

'On schedule.'

'And Yuri Dushkin?'

'He left Berlin this morning and is due back from Zurich tonight. He flies into London tomorrow.'

Malenko returned to the original subject. 'What about Sherenko?'

'As I said, everyone's looking for him.'

Early evening in Moscow was warm and the Old Arbat was crowded with locals and tourists. The area was cobbled, cafés and shops along either side and in the side streets off it; McDonald's, clubs and a theatre, photographers offering Polaroid shots and a band playing somewhere. The currency exchange offices, tucked into buildings or offices every hundred metres or so, were busy, people queuing to change dollars.

Sherenko drifted near the exchange he had selected and waited.

It was the wrong way to do it. For this sort of job you needed days of observation and preparation. Identify the routine of the armed guards delivering and collecting the money then analyse it for weaknesses. Confirm how many of them there were and what each did; the weapons they carried and whether they appeared prepared to use them. Where and how the bagman went: behind or in front of his escorts.

No option, though.

Inside would be no good. Inside each booth there were two armed guards, either private or militia, and the cashiers were locked behind secure walls with bullet-proof glass and panic buttons, so there was no way you could get to the money. Therefore outside, as the guard or guards and the bagman moved from the money exchange to the security van. Okay, guards still inside the exchange and driver still sitting in the vehicle, and all of them only metres away, but if he got it right it would be over before they realized. As long as the guard or guards did nothing unusual; as long as there was no police car too close and no one did something and got in the way; as long as the mafia weren't looking after their own tonight, because the mafia had a stake in the currency exchanges just as they had a stake in everything.

So how had Kosygin set him up so effectively? The question thumped in his head like a hammer.

Forty metres away the security van turned into the street and began to reverse up, dark green bodywork, thick plate glass windows and lights blinking. Men stepping out of its way and women pulling their children back. The van stopped and the two men got out the side door: the guard was young but big build, blue uniform, helmet and bulletproof vest, Uzi in his hands; the bagman was slightly older, also big build, uniform, helmet and bulletproof vest, and carrying a leather satchel-style bag, no security chain round his wrist. The door of the van was already shut, and the two men were moving quickly, the guard in front to make sure no one got in their way. A mistake, Sherenko knew, because in front of the man you were supposed to be protecting you couldn't see what was happening to him. So if they left the exchange in the same way . . .

The street settled again. Sherenko eased forward and glanced at the van driver, swept the street again, made sure that his way in wasn't obstructed and that his way out was clear. The door of the currency exchange opened and the guard came out, checked the street, turned back, nodded to the bagman, and ran for the van. Different movement this time, different tension. Uzi held high and eyes on the door of the van. The man with the money satchel three paces behind him and running as fast as he could. The bagman glanced round: no gunmen, no mafia, thank God. Woman with pram – the guard half-noticed: woman pulling child away to her and man near her, but no gun, so no problem.

Sherenko exploded. Three paces and right fist clenched tight. The fist smashed into the guard's face, broke his nose and cheekbone, and knocked him out. The bagman was too close behind to stop. Sherenko's strength and power took him on as if the guard had not existed, fist driving into the bagman's face, the bagman's hands coming up and his fingers slipping from the handle of the bag. Sherenko slowed marginally, seized the bag and disappeared into the maze of side streets.

Red Square was almost empty, the moon above St Basil's and the Kremlin walls eerie in its light. Kincaid sat on the edge of the pavement outside the GUM department store and stared across toward the Lenin mausoleum.

The cellphone rang. 'You'd better come back,' Riley told him. Fifteen minutes later Kincaid joined the others in the conference room. In the main office outside the teams were already assembling.

'Sherenko's made contact with a car dealer.' Gerasimov showed no emotion. 'He's turning up tomorrow morning. The boys will be waiting for him.'

'How do we know this?'

'How do you think we know?'

'You want me to be there?'

Jameson looked at him. 'I don't think that would be a good idea, Jack.'

The night was warm around him, rats nibbled somewhere in the wall against which he now rested, and the light of the moon glinted through the dust and grime of the window. Sherenko lay on the makeshift bed and catnapped. In the last half-hour the calm had ebbed slightly and allowed the anger and the emptiness in. For one moment he was back in Boston five years ago, Hurricane Bob sweeping through the city centre. For one moment he was opening the door of the safe house, stepping outside, the wind and the rain like nothing he had ever experienced, and running in anger in the eye of the storm. Alexei Kosygin had set him up, so why wasn't he trying to analyse how Kosygin had done it? It was three in the morning. He rolled out of the half-sleep and shut out the question.

* * *

Gerasimov began the penultimate briefing at three-thirty, the room filled with cigarette smoke, and the teams which would lead the operation concentrating on the wipe-board on which Gerasimov had drawn the street on which the car dealer who called himself Gino had a garage, plus interior details of the premises themselves. Omega men to be inside the garage, eyes and back-up on the ground floor of the premises opposite, and additional back-up in cars three blocks away. No one to take any chances this time.

When he finished the teams brewed coffee, thick and sweet. Gerasimov and Jameson went to Gerasimov's office, and Kincaid and Riley took their mugs to the conference room and slumped in the chairs. The light was beginning to filter into the room. They lapsed into silence, occasionally into a fitful sleep; jerked awake, checked the time, then tried to make themselves comfortable again. The final briefing was at six, the tiredness suddenly gone and the nerves pumping. At six-fifteen, two and a quarter hours before Sherenko was due at the dealer's, the teams left. Kincaid went to the kitchen, washed some mugs and made fresh coffee. Outside the sky streaked pink. Gerasimov and Jameson were locked in conference, Riley at his desk.

Kincaid rose and went to the door. 'Going to the kitchen,' he told Riley.

'You've just been.'

'I know.'

Riley stared at him. 'Don't go in till it's over, Jack.'

Kincaid nodded and left the building. The Sig Sauer hung in the shoulder holster, the spare magazines were in his left coat pocket and the cellphone was in the right. Two blocks away he waved down a Lada and negotiated a price to a street three from the car dealer's.

Gino's garage was on the left, the street sloping slightly; industrial buildings on either side, and the pavement and road were pock-marked with holes. The door to the premises on the right, and forty metres from the garage, was padlocked. Kincaid forced the lock and slipped inside. Thirty minutes later the sun rose over the tops of the buildings, the street began to warm, and the first people and the first cars began to appear.

It was seven-thirty. Kincaid felt the weight of the Sig Sauer and waited.

It was eight o'clock. A 500-series BMW stopped at the garage and a man – Kincaid assumed the car dealer called Gino – stepped out, unlocked the door, rolled it open, and went inside. No minders or workmen, Kincaid noted. Omega clearing the area, the Omega men inside already dressed as mechanics.

It was eight-thirty, time for Sherenko. Kincaid checked the Sig Sauer and waited.

It was eight forty-five, going on nine. You're late, Nik, and you're never late.

He heard the Lada before he saw it, the engine spluttering slightly and the car approaching from outside his vision, to his left. He eased the door open. Personal, Sherenko. Between you and me. The guys waiting for you are waiting because it was their friends who died yesterday, but I'm waiting because it was me who was supposed to die as well. The Lada slowed and stopped, the woman got out and the car pulled away. Kincaid eased the door shut again and waited.

It was nine going on ten. Nikolai Sherenko slid the metal strip between the window and the rubber mounting on the driver's door of the Mercedes, clicked open the lock and withdrew the metal. Then he slipped into the driver's seat, jammed the slide hammer into the ignition, tapped it sharply, pulled it out, extracting the ignition barrel, pushed a screwdriver in its place, heard the engine roar into life, and eased away.

The car dealer Gino had always been good, best cars at the best prices, but he had also been known to the FSB. So when the word had gone out, Gino would have done a simple calculation: ten grand from Sherenko, or immunity from the security services. The night before, therefore, Sherenko had taken his place on the top floor of the building opposite the garage. Had watched the Omega boys arrive six hours later, then vanished by a rear door.

And if the word had gone out so quickly and effectively that it had filtered down to someone of Gino's level in Moscow, then it would have already gone to the faceless men running the smuggling rackets through the Baltic. Thus the Baltic route out of Russia was off, even though it was his preferred option.

Ten minutes later he stopped, removed the registration plates, and screwed another set in their place. Fifteen minutes after that he cleared Moscow and turned west toward Brest and the border of the former Soviet Union with Poland.

It was eleven o'clock. The street on which the garage was situated was busier – more cars, more people. Kincaid stretched the stiffness from his back and peered through the grime of the window. The Omega teams were still in position, but Sherenko wasn't going to show. Sherenko was no longer in Moscow, because Sherenko would know that, quietly but efficiently, Moscow was being torn apart in the search for him. Sherenko's call to the car dealer was just a test, to see how far down the word had spread. So where the hell was he?

Kincaid checked the street through the dust on the window, opened the door, and slipped away. Twenty minutes later he was back at the Omega offices. Gerasimov was at the Kremlin and Jameson was at the embassy, both carrying cellphones, Riley and Igor Lukyanov were in the main office, and the office manager and a couple of Omega boys lounged in the outer area.

'Long time in the kitchen,' Riley suggested.

'What happened?' Kincaid asked in reply.

'You tell me.'

'Nothing. When I got there the street was quiet, I assume the boys were in position. I wasn't in communication with them, remember. I find myself a place and wait, but no Sherenko.' The percolator was empty. Kincaid filled it and switched it back on. 'What are the boys reporting back?'

'Same as you.' Riley opened the desk drawer and threw Kincaid an electric razor.

The percolator began bubbling. Kincaid poured three mugs, settled at the desk, and began to shave.

'You hear about the robbery on the Arbat last night?' Lukyanov asked him. Lukyanov was busy on his computer. Lukyanov lived for his computer.

'What robbery?'

'Somebody took out a guard and bagman collecting from a money exchange. Interesting job, one guy apparently, no guns even though the guard was carrying. Description sort of matched Nik.'

'How much did they get?' The tiredness began to come over Kincaid.

'Twenty grand in US dollars.'

'So it wasn't Nik, because why should he risk so much for so little if he has a quarter of a million stashed in Vienna?'

'Precisely.'

Kincaid finished shaving, gave Riley back the razor, and poured himself another coffee. The tiredness was overwhelming him now; or perhaps the anticlimax after the wait at the garage.

Lukyanov leaned over and tossed a file on to his desk. 'Nik asked for this couple of days back.'

Kincaid yawned and looked at it. The file was for a Yuri Dushkin. Pinned to the top right corner was a business card. He read the details on it, saw Dushkin's name hand-written on it, then read the details on the file. It seemed thin, like Kosygin's. So where are you, Sherenko; what game are you playing, you bastard? Where the hell to start looking for you?

Ed Miller rose at five, London time. At six he spoke with the chief of station in Moscow, at seven he attended a briefing at the American embassy in Grosvenor Square. At seven forty-five, together with the London CoS and the team who would accompany them, he was driven up the M40 to the manor house, tucked discreetly in the folds of the Oxfordshire countryside, where the security conference was to be held. By ten he was taking coffee in the book-lined music room and shaking hands with those who were not simply his country's traditional friends, but also those who were its former enemies.

The majority of those in the room were male. Even though all were dressed in suits the politicians stood out from the diplomats and civil servants, who in turn stood out from the policemen and the spooks. Miller spent two minutes with the American ambassador, shaking hands with those to whom the ambassador introduced him. The London chief of station was in a corner by the windows, talking to three men. Miller excused himself and joined them.

'Ed Miller, Vitali Bukovski, London *rezident*.'

Miller and Bukovski shook hands.

'Strange meeting.' Miller glanced round the room.

'Probably looked good when some politician suggested it.' The *rezident*'s English was flawless. 'Someone I'd like you to meet,' he suggested. They crossed the room. 'Ed Miller, Soviet Division,' the *rezident* did the introductions. 'General Malenkov, from the Foreign Intelligence Service.'

The two men shook hands.

'You know Miles Wightman, Assistant Secretary of State from DC.'

The handshakes continued, some smiles diplomatic, others not.

'General Malenkov, do you know Sheila Harrington?' It was the British ambassador to Moscow. He was tall, slightly stooped shoulders, with white hair swept apparently carelessly back.

'Good to meet you again, Mrs Harrington.'

Sheila Harrington wore a dark pinstripe jacket and matching skirt. Her hair was ash blonde and her eyes were a penetrating blue.

'You too, General Malenkov.'

'We met at the United Nations last October,' Malenkov explained to the ambassador.

'Of course.'

Miller looked at the group from across the room. Sheila Harrington from Riverside, the London chief of station informed him. Perhaps because he thought Miller might not know, perhaps to show that he himself knew.

Jameson returned to the Omega offices shortly before twelve, Gerasimov fifteen minutes later. They would keep the teams at the car dealer's, they decided: perhaps there was a reason Sherenko had not yet shown. Kincaid fought against the circles of sleep swimming in his head and tried to concentrate on the case log.

'Any chance of Sherenko's phone records over the past week?' he asked Lukyanov.

'Home or cellphone?'

'Both.'

Sherenko had asked Igor Lukyanov to pull the file on Yuri Dushkin the morning after the meeting with Kosygin. The request was entered in the log in Sherenko's handwriting. Kincaid flicked back a page and checked Sherenko's account of the dinner meeting at the Tokyo restaurant. The entry detailed the time and place of the meeting, plus those present: Alexei Kosygin, some women (unnamed, Kincaid supposed, because Sherenko had considered them irrelevant to the enquiry), and Yuri Dushkin.

'Nik's phone records.' Lukyanov dropped the computerized sheets on Kincaid's desk.

'Thanks.'

'You eating?'

'In a minute.'

The records weren't going to reveal anything, Kincaid was aware; Sherenko was too good, too careful. But perhaps before he had changed sides he had done something, contacted someone, which might give a lead. Perhaps . . . Kincaid almost laughed at himself, then placed the phone records on the desk, one pile for Sherenko's home number and one for his cellphone, examined each in turn, and eliminated those numbers he could identify: his own, the Alpha office, Gerasimov's and Jameson's mobiles, and the ConTex office. There was no record of calls to Vienna, but Sherenko wouldn't be that obvious. He pulled a telephone directory, checked the numbers of airlines and travel agencies, and ran them against Sherenko's phone record. No way Sherenko would do something so obvious, he told himself again.

He checked the Dushkin file again, glanced at the business card pinned to it, and focused on the telephone records.

During the relevant period Sherenko hardly used his home phone. So what did he mean by the relevant period? After he and Sherenko had started on the ConTex investigation, he assumed. He placed the home list to one side and concentrated on the numbers Sherenko had called on the cellphone, then cross-checked them against key events as recorded in the case log. Define key events, he told himself.

The ConTex VP at Nite Flite. Sherenko meets with Kosygin. Maddox's secretary goes missing. The meeting with the Moscow girlfriends of Whyte and the other courier. The moment Sherenko had cried off from that meeting.

The meeting with Kosygin. Does spring follow winter?

He checked the case log, found Kosygin's number, and ran it against the records. The number did not appear. Why not, he asked himself. Because Sherenko had made the first call from the office, and if Sherenko made more calls later he hadn't made them on the cellphone or from his apartment. He could get the phone record for the office, of course, but Sherenko would have been more careful than that.

The others had gone through to the dining-room off the far end of the corridor from the outer office. He thought about joining them, and ran through the cellphone calls for the day after the Kosygin meeting, accounted for them, and came back to the start point: the evening he and Sherenko had been scheduled to meet the girlfriends of the two couriers. Something's come up, Sherenko had said; could Kincaid cover for him. So what had come up?

He checked the phone records and confirmed the call to his own cellphone. There were no calls listed immediately before it which might explain Sherenko's call to him, one immediately after, and no other calls that night. You're going in circles, he made himself admit. He noted the number and checked whether Sherenko had called it again the following day. Better luck next time. The tiredness was coming in waves now. Time to eat, he told himself. He left the office and joined Riley and Lukyanov. Was halfway through when he thought he saw it.

Sherenko meets Kosygin – his logic was suddenly on automatic. Sherenko has the business card of an Anna Buskova with Dushkin's name on the back in Sherenko's handwriting. Sherenko only met Dushkin once, at the dinner with Kosygin. Ipso facto Anna Buskova, whoever she was, was one of the women present at that dinner.

Finish eating, he told himself. 'Excuse me.' He rose and returned to the office.

The telephone records were on the left of his desk and the Dushkin file was on the right. He checked the number Sherenko had called on the evening he had pulled out of the meeting with the couriers' girlfriends, then looked at the business card pinned to the Dushkin file. The details on the card were in Russian one side and in English on the other. Nice card, he thought; must have been expensive to produce. He checked the office number, ran it against the number Sherenko had called immediately after he had pulled out of the meeting with the couriers' Moscow girlfriends, and felt the sudden charge of electricity.

Okay, he told himself, try this: Sherenko investigates the missing ConTex money . . . Sherenko meets with Kosygin about the money . . . Sherenko and Kosygin do a deal, probably after the first meeting, otherwise Sherenko wouldn't have mentioned the ten per cent, and probably with Sherenko getting more than the ten per cent . . . Except both Kosygin and Sherenko would be careful, would have built in the cut-outs so they weren't directly linked. And the cut-out would be someone they both knew. So who was the cut-out, Yuri Dushkin or Anna Buskova? Anna Buskova, because Sherenko had asked for a file check on Dushkin. Except Sherenko had forgotten the business card he'd given Igor Lukyanov . . .

He leaned forward and called the number.

'Computer Systems, how may we help you.' The voice was female, friendly and efficient.

'May I speak to Anna Buskova?'

'I'm sorry,' the receptionist told him. 'She's away. Do you want her secretary?'

'Yes, please.'

He was connected to the secretary.

'Good morning, I was hoping to speak to Anna Buskova . . .'

'Anna's out of town at the moment.'

Interesting, Kincaid thought. 'Anywhere nice?' The tone suggested he knew her.

'London.'

'*Very* nice. When did she go?'

'Yesterday morning. Can I help?'

'I was hoping to see her rather urgently. You have a number for her?'

'She's staying at Brown's Hotel.' The secretary read him the number. 'Who can I say called?'

'Don't worry. I'll call her.'

Try this, Kincaid told himself again:

Sherenko does a deal with Kosygin. Sherenko and Kosygin use Anna Buskova as a cut-out. Anna Buskova leaves Moscow for London on the morning of the hits. I mean, is that a coincidence or is that a coincidence? So what does it say about where Sherenko might be? Hypothesis, Kincaid told himself, pure speculation. Except it was all he had. He checked the case log and called Kosygin's number.

'This is Jack Kincaid from Omega. I'd like to speak with Alexei.'

'Mr Kosygin isn't here at the moment.'

'Any idea when he's due back from London?' The question was instinct, years of training and too many years of living on the edge.

'I'm not sure,' Kosygin's secretary told him.

Which might or might not be confirmation that Kosygin was in London.

Any chance of a check on whether Alexei Kosygin is on airline and immigration records as having flown to London in the past two days, he asked Lukyanov. Kosygin flew to London twenty-four hours ago, Lukyanov informed him thirty minutes later.

Sherenko and Kosygin . . . Sherenko and Kosygin, with Anna Buskova as cut-out . . . Kosygin and Buskova in London, and no way Sherenko could still be in Moscow. Therefore the chances were that . . .

One hell of a flyer, my friend. You got anything else, though?

The office was still empty. He copied the relevant details of the case log into his notebook – telephone numbers and addresses, flight and immigration details of Sherenko's trip to Vienna plus details of the bank account there. Then he photocopied all the relevant documents, including the ticket carbons and bank slip found at Sherenko's apartment, plus the FSB files on Alexei Kosygin, Yuri Dushkin and Anna Buskova, including their photographs, waited for the others to return from lunch, gave Jameson time to settle then went to see him.

'You're looking tired, Jack.'

'You should try it from this side. I was thinking of taking a couple of days R and R.'

Jameson nodded. 'Time you were out of Moscow anyway. Where you thinking of going?'

'Nothing too exciting. Perhaps touch base in Amsterdam.'

'Do it,' Jameson told him.

The London conference, so-called even though it was held in Oxfordshire, broke for lunch at one. The morning session had begun formally at ten-thirty, the delegates seated along four sides of a square formed by beige-covered tables. Oil paintings hung on the panelled walls of the reading room, logs lay unlit in the massive stone fireplace in the west wall, and a glittering chandelier hung resplendent from the patterned ceiling. That afternoon and the following day would be taken up by individual subjects – narco-terrorism, arms trafficking, the threat of thefts of nuclear material – sometimes in full session and sometimes in working parties.

The lunch was typically English, Miller thought. He left the room, went to the suite assigned to the American delegation and phoned Moscow.

'Just checking to see how things are going,' he told Jameson.

When he returned to the conference room the afternoon session was just beginning. It was at eighteen minutes to four (the American chief of station noted such things) that a Russian aide entered and slipped a note to the Russian *rezident*, who read it and left. Two minutes later the same aide returned and passed a note to Malenkov. Malenkov read it, folded it, placed it in his right coat pocket, and followed the aide out. Nine minutes later Malenkov and the *rezident* returned and took their places again.

The afternoon session closed at five and the delegates prepared to leave. That evening there would be a reception in the Foreign Office off Whitehall. 'Perhaps we might have a word,' the Russian *rezident* suggested to his American counterpart, then repeated the suggestion to one of the pinstripes from Riverside.

'What's running?' Ed Miller asked his London CoS.

'Not sure.'

'You want me in?'

'Wouldn't do any harm.'

The other delegates were beginning to leave.

'What was that about?' Sheila Harrington asked the pinstripe.

'I'm not sure.'

'Any point served if I was there?'

'Could be.'

The meeting took place ten minutes later, in the study of Chansom House. The windows looked out across the gardens to the south, and ancestral portraits stared down from the deep green of the walls.

'We might have a problem.' The Russian *rezident* was seated to Malenkov's right. 'Earlier this afternoon I was informed that two men suspected of being associated with the Russian mafia have left Moscow and are presumed to be in Europe. According to the FSB the two are also suspected of being involved in the theft of six million dollars from Sheremetyevo airport, plus the deaths of a number of private security personnel in Moscow yesterday morning.'

So why tell us – it was in the face of the American chief of station.

'According to the FSB, though this has yet to be confirmed, the two men may also be involved in the laundering of mafia money, and one of them might also be involved in the smuggling of nuclear items.'

The eyes in the room were suddenly more focused.

The *rezident* hesitated. 'One of the men involved, Nikolai Sherenko, is a former member of the KGB.'

Oh Christ – it was in all their faces.

The London chief of station leaned back in his chair. Lean forward and it showed interest, back and it said you were relaxed about the whole thing. 'Interesting. I have to ask, however, how that affects us.' How that affects the United States of America.

The *rezident* looked at Malenkov and waited for the general to speak.

'The other man concerned is Jack Kincaid.' Malenkov told them.

Miller's response gave nothing away. One glance, slow and

deliberate, so they would all see, at his CoS, then the eyes staring at Malenkov again.

Sheila Harrington's eyes did not move. Kincaid was ex-Soviet division – Kincaid had been the baby-sitter, what the Americans might call the point man, on the Joshua affair; Kincaid had been flown up from Miami to hold Joshua's hand. Kincaid had been waiting in the restaurant on East 54th when Joshua had been blown away. Kincaid had faced her when she had ridden shotgun for Riverside in the inquisition which followed the Joshua fiasco.

'Impossible,' Miller told Malenkov.

'Why impossible?'

'The two men you name, Sherenko and Kincaid, are working for a private company, Omega, investigating the theft of the money you also mention. Yesterday morning there were gun attacks on both of them. The belief in Moscow is that Sherenko has changed sides and organized the attacks himself. Sherenko has now disappeared.'

'So . . .' Malenkov returned his stare.

'So what?'

'So doesn't it strike you as a coincidence that Sherenko and Kincaid are both intelligence professionals, working together on the theft of a relatively large amount of money, and that both survive gun attacks on them?'

Possibly – Miller's silence conceded.

'Point taken.' Harrington's accent was Cheltenham Ladies College and Somerville, Oxford. 'So why have you asked us here?'

'Because they might be heading for the United Kingdom.'

'And what are you suggesting Riverside does?'

'Start looking for them.'

'You're asking a lot, General Malenkov.'

'I thought that was what this conference was about, Mrs Harrington.'

Harrington stared at Malenkov, tapped her fingers on the arm of the chair and switched her focus to Miller. 'What do you think, Ed?'

Miller shrugged.

Harrington stood, crossed to the desk, and lifted the telephone. 'This is Sheila Harrington. Get me Special Branch and Organised Crime as priority.'

Anna returned to Brown's Hotel at six-thirty. The day had been busy but successful: two more clients and a new dress designer. She slipped off her shoes and dress, and checked if there were any messages for her. Where are you, Nikolai Alexandrovich; why haven't you called me? She showered, checked the numbers, and called Sherenko's apartment in Moscow. Sat on the edge of the bed and heard it ring. Heard the male voice.

'Nik?' she asked.

'Who's that?'

Not Nik.

'Sorry, wrong number.'

She began to call again and stopped, called reception and asked them to check on her computerized telephone billing for the number she had just called. Why – she asked herself. Not just because someone else was answering Nik's home phone, assuming she hadn't misdialled. Something about the way the other man had answered.

The receptionist confirmed the number. Anna pulled the dressing-gown tighter round her and called Sherenko's cellphone. The number she had called was not functioning, a recorded voice informed her. She checked the numbers again and called the Omega office. There was no answer. Mid-evening in Moscow, she reminded herself. So who had answered Nik's home number? Perhaps she should have asked for Nik, perhaps she was wrong in thinking there was something about the voice.

The phone rang. Nik, she knew. 'Yes,' she said, and began to relax.

'Anna, it's Yuri.'

'Hi, Yuri. When are you in town?'

'Tomorrow. See you for lunch twelve-thirty, the Sakura on Hanover Street. And save the evening. I have something you might enjoy.'

Sheila Harrington left home shortly before seven.

The house – three floors including basement, where she had the kitchen – was in a cul de sac near Primrose Hill. Small garden at the back, large sitting-room, her bedroom at the top and in front, and the smaller room she used as a study next to it at the rear. The house had been part of the divorce settlement, plus a healthy financial arrangement in her favour. Everything civilized, of course, everything amicable. Christ, she and Edward *were* adults, therefore nothing had been allowed to stand in the way of their respective jobs. She'd screwed the bastard for as much as she could, though. Edward was old money making lots of new, Edward had been the one playing games. And a girl had to do what a girl had to do.

Twenty-three minutes later the car dropped her at the Foreign Office. She passed through security and was conducted to the state room where the reception for the London Conference was being held. The Foreign Secretary was already present, plus ambassadors, the delegates at Chansom House, and the inevitable political hangers-on. At eight the PM would attend, shake the usual hands and entertain the usual attempts to lobby his patronage.

Miller saw her enter, and watched as she spent two minutes laughing at what he assumed was a boring joke from a Permanent Secretary. The Russians, with the exception of Malenkov, were keeping to themselves. Miller nodded his agreement at something one of the Paris boys was telling him and looked back at Harrington. Harrington was good, Harrington was one of the best, but Harrington was as far up the ladder as she would go. The Boys' Room would see to that. Harrington had known that the first time she and Miller had met. He moved on, smiled and chatted and nodded. Listened in and said little. Reached Harrington the same time as Malenkov, the convergence natural and unnoticed.

'Just heard.' Sheila Harrington smiled as if they were indulging in small talk. 'No sign of Sherenko, but Kincaid's popped up in Amsterdam.'

There was a stir at the door and the Prime Minister came in.

Sherenko drove steadily, the Mercedes eating through the kilometres. The sun was a golden ball in front of him, the trees ran on either side and the road was curving, the surface slightly pock-marked. An hour ago he had cut north, avoiding the main border crossing between Russia and Belarus. The false plates he had put on the car in Moscow, registered to a similar model Mercedes, meant that the car was not on the stolen register, and the two $100 bills slipped to the border guard who had apparently checked his passport had ensured that the wave through was automatic. Another $200 on the other side of the border, and he had entered Belarus. Then he had cut back south and picked up the main Moscow–Minsk–Warsaw highway.

. . . So how had Alexei Kosygin managed to set him up so efficiently and in a manner which had convinced Gerasimov? Bank payments in Vienna, airline tickets and official records, Gerasimov had said. But all the time in question he had been on the ConTex investigation with Kincaid. Except he hadn't, of course – the logic was a night tide creeping in on him. For thirty-six hours – for what he must assume were the relevant thirty-six hours – he had been out of circulation. From the time he and Kincaid had been due to meet the girlfriends of the couriers until minutes before the hits on himself and Kincaid he had been with Anna. So Kosygin had used the period when he had been protecting Anna to incriminate him . . .

The sun was dropping, the descent suddenly rapid as it closed on the black line of trees which was his horizon. The engine was running smoothly and he felt no tiredness. Seventy minutes later he cut south, off the main highway and on to a network of increasingly narrow country roads. He had been here before, crossed the Polish border in the way he would cross it tonight, occasionally tried to stop others crossing it. Always exercises, of course, but the routine and the locations were logged in his mind as if they had been for real.

The lane was rutted by tractor tyres and the mud was hard. He bumped along it, leaving no marks, picked up the broken tree, and pulled left. The main crossing into Poland was six kilometres to the north. Not that it mattered unduly, because the West still considered Poland as part of the old eastern bloc, therefore the main security was at Poland's border with Germany. He cached the car, took the black heavy-duty polythene bag, the Makharov and the Uzi, and left the area, checking in the last of the light that no indication remained of his presence there, or of the Mercedes. The moon was rising above the firs. He headed west, moving quickly and easily, came to the river, and sat without moving for twenty minutes, eyes and ears straining for signs of border guards. Then he cached the Uzi, cut a series of small branches, undressed, sealed the Makharov, his clothes and money in the bag, tied the branches on to it as if they were a piece of flotsam and leaving a loop of cord to go around his shoulders, closed on the bank and checked again that he was not being observed.

. . . Alexei Kosygin set him up – the night tide was black around him. Kosygin had used the period he was with Anna. Except that relied too much on coincidence, on Kosygin seizing an opportunity. So it was more than that. Kosygin had arranged for him to be with Anna at the relevant times, Kosygin had set Anna up, set up the mafia threat to Anna, to set him up. But even that relied too much on coincidence, because Kosygin would need to have predicted their relationship, to have known that Anna would turn to him when the no-necks called. The first whisper of the hurricane swirled in his head. Kosygin had set him up and Anna had helped. Perhaps Kosygin *and* Anna had set him up, accessed the ConTex money, agreed on their percentages, and used him as cover. Why are you thinking this, Nikolai Alexandrovich Sherenko – the thin shaft of sunlight tried to fight through the blackening grey of the hurricane. You don't really think I set you up, you don't think we could talk with each other, make love with each other the way we did if it wasn't for real? The hurricane filled his mind and blotted out the sunlight, the epicentre closing on him and cutting him off . . .

The water was not as cold as the first time he had crossed, but then it had been April, and the waters were still freezing from winter. He checked again, slid in, and swam diagonally right, so that the current wouldn't carry him too far down river, yet not too diagonally, so that the drift of the flotsam on the bag would appear natural. The moonlight was silver on the water and the current rippled against him. Twice he stopped and checked round him, the shape of his head lost against the foliage on the bag. He came to the bank, allowed himself to drift with the current and surveyed the ground in front of him. Then he pulled himself ashore, climbed up the bank on the Polish side of the river, cleared the immediate border area before stopping and dressing, and ran at an even pace for another thirty minutes, the terrain as familiar as it had been on the other side.

The Yamaha was where he had cached it in the old days, the plastic fuel can was fifty metres from it, and the heavy duty polythene bag containing the handful of items he would need to change his appearance, plus two false passports, one American and the other Dutch, fifty metres in the other direction. Alpha training had always been good, Alpha had been based and structured on the British SAS. Similar philosophy, similar emphasis on planning ahead.

. . . Kosygin *and* Anna had set him up. He was still back in Boston five years ago, leaving the safe house and running into the eye of the storm. You don't really believe this, Nikolai Alexandrovich – the voice was fainter now, almost gone. You don't really believe I could do this to you . . .

By seven in the morning he was in Warsaw. He hid the Yamaha in an outer suburb and caught a tram to the centre. At a boutique he bought a fresh set of clothes, paying in dollars; at a hotel near the central railway station he shaved and showered, then went to the hairdresser. When he took a cab to the airport fifty minutes later it was as Franz Zeegers, engineering consultant, of Utrecht in Holland, his appearance changed slightly but significantly to match the photograph in the passport – cheek pads, tinted contact lenses, and hair coloured slightly.

. . . Anna Mikhailovna I thought I could trust – the hurricane swept for the last time through his mind and his body and his soul. But Anna Mikhailovna betrayed me just as the bastards who ran me five years ago betrayed me. Because I know that the job in New York was connected with the Gorbachev putsch and the attempt to bring back the old days. And I did it for them, played my part in trying to stop the reforms I believed in.

It's more than that though, isn't it, Nik?

Okay, so it's more than that.

So what is it?

You want to know, my friend? You *really* want to know?

Yeah, Nik, I *really* want to know.

Anna Mikhailovna betrayed me in the same way that the Kremlin betrayed the boys in Afghanistan. Anna Mikhailovna betrayed me in the same way that the reforms and the new Russia betrayed me. Anna Mikhailovna I thought I loved, Anna Mikhailovna was my life and my future and everything I could trust and believe in. Just like the new Russia after '91. But the new Russia betrayed me as it betrayed most people. Okay, not just the new Russia. The new world. So it gave us fast food and new banking and international investment. But the ordinary people got poorer and the fat cats got fatter. And I hit the bottle, lost my wife and children, lost myself. And eventually, one awful cold wet goddam morning, I went to the morgue on C'urupy Ulica and pulled out the body of the daughter of my best friend. And that's how Anna Mikhailovna has betrayed me. On that scale and with that enormity.

8

Sheila Harrington left home at five-thirty. The streets were wet with overnight rain and the smell of freshness lingered in the air. Thirty minutes later she held her first briefing of the day at Riverside, at six thirty-five she was driven to New Scotland Yard. As she arrived, Malenkov's BMW pulled through the security barriers at the front of the building.

The meeting was in a room on one of the upper floors. The room itself was comfortable though plain, prints on the walls and conference table down the centre. In Moscow, Malenkov thought, there would be bugs all over the place. Perhaps there were, even in London. Which today was no problem, which today actually made it better.

Miller and the two policemen who would attend, the Metropolitan Police commanders for Special Branch and Organised Crime, were waiting. As soon as the meeting was over they would drive to Chansom House in Oxfordshire, police escorts cutting their way through the London traffic.

Harrington shook hands, declined coffee, sat at the head of the table, thanked them for attending, the two policemen in particular, and moved succinctly on to the agenda.

'Late yesterday afternoon Riverside was informed by the FSB that two men believed to be associated with the Russian mafia were running in Europe. I say that we received it from Moscow, it would be more accurate to say we received it after close of play at Chansom House.'

We were there – she read it in the policemen's faces. So why didn't you tell us then?

'The FSB believes that one or both of the men are involved with the theft of six million dollars, plus the deaths of a number of investigators enquiring into that money on behalf of the company involved. According to the FSB it is also possible, though not yet confirmed, that one or both of the men may be involved with the laundering of mafia money. One of them might also be involved in the smuggling of nuclear items, though as yet this is also unconfirmed.'

'So what's the problem?' Elwood had run Special Branch for the past eighteen months.

'Why should there be a problem?' Harrington came back at him.

Elwood smiled. A thin smile, which suggested she stopped playing her games. 'Because there has to be, otherwise why are we sitting here?' Two of Britain's senior police commanders, a senior officer from Riverside, and two top-rankers from the intelligence communities in Washington and Moscow.

Harrington looked at the file in front of her then up again. 'One is named Sherenko, the other is named Kincaid. Until late 1991 Sherenko worked for the KGB and Kincaid worked for the CIA.'

Oh shit – it hung in the air.

'What did they do?' Elwood took out a packet of cigarettes and saw there was no ash tray.

Harrington looked at Malenkov.

'Sherenko was in Alpha.' Malenkov spoke carefully, as if he was reluctant to disclose the information. 'Alpha was the KGB's Special Forces and anti-terrorist unit, the Russian equivalent of your SAS. Everyone knows about it now, no one did then.'

'And Kincaid?' Elwood turned to Miller.

'Kincaid was in the Agency's Soviet Division.'

'Field or desk?'

Miller hesitated. 'Kincaid was clandestine ops.'

Christ – the two policemen glanced at each other. 'What the hell are they doing working together?' It was the head of Organised Crime this time.

Malenkov nodded his understanding of the policeman's surprise. 'Officially they were both working for the security company in Moscow investigating the theft of the six million.

207

Unofficially the feeling is that they go back a long way together. Probably crossed each other sometime. You know how it is. Probably decided there was a future if they worked together.'

'So what's the problem?' Elwood asked again.

'The problem is that we think they might be en route to London.'

'What do we think they'll be doing in London?' It was still Elwood.

'We can't be sure, but we have to assume it's to liaise either with Russian mafia figures in town, or with international buyers of whatever they have to peddle.'

'So where are Kincaid and Sherenko now?'

Nik's cellphone was still down and there was no answer on his home number. In Moscow it was mid-morning. Anna checked the business card Sherenko had given her, called the Omega number, and heard the ringing tone. Heard the answer: no name, but with an organization like Omega there wouldn't be, just the confirmation of the number.

'May I speak with Nik Sherenko?'

Be there, Nik – she was unsure why she felt frightened. Be okay.

'One moment,' the man told her. The man who'd answered Nik's home number last night, she thought.

'Who is this?' It was another voice.

She put the phone down. Nik was okay, she told herself, Nik was a big boy and could take care of himself. She was misunderstanding things, making too much of simple things like his cellphone not working and the fact that someone had probably stayed in his apartment.

Her first business meeting of the day was with a computer company trying to sell her hardware and her second was with the export manager of a textile manufacturer wishing to know about setting up in Moscow and worried about the mafia. Between the two she squeezed in forty-five minutes at a fashion house. Shortly after midday she took a cab to the Sakura Japanese restaurant on Hanover Street.

Yuri Dushkin was waiting for her.

'You're looking good.' He kissed her on the cheek and held a chair for her.

'You're looking like you've got something running.' She kissed him back.

They ordered sushi and Asahi beer.

'When did you get in?' she asked.

'Flew in this morning. You've seen Alexei?'

'Not yet. He's booked in at his hotel but nobody knows where he is.'

'Typical Alexei.'

'Yeah, typical Alexei. So what's up? Why must I save you this evening?'

They took their time over lunch, exchanging anecdotes and gossip, then left the restaurant and crossed to New Bond Street. The weather was hot, the street was busy, and the flags of some of the world's most prestigious jewellers, fashion houses and fine art galleries were draped above the pavement like mediaeval pennants. Dushkin turned into Sotheby's, nodded at the commissionaire and led her through the foyer, through the reception area – green carpet and subdued lighting – through the doors at the end, and left up the stairs to the main gallery.

The room was burgundy red, the reception desk was on the right as they entered, and there were more porters and security guards than Anna assumed was usual. The central partition had been removed to increase the size of the room, the auctioneer's rostrum was near the far wall, and the assistants' desk to its right, Anna's left as she looked at it, though as yet there were no seats in the centre of the floor area.

Dushkin bought a catalogue and presented it to her. Where are you Nik – the slightest trace of anxiety still clung to her. 'When's the auction?' she asked.

'This evening.' Dushkin held her arm and steered her toward a Van Gogh. 'It's a Part One.'

'What's a Part One?'

'Part Twos are general auctions, open to anyone. Part One auctions are invitation only, the big spenders and the really big money. Fifty or sixty paintings, no more. Black tie affair, the rich and the famous, though only a handful will be buying.'

'And we're invited,' she teased him.

'Of course.'

They admired a Renoir and walked on.

'So are we buying or selling,' Anna asked.

They stood before a Gauguin and decided it wasn't for them.

They came to Lot 17.

Chagall: oils, early period.

She stood and looked at it, stepped back from it so she could view it from a distance; stood close to it again and almost wanted to touch it, to run her fingers across it. Found herself riveted by it. She looked at Dushkin and saw the way he was looking at her.

'This is why we're here, isn't it?'

'Perhaps.'

'You're not buying, are you?' This one, she meant. The Chagall.

'No.'

They left the gallery and walked down the stairs.

'So you're selling?'

He shrugged.

'How much?' she asked, and knew Dushkin would tell her.

'The reserve is one and a half million.'

'Dollars?'

'Pounds sterling.'

The morning topic at Chansom House was narco-terrorism, with special emphasis on the prospect of South American drug barons extending their operations into Europe, including Russia, and the proceedings dominated by civil servants and guest academics. At five minutes to one, five minutes before the session ended and the delegates retired for a working lunch, Harrington was called outside. When Malenkov and Miller left she was waiting in the lounge. As Elwood and Fenton passed she caught their eyes and they joined the group.

'Kincaid's en route for London.' Harrington paused while someone passed by, then continued. 'He left Amsterdam by train this morning, travelled to Brussels, and purchased a return ticket on the 12.31 Eurostar. He's due at London Waterloo at 14.43.'

*   *   *

The Belgian and French countryside passed in a blur. At seventeen minutes to three, exactly on time, the Eurostar express slipped into the international section of London Waterloo. Kincaid collected his travelling bag and left the train. The first tail picked him up as he stepped through the exit gates.

'Green One. Emir is wearing a light blue suit and carrying a brown leather bag.' The tail was five-eight tall, good figure and blonde hair, which was to say a blonde wig, and her clothes were stylish without being especially noticeable. The microphone was concealed in the light wool cardigan she wore, the earpiece lost beneath her hair, the battery of the set was strapped to her body below her left armpit, and the operation was her first as team leader.

'Emir turning left towards cab ranks.'

The target coded Emir because that suggested someone of Middle East origin and appearance, certainly not white American male.

'Green Two. Emir taking cab.'

'Hotel Pastoria in St Martins Street,' Kincaid told the driver.

The cab pulled away, the tails behind and in front: London black cab, Vauxhall Cavalier and BMW motorcycle, plus Senator for the leg men if it became necessary. The vehicles shifting and changing, running in front and behind, everything low key at this point.

The Pastoria was at the heart of the West End, just off Leicester Square. Thirty minutes later, having showered and changed, Kincaid left the hotel and turned right toward Trafalgar Square, the tails moving quickly and efficiently around him.

'Green Three. Emir at the National Gallery . . .'

Go, the controller ordered the bugging team.

'Green One. Emir leaving China Town towards Charing Cross Road.'

Central London wasn't the place to go if you thought you'd picked up a shadow and wanted to lose it, the team leader knew. There were too many people to spot a tail. If you thought you had a tail and wanted to launder it, then the place to do it was the suburbs, and even then there were ways of doing it.

Kincaid stopped at a telephone kiosk and went in. The floor

was dirty and the wall in front of him was covered with cards advertising a range of services. *Leather and lace. Sexy blonde transvestite. Man to man.* He looked at them, called one of the numbers, let it ring ten seconds then hung up.

Beautiful English brunette – Kincaid ran down the cards on the wall of the kiosk and called again. *Beautiful black mistress. Top class Thai massage.*

The dirty bastard – the team leader chuckled to her driver.

Kincaid rang off, appeared to check the cards, and called again.

'Brown's Hotel . . .'

'Miss Buskova, please. She's staying with you. I'm afraid I don't have her room number.'

He waited.

'I'm sorry,' the operator informed him. 'No reply from Miss Buskova's room.'

So Anna was still in London, still his way in to Sherenko.

He left the phone kiosk and walked north. In a radio shop in Tottenham Court Road he bought a pocket-size radio and head set, paying cash and wearing it when he left the shop, the set tuned to London News Talk. Then he returned to the hotel, went to his room, and telephoned the escort agency, the theatre and the restaurant, in that order.

The Air France 737 landed at Paris Charles de Gaulle two minutes late. Sherenko took a cab to the city centre, and the two o'clock train out of Paris Nord to London Victoria via Calais and Dover, paying in cash and again using the name Franz Zeegers of Utrecht.

The Netherlands was a member of the European Union, therefore within Europe, and excluding Britain, travel across its borders was straightforward. No one except the Dutch spoke the language, especially immigration officers at entry points into places such as Britain. And most Dutch spoke English, therefore any questions would be in English and any hint of an accent on his part would be immediately explained away.

*   *   *

Kincaid came out of the hotel and turned left. The radio was in the inside pocket of his jacket, the wires running to the headset, Kincaid making no effort to disguise the fact that he was listening to a radio or a cassette or CD player. He ignored the early evening West End bustle around him and concentrated on the programme being transmitted by London News Talk.

'Emir leaving hotel and moving north towards Leicester Square.'

He thought he heard it and walked on.

The surveillance team leader had changed clothes and was now wearing trousers plus reversible jacket – green one side, pale yellow the other. Hell, the stiff really had no idea, Christ only knew why they were watching him. Perhaps it was an exercise, except the target in an exercise would have made it more difficult, and they'd been told it was for real.

'Green One. Emir in Leicester Square.'

Kincaid thought he heard it again.

The team leader dropped away from him and the tail on the other side of the road picked him up.

'Green Two. Emir heading east along Piccadilly.'

Definitely, Kincaid knew.

The stake-out and back-up cars cut against the evening traffic, the motorcycle already through and in position in Dover Street. Kincaid turned into the Ritz, settled at a table in the bar just inside the foyer and ordered a Cesar Ritz.

'Green Two, Emir has entered the Ritz.' And everything on schedule. The target meeting the woman from the escort agency: the place and time picked up by the taps on his hotel phone. The tail walked confidently into the hotel and sat at a sofa in an alcove between the bar and the restaurant. 'Green Three. Emir in bar.'

Kincaid disconnected the radio and picked up the newspaper.

'Jack, I'm Elaine.' The woman was early thirties, tall, good-looking and well-dressed.

Kincaid rose, shook her hand, thanked her for coming, and offered her a drink.

'What are you having?' the woman asked.

'Cesar Ritz.'

'Sounds good to me.'

'Green Three. Emir joined by woman. Looks like the escort agency job.'

So what do you have in mind for this evening, the woman's look said.

'I've booked tickets for the theatre. Dinner after at Wheelers. Hope that's okay with you.'

She was going to enjoy this evening, the woman thought. Sometimes she did, sometimes she didn't; but the client had paid the agency by credit card, confirmed his hotel and all that, so she felt safe.

Anna checked the time, left her room and gave her keys to the concierge. Yuri Dushkin was waiting in the lounge. He was wearing an evening suit, the bow tie a slightly extravagant purple.

'You're looking good,' Anna told him, and allowed him to kiss her on the cheek.

'You're looking stunning.'

Stop worrying about Nik, she had told herself; Nik's fine, Nik's probably doing one of his crazy jobs and will phone you when he can.

They walked the two minutes to Sotheby's. As they arrived a Mercedes pulled away and a Rolls Royce took its place. Dushkin showed their invitations to the commissionaire, then they walked through the hall and took the stairs to the main gallery. The seats, set out after the house had closed its doors, were numbered, most of them already taken. The auctioneer's dais was in front, against the end wall, the computerized monitor which would show bids in a range of international currencies behind and above it, and the staff who would take telephone bids were seated behind a cloth-covered table against the wall on the right.

The auctioneer welcomed those gathered in front of him and moved briskly to the first lot.

Malenkov had changed into an evening suit in the back of the car. When he entered the main gallery the auctioneer was on Lot 10. He settled in his seat and waited. At three minutes past seven the auctioneer closed the bidding on Lot 16, took a sip of water and waited as two porters held the Chagall in place on the stand to his left.

'Lot 17, the Chagall.' Auctioning was an art, auctioning was acting. Therefore he had thought it through carefully, where to start the bidding and what to do if it looked like failing to reach the reserve.

'Six hundred thousand pounds.'

The first eye was raised.

'Six hundred and fifty thousand . . . Seven hundred thousand . . . Seven fifty, eight hundred, eight hundred and fifty . . .'

The bidding slowed slightly. 'Eight hundred and fifty thousand pounds. With you, sir. Against you on the telephone . . .'

A long way to go to the reserve.

'Nine hundred thousand.' The auctioneer glanced around the room, glanced at the telephone bidders. 'Nine hundred thousand. And twenty-five. And fifty.' He scanned the room. 'Nine hundred and seventy-five thousand pounds.' And still way below the reserve. He picked up the movement of the catalogue. 'One million pounds.'

Malenkov saw Yuri Dushkin three rows in front of him and to his left. No problem, though. Dushkin didn't know him.

'One million pounds.' The auctioneer scanned the room again. Still five hundred thousand below the reserve – it was in the computer of his brain, in every nerve and sinew of his body though he did not show it. 'One million pounds on the telephone. One million, one million.' He searched for the slightest movement of an eyebrow or a finger or a catalogue; scanned the faces of the women handling the telephone bids. 'One million pounds, one million pounds.' The auctioneer's voice and manner concealed the tightening in his stomach. He looked round the room again, looked at the telephone bidders.

'One million and fifty thousand pounds.' Nobody in the room had moved. 'With me at one million and fifty thousand pounds.' The figure still below the reserve, and the auctioneer placing a bid on behalf of the seller to ensure that the painting did not sell below that price. 'One million and fifty thousand pounds.'

A bid on behalf of the seller at one million and fifty thousand pounds and the next bid from the floor, assuming there was another bid, would be at one million one hundred thousand. Still below the reserve, so the auctioneer would bid on behalf of the seller at one million two. The next bid from the floor would be at one three, and the auctioneer would come back at one four, so that any subsequent bid from the floor would have to be at one million five hundred thousand, which was the reserve. If the auctioneer had come in on one million one hundred thousand, on the other hand, it would be he, rather than a buyer from the floor, who would reach the reserve first. 'With me at one million and fifty thousand pounds.' He stopped himself playing with the gavel. 'One million one hundred thousand pounds. Yes, with you on the telephone.' He felt the relief.

Still four hundred thousand short of the reserve, though. Anna glanced at Yuri Dushkin and saw the fear in his eyes.

Malenkov watched carefully; perhaps Dushkin had been greedy, perhaps they had allowed Dushkin to be too bullish.

'One million two hundred thousand pounds.' A bid from the floor. 'One million three hundred.' On the telephone. 'One million four hundred thousand.' The floor again, but still short of the reserve. The auctioneer worked the room, tried to pull another hundred thousand from the underbidder. The women on the telephones were talking quietly, relaying not just the bid but the atmosphere in the room. The auctioneer looked at them, saw the shake of the head from one, began to turn to the floor and picked up the flick of the pen from another of the women on the telephones.

'One million five hundred thousand pounds.'

The reserve.

Anna grasped Yuri Dushkin's arm.

'One million six hundred thousand.' The flood broke. One seven, eight, one nine ... One million nine hundred thousand pounds ... Two million pounds.'

Malenkov watched Dushkin, watched the faces round him.

Two one, two two, two three ...

'Selling for two million three hundred thousand pounds.'

The auctioneer tapped the gavel down, watched as the porters removed the Chagall, and poured himself a fresh glass of water.

Dushkin leant closer to Anna. 'Ironic, isn't it?'

'What's ironic?'

'The Chagall came from Russia, now it's going back there.'

'How d'you mean?'

'The man who bought it is a big player in Moscow.'

Dushkin staying three more lots before leaving, Malenkov noted. Dushkin not leaving immediately after the item in which he had an interest, because Dushkin was a pro. Dushkin leaving with a woman.

Malenkov saw her face.

Wrong time, wrong place, my lovely Anna. Saw you on the flight over, of course, though you don't know me, as Yuri doesn't know me. But seeing you on the flight was fine, because there were plenty of reasons why someone like you should be coming to London. But wrong time, wrong place; three times now. At the Tokyo restaurant when Sherenko met with Alexei Kosygin; then screwing with Sherenko; now turning up at the Chagall sale with Yuri Dushkin. Too many links between the present now, too many roads leading to Moscow USA. And you're one of them.

'Green Three. Emir moving.' The microphone was concealed beneath the tail's lapel. 'Emir and companion turning east.'

'Green Four. Emir moving east along Piccadilly.'

'Green One. I have them.'

The pavements of London's West End were crowded; Kincaid held the woman's arm and guided her through.

'Green One. Emir entering the Prince of Wales theatre.' Which figures. Escort agency pick-up, then theatre. Circle seats, just as the phone tap on the hotel room suggested, and restaurant after. The team leader allowed them to go inside, then checked the streets round the theatre. The Prince of Wales occupied half of a four-storey block on the corner of Leicester Square, separated from the next block by a narrow alleyway. She positioned the tails and stake-out cars to cover the main door, the emergency exits and the stage door, returned to the Senator, and poured herself a mug of coffee.

*   *   *

Sheila Harrington briefed the Wise Men at eight. Everything looked good, they agreed. Riverside had established new connections with the Russian SVR and FSB. Riverside had also accessed a possible route into one of the areas now regarded as a major and global threat, so perhaps they should consider letting Sherenko and/or Kincaid run; perhaps Riverside might even consider recruiting them. No one else knowing, of course, but that was the game after all. Plus Riverside had covered itself by involving the police. So if anything went wrong, by which they meant if there was a shoot-out or some similar fiasco, then it would be the police who would take the flak.

Ed Miller met the London chief of station at eight-thirty. You don't like it, Miller agreed, I don't like it. Because Jack used to be Agency, therefore Jack was family. But everything points to the fact that Jack's gone off the rails, and if that's the case, then we – you, me, the Agency – have to act on it.

Malenkov's meeting with Vorkov was at nine, in the apartment near the Regents Park canal. Vorkov had flown in on that evening's British Airways flight.

'Today I think champagne.' Malenkov lifted the Bollinger from the ice bucket.

'How much did the Chagall fetch?' Vorkov asked.

'Two three. Bit of a scare at one million fifty thousand; the bidding stuck till the hammer was about to go down. I thought there were going to be a few heart attacks.'

'You went?'

'Of course.' Malenkov eased out the cork and poured them each a glass. 'What happened in Moscow?'

Vorkov told him.

'What about London?' Malenkov asked when Vorkov had finished.

'Kosygin is in Britain, actually Scotland, buying up some property; he's due back in London in a couple of days. Sherenko is missing. Our assumption is that he thinks Kosygin set him up. If he knows that Anna is in London he might be using her to get to Kosygin. Kincaid left Moscow for Amsterdam, possibly en route for London, which we've already discussed.'

Malenkov finished the glass and poured them each another.

'Kincaid arrived this afternoon. Special Branch were waiting for him.'

Of course, Vorkov thought. 'So what do you suggest?'

'You finish here what wasn't finished in Moscow. Special Branch have tails on Kincaid, so we'll always know where he is, and Kincaid will lead us to Sherenko. Therefore you've got your way in, and we've got a cover. Riverside and the police think Sherenko and Kincaid have gone over to the other side. When your people send Sherenko and Kincaid, and whoever else, to kingdom come, the authorities will assume it's just part of an internal mafia war.'

Vorkov ran the champagne round the glass. 'You used the words *whoever else* . . .'

Malenkov checked the time and stretched for the bottle. 'Alexei Kosygin . . . Kosygin was Sherenko's access point into all this; if it hadn't been for Kosygin we wouldn't be working out what to do now. Kosygin is dispensable. Plus he's extra cover. If Kosygin is killed with Sherenko and Kincaid – I mean actually physically together with them – and Kosygin is on file as a known mafia boss in Moscow, then it's direct confirmation that the mafia was involved and indirect confirmation that Sherenko and Kincaid were involved with the mafia.'

Vorkov drained the glass. 'Anyone else?'

Malenkov stared at the champagne bottle. 'Anna Buskova.'

The restaurant was busy. Dushkin allowed the waiter to pour them both a Krug and raised his glass. 'To Marc Chagall,' he suggested.

'Marc Chagall.' Anna drained the glass and allowed Dushkin to pour her another. 'You're off to New York in the morning?'

'Los Angeles first.'

'Another Chagall?' Her eyes sparkled at him.

'Actually no.'

His cellphone rang. He apologized, answered it, and recognized the voice immediately.

'Just phoning to offer my congratulations on this evening's little success,' Vorkov told him.

'My pleasure.'

'I gather there was an awkward moment round the million fifty mark.'

'For a moment,' Dushkin conceded. How did Vorkov know – it was a trickle of apprehension on the farthest horizon of his mind; because Vorkov hadn't been there. 'The million actually. The fifty thousand was the house covering itself.'

'Whichever way, I'm glad it worked.'

Dushkin sipped the champagne. 'It happens. There was never a chance we weren't going to make the reserve.'

Vorkov laughed. 'I'm in London for a couple of days, usual numbers if you want to get hold of me.'

Anna studied Dushkin's face as he put the phone back in his pocket. 'Who was that?'

Dushkin shrugged.

'Something about the auction this evening?' She pressed him slightly.

What makes you think that – it was in the way he tried to laugh it off.

'Obvious,' she told him and poured him another glass. 'So who was it?' Her eyes sparkled at him, teased him. Go on, Yuri, her laugh said; we're friends, we go back to before Time. And if you can't relax with friends, then who the hell can you relax with; who the hell can you tell that your boss, or whoever you work to, has just phoned to congratulate you. Because it's all over your face and your body language.

Dushkin laughed. 'Actually it was someone I work with.'

'I thought you worked by yourself.'

'I work for some people.' Perhaps it was the champagne, perhaps the adrenalin. 'Actually I don't know who the hell I work for.' He drained the glass and poured them each another. 'I work through a middleman.' It's the business, the shrug said again. I don't know, and don't want to know.

'And that was the middleman?'

'Yes.'

'Phoning to say congratulations.'

Dushkin waved for another bottle. 'Yes.'

'So someone you work for was at the auction?'

The sliver of caution cut through Dushkin. 'How can you say that?'

'Because they knew about the glitch when the bidding reached a million.'

'Probably,' Dushkin conceded.

'Tell me, Yuri.' Anna teased him, taunted him. Because you know you want to. 'One of the people you work for but not the middleman,' she suggested.

Dushkin had relaxed and was enjoying himself. 'Explain.'

'There was nobody at the auction you knew. And if it wasn't the middleman, it must have been someone above him.'

Dushkin's eyes sparkled. Close it, his brain told him. Shut the doors before you say something you regret.

'So how do you manage legal-wise?' Anna asked.

'How do you mean, legal-wise?'

'You know what I mean, Yuri. You're a wheeler-dealer. Hell, Yuri, you're not just a dealer. You deal in millions. You sell Chagalls. You come to Russia, somehow you ship items out of Russia. I mean, everybody does it, but only if they have the money and know the right contacts.'

'Items out of Russia?' Dushkin returned her laugh. 'The Chagall was legit, it had a certificate from the Chagall committee in Paris.' He pretended to think. Wanted to tell her, see her appreciation, but pulled himself back, though only partly. 'Let's see, where do other such things come from? Perhaps they come from Germany or Switzerland. Switzerland is a very good place for things to come from.' He waved a hand in the air.

Believe me I know my business, he told Anna. I do my research, know what's in demand, what will be easy to shift. Not always Chagalls, of course, because you can't do that sort of thing too often. But a few items moving at around fifty grand ten times a month and spread around Europe and the United States soon adds up. A watch, a book, a nice little Fabergé. A rock – he used the trade jargon for a diamond. Which was one of the reasons he was going to the US. Though rocks, or items like rocks, or items which come from the same place as the rocks, are subject to more cuts along the way, more people taking their commissions. At either end and in the middle.

He waved his hand nonchalantly in the air again. *Takova zhizn*. Such is life

The curtain came down for the interval, and Kincaid and his companion joined the move to the circle bar. Kincaid had already placed the order for the interval drinks, so that the glasses were in place with his name beside them.

'Interesting performance,' he suggested.

'Interesting evening,' his companion told him.

The pay phone was on the landing outside. He apologized that he had to make a business call, asked her to excuse him, and returned two minutes later. 'I'm sorry,' he told her. 'My firm has some clients coming into Heathrow, their flight's been delayed and I have to meet them.' He kissed her on the cheek and noted that she didn't pull away. 'I really am sorry.' He held her hand, not tightly, and noted again that she didn't remove hers. 'Look. Don't take this the wrong way. The table's booked for ten-thirty, why don't you go and enjoy it, have a drink on me.'

Normally it was her telling a client she had to leave, she thought. Okay, sometimes not, but that was the business. But never a client apologizing to her for leaving, then sliding two $100 notes into her bag and telling her to make sure the wine she had on him was a good one.

'You're sure?' she asked.

'Sure.'

She wrote her name and number on the programme. 'Next time you're in town.' She kissed him on the lips and allowed him to walk her back to their seats. The bell was ringing for the second half. He kissed her on the cheek again and walked to the rear of the circle seats and out the door to the stairs. The area was busy with people returning from the bar. Right, and the stairs went down to the foyer. Kincaid turned left, up one flight, then right, through a door bearing the names of theatrical offices, up another flight, past the offices, and up another flight. The door on the left was bolted on the inside. He slipped the bolt back, went through, and shut the door behind him. He was now in a narrow well, the open sky above, walls rising ten feet on all

222

sides and a black-painted door at the far end. A ladder ran up the wall on the right of the door. He climbed it and stepped on to the roof of the theatre. The night was grey around him, from below came the sound of police cars and fire engines. He ignored it and crossed the roof. A second ladder led down to a small area from which there was a connection to the next block. He ignored it because it could be seen from the street below, lowered himself over the edge, dropped to the flat area beneath, and crossed the two metres to the next block, keeping his body low.

The office in the other block was empty of furniture and fittings, and the windows were secured only by old-fashioned metal handles. He broke the glass, opened the window and pulled himself inside, padded across the office, broke the lock on the door into the passageway outside, and followed the emergency exit signs down the stairs. At the bottom he pushed through a door into the other half of the block and found himself in a concrete corridor. Left was the emergency exit on to the alleyway at the rear of the theatre. He turned right, into the nightclub which occupied the ground floor in that half of the building. The bars were busy. He drifted for three minutes, attached himself to a group who were leaving, and exited with them through a door on to Panton Street, one block from the Prince of Wales.

The radio was still in his pocket. He switched it on, plugged in the ear piece and listened for the faintest interference with the London News Talk transmission which nobody else would notice. The sound gentle, almost a whoosh, as the tails around him talked to each other. The frequency they were using was so close to the frequency on which the station broadcast that even on low power they interfered slightly with the transmission. Not that you'd know unless you were listening for it. And not that he'd been able to spot the vultures who'd been sitting on him since he'd arrived at Waterloo yesterday. The Special Branch tails in London were among the best.

Perhaps he had been too long in the game not to think someone would be waiting for him, he supposed; perhaps he was running more careful after Moscow; perhaps he remembered that five years ago Joshua had thought that because he'd cleared the cut-outs he wasn't being tailed.

Thirty-five minutes later he was in a cheap hotel in the Paddington area: single room, television that didn't work properly and shower and toilet on the next floor down. Cash payment in advance and no check on the name and home address he gave.

It was ten-thirty. He sat in the room and tuned in to London News Talk. In the West End the crowds were pouring from the theatres and the tails around the Prince of Wales were suddenly alert again. Kincaid listened carefully and picked up the faint *whoosh*.

'Green One. See the woman.' Everything going to plan, everything going to the schedule they'd been led to expect. 'Green One. No sign of Emir.'

'Green Two. Woman crossing road and heading east. Still no sign of Emir.'

'Green Three. Woman entering Wheelers.'

What the hell's happening, the team leader asked them. Where the hell was Emir?

'Mr Kincaid's table,' the woman told the waiter at the reception desk. 'It was booked for two, but I'm afraid there's only one.' He smiled at her, took her coat, and escorted her to the table in the window. Here's to you, Jack, she thought. She asked for the wine list and chose a Montrachet. In the room in Paddington Kincaid heard the momentary break in transmission as the tails turned up the power and informed Control that they had lost him.

Sheila Harrington returned home shortly before fifteen minutes to eleven. The light in the lounge was on, the curtains drawn, and Ricky's turbo Saab was parked outside.

Ricky had been at Winchester with Edward, gone up to Oxford with him. After the divorce Ricky had become once a week, plus weekends. Ricky was also acceptable: right school, right job in the City, right clubs, right sort of divorce, certainly no suggestion he played the field or preferred chaps. Once Ricky and she had come to their arrangement, therefore, she had let it be known to those at Riverside who needed to know such things. Ricky was also a last payment on the divorce settlement, a final retribution against her husband's peccadillos. Edward had always joked about his being small but pretty. At Winchester, on the other hand, Ricky had been known as Donkey.

A girl, after all, had to make her own way in life. Cover herself with those who considered themselves the great and the good, but play her games as well.

'Good day?' Ricky poured her a large Scotch on the rocks.

'Better than some.' They never discussed her work, just as she and Edward had never discussed it. She took the drink to the bedroom, undressed, slipped on a dressing-gown, then went to the bathroom, turned on the shower, slid off the dressing-gown, and stepped in. The shower was a luxury – massaging jets from three sides as well as from above. She felt the needles bite into her and relaxed, heard the sound outside, then the shower door opened and Ricky joined her. Stood behind her and soaped her back, soaked her neck and her shoulders. She felt his column growing, moved back against it, and heard the telephone. 'Shit.' She stepped from the shower, pulled a towel round her, and took the call on the cordless. 'Yes.' At home she never identified herself.

'Daphne, it's Frank.' The codes from the office.

She left the bathroom, went to the study, closed the door, and unlocked the cabinet concealing the encryption unit. 'On secure,' she told the office.

'Problems,' the duty officer informed her. 'Special Branch have just been in touch. They've lost Kincaid.'

Christ – she breathed out sharply. 'Anything we can do about it tonight?'

'No. They suggest a meeting tomorrow morning.'

'What about Malenkov and Miller?'

'Being informed through the *resident* and the CoS.'

She replaced the unit in the cabinet and returned to the bathroom. Ricky was sitting at the base of the shower, the water cascading over him and his column erect in the stream. She closed the shower door and lowered herself on to him.

Miller had always liked Whyte's. If he had been British, by which he meant the right sort of British, Whyte's would have been the sort of club he would have lobbied hard to become a member.

Discreetly, of course, because that was still the way certain things were still done. His host that evening was a Washington hand from the old days turned merchant banker. An enviable combination, Miller had suggested over the Havana and cognac.

A porter appeared as if from nowhere, coughed discreetly, and informed his host that Mr Miller was required on the telephone. Miller excused himself, followed the porter out of the room, picked up the phone and identified himself because there was no reason not to.

'Ed, it's Dan.' The London chief of station. 'Ed, I just heard from our fishermen friends.' The conversation was on an open line, therefore veiled. 'They lost the fish.'

Malenkov looked up into the dark. The champagne bottle was empty and the woman above him rode with his movement. The cellphone rang. He rolled her off, picked it up, growled a *yes* without identifying himself, and listened carefully.

Thanks, he told the *rezident*. Typical British losing Kincaid – it was in his tone.

Special Branch's fault – he could imagine how Harrington would react to the news. Riverside covered in the overall game, though, and Harrington herself covered back and front within Riverside itself. Anna Buskova still the way to Sherenko and Kincaid, because both Sherenko and Kincaid thought that Anna was their way in to Kosygin, plus the hit on Sherenko and Kincaid with Kosygin as a veil.

Everything and everyone covered.

Everything going to plan.

Sherenko's ferry docked at Dover on time. He stood in line with the other foot passengers at immigration, handed over the slightly dog-eared passport and was nodded through just as the passengers from the next ferry entered the checkpoint. By eleven-thirty he was in a bed and breakfast establishment in south London.

Vorkov's meeting with Kosygin was shortly before midnight, in the Park Lane Hilton. Kosygin had flown in to Heathrow on the last flight down from Scotland. In the past three days he had acquired two estate properties for knock-down prices, each of which he could develop or sell on at a profit when the market turned up, or which he might use for collateral or for other purposes, which some might call money laundering.

He waved to a waiter and asked for champagne.

Champagne seemed to be everyone's drink this evening, Vorkov thought wryly. He waited for the waiter to pour them each a glass, then began the process of drawing Kosygin in.

'You're in London tomorrow, then you fly back to Moscow the day after?'

Perhaps Kosygin was already alert, despite his manner; perhaps it was at this moment that he came on guard. 'Couple of business appointments tomorrow, dinner with a friend in the evening, then fly back the following morning.'

'Anna Buskova . . .' Vorkov said the name casually, almost as if it was irrelevant. 'Do any of your plans tomorrow include her?'

Kosygin's immediate reaction was to ask how and why Vorkov knew of Anna Buskova. Instead he nodded, as if they both knew he and Anna were friends.

'There's a problem.' Again Vorkov made it casual. 'Nikolai Sherenko. He saw you about the ConTex money.'

'Why is that a problem?'

'A couple of days after you met him there was an attempt on his life. Sherenko thinks you arranged it. He's here looking for you. Actually, there are two of them: Sherenko and a fellow investigator, an American called Kincaid.'

'So?'

'So we think it would be appropriate to remove them while they're in London.'

'How?'

'Put them in a situation which they think they control, but which we, in fact, have set up.'

'And how do you get them into that situation?'

'We set them up via Anna Buskova.'

Kosygin's eyes narrowed slightly, even though he tried to conceal it. 'Why should they go for that?'

'Because Anna's the way they're getting to you.' It was still quiet, still almost a throw-away.

'Why should Anna be Sherenko's way in to me?'

Vorkov changed the terms slightly. 'You mean why should Anna Buskova lead Sherenko to you?'

'Yes.'

Vorkov put down the glass. Happens to all of us, it said; pity, but a fact of life. What do the Americans say? Shit happens.

Why – it was in the sudden dark of Kosygin's face.

Vorkov clanged the trap shut. 'You know what the girls are like, Alexei. Sherenko's screwing her like there's no tomorrow.'

9

Kincaid woke at five. At six he showered and dressed. At seven, at a shop on a corner two blocks away, he bought toiletries to replace those he had left in the Pastoria Hotel. By seven-thirty he was in Albemarle Street.

The front of Brown's Hotel was an appropriate light colour, there was a white façade around the main door, and a Union Jack hung from a flagstaff above it. The pavement was swept clean, black-painted iron railings along the inside of the pavement protecting the steps going down to a basement.

On the other side of Albemarle Street was a row of shops and an antiques arcade. A small café, the Bon Appetit, was tucked between the shops and opposite the main door to the hotel. He ordered breakfast, sat at the second table from the window, and checked the photograph which he had brought from Moscow.

A cab stopped outside the hotel. An elderly couple came out, a concierge carrying their baggage, and the cab pulled away. The street was getting busy now – early morning busy in a city centre. A few cabs, delivery vans, bleary-eyed faces. He ordered another coffee, saw the concierge come up and wave down a cab, and recognized Anna Buskova immediately.

The cab was already pulling away. Kincaid left the Bon Appetit and flagged down the next. Ten minutes later he followed Anna through the reception area of the Savoy Hotel and into the breakfast room. Smart operator, Kincaid thought: power breakfast at one of the best tables at one of the most famous hotels in London, every male in the room looking at her, and the two businessmen she was now with happy to sign anything she put in front of them.

*　　*　　*

Sherenko lay awake and stared at the ceiling. It was six in the morning, the light pouring through the faded net curtain at the bedroom window. He rolled off the bed, showered in the brown chipped unit two doors along, passed on breakfast and left. By eight he was in the overgrown cemetery in Stoke Newington, in north London; by eight-thirty, having confirmed that he was not being observed and that the cache had not been disturbed or was under surveillance, he had removed the Sig Sauer, holster and ammunition, and concealed the cache again. By nine he was in Central London. Leicester Square was almost empty; he walked across it, used a pay phone, and telephoned Brown's.

'Mr Kosygin, please.'

'I'm afraid we don't have a Mr Kosygin,' the switchboard operator told him.

He thanked her, rang off, then phoned again and asked for reception. 'This is Henley Florists. We have a delivery for Miss Buskova. We just wanted to confirm she's staying with you.'

There was the slightest hesitation. 'Yes. Room 220.'

'Thank you.'

He left Leicester Square and walked along Piccadilly. The streets were still quiet, only the first handful of tourists of the new day, and the last homeless of the old night, plus the pigeons. He turned up Albemarle Street and came to Brown's. A concierge – black uniform, gold lapel badge – was carrying two suitcases out for a pair of Texans. Sherenko nodded at the concierge and went in.

The foyer was wood-panelled; the concierge's desk was on the left, a dining room beyond it; to the right was a lounge, a passage-way leading through it to a bar. The main hallway ran from the front door to the rear entrance on Dover Street, a smaller hallway off it to the left. On the right of the smaller hallway were a guest lift and service lift, and the stairs at the end led to the upper floors.

The room keys were in pigeon holes behind the concierge's desk. Key 220 was in place, therefore Anna was out. Sherenko smiled as if he belonged and took the stairs.

Room 220 was on the fourth floor, at the front of the building and opposite the lift. The door was open and a chambermaid was cleaning it. He decided against going in, and spent the next ten minutes examining the interior layout of the hotel.

The bedrooms were on five floors, one set of rooms at the front of the hotel and a separate set at the rear, no connecting passageways from front to back on the lower floors. There were guest lifts and stairs both front and back, a staff lift at the rear, and a staff entrance from a basement door in Dover Street, plus a basement door for refuse disposal.

Sherenko returned to the fourth floor, confirmed the location of Anna's room, and checked again for the ways in and out. He hadn't eaten since the cross-Channel ferry the previous afternoon, he remembered. He left the hotel, crossed to the café opposite the main door on Albemarle Street, and ordered breakfast.

Malenkov and Vorkov met at six, in the honey pad near Regents Park canal. The woman Malenkov had hired for the previous night was still asleep in the bedroom, and fresh coffee bubbled in the percolator.

Malenkov poured them each a mug. 'How was Kosygin?'

'He bought it.'

'And you've worked it out?'

Vorkov sipped the coffee and nodded. 'What we need is a location where Kosygin will be and where Anna will lead Sherenko and Kincaid to him. I suggest a restaurant dinner for Kosygin and Anna Buskova. We arrange for Sherenko and Kincaid to discover the time and location, give them enough time to check the place out and make their own arrangements, then we leave them to their devices. And when they do, we take them out.'

'How?' Malenkov asked.

'An explosive device in the car they'll use.'

'When?'

'It has to be today, tonight at the latest. Both Kosygin and Anna fly back tomorrow.

Fifteen minutes later Vorkov left, thirty minutes after that a cab collected the woman with whom Malenkov had spent the night; eight minutes after that Malenkov was driven to New Scotland Yard.

The others were already waiting:

Elwood from Special Branch and Fenton from Organised Crime, both tight-lipped. The American chief of station and the Russian *rezident*, neither giving away even the slightest scintilla of thought or expectation. Ed Miller, impassive and apparently relaxed. So somebody fucked up, his demeanour said; but that's history, so let's work it, let's move it on. Sheila Harrington, layers of blue in her eyes and all of them cold.

Everything up and running, exactly as planned. Better than that. Everything official and in the open. The best cover of all.

'So what happened last night?' Harrington asked the Special Branch commander.

Anna's second meeting of the day was on the fifth floor of a modern glass-fronted office block in the City of London. She should have telephoned Nik this morning, she thought; should have tried to make contact with him. Okay, last night she had decided that Nik was a big boy and could take care of himself. Last night she had tried to convince herself that nothing was wrong, and that there was a logical reason for the fact that Nik's cellphone wasn't working and that someone else had answered his home number. Nik was a big boy and she was a big girl, and there was a simple explanation for everything. Nik was out of Moscow, Nik was on a job and away from home. And given the delicacy of his work, it wasn't surprising that the office had reacted the way they had when she'd phoned and asked to speak with him. So Nik was okay, she'd told herself last night. And Nik would phone her when he could.

Kincaid settled in a café opposite – one of those that had a handful of tables but which also catered for take-out sandwiches and drinks for office workers – and ordered coffee.

Sherenko left Brown's, changed $2000 at American Express, and took the Piccadilly line to Hammersmith Broadway. Hammersmith was west London and dissected by the main dual carriageway toward Heathrow. Parts of it were expensive, parts not.

Hammersmith was also on the river and Sherenko liked rivers because they gave him another way out.

He left the underground station, checked out two property letting agencies near the Broadway, then crossed the bridge, the Thames glistening below him and rowing eights sliding easily across the silver water, and enquired at an agency two blocks down, in a row of shops. Nothing large, he explained: bedroom and lounge plus kitchen and bathroom or shower room.

Of the five addresses the agency supplied him, Arundel Terrace was the third he checked. It was a hundred metres and two streets from the river. It was also a cul-de-sac, large wooden gates across the road at the end and a high wall protecting the Gothic red brick edifice that was the Harrods furniture depository. The apartment itself was on the first floor in a terrace of small houses on the right. No easy way in to him – Sherenko ran the check list. Cul-de-sac, so difficult for surveillance vehicles. Good way out – drop one floor, cut left through the gardens and over the wall into the vast meandering grounds of the furniture depository, the area itself joined on the south side by a housing construction site, on the east by an undeveloped area of land including what seemed to be gravel pits, and on the north by a towpath and the river.

Thirty minutes later Sherenko moved in. When he left for the West End fifteen minutes after that, it was only after taking the usual precautions, even though no one else knew of the existence of what he already mentally referred to as a safe house.

The West End was alive with tourists now. At Leicester Square he bought a phone card, telephoned Brown's, and asked for Anna.

'I'm sorry, Miss Buskova isn't in the hotel at present,' the operator told him. 'Are you a business colleague?'

'Yes.'

'Putting you through to reception.'

He waited.

'Good afternoon. I'm a colleague of one of your guests, Miss Buskova. The switchboard put me through to you.'

'Miss Buskova left a message if anyone called. She's not available during the day, but she'll be at Laycock's restaurant from seven-thirty this evening.'

Anna being efficient – Sherenko's thought process was automatic. Anna getting her business out the way during the daytime and assigning her social affairs to the evening, but not missing a trick in case a potential business colleague called. He checked the number with directory enquiries and called the restaurant.

'I'm having dinner with a friend this evening, and just wanted to confirm she'd booked the table.

'The lady's name, sir?'

'Buskova.'

There was a slight delay.

'Sorry, we don't have a reservation in that name.'

'What about Kosygin?'

There was another slight delay.

'Yes. Mr Kosygin. Seven-thirty.'

Sherenko left Leicester Square, took the underground to Sloane Square, and walked west. King's Road was busy: shops, boutiques, and the Duke of York army barracks set slightly incongruously off to the left. He walked another hundred metres and turned right into Guildford Street. Laycock's was on the left, amongst the boutiques, antique shops, pub and wine bar, and already busy with lunch-time customers. He walked past without stopping, checked up and down the street, then skirted to Wiltshire Street, at the rear.

Wiltshire Street was narrow, no shops, merely the rears of those premises fronting Guildford Street on one side, a small arched entrance to a cobble-stoned mews half way up on the other side, and the name Laycock's painted neatly in white on a black door opposite it. Single yellow lines, plus pull-in for a couple of cars near the rear of Laycock's, but both spaces taken. He checked the rest of the street, confirmed it could be entered and exited at both ends, then returned to Guildford Street at the front, swept the street again, the precaution routine rather than necessary, and went into the restaurant.

A small hallway led past the reception desk to the dining rooms on the right. 'Looking for a friend.' He smiled at the receptionist. 'Okay to see if he's here?' He went through. The walls were white and hung with paintings, the floor tiles were blue and white, and the tablecloths were crisp and immaculate.

There were some ten tables in the front section, slightly fewer in another room to the left. A corridor at the rear led to the washrooms and an emergency exit at the end. He confirmed the door opened, checked Wiltshire Street, then closed it. Almost too easy, he thought. He left Laycock's and cleared the area.

The man in the wine bar on the opposite side of the road watched as he left then took the cellphone from his pocket. 'Our fish has bitten,' he informed Vorkov.

Anna Buskova's third meeting of the day was at the Tower Hotel, her fourth, with a software company who wished to become one of her suppliers, was over a light lunch near the National Gallery, and her fifth, which lasted two and half hours, was in Knightsbridge. After it she spent forty minutes in Harrods then took a cab back to Brown's. The message light on her telephone was blinking.

Knew you'd phone, Nik; knew you were okay. She kicked off her shoes and called the concierge's desk. A Mr Kosygin had phoned and left two numbers, she was informed. She told herself that the disappointment was illogical and called the Park Lane Hilton, then the cellphone.

'Alexei, it's Anna. I thought you'd abandoned me.'

'Only just got back to town. I phoned and left a message as soon as I got in.'

'So when are we meeting?'

'Dinner at seven-thirty. Nice little place I've found. Laycock's. It's new so you probably haven't been there. I'll pick you up at seven-fifteen.'

'Look forward to it.'

It was almost six. Nine in the evening in Moscow. Why wasn't it you leaving a message, Nik, why haven't you phoned me? Nothing wrong, is there? She helped herself to a soft drink from the minibar and carried the drink to the shower. Nik's fine, she told herself; her fears were totally irrational. She showered, dried herself briskly, pulled on a dressing-gown and telephoned the number in St Petersburg.

'Hello, Mama, it's Anna.'

'You're well . . . ?' already the first anxiety crept into the woman's voice, the first tell-tale sign.

'I'm fine. London's good. I'm doing a lot of business. How's St Petersburg?'

They talked. Minor things: the weather in the two cities, what her mother had been doing, what Anna was doing that evening and who she was seeing. When Anna was returning to Moscow and when she would visit St Petersburg again. The present she had brought for her mother in Harrods.

'You're okay, Mama?' Anna asked. 'What did you do today? Have you seen your friends, have you taken tea with them as you do?'

'I walked to the cemetery, laid some flowers.'

Anna could imagine her mother, kneeling and talking in her soft lilting voice. 'So what are you doing now?'

'I've had a tea, now I'm going to bed.'

'Take care, Mama. See you soon.'

The vehicle Sherenko chose was a Ford Escort. XR3i so it was fast, with quick acceleration and good road holding if he needed it, and hatchback, so there were no rear passenger doors which someone sitting in the back could use to get out. It was parked on the third floor of a multi-storey in the West End, and the ticket in the glove compartment showed it had been left half an hour before, so whoever had dropped it was probably going to the theatre or a cinema and wouldn't be back till late evening.

He checked round him, forced the thin metal strip between the glass of the driver's window and the rubber mounting, hooked the end round the lock, pulled gently, and opened the door. Then he checked round again, sat in the driver's seat, wrenched the steering wheel violently both ways, and broke the steering lock. Someone walked behind the car. He pretended to ignore them, waited till they had gone, then felt underneath the dashboard and connected the two live wires. The dash lights came on. He touched the starter wire against the live wires and the engine throttled into life. Fifteen minutes later he was in Wiltshire Street.

Someone was holding a drinks party in one of the flats in the mews and the parking spaces behind the restaurant were still occupied. He parked on a single yellow line, three metres from the rear door and facing down the hill, so that the driver's seat was furthest from the door, tilted the front passenger seat forward and rehearsed the procedure.

Enter the restaurant by the front door. Lift Kosygin and Anna, and leave by the rear. Unlock car, Anna into rear seat. Front passenger seat down, Kosygin across it to driver's seat and Sherenko covering both from front passenger seat.

He left Wiltshire Street, checked the front of the restaurant again, and cleared the area.

Vorkov briefed Malenkov at seven.

'Sherenko put his getaway car in place seventeen minutes ago and cleared the area. The boys went in ten minutes ago.'

'What did they use?'

'Half a pound of Semtex under the car, which is more than enough, a mercury tilt switch and a simple arming device. They have also now cleared the area.'

'Tails on Sherenko,' Malenko asked. 'Eyes in the area?'

'No tails. Only one set of eyes, in the wine bar opposite. Sherenko set everything up, Sherenko will be back; therefore we do nothing which might alert him.'

'What about Kincaid?'

'If Sherenko's around, Kincaid can't be far away.'

Malenkov sat back and thought it through. 'Résumé: we want Sherenko and Kincaid out. We're using Kosygin as bait and Anna as their route in to Kosygin. We know Sherenko's and Kincaid's plan: they enter the restaurant, lift Kosygin and Anna, exit to the car they've put at the rear, and *boom*.'

'Correct.'

'So what do we do if something goes wrong?' The question was rhetorical. 'Sherenko and Kincaid are the danger points, but what do we do if we don't remove them tonight?' Malenkov rose, paced the room, eyes locked in concentration, then sat down again. 'We want to remove Sherenko and Kincaid because we fear they might find their way into Moscow USA, even though they're not even aware of it at the moment. If we miss Sherenko and Kincaid, the priority is still to remove that route.'

So . . . Vorkov waited.

'Anna is still one way in.'

'Even though she has no knowledge of her father's connection with Moscow USA, nothing to link her to the place?' Vorkov asked.

'Even though she doesn't know,' Malenkov agreed. 'So no matter what happens tonight, we remove Anna. Even if we miss Sherenko and Kincaid, we take Anna out. Kosygin with her as cover.' He sat forward. 'You have enough back-up?'

'Just.'

'Okay. If it doesn't go down at the restaurant, lift Kosygin and Anna Buskova. Do it quietly, it might be an idea to let them get back to their hotels, so have the boys check the locations first. Then deal with them. Either together, or put them together after. Make it look like an internal mafia job. Kosygin was the target and Anna was someone who got in the way.'

Kincaid checked his watch again. Anna Buskova had been in the hotel over an hour, so perhaps she was dining in tonight, perhaps she was taking room service. Perhaps he himself was in the wrong place. The coffee in front of him was cold and he was aware of the Sig Sauer hanging in the shoulder holster. A black cab stopped and let off two passengers. Nobody to interest him. Another black cab came up the street, from his left. He crossed to the hotel, turned left past the concierge's desk and checked the restaurant, then turned right into the lounge. A pianist was playing, a waiter was serving cocktails, and Anna Buskova was sitting by herself. He turned to leave and brushed against someone coming in. Alexei Kosygin – the recognition was immediate.

So either Buskova, Kosygin and Sherenko were meeting at Brown's, in which case Sherenko wouldn't be far away, or they were meeting somewhere else. The latter, because Sherenko would have built in his cut-outs. His palms were suddenly sweaty. He went outside and saw the cab, door open and engine running. Another cab pulled in and dropped three guests. Kincaid gave the second driver a ten pound note and told him to wait. As he went back into the hotel Anna Buskova and Alexei Kosygin passed him and stepped into the first cab.

Guildford Street was crowded, some of the shops still open and people spilling out of the pub and standing on the pavement, drinks in hand. Sherenko swept the street. There was no sign of tails but if they were professionals he wouldn't spot them anyway. No reason for there to be tails, though, because no one knew where he was or what he was doing.

Most of the tables in Laycock's were already taken. He left Guildford Street and walked to the rear. Wiltshire Street was clear, the sounds of the drinks party still coming from the mews. One of the parking spaces was empty. He considered moving the car then decided against it. It was twenty-eight minutes to eight. He left Wiltshire Street and lost himself in a crowd outside a wine bar on the King's Road, opposite the turning into Guildford Street. The cab pulled into Guildford Street, stopped outside Laycock's, and he saw Kosygin and Anna step out and go inside.

Drive past and stop at the corner, Kincaid told his driver. No Sherenko yet, unless Sherenko was already inside, but Sherenko wouldn't arrive first because that wasn't his style. He lost himself in the general bustle and imprinted the lay-out of the street on his mind: the shops and restaurants, the people outside the pub close to Laycock's and the wine bar opposite. Check the area, he reminded himself; Sherenko was a pro, therefore he'd not just have a front way in, he'd also have a back way out. He left Guildford Street, turned left at the top and left again into Wiltshire Street.

The street was clean, no signs of tails or stake-outs. Sounds of a party from the mews on the right, and a door with the name Laycock's on the left. Ford Escort XR3i parked next to it. He walked down the street, checked the exit at the bottom, then returned to the top of Guildford Street.

Time to do it, Sherenko decided: Kosygin and Anna had been in place fifteen minutes and the traffic was lighter now, therefore wouldn't impede his exfil from the area. He left the wine bar, dodged the traffic on the King's Road, and crossed to Guildford Street.

Kincaid saw him immediately.

Personal, you bastard, not business. You and me and nobody else. Okay, Joshua. Okay, making up for what I couldn't do for Joshua five years ago, even though you don't know Joshua.

Last check around him – Sherenko swept the street. Last confirmation that Kosygin wasn't carrying shadows.

Kincaid left the cover of the bustle outside the wine bar. Last check for any tails, last thoughts on his way out after he'd dealt with Sherenko.

Sherenko reached the restaurant and glanced through the window.

Kincaid crossed the street. Sherenko looking away from him, Sherenko exposed. Everything like ice, everything controlled. Hand toward Sig Sauer. Sherenko about to enter restaurant.

Sherenko sensed the shadow on him and turned, away from the door. His body dropped and coiled, and his hand reached automatically inside his jacket.

Christ – Kincaid realized. 'It's a set-up, Nik.'

'I know. I've just seen it.'

'Leicester Square tube station, thirty minutes.'

'See you there.'

Target at door, the eye in the wine bar opposite whispered in the cellphone; target joined by second man. Going down, Malenkov and Vorkov understood: Sherenko joined by Kincaid. Target not entering, the eye updated them; target walking up street and other man walking down. So what the hell were Sherenko and Kincaid playing at, Malenkov whispered. Anything suspicious? Vorkov asked the eye. Nothing suspicious, he was informed: target and other man are walking slowly. The back-up teams are standing by to take out Anna and Kosygin? Malenkov asked. Standing by, Vorkov confirmed.

Kincaid reached the King's Road and turned left, waved down a cab and took it to Knightsbridge underground station, took the tube and began the switches.

. . . Everything logical, everything in place and pointing to Sherenko: the bank account, the airline tickets, Sherenko even seen on his way in from Sheremetyevo, which was a bonus for whoever had set it up but which was also one of the give-aways.

Because the Vienna bank slip and the airline ticket counterfoils had been found in Sherenko's apartment before they'd spotted Sherenko on his way in from the airport. Which they'd all failed to see, himself included, because they were all so uptight after the carnage outside Sherenko's apartment and the attack on himself. Plus Sherenko had called Gerasimov immediately after the first attack. Get Kincaid off the streets, Sherenko had told Gerasimov; get him under cover in case it's related to ConTex and they go for him as well. Except the other evidence, the other circumstantial stuff, had been so strong they'd forgotten about Sherenko's warning or thought it was Sherenko setting up a cover for himself. And the robbery in the Arbat, which Igor Lukyanov had told him about. Someone answering Sherenko's description – more or less – and acting like an Alpha man, except why should Sherenko risk a robbery if he'd already heisted all or part of the ConTex money? But what the hell were you doing in the missing hours, Nik? How the hell did someone fix it for rounds from your weapon to be found in the bodies of two mafia stiffs suddenly and miraculously alleged to be responsible for the original ConTex heist . . .

Sherenko turned right at the top of the street, cut right then left, waved down a cab and checked if anyone or any vehicle followed. Gave the driver one location then told him to stop at another. Disappeared into the underground and continued the switches.

. . . Are you a business colleague of Miss Buskova, the hotel had asked. Miss Buskova can be contacted at Laycock's restaurant at seven-thirty. Except why should Anna leave such a message, because Anna was efficient, therefore the first thing she would have done in London would have been to rent a cellphone, therefore there was no need for her to leave the name of the restaurant where she would be that night or the time she would be there. Plus the set-up at the restaurant: Kosygin and Anna, front door in and back door out. The get-away car as he had left it, no shadows in the street and no smell of stake-outs in the air. All too neat, all too easy . . .

Alexei was looking nervous, Anna thought; Alexei wasn't his normal confident self. He was trying, of course, but it wasn't working and the fact that he was trying made it even more obvious. Twice already she had asked him about it; the first time he had said there was nothing wrong, the second time he had corrected himself and admitted it was business. Except Alexei had never allowed business matters to impinge upon his state of mind in the past. So what is it, Alexei? Why do you keep looking towards the door?

The entrances to Leicester Square underground station were busy. Sherenko saw Kincaid on the other side of the road, almost lost in the crowd. He turned back up Charing Cross Road, Kincaid covering him and trying to check for a tail. Kincaid passed him, still on the other side of the road, and turned right then sharp right again, into an alleyway, and left at the end. Sherenko checked for shadows, crossed the road and walked up the left pavement, in the direction Kincaid had taken but one street over. Kincaid was waiting a hundred yards up on the right. No obvious tails, no legmen or cars or motor bikes, but in a busy area like the West End they'd be difficult to spot.

The pub was on the right. Sherenko walked in. The interior was cavernous and echoing with music, and most of the drinkers were young, few older than their mid-twenties. Sherenko stood at the bar and asked for a Guinness. Kincaid passed him without speaking and checked the back door out. No tails coming in behind him, Sherenko noted; no one pussy-footing around outside. He left the bar and took a table in the front of the two rooms, away from the door. Kincaid came back in, bought a bitter, and joined him, sat so that Sherenko could observe the entrance at the front and he himself the exit at the rear.

'So what are you doing in London, Jack?'

'Looking for you, Nik.'

Sherenko's face showed no reaction. 'What happened in Moscow?'

'After the shooting outside your apartment they came for me. I assumed it was you. Or at least that you were behind it.'

'I tried to warn you, I told Gerasimov to pull you off the streets.'

'I know. It got lost given everything else that was running.' He sipped the beer. 'So what are you doing in London?'

'Trying to get to Kosygin.'

'Why?'

'Because I was being set up and I assumed he was behind it.'
They went into details.

'Two questions, Nik. Where were you all that time?'

Sherenko told him about Anna.

'And why were you coming in from Sheremetyevo?'

'Anna was flying to London. I took her to the airport.'

'Why didn't you tell me, Nik? Why didn't you explain when
you asked me to cover you?'

Sherenko shrugged. The old Sherenko shrug, Kincaid thought.
'I guess because none of us knew at the time what else was going
down.'

Any sign of the targets? Vorkov requested the eye. No sign,
the stake-out updated him. Back-up still on readiness to take out
Anna Buskova and Kosygin? Malenkov asked again. Back-up
standing by, Vorkov confirmed.

Sherenko checked there was nothing and no one behind Kincaid. 'So you thought you could get to me through Kosygin, and
you could get to Kosygin through Anna?'

'Something like that. Same as you, I assume.'

'Something like that. What about this evening? Why were
you outside Laycock's?'

'I tailed Anna. Kosygin picked her up at her hotel. And you?'

'There was a message at reception, apparently from Anna to
any business contact who called, giving the time and location if
anyone wanted to get in touch.'

'Sounds implausible.'

'Precisely,' Sherenko agreed.

'Which is why you didn't go in.'

'Except I almost saw it too late.' The music seemed louder;
they changed tables, away from the speakers. 'Why did you say
it was a set-up?'

Kincaid checked behind and around Sherenko. 'Everything was
suddenly too easy, just like the first Kosygin phone call. I assume
the Escort was yours.'

'I put it there an hour before, which is what they assume I'd
do. They tell me where Kosygin will be. I check it out, look for

the back door, and place the getaway wheels. I go in, lift Kosygin, and take him out the back.'

'Plus me,' Kincaid suggested.

Sherenko sipped the Guinness. 'So the two of us. We lift Kosygin and leave through the back. The car wired for a bomb, probably tilt device. Easy to put in place, easy to spot if you're looking for it, but we're not, because we think nobody else knows we're there and we're in a hurry.'

'Sounds about right,' Kincaid agreed.

Sherenko laughed. 'You want to check it out?'

Kincaid shook his head. 'What about the car?'

Do we leave it, because that's the sensible thing to do, because that says we didn't know they'd wired it, therefore we don't tell them we know they're on to us. Except what happens when someone moves it? We want that on our hands?

They left the pub. Sherenko used a pay phone, taking care not to leave his prints and disguising his voice, and called 999. So the three of them in the car, they agreed, the two of them plus Kosygin. The car goes boom, and somebody's problems are solved in one go. Kincaid saw the moment the colour drained from Sherenko's face.

'It wouldn't have been three of us.' Sherenko's features were death white. 'It would have been four.'

Anna sipped the champagne and looked across the table. Alexei was still looking nervous, still glancing at the door. What is it, Alexei, what's running? The sirens split the air. She looked through the window, and saw the police cars and the white Range Rovers with blue lights flashing from them. A police Rover screeched to a halt outside and a uniformed inspector came in and asked for the manager, more police following him. A suspect car had been found in the street at the rear – the inspector addressed them all, the manager at his side. Premises in the immediate vicinity were being cleared as a precaution. A bomb – Anna heard someone muttering. The police wouldn't be clearing the area if it was merely a suspect vehicle. Bloody IRA. What is it, Alexei, why do you look as if you've seen a ghost?

'Drink back at my hotel?' Kosygin suggested. His face was ashen and he chewed nervously at his upper lip.

'Had enough,' she lied. 'Early start in the morning, got some business before the flight. I'll get a cab back to Brown's.'

Police and emergency services in the target area, the eye informed Vorkov; the police are clearing the premises including Laycock's. There's a suggestion that a suspect vehicle has been found in the street at the rear.

'How far are the back-up teams from Kosygin and Buskova?' Malenkov asked.

'Assuming Kosygin and Buskova return to their separate hotels, and assuming they stay there, we could have them covered in five minutes.'

'Do it,' Malenkov ordered.

The cab stopped outside the Albemarle Street entrance to the hotel. Anna paid the driver and went inside. Kosygin's cab pulled in to the Park Lane Hilton. He paid the driver and hurried inside. The men left the Ford Granada and followed him in. Anna collected the room key from the concierge's desk, considered going to the bar for a drink, decided against it and walked to the lift. The second Granada car turned left off Park Lane into Piccadilly. The lights in front of them changed to red; the driver considered jumping them and decided against it.

The lift door opened. Anna stepped in and pressed the button for the fourth floor.

The traffic lights changed and the Granada accelerated through and swung left. 'Stop at the Dover Street door,' the *komandir* instructed the driver. 'You two go in that way,' he ordered the men in the rear seat. 'Give it twenty seconds between you. I'll go in the front, so allow me a minute to get round the block. If we can, we bring her out to the car; if not we leave her in her room.' The car stopped and he slid out.

Anna left the lift, went through the doors to the corridor at the front of the hotel, and turned diagonally left to Room 220. Why did Alexei react the way he did when the police cleared the restaurant because of a suspect car at the back? She slid the key into the lock. Something to do with Moscow – the apprehension seeped into her; something to do with the fact that Nik had been out of contact – the fear crept upon her like a fog. She turned the key, sensed the shadow behind her and felt the hand over her mouth. The terror bit into her then she saw the face.

What the hell is it, Nik? What the hell are you doing?

Sherenko put a finger to his lips.

She fought against the fear. I understand – she nodded. What is it Nik, what's going on?

It's okay – Sherenko mouthed.

Okay – Anna nodded again.

Sherenko took the hand from her mouth. Anna almost collapsed, then saw the second man. Christ, she thought, they were both carrying guns. This isn't London, this is Moscow. The door was slightly open. Sherenko crashed it back against the wall in case someone was behind it, and Kincaid burst past him, Sig Sauer in front of him in the combat position, then cleared the door space for Sherenko to enter behind him, sweeping the room then moving quickly to check the bathroom.

What is this, Nik – Anna was too frightened to speak. What are you playing at?

Sherenko stepped outside and put an arm round her, Kincaid checking the corridor. Why are we having this conversation in the corridor – she looked at him. Because the room might be bugged, she understood. Christ, this really was Moscow not London. 'No time to explain.' Sherenko told her. 'Collect what you need, but make it fast.'

The *komandir* entered the hotel. The key to Room 220 was missing from the pigeon holes at the rear of the concierge's desk, therefore the target was in her room. In front of him the first of the no-necks entered by the Dover Street door, walked through and went to the lift.

Anna pulled a travel bag from the wardrobe and began to pack it. What's the hurry, Nik; what's the rush? Don't ask, she told herself, just pack.

The second no-neck entered by the Dover Street entrance and took the stairs.

Anna took the photograph from the bedside table and put it in the bag, put in a handful of other personal items, put in her laptop. Money, passport, credit cards? Already got them, she confirmed. Her father's letter – the last one he had written to her – where was it? She checked she had it, stuffed in some

246

more clothes and closed the bag. Ready, she nodded at Sherenko. Somebody had gone for her and Alexei at the restaurant – the fear and the cold and the panic hit her. That was what the car bomb behind the restaurant had been about. And whoever it was would come after her again.

The *komandir* walked down the hallway and took the stairs.

Kincaid checked the corridor. Clear – his nod began to confirm. Someone coming up the lift – the look changed. Sherenko pulled Anna out of the room, hurried her left along the corridor and through the glass fire door fifteen metres away, Kincaid covering them. Christ, someone was coming up the stairs as well. Kincaid backed through the fire door and closed it behind him.

The lift stopped and the first no-neck stepped out, the second melting from the main stairs and the team leader three seconds behind.

Just beyond the fire-door was a set of stairs, one flight leading down and the other up. Sherenko turned right, up the stairs, Anna tight behind him and Kincaid behind her. What are you doing, Nik – Anna looked at him. Why are we going up not down?

The *komandir* checked the room numbers, eased open the lock of 220 and slid in, the other two moving fast past him. *Chert* – he swore. Items on the bed and clothes on the floor, so someone leaving in a hurry, but the target must only just have arrived. 'Target not in room but might be leaving,' he told the driver on the Motorola. 'Target not exited yet,' the driver informed him. The target couldn't have used the main stairs or the lift – the team leader was thinking automatically now, therefore there must be another set of stairs. You check that way – he ordered the first gunman to go right; you the other – he ordered the second left. 'We've got the back door covered, I'll take the front.'

Sherenko bundled Anna up the stairs and into a corridor leading toward the rear of the hotel.

The first gunman pushed his way through the glass door and saw the stairs, one set going up and another going down. Not the sort guests would use. He indicated to the team leader and took the stairs down.

Sherenko pulled Anna along the corridor. The passageway was

narrow, with a dog-leg, and not as well decorated as the corridor at the front of the hotel. Staff quarters, he had assumed when he had recce'd the hotel the previous morning.

Same this end, the second no-neck indicated. The team leader nodded and ran down the main guest stairs to the foyer.

Sherenko dog-legged again, hurried another ten metres, and stopped at a door on to the well-decorated corridor serving the guest rooms at the rear of Brown's.

No sign of the target – the team leader saw the driver shake his head at the Dover Street door. No sign of the target on the stairs down from the end of the corridor – the first gunman appeared.

Sherenko paused and checked the rear corridor. The guest lift was past two bedrooms to the right. He checked the corridor again, turned left and called the service lift. Go – he nodded and pulled the doors open, pushed Anna in and stepped in behind her, Kincaid in last.

The hotel was in two sections, the team leader thought, formal guest stairs and lift by Dover Street entrance, but the target hadn't left that way, and couldn't have left by the Albemarle Street entrance because to do so she would have passed them on the stairs or the lift. Therefore the target was still somewhere in the hotel. Cover the front, he told one man; you and I check the rear, he told the second.

The service lift bumped to a halt in the basement. Sherenko pulled the doors open. The corridor outside was tiled white and the hotel kitchens were in front of them. They turned right and walked twenty metres to the staff changing room, took three coats, then crossed the corridor, went through one door leading toward the rear of the hotel, walked another five metres, clicked open the lock on the service door, and stepped into the area used for refuse collection outside.

'Any movement?' the team leader checked with the driver on the Motorola. 'Nothing.' The driver left the pavement and stood inside the doorway.

Twenty metres from him the three figures emerged from the basement steps and strolled apparently casually down the street.

*   *   *

248

Three hundred yards from the hotel, they picked up a black cab and took it north in case whoever was looking for them traced the driver and established their approximate destination, then they split into two groups, Sherenko going with Anna, and took a series of cabs and underground trains south and west to Hammersmith.

'What the hell's happening?' Anna asked. 'What the hell is this all about?'

'Later,' Sherenko told her.

Hammersmith station was quiet; Sherenko and Anna took the steps at one end of the platform and Kincaid the steps at the other end. The shopping mall above the platforms was empty, the shops closed and shuttered. They left the station and cut south towards the river. What's the address? Kincaid asked. Sherenko told him. Over the bridge and third on the left.

'Official or unofficial,' Kincaid asked.

'Unofficial.'

The Thames was ebbing, laughter and conversation drifting from the pubs along the river, and rowers gliding like fireflies over the water. Kincaid crossed, disappeared again, and waited. Five minutes later he saw them – two figures, one male, one female. No tails. He waited till they had cleared him, walked quickly to the street on which the safe house was situated, and waited another ten minutes before he saw Sherenko and Anna approach. Still no tails, but at this stage tails would be screwing themselves with caution.

'Stay with Jack,' Sherenko told Anna. 'Give me ten minutes,' he told Kincaid. 'Two rings, three, then one.'

The light was gone now and the street lamps were beginning to glow. He unlocked the door and stepped inside. Took out the Sig Sauer. The specks of dust he had placed on the carpet against which the door to the safe house would open were still in place. He unlocked the door, went up the stairs, and confirmed the apartment was clean. The doorbell rang twice, three times, then once. Clear, he told Anna and Kincaid as he let them in.

'So . . .' Anna sat on the sofa and waited. Her hands had begun to shake, and she clasped her fingers tight to control them.

Sherenko poured them each a large malt, then they told her.

The ConTex investigation and the assassination attempts on them in Moscow; the alleged bank account in Austria, the airline tickets and the computer confirmation that Sherenko had made the trip; the tails in London and the car bomb at Laycock's two hours ago. How and why they had both come to London.

The fear seeped back into Anna. I don't believe this, she thought; I can't believe this. This sort of thing happened in the old days, this sort of thing happens in the new Moscow, but not to people like me. She tried to calm herself, tried to fight the fear. 'Originally you thought Alexei was responsible for the attacks on you because of the ConTex money,' she asked.

'Correct.'

'Now you say that Alexei was used to set you up, and that something else and someone else was behind everything.'

'Correct again.'

'Why?'

'No idea.'

The fear grew in her again. I don't believe this is happening to me – the thought cut like an ice pick through her brain again: I can't believe this is happening to me.

'You're also saying that the decision to kill you both was made only after you asked for the file on Yuri. So the reason why someone wants you removed is connected to Yuri.'

'So it would seem.'

'Why kill me as well, though?' The fear gripped her like a vice. 'I don't know anything, don't have any connections with anything.' Hold me, Nikolai Alexandrovich, she wanted to say; pull me back from wherever it is that I am sinking. Except there's something I have to ask you first; something I don't want to ask you.

'Tell us about Yuri,' Sherenko asked her.

'I told you in Moscow.'

'Tell Jack.'

'Not now, Nik.' Anna's eyes were rimmed with red and the question thumped in her head. 'Something I have to ask.' She turned to Kincaid. 'You came to London because you thought Nik had set you up for the assassination attempt in Moscow?'

'Yes.'

She locked her eyes on Sherenko. 'What about you? Did you also think I'd set you up?'

What are you going to say, Nik? What are you going to tell her?

'You mean that during the time I was out of circulation in Moscow I was with you, therefore that I thought you were part of it,' he asked.

'Yes.' Anna's eyes were still locked on his.

'And that I thought you were therefore the way into Kosygin, just as Jack thought Kosygin was the way into me?'

'Yes.'

Tell her what you have to, because nothing else counts.

'Yes.' He wanted to lower his eyes but couldn't. 'At one stage that's what I thought.'

Bastard, she wanted to scream at him. After what we did together in Moscow. After the way I worried about you. 'Nice friends, heh.' The cold trespassed deeper into her body and her soul. 'So you also assumed that everything that happened between us in Moscow was part of it?'

'Perhaps,' he conceded.

She locked tight with the cold and the fear. 'Now you're saying that another friend, Alexei, set me up tonight.'

'I'm saying that Alexei used you to allow me to get to him.'

'But you're now saying that someone also set Alexei up. That we were all going to be blown up.'

'Yes.'

How could she believe the rest of his story? Anna asked. There was a message at hotel reception informing business callers where she could be contacted after seven-thirty, Sherenko told her. If she wanted she could check herself; call reception in the morning and ask to speak to whoever was on duty yesterday. And if she hadn't left it, then someone else had.

Anna stared at him bleakly. 'I'm tired, Nik. I want to sleep.'

She left them and went to the bathroom. When she came back she wrapped a blanket around herself and curled up on the sofa.

The night was grey rather than black. She was standing at the grave, the August heat on her back and her father's body cold in the mother earth. She was driving back from Sheremetyevo in

Nik's car and turning into the road where Nik lived; was parking the BMW, crossing the pavement, and hearing the first car coming in, then the second. Was in the restaurant in London, the explosion deafening her and the shock waves and the flames engulfing her even though she knew it was illogical that she should be aware of them, because by that point she was already dead. She was standing again at her father's grave, the snow upon her shoulders and the last letter he had written to her open in her hands.

Sherenko and Kincaid were on the pull-down bed, their breathing shallow and the light splintered across them. She left the sofa, shook Kincaid's shoulder, and stepped back slightly because she was unsure how he would react; saw the way his eyes flicked to her and realized that neither of them were sleeping. Kincaid rolled off the bed, wrapped the blanket round him, took her place on the sofa, and Anna slid into the warmth he had left.

'Hold me tight, Nikolai Alexandrovich.'

They rose at six. By six-fifteen each of them had showered and dressed, and Sherenko had made fresh coffee.

'You asked about Yuri Dushkin.' Anna wrapped her fingers around the mug. The cold had gone but the fear still ate into her. 'Yuri works in antiques and art, mainly Russian or coming out of Russia, so he comes to Moscow regularly. He doesn't work for himself. He's an intermediary for someone. Two days ago a Chagall fetched over two million pounds at auction here in London. Yuri was the front man for the deal.

'Who does he work for?' Sherenko asked.

'Because whoever he works for are the people who are trying to kill us?'

'If we're right and Yuri is the reason someone is after us.'

'Yuri doesn't know who he works for. He goes through a middleman, an intermediary.'

Kincaid poured her another mug. 'How'd you know?'

'The evening after the sale Yuri and I went for dinner. Alexei was supposed to be there but didn't make it. Someone phoned halfway through dinner. Whoever Yuri answers to.'

'You don't know who Yuri was speaking to?'

'No.'

'But?'

'One of the people above the middleman was at the auction.'

How can you say this – it was in the sharpness of Sherenko's look.

'There was a problem at the auction, the middleman knew about it.'

'How do you know the middleman wasn't at the sale?'

'Yuri would have seen him.'

It was eight in the morning. Sherenko went to a supermarket off Hammersmith Broadway, on the north side of the river, Kincaid covering him for tails, and bought bacon, eggs and bread. Eat now, stock up now, because you don't know when you'll next have time. Anna made fresh coffee, Kincaid cooking the breakfast, then they sat round the table again.

'So where does this leave us?' Anna asked.

'Where it always left us.' Sherenko spoke quietly.

'Where's that?'

'No matter what happens, we're dead.'

'Literally or metaphorically?' Anna asked.

'Both.'

Her face paled. 'You're not joking.'

'No, I'm not joking.'

She turned to Kincaid and saw the grimness mirrored in his face. 'So what are we going to do about it?'

'*We* . . . ?' Kincaid asked.

'*We*, Jack. I was also supposed to be in the car last night. As far as whoever's trying to kill us is concerned, I may not be important, but I am expendable.'

'So we go after them.' It was Sherenko.

Because it's the game . . . Because in Moscow we thought we were the hunters, but all the time we were the hunted . . . Because now the opposition still thinks it is the hunter, but in fact we are . . . So the game has changed . . .

Anna's face was still pale. 'But no matter what we do, you're still saying that at the end we're dead?'

'Yes,' Sherenko told her.

'Why?'

'Because that's the game.'

She shook her head in disbelief. 'Where do we start?'

'With Yuri.'

This I don't believe – the thought still flowed like electricity through her mind. This I cannot believe. Okay, in Moscow we all played games, in Moscow the mafia killed people. But this game is different. 'What about Alexei?' she asked.

'What about Alexei?' Sherenko came back at her.

'You say he set you up, so he must know who ordered or paid or persuaded him to do that.'

'I imagine that by now Alexei's met his maker.'

'Why?' She knew what Sherenko was going to say and answered her own question. 'Because of what or who he knows.'

'Where do we start?' she asked.

'Yuri's our way in. Yuri's in America, so it has to be America,' Kincaid suggested.

They finished eating and cleared the table. So how did they get through Yuri to his controller – Sherenko led the discussion. How did they get to whoever was behind Yuri's cut-out. How did they establish Yuri's movements in the past, which might give a clue to the future, without whoever was trying to kill them knowing?

Anna looked at them both. 'That may not be a problem.'

As long as they were lucky.

'Why not?'

She told them.

Sherenko sat forward. 'One other thing. Money. I have under ten thousand dollars left.' Left from what he didn't say. 'That won't be enough.'

'That may not be a problem either,' Kincaid told him. As long as the gods were with them and the cut-out, or his masters, had been too busy to undo what he or they had set up.

They made fresh coffee and ran through the next twenty-four hours.

'You're sure?' Anna asked.

'About what?'

'That someone in Moscow is setting all this up, involving the security and intelligence services, just to protect an antique and art scam? Because that's what we're saying.'

'How much did the Chagall go for yesterday?' Sherenko asked her.

'Two million three hundred thousand pounds sterling.'

Three and three quarter million dollars on one scam, Kincaid's look said. So why do they need another reason?

Los Angeles was hot and sticky. Yuri Dushkin checked out of his hotel and settled back in the cab. With him he carried his travel bag and a briefcase containing his TravelMate 5000. His cellphone was in the inner pocket of his jacket.

Dushkin had spent the last two days visiting some of the dealers with whom he did business on the West Coast. Most of the items he had sold in that period were one-offs: a set of Shostakovich letters, various smaller oils, some small but exquisite imperial porcelain pieces, various Fabergé items including an imperial photo frame, a tie-pin and a set of cufflinks. Some malachite pieces and a number of smaller icons. Plus the rest: a tenth-century Byzantine cross, a miniature in the manner of Grigori Musikiysky, a smaller Repin. Not as spectacular as the Chagall, or what he would set in motion this morning, but four hundred thousand dollars on purchases made in Russia for fifty thousand was more than most businesses would have considered satisfactory.

The bank was off Rodeo Drive. He stepped into the air conditioning, went to the enquiry desk, and informed the clerk he wished to access a safety deposit box. Ninety seconds later he was escorted to the office of a deputy manager and had his identity and authorization confirmed, then he followed the deputy manager through the security checks, signed the relevant authorizations, waited while the manager opened the first lock then retired, opened the second himself, removed the single package the courier had hand-carried from Europe, locked and returned the box, and passed back through the security systems.

Thirty minutes later he was at the airport.

Of the two calls he made on his cellphone in the next ten minutes, the first was to Vorkov in London, informing him he had made the pick-up. When he tried the second number it was engaged. Dushkin checked the flight boards and tried again.

Area code 208 followed by the local prefix 882 then the standard four digits.

The airport was busy, minor delays on certain incoming flights, though his outgoing flight, and the connection at Portland, were on time. Two and a half hours later he arrived at his destination. The airport was small and single storey: check-in counter at one end, and the bathrooms, coffee and candy machines, pay phones and mail box at the other.

Sobolev was waiting.

Yevgeni Sobolev was mid-fifties and dressed like the university professor he was. After the authorities had granted him and his wife permission to leave the USSR in the late 1970s, Sobolev had taught economics at the University of Sussex, in England, before moving to the USA. In their new home the Sobolevs had settled easily and quickly; Sobolev himself had established a professional reputation at the university, and his wife had built up new circles of friends. Which was no more than those who had recruited and sent him had expected.

Sobolev's Landcruiser was in the parking lot outside. They left the airport and turned east through the grain fields. Four miles on they hit the shopping mall and the strip of motels and fast food restaurants, came off Pullman Drive, then passed the used car lots and came to 3rd Street; slowed at the lights then turned into Jackson Street, past the offices of the local *Daily News*. As they left town the grain silos glistened in the heat to their right, and the tarmac of the road to Genesee shimmered in a heat haze in front of them.

Two miles past the city limit they cut right, up a track, towards the white-painted wooden farmhouse at the end. The fence to the right was broken and the farmhouse beyond it was deserted.

'Family called Sherman used to live there,' Sobolev told Dushkin. 'Good couple, nice daughter. Bank foreclosed on them four years back.'

10

The security meeting began at seven, on the upper floor at New Scotland Yard. Sheila Harrington declined coffee and brought the meeting to order. 'Perhaps you could update us . . .' It was to the Special Branch Commander.

No interruptions, Elwood had ordered; no telephone calls unless they were both relevant and important. 'We still have no information on the whereabouts of Sherenko and Kincaid. We know that as of two nights ago Kincaid was in London; we do not know if he is now, or whether Sherenko has joined him.' He moved to the next item. 'The car bomb behind Laycock's restaurant yesterday evening. The explosive used was Semtex, tilt device for when the car was driven away. The device was neutralized following a 999 call. The call was made from a public kiosk in the West End. The voice was disguised and the handset of the phone from which the call was made was clean of fingerprints.'

The American chief of station raised his hand. 'What has the Laycock's restaurant bomb to do with why we're here this morning?'

'Present in Laycock's yesterday evening was a Russian, Alexei Kosygin. According to Moscow, Kosygin is linked to the Russian mafia. According to immigration records, he entered Britain on a valid business visa and is due to leave this morning. He has been staying at the Park Lane Hilton. As of last night, Kosygin is missing.'

He shuffled his file slightly. 'Kosygin was at Laycock's in the company of a woman. Telephone calls listed to Kosygin's room at the Hilton included a call to Brown's Hotel. The guest list at

Brown's includes a Russian, Anna Buskova. As of last night Miss Buskova is also missing.'

'You're suggesting there's a connection with Sherenko and Kincaid?' It was the American CoS again.

The SB commander was careful in his answer. 'I'm suggesting we look at that possibility.'

'But do we have any evidence of such a connection?' The Russian *rezident*.

'Not at present.'

Ed Miller sat forward, elbows on the table. 'Except it would seem one hell of coincidence if there wasn't,' he suggested quietly.

One of the telephones rang. Elwood picked it up, snapped his name, listened attentively, then replaced it. 'We've just found Kosygin. He's dead. Every indication he was executed. Hands bound behind back, tape over mouth, and single shot in the back of the head. No money or credit cards taken.'

'Where?'

'The river.'

'What about Anna Buskova?' Miller asked.

Elwood shook his head.

'Interesting . . .' It was Harrington, almost in a whisper. More a thought which had found its way out than a statement to be heard and acted upon.

'Why interesting?' Malenkov asked her.

'Kosygin and Buskova appear to be connected. They both disappear, then Kosygin pops up dead and we ask why Anna Buskova didn't pop up with him.'

So . . .

'We're assuming that Anna Buskova was also a victim, but suppose she wasn't?'

The Organised Crime commander leaned forward. 'What else could she have been?'

'Suppose she was bait,' Harrington told him.

'For whom?' Miller asked.

'Kosygin.'

'On whose behalf?'

'Try Sherenko and Kincaid.'

'Sherenko and Kincaid working for whom?' Malenkov.

'Another mafia faction. Which was suggested on the original intelligence reports.'

Miller glanced at the clock on the wall. Time to catch a plane, the movement said. The Russian *rezident* and the American CoS to act as liaison points with the police, they agreed; names and details circulated to all points of exit from the country, including main line stations with international connections and the Eurostar section at Waterloo. Photographs of Sherenko and Kincaid as well, plus Anna Buskova when the FSB came up with one.

Kincaid left the safe house at fifteen minutes to ten. If he tried to phone, the line would probably be engaged, Anna had warned him.

The room was quiet, the first sun slanting through the window. Anna placed the laptop on the kitchen table, pulled the telephone lead from the wall socket, and replaced it with the computer lead. Sherenko crossed the room and looked over her shoulder.

'We have to get in and out fast.' Anna glanced up at him. 'The one thing we don't want is for Yuri to dial up his computer line and find it's engaged.' She switched on the Toshiba and clicked on the modem icon. 'The first problem is finding the telephone number Yuri uses for his computer.' She keyed in Dushkin's telephone number in Berlin and instructed the Toshiba to dial up an ongoing sequence to scan telephone numbers close to Dushkin's phone number. The computer dialled up the first number, she heard the hello as someone answered. and the computer dialled up the second. She heard the ringing sound, then the almost grating sound as the modems synchronized, and the number appeared on the screen. 'Modem,' she told Sherenko. Five minutes and twenty-three seconds later the Toshiba prompted her that the task was complete.

There were sixteen phone numbers with modems. She highlighted the number closest to Dushkin's telephone number, clicked on it, and shook her head. 'Dial-in travel service,' she told Sherenko. She highlighted and clicked on the next, then the next. 'Internet service numbers.' She highlighted and clicked on the next. 'Looks good. We might have it.' The words *system connection established* flashed on the screen, then the log-in prompt. 'Firewall,' Anna told Sherenko. 'Security barrier to try to stop us getting in.'

Underneath the words were ten dashes. 'Careless, Yuri . . .' it was little more than a whisper to herself.

'Why?' Sherenko leaned forward slightly.

'Because the number of dashes gives me the maximum number of characters in the password.'

She reduced the screen, went into her own hard disk, called up the password cracker that she had acquired from a computer nerd in Syracuse via a contact in Moscow, and opened it up. 'Could take time,' she told Sherenko. 'There's a system now which worms its way through the firewall and comes up with the password the target is using. Pity I don't have it.' She connected the breaker to enable it to network, highlighted the external hard disc icon, instructed the breaker to run an alpha-numeric sequence up to ten characters, and hit return.

'The breaker will try a sequence of passwords and keep re-dialling until it cracks the right one.'

'How long?' Sherenko asked.

'How long is a piece of string?'

She began making the coffee, glancing across occasionally at the screen, and saw the moment it flashed *connected*. 'We're in,' she told Sherenko. 'You make the coffee.' She reduced the screen again and went back into the password breaker. The words *Trial 1* and *Master* were listed at the top of the screen. She went into her C drive, labelled Dushkin's hard drive F, double-clicked on F, opened up Dushkin's hard drive, and began trawling.

'This isn't what we want.' It was the whisper again. She checked for hidden files, then went back to the root directory. 'Nice,' Sherenko heard her say.

He gave her the coffee. 'What's nice?'

'Yuri's split his hard drive.'

She labelled Dushkin's D drive to her G and double clicked. *Please enter password*, the screen requested her. 'Getting there . . .' She smiled at Sherenko, and went back into the breaker sequence. *Trial 2. Margarita*, the screen showed seventeen minutes later. 'Okay.' The excitement was in her voice now. 'We've got a pattern.'

Sherenko picked up on it. *'The Master and Margarita.'*

The novel by Bulgakov.

So future passwords would almost certainly refer to the book, because passwords were always in a logical sequence so that users could remember them.

Anna entered *Margarita*.

'We're in,' she told Sherenko and checked the time. 'Don't want Yuri to call in and find the line engaged,' she reminded him. She stored the material on her own hard drive without even looking at it, then exited the databases and checked whether Dushkin had a log-in file. The time and duration of her access was logged. She erased the file dated that day and closed out.

If Langley had done its homework then Langley might have remembered the account, Kincaid was aware. And if they did, then Langley might have informed Riverside and the gorillas might have been waiting for him. Except the account was one of many Kincaid had set up to confuse those who might be trying to trace how and where he might be moving that part of the Agency's money. Tucked away, nice and quiet. And when he'd left the Agency he'd kept it running. Forgotten to mention it to anyone at Langley, of course. Used it a few times when he'd gone private, even after Jameson had recruited him into ISS. Different name. Not that the name mattered. The only things that mattered were the codes and numbers for the account.

Kincaid stepped from the cab and walked up the street. Eight minutes later he sat in the deputy manager's office and detailed his instructions. Two hundred thousand dollars to be transferred from a specified bank account in Vienna to the account in London, via a series of cut-outs including Jersey and Liechtenstein. As long as the opposition hadn't removed the money from the account they'd used to set up Sherenko; and if they had he'd simply bluff his way out.

Eighteen minutes later $200,000 was assigned to the account in London, thirteen minutes after that Kincaid left the bank with $175,000 stacked neatly in an unobtrusive briefcase. Fifty-seven minutes after that, having run the standard checks for tails and stake-outs, he was in the kitchen of the safe house in Hammersmith.

Anna was bent over the computer, Sherenko watching her.

'Accessing Dushkin's cellphone records,' she told Kincaid. 'He's never off his cellphone. Uses it everywhere he goes.'

Kincaid nodded. 'How are you getting in?'

'Through the back door.'

When engineers set up mainframe systems like the telephone company's, she explained, they built in firewalls at the front, but left a back door in case they needed to get back in to adjust or correct the system. Password-protected, but phone companies were favourite targets for geeks. So she'd got in via a computer geek in Moscow to another in Berlin. Handles only, no real names. Covered herself, and the reason she wanted to access the phone company, by explaining that she'd run up a big bill and wanted to reduce it. Tough luck, the geek had told her; once she was inside the data was *read only*, therefore she couldn't change anything. Had given her the number and password anyway.

'I'm in.'

She keyed in Dushkin's account number, obtained from his own computerized files, and snapped her fingers.

'Yuri Dushkin's cellphone charges for as long back as you want.'

An hour later they left the safe house. Kincaid first, Sherenko and Anna ten minutes after him. On the north side of Hammersmith Bridge Sherenko and Anna picked up a cab to the station at Clapham Junction, Kincaid confirming there were no tails on them then doing the same. If the watchers were looking for them, they would be at exit points from the UK, including the Eurostar terminal at Waterloo. And at Waterloo the watchers might drift, take a coffee while someone else took their place, might go on to the main concourse. Leave from a main line station like Waterloo, therefore, and there was a risk. Pick up a train outside London, however, by which they meant outside the main London terminals, and you were clear. At least for the moment.

At Clapham Junction they bought tickets to Exeter, in the

West Country, got off at Woking, where the lines split, bought new tickets, took the service via Southampton to Weymouth, and changed at Brockenhurst, in the middle of the New Forest, for the branch line to Lymington, on the south coast. When they arrived it was late afternoon. The jetties on the river were busy with pleasure craft and spectators, the yacht halyards jangled in the breeze, and the town itself was crowded with tourists. At a chandler's shop they bought a set of charts, plus navy blue slacks for Anna, jeans for themselves, casual yachting tops and Henri Lloyd deck shoes, changing in the toilets near the main jetty.

The marina was downriver, to their right. Anna stayed at the jetty, and Sherenko and Kincaid walked to it. The pontoons stretched like fingers into the water, security cameras scanned the entire area, and there was a guard on the gate.

Sherenko and Kincaid walked confidently, as if they belonged, each looking for the same thing. A motor boat that hadn't been used for a few days. As far from the offices as possible, not near the fuel jetty, and with no one taking a drink or doing maintenance on any boats near it. Twin-engined for reliability. Fuelled up, which they wouldn't know till they got on board. And fast.

The Sunseeker Portofino 400 was moored at the end pontoon. It was forty feet long and sleek, white body with dark blue flash along the sides. Large cockpit, dinghy with outboard hanging on a davit at the stern, and shore power leads plugged in, so the battery was charged. Two Mercruiser V8 outdrives, top speed of 36 knots and a cruising speed of 30, which was of importance to them. Double berth en suite state-room below, plus second bedroom and luxury saloon, which was not.

Kincaid stepped aboard as if the boat was his, opened the flap of the awning over the cockpit, and checked the gas locker at the stern. The key to the door to the saloon was inside. He saw Sherenko nod that the pontoon was still clear, unlocked the door to the saloon and dropped down. The ignition keys were in the top drawer under the sink on the left of the galley. He flicked on the battery switch, went back on top, inserted and switched on the keys and checked the fuel. Pity Anna wasn't with them now, he thought.

It was almost six. They collected Anna and walked back to the marina, walked along the pontoons and checked there was still no one on or near the Sunseeker, Anna holding back slightly. Kincaid slipped through the flap of the cockpit awning, took the key from the locker at the rear, and unlocked the door to the saloon. Took the ignition keys from the drawer under the sink, went back on top and put them in, one key for each engine. Still clear, Sherenko confirmed. Kincaid opened the engine hatch, slid inside, checked the engine oil and water, and opened the sea cocks which would supply the water, through two sets of valves, to cool the engines.

Still clear – Sherenko nodded. *'Vpered.'* Let's do it. He stepped on board and unclipped the cockpit awning. Anna walked along the pontoon, climbed aboard, and sat back in the cockpit as if the boat was hers. Kincaid turned the keys and the Mercruisers purred into life. Sherenko cast off and jumped back aboard.

Someone was watching them. They waved at him and followed the line of port and starboard markers out from the marina. The marshlands were flat on either side and the Isle of Wight was in front of them. They reached the last marker and swung right up the Solent. A light aircraft flew overhead, the white teeth of the Needles glistened to their left, small yachts dotted the blue around them, and a cross-Channel ferry inbound from France loomed larger in front of them.

Kincaid eased the throttles forward gently and Sherenko pulled out the charts. 'One eighty-five degrees,' he told Kincaid.

'How long?'

'In this thing we should make Cherbourg in two and a half hours maximum.'

Kincaid passed the Needles, cleared the shipping channel, swung the wheel slightly on a 185-degree course, and opened up the throttles.

An hour later the breeze off the water was chilled, the light was beginning to go, and the Channel was suddenly emptier around them. Kincaid eased the power back and Sherenko climbed on to the dinghy, confirmed the paddles were in place, checked the fuel tank and test-started the outboard. Anna checked that the name of the boat wasn't on the life-jackets and threw them overboard; Sherenko found the life-raft, ripped it with a knife, and dropped it over the side. Then Kincaid eased the throttles forward and the bows of the Portofino picked up. In front of them they saw the smudge of the French coast, then the lights of Cherbourg. Two hours and ten minutes after leaving Lymington, Kincaid steered through the outer harbour at Cherbourg and into the inner section.

The last of the light was about to go. Kincaid dropped Sherenko and Anna at the visitors' pontoon and pulled out of the harbour. When he returned twenty minutes later Sherenko was waiting. They were checked in at two small hotels, Sherenko told him: himself and Anna in one and Kincaid in the other – if the authorities were searching for them they would be looking for three of them travelling together, at least two men travelling together.

They left the harbour and motored west along the coast.

A motor boat missing from a British marina and the police would assume it had been stolen. A missing power boat turning up in France and London might suspect their involvement. Sink a boat where she might be recovered and the authorities would certainly suspect; ditch a boat where there was a lot of tide, somewhere like the Alderney Race, and within five minutes she wouldn't be intact. Dump her at night and in slack water, though; allow time for her to sink and you to get ashore . . .

They were two miles from the point and a mile and a half off the land. Kincaid eased the engines into neutral, and Sherenko opened the engine hatch and dropped down inside. The sea cocks, through which the water to cool the engines had pumped, were against the stern. He turned them off, removed the filters, disconnected the taps, and turned the sea cocks back on. The seawater spurted from them and began to flood the floor of the engine room. The night was quiet around them, the sea barely rolling. Sherenko went through the saloon to the two toilets, disconnected the stopcocks, and watched the seawater seep across the floors. Kincaid eased the throttles forward, the Portofino picked up speed and the water rose in her engine room and saloon.

In the sky above them they heard the sound of an aircraft, to their left lights sparkled on shore. The Portofino was sluggish now, settling into the water. They reached the Alderney Race, checked there were no boats around them, switched off the lights, stepped up to the dinghy, started the outboard and drifted away. The Portofino was settling deeper in the water and beginning to go down, only its deck and radar bridge above the surface. Sherenko looked at her once then turned the dinghy for the shore. Half a mile from the beach they stopped the outboard and dropped it over the side – outboards had serial numbers and serial numbers could be traced back. The beach in front of them was slightly rocky. They paddled quickly, confirmed the beach was deserted, then grounded the dinghy, knifed through its tubes, smashed the fibreglass floor, and pushed it out to sea again.

Five hours later they caught the 5.53 to Paris, buying their tickets separately, and arriving Paris St Lazare at 9.29. Two hours after that they caught the 11.27 from Paris Nord, again buying their tickets separately, and arriving Brussels Midi at 13.10. By two that afternoon they had checked into two separate hotels; by three they had showered, changed and eaten. By four Kincaid and Anna had changed their appearances for the passport photographs. At four-thirty Sherenko left them, saying he would be back mid-evening.

Anna's bag was still packed. She opened it, but took from it only what she needed. The rest – the few clothes she had brought with her from London and the personal items like the head of the porcelain horse, plus her father's letter, now stayed in the bag in case she had to move quickly again. Then she plugged in and switched on the laptop.

'How far back do you want Yuri's cellphone records?'

'Two weeks,' Kincaid told her. 'We can go back further later.'

The details flicked on to the screen. Anna scrolled up the list, to the date two weeks earlier, found a sheaf of hotel letter paper in the drawer and wrote down the numbers, then Kincaid laid the sheets on the bed and ran through them.

There were calls to Moscow, as well to other parts of Russia; calls to Germany and Switzerland; calls to numbers in London, and calls to the United States. Plus an occasional call to other parts of the world, including Japan and Israel.

He took another sheet of paper and separated the calls to the United States.

Most fell into two groups: East Coast and West Coast. He could tell by the area codes. 212, 202, 213 and 415. The Manhattan area of New York, Washington DC, part of Los Angeles, and San Francisco. Plus a number of calls to Chicago, area code 312, and two to the same number, area code 208, which he didn't know.

'Back soon,' he told Anna.

'Where are you going?'

'Check out these numbers, but it's best if I don't do it from here.'

He left the hotel and went to a telephone shop on the Boulevard de l'Impératrice. The shop was busy, mostly young people. He was assigned a booth, shut himself in, and began calling the American numbers, beginning with Los Angeles because that was where Anna had said Yuri Dushkin was going first.

'Beach Antiques . . . Levi's Clocks and Watches . . . West Side Art Gallery . . . Sheraton Hotel . . .'

'Good morning. Mr Dushkin, please. He's a guest with you.'

There was a pause. 'Sorry, sir. We have no one of that name.'

So either Dushkin hadn't stayed there, or had phoned someone staying at the hotel. Or Dushkin had stayed and left, or hadn't arrived yet. Kincaid thanked the switchboard operator and asked for reception.

'Good morning. I'm phoning from Europe.' Which always helped. 'I'm trying to locate a business colleague, but I wasn't sure when he was supposed to be with you.'

'What's his name, sir?'

'Dushkin.'

There was a three-second pause while she ran the name on the computer. 'Mr Yuri Dushkin?'

'Yes.'

'Sorry, sir. He checked out yesterday.'

Kincaid thanked her and continued.

Antique and art galleries in San Francisco, but no hotels . . . Art and antique dealers in Washington DC and Chicago . . . A hotel in Chicago and Dushkin booked in for three days' time . . . Art galleries and antique dealers in New York . . . Sotheby's auction house and a diamond dealer . . . What the hell was Dushkin doing phoning a diamond dealer?

He phoned the last Manhattan number.

'Netherlands Hotel.'

'Reservations, please.' He listened to the computerized music and waited. 'Good morning. I'm confirming a reservation for a Mr Dushkin.'

There was a brief pause.

'Yes, Mr Dushkin. You have a room reserved today and tomorrow.'

Which left just the one number. Area code 208, local prefix 882, then the four-digit number.

He called the number, waited and heard the ringing tone; allowed it to ring for thirty seconds then hung up, called the international operator, asked for the US supervisor for area code 208, and waited as his call was switched.

Why bother, he asked himself. He had the rest of Dushkin's contacts; he knew where Dushkin was coming from and going to, so why waste time? He began to hang up, then the voice told him he was being connected. Sorry to trouble you, he told the supervisor; he was phoning from Europe and hoped she could help. Area code 208, local prefix 882. Where was that for?

Main Street, Moscow, Idaho, was busy in the way that it was always busy mid-morning. Sobolev and Dushkin turned left, Sobolev waving to someone he knew, then they drove out of the city and headed west past the university and shopping mall to the airport. Sobolev pulled into the drop-off zone, Dushkin got out and they shook hands. Behind them a family were getting out of a battered station wagon and saying their farewells. Dushkin watched as Sobolev pulled away, then went inside.

The airline desk was to the left, the X-ray machine straight in front and the bathrooms were to the right, coffee machines, pay phones and mail box next to them. Dushkin checked in, bought a black coffee from the machine, and flicked through the auction catalogue.

Sotheby's New York. Lot 57 the following morning.

Kincaid chose a seat in a café off one of the cobbled squares in the heart of Brussels and ordered a beer. The pavement cafés and the streets were alive with tourists, even at ten in the evening.

Why . . . The question hung in Kincaid's mind. In Kincaid's body and Kincaid's soul. What the hell are you doing, Dushkin? What game are you running? Why in the name of the Almighty are you in contact with a number in Moscow, Idaho? Because that was where Joshua began his last journey five years ago.

And what do I tell you, Nik? Do I tell you anything?

He checked his watch and realized he should have been back at Anna's hotel an hour ago.

Where are you, Nikolai Alexandrovich – Anna glanced at the door and tried to concentrate on the screen of the laptop. Sure you can look after yourself, but you said you'd be back mid-evening, and mid-evening was two hours ago. She focused on the details on the screen and copied out the details of Yuri Dushkin's other telephone records. Pity she didn't have a printer, perhaps she should get one in the morning. Where are you, Nik, what am I doing here? Why aren't I safe and secure with my friends in Moscow? She heard the knock on the door, checked through the security hole, saw Kincaid, let him in, and locked the door behind him.

'What's wrong, Jack?'

'Why?'

'You look as if a ghost's flown over your grave.'

'No ghosts in Brussels. A few other things maybe, but no ghosts. No Nik yet?'

'No. What about the phone calls?'

He told her. About the dealers and the galleries and the auction houses. About the hotel Dushkin had stayed in in Los Angeles and the one he was booked in to in New York. But not about Moscow USA. Because some things you don't talk about, even five years on. Because some things are sacrosanct and should remain so.

He heard the knock on the door. Three taps, one, then two. Anna crossed the room, unlocked the door, and let Sherenko in.

'Problems?' she asked.

'The ink on one of the stamps was wrong and had to be done again.'

He gave them the passports and sat on the edge of the bed. Anna returned to the computer and Kincaid settled in a small armchair next to the window and examined the passport. 'Looks good.' Good detail, nice feel of it being slightly used.

Should look good given how much it cost, Sherenko told him. He reached across and took the new telephone numbers. The list was for the seven days before Dushkin had flown to London, including his time in Moscow, and ran to three pages. 'Must have a hell of a phone bill.' It was half to himself, half to the others. He turned the page and ran down the numbers on the second sheet, turned the page again and began to run down the third sheet, then turned back. *Chert.* Kincaid saw it in the way Sherenko's eyes narrowed, the way he scoured the other pages, quickly and differently, then turned back to the second page.

Anna was still sitting in front of the computer. Sherenko stood and crossed to her. 'This number . . .' he indicated the number two-thirds down the page. 'Show me.' He hunched over her right shoulder. Anna swivelled in the chair, called up the file again and scrolled down the pages till she found the number.

'See if it's a one-off or whether Yuri called the number again,' Sherenko told her.

The room was almost silent, just the hum of the computer. Why – Anna turned slightly and looked up at him.

'If it's a one-off it might have been a mistake.'

The light from the street lamps outside was tinged with orange and the numbers on the screen were like ghosts. Kincaid rose and stood behind Sherenko. What is it, Nik? Why are you suddenly on edge?

'How far do you want to go back?' Anna focused on the monitor.

'As far as we have to.'

She typed in the last seven digits of the number. The figures on the screen flicked on and off, then the screen showed a separate table, dates on the left and the number, with a range of dialling codes prefixing it, in the centre, the time and duration of the call next to it and the charge on the right.

Sherenko locked his eyes on the screen then straightened, stood back as if he was about to walk around the room, as if he needed time to assimilate what he had just seen, or as if he needed time to work out what and how he would tell them.

'We thought we might be dealing with someone from the FSB . . .'

The internal security people.

'Yes.'

'We're not.'

'So who are we dealing with?'

'The SVR.' The Foreign Intelligence Service. 'The number's Yasenevo. One of the numbers Dushkin has been calling is First Chief Directorate.' What had been First Chief Directorate before the Soviet Union had broken up and the KGB had been dismantled.

Chert. Kincaid looked at the details on the screen. 'You know whose number?'

'No, but it's Yasenevo.'

'Yuri phoning his cut-out.'

'Probably,' Sherenko agreed.

'Unless there's a reason for Yuri to know somebody else in the SVR.'

'I don't think so.'

Anna had swung round from the computer; now she sat with her knees drawn up, arms wrapped round them, and her heels on the edge of the chair.

'What are you thinking?' Sherenko asked her.

'Yuri's cut-out is SVR. If the cut-out reports to someone on the commercial side, how likely is it that he reports to the same person on the intelligence side?'

'It's logical,' Sherenko agreed.

'So find out whose number he's ringing, find out who that person reports to . . .'

'Logically,' Sherenko agreed again.

'But?'

'We're talking Yasenevo here.'

'What about your contacts?' It was still Anna. 'Can't they find out whose number it is?' She shook her head. Because everybody who might have been a contact – SVR, FSB, Alpha, Omega – were all looking for them. And give the number to someone and you risked telling the opposition how close you were to them.

'There's another way in to Yuri's controller.' It was as if she had suddenly broken out of a trance. 'The dinner I had with Yuri in London, the night the cut-out called. Whoever was calling told Yuri he could be contacted at the usual number.'

'Moscow?'

'No. London.'

'How do you know?'

'The tone of Yuri's reply, the way Yuri reacted.'

'So?' Sherenko sat on the edge.

'So I check what numbers Yuri called in London between the dinner and when he left.'

'Assuming he made the call,' Kincaid suggested.

'You have a better idea?'

Anna swung back to the laptop and called up the details on the screen. Then her shoulders dropped and the cloud settled on her. Good try, Kincaid told her.

It was one in the morning, going on two. Come with me, Anna told Sherenko; finish with me now. You always make love like that, he asked her? Only with you, she told him; what about you, she asked him. Never before I met you.

It was three in the morning, going on four. Still feel you in me, Nikolai Alexandrovich, still feel myself climaxing, still feel you cascading inside me. The light from the street lamps penetrated the crack in the curtain. She slid from the bed and switched on the laptop.

Kincaid checked out of his room at seven; at seven-thirty he was in position in a doorway opposite Anna's hotel. At seven forty-five he saw her leave, followed her, and checked there were no tails on her, Sherenko in his turn checking on Kincaid. At eight-thirty they joined Anna in a café off the Grand' Place, the table against a wall and in a position where they could observe both the door and the street.

Yuri Dushkin was still the key; therefore they would keep to their original plan; therefore this morning they would fly to Frankfurt and make the connecting flights to North America, travelling indirectly via Toronto and driving south, then picking up on Dushkin when he was in New York. They would book separately, at different travel agents, and pay cash, which was the sort of thing airlines were always looking out for, but which travel agents would accept without query. Kincaid and Anna would travel to Frankfurt on one flight, though not together, and Sherenko on another. Sherenko and Anna would then take Air Canada to Toronto, Anna travelling business and Sherenko economy, and Kincaid would take Lufthansa.

The café was beginning to fill, the first tourists milling in the square outside. 'There's one other thing,' Anna told them. 'You remember I said Yuri had a number in London where he could contact his controller. Yuri didn't call any London numbers after he'd spoken to his controller, but he did call London from Los Angeles. I checked last night. It may or may not be the one we're looking for. I also checked back through his previous records. He's called the number eight times, some of them when Yuri himself was in London.'

She gave Sherenko the number.

They left the café and split up, each going to a separate travel agent. Sherenko booked his tickets then went to the telephone shop on Boulevard de l'Impératrice.

Probably nothing, part of his mind told him; probably some sophisticated telephonist telling him he was calling Sotheby's or the Park Lane Hilton. He checked the code for the UK and called the number.

The apartment overlooking the canal near Regents Park was silent, the morning sun angling through the windows. Vorkov set the voice mail and was halfway to the door.

Sherenko heard the ringing, then the voice mail cut in and invited him to leave a message. No name or number identified, he noted, the voice itself bland and neutral.

Vorkov heard the ringing, walked the five paces across the room, and lifted the telephone.

Sherenko began to put the phone down then the voice cut in across the recorded message. Five years ago he had made another call – the ice in his brain mixed with the numbness. Five years ago the voice he was now hearing was phoning him, telling him where to go and what to do. Impossible, he knew. He listened, not speaking, then the line went dead.

Vorkov shrugged, made sure the voice mail was still working, and left the safe house.

Sherenko hung up and stared at the wall in front of him. The telephone shop was busy around him. He shut out the bustle and heard the voice again. He was wrong, he told himself; the voice in London wasn't the voice he thought it was; the voice in London had been on the line for too short a time for him to identify it.

He struggled out of the numbness, punched the number again, and heard the neutral voice of the voice mail asking him to leave a message. The numbness was seeping away. He checked the number in Moscow, worked out the routine in case he was told he was being connected, and punched in the code, then the number at Yasenevo,

'Is Vorkov there?'

'Sorry, he's not here.' The secretary was careful as always.

'When's he back from London?'

'I'm not sure. I'm afraid he's been delayed.'

Who wants him, she began to ask; could she take a message. He said he'd phone back, thanked her, and put the receiver down.

So what's running, Vorkov? Why the hell, five years on, is Yuri Dushkin phoning you? What the hell's this all about? What do I tell you, Jack? Do I tell you anything?

He left the telephones and returned to the café off the Grand' Place. Anna was waiting.

'Everything okay with the tickets?' he asked.

'Everything was fine.'

He called a waitress and asked for a large expresso.

'What's wrong?' Anna stared at him.

'Why?'

'You look as if you've seen a ghost.'

He shook his head and laughed. Anna stared at him. What is it, Nikolai Alexandrovich; what's just happened that has shaken you to the core? Because you have the look in your eyes which Jack had when he returned to the hotel last night. She saw Kincaid coming and waved to the waitress for a third coffee.

274

No problems with the tickets, they confirmed; just time to get to the airport.

So what about it, Nik? Because it's part of the past you want to keep hidden away, but it's also part of the present.

He glanced around. 'I know who Yuri Dushkin's cut-out is.' He glanced around again. Not that any listeners would be needing to sit behind him, because directional mikes could pick up a conversation a couple of hundred metres away, depending on the angle and the environment.

'Dushkin's contact man is called Felix Vorkov. I phoned the number in London, was getting a voice mail message, then someone answered. It was Vorkov. I know this because I know Vorkov. I once worked with him.'

He sipped the expresso.

'I confirmed this by trying the number at Yasenevo and asking to speak to Vorkov. A secretary told me he wasn't there, which I took as confirmation that the number was Vorkov's. When I asked when he was due back from London she said she wasn't sure, and that he'd been delayed, which I took as confirmation that he was in London.'

And that's as much as I say. Because some things you don't talk about. Some things are *svyato*. Even after five years.

Manhattan was hot and busy. Dushkin was at Sotheby's by eleven. He went through to the auction room; hovered on the edge, not sitting down, and checked the faces of those present.

The auctioneer edged closer to Lot 57.

Shipped out of Russia eleven months before. Usual origin, route and precautions. Everything done through a cutter, therefore everything secure, because rocks were submitted to auction in the name of the cutter, and the cutter never identified his source. In return for which a cutter would take up to 30 per cent, which might seem an arm and a leg, but there were only half a dozen cutters in the world you could really trust. Because one slip and a rock that might be worth three million dollars might be down to two hundred thousand. Plus a lot of other people taking their percentages. Percentages being the wrong term, because they were paid up front: officials from the regions, the relevant officials in Moscow. Not even Vorkov, or whoever was above Vorkov, could pull the diamond stunt too often, though. But when they did come out Yuri Dushkin would check the market and run them through Tel Aviv or Amsterdam or London or New York. New York was favourite, of course. Just like the rock on sale today. And in a few days, perhaps a few weeks, Yevgeni Sobolev would leave Moscow, Idaho, take the flight to Seattle and the connection east, slip quietly into New York with the uncut rock Dushkin had given him two days ago, and the process would start again.

The auctioneer wiped his brow, took a sip of iced water, and came to Lot 57.

Frankfurt airport was busy. They sat in one of the cafeterias and ran through the last arrangements.

What are you two hiding from me – Anna glanced between Sherenko and Kincaid. What are you hiding from each other? Because you may not be aware I know, or how I know. But I do. By instinct or intuition, call it what you wish. Except that's the way you play the game, that's how you've both survived. So I guess I have to accept it.

She switched back into the discussion:

Vorkov was SVR . . . Vorkov reports to someone on the commercial side, therefore it was logical that Vorkov reported to him on the intelligence side . . . Therefore find who Vorkov reported to and they were on their way into the opposition . . .

Sherenko checked the time. 'Running an enquiry through Moscow would be difficult. How about Langley. You know someone?'

'Yeah,' Kincaid told him. 'I know someone.'

The flight board was showing the gate at which the Air Canada flight would be boarding.

'Time to go,' Sherenko told Anna. 'Me first. Do whatever Jack tells you.'

They separated, Kincaid drifting through the crowd and watching Sherenko's back, Anna staying near the cafeteria and watching Kincaid's.

Check-in . . . Sherenko smiled at the clerk and Kincaid watched her face for the tell-tale flicker which would suggest that the name on the computer had been flagged. Sherenko thanked the woman and moved off, Kincaid still studying her face and waiting for her to lift the phone and alert security. First check going air-side . . . a uniformed official asking for boarding passes, armed police nearby, but no problems. Baggage inspection . . . again no problems, but again there wouldn't be. Passport check . . . Sherenko shuffled forward, and handed over the Dutch passport. Standard routine: check details, then check face against photograph, then the nod to go through.

Kincaid waited another thirty seconds then returned to Anna.

'Nik's through. There were no problems. Don't talk to him, either in the departure lounge or on the plane. When you're at the departure gate itself, let him go first. If anything happens, don't try to go through. If they pick Nik up, go back to the departure lounge and wait for me.'

He watched her through, checked the time, and took the S-Bahn to the central railway station. Old hands, old habits. Cover what you're doing and where you're doing it. Even amongst friends.

The station was busy. He bought a phone card and went to the international phones. So Bram or Ed Miller, because both men were in positions to help him. He punched the number. On the Eastern Seaboard it was eight in the morning. He heard the ringing tone and imagined the wood shingle house by the dunes on the Chesapeake Bay, Bram with his flowing white hair, his crystal eyes and his mind like an IBM mainframe.

Thought I'd got rid of you, Joshua, now I'm phoning the man who pulled me into the case five years back.

The phone was still ringing. Perhaps Bram was out sailing, perhaps he and Mary were away for a few days.

Kincaid hung up and called the second number. 'Morning.' He made it sound as if he still belonged. 'Ed there?'

It worked as he knew it would. 'Sorry, Ed's in a meeting.'

The secretary looked through the glass partition. Miller and his section chiefs were spaced round the table at the end of his office farthest from the window. Standard morning conference, the division briefing Miller before Miller briefed the Deputy Director, Operations before the DDO briefed the Director.

'Does he look as if he's going to be long?' Kincaid still made it casual but informed.

'Who wants him?'

'Jack Kincaid.'

Sorry to interrupt, the secretary told Miller. There's a Jack Kincaid holding for you. You want to speak with him or should he call back?

Give me five, Miller told the meeting. He waited till they left then walked to his desk, activated the tape recorder, and lifted the telephone.

'Jack, good to hear from you. You all right? Grere told me about Moscow.'

'Thanks, Ed, I'm fine.'

'Anything I can do?' Miller asked.

'Actually, Ed, there is one thing. Guy called Vorkov. Ex-Opposition. I need to know who he is, where he is now and who he's working for.'

'Problems, Jack?'

Anything affecting the Agency, the question meant; anything Miller, as chief of division, should know about.

'Just routine commercial. He might be doing something for us in Moscow and the people who could normally tell us are out of town.'

'Give me a number where I can call you.'

'I'm on the move. I'll get back to you.'

'I'm on the Hill for the rest of the morning. Make it this afternoon or tomorrow.'

Miller sat back in his chair, rewound the tape, listened to it again, then called security, requested a trace on the call he had just received, and reconvened the morning's briefing. When the meeting ended he phoned London, asked to speak to Sheila Harrington, and waited ten seconds.

'I'm going secure,' he told her.

'Secure.'

'Kincaid just called.' Miller held the set close to his mouth out of habit. 'He wanted information on a Felix Vorkov. Specifically, he wanted to know who Vorkov is, where he is now and who he's working for.'

He went into detail.

'Any mention of Sherenko?' Harrington asked.

'None, and for obvious reasons I didn't ask.'

'Where was he phoning from?'

'Frankfurt railway station.'

Ten minutes later Harrington left Riverside and drove to the Park Lane Hilton. From one of the public phones there she called Malenkov's number in Moscow, then she left the Hilton and walked up Park Lane to the Grosvenor House.

Standard procedure when lines weren't secure or you didn't want a call to be logged. Ring a contact, include a pre-ordained code in an otherwise straightforward conversation, then use another public phone to call the public phone where the contact would be waiting.

Twenty minutes later she called the number of one of the public phones in the foyer of the Intourist at the bottom of the Tverskaya. Malenkov answered on the third ring.

'Going secure,' Harrington told him.

'Secure.'

'Kincaid's been in touch with Ed Miller. He asked about Vorkov, where he is now and who he reports to at Yasenevo.'

Chert – she could almost hear Malenkov swear. 'How does Kincaid know about Vorkov?' he asked.

'One way would be through Yuri Dushkin's telephone records.'

'So Sherenko and Kincaid are far enough down the line to be asking who Felix works to.'

'So it would seem.' Harrington swept the foyer. Casually, nothing anyone would pick up. 'The problem is: if they got this far through Dushkin's phone records, they may also have picked up his calls to Moscow.'

To Moscow, Idaho, Moscow USA.

Chert – she could almost hear Malenko swear again. 'Where was Kincaid phoning from?' he asked.

'Frankfurt railway station.'

279

'Why Frankfurt?'

'They might be en route to Berlin. Access Dushkin's apartment and see what they can find there. Travelling by train because it's more secure.'

'And Kincaid's phoning back this afternoon or tomorrow morning. So we'll have an update then on where Kincaid and Sherenko are.

'Yes.'

'Good. The boys will be staking out Berlin within the hour.'

Harrington left the Grosvenor House, walked the two hundred metres to the Park Lane Hilton, called international directory enquiries and asked for the number in New York.

Civil Service salaries weren't what they were cracked up to be, and a girl had to look to the future. Retirement was still a few years off, but the Boys' Room would make sure that another woman didn't rise to the highest of the heights. And with the end of the Cold War even Riverside was being made to cut back. Wrong policy, because the future was even bleaker than the past, but the penny-pinchers in Whitehall and the policy-makers at Westminster wouldn't understand that. A girl had to remain a patriot, of course, a girl would wish to remain a patriot, do nothing to harm the nation, continue to do everything to support and serve the nation. But the Boys' Room was a different matter. The Boys' Room would take care of themselves after the service, as they did so inside it. The Boys' Room told her how much they sympathized with her over her divorce, then the Boys' Room rubbed shoulders with Edward at the same clubs and quietly laughed at her behind her back. Without knowing how she'd screwed him financially, of course, but the Boys' Room wouldn't like to admit it even if they did know. Nor would the Boys' Room like to concede that the financial settlement to which Edward admitted gave her the cover she needed for her own little games. And over cigars and brandy in their clubs, the Boys' Room would laugh at the fact that she was being fucked by the biggest dick in London, without even acknowledging that it was the one thing guaranteed to screw Edward's peace of mind till the day he died, or the fact the decision was hers and hers alone.

So a girl had to be a patriot, but she certainly didn't have to lie back and think only of England.

She called the number in New York.

'Lot 57 . . . ?' she asked.

11

The 747 descended from the Canadian sky. Why the nerves, Jack, why the feeling like the old days? Okay, the game had changed. Not the game he and Sherenko thought they had been playing, however, because there was another game, one that went way back. And now he and Sherenko and Anna had begun the road to playing it out, even though none of them knew what it was. You're crazy, he told himself; you've been off the edge for five years and can't cope with being back on it. Perhaps. But why the hell was someone or something taking them back to Joshua? The wheels bumped down and the engines screamed in reverse thrust. At least he'd know the next stage soon, at least Ed Miller would come up with the name of whoever Vorkov was working for.

The 747 eased on to the gate and the jetbridge was connected. He left the aircraft and picked up the arrivals signs. The immigration desks were busy, queues tailed back at each. He shuffled forward and told himself to remember the drill from the training courses. The line edged on. He stepped to the desk and handed over the passport Sherenko had acquired in Brussels. The official glanced at it, checked the photograph, and allowed him through without even consulting the negative database. Ninety seconds later Kincaid cleared customs and stepped through the doors into the main arrivals area.

Anna was waiting.

Kincaid ignored her, walked through the terminal, picked up the signs to the car park, stopped at a set of pay phones, and saw Sherenko, anonymous in the crowd. Anna passed him and he followed her to the parking lot, saw her take the elevator, watched till the lights stopped at the third floor, then walked to the second.

Two minutes later the Chevrolet eased to a halt. He slid in, closed the door behind him, and Anna pulled away.

'Good to see you.' He kissed her on the cheek. 'Everything okay?'

She smiled at him. 'No problems. You?'

'No problems.'

They passed the Oldsmobile, Sherenko's head not turning but Sherenko's eyes and brain checking for tails. The exit roads were busy; they left the airport and picked up the route signs for Queen Elizabeth Way. Toronto was a haze to their left. They passed through Burlington and Hamilton, Lake Ontario on their left now, and closed on the border. In front of them Kincaid saw the signs for the United States, then a line of gas stations, motels and fast food diners. Anna indicated right and pulled in.

Sherenko was waiting.

Good to see you – he laughed at Kincaid. Everything okay – he stood with his arm round Anna and hers round him. Kincaid took the number of the pay phone in the entrance to the diner, went to the gas station two blocks down, called the number and confirmed it took incoming calls, then Sherenko left and they waited, Anna sitting in the car, face tight and window open so she wouldn't miss the ring. Kincaid fetched them coffee. Anna left the car, walked round it, checked the time and sat inside again.

The phone rang.

'No problems,' Sherenko told Kincaid. Nothing else, no indication who or where he was, because nothing else was necessary.

They left the diner and drove to the line of immigration booths at the border, settled and waited, then eased forward and stopped again. Fifteen minutes later they were through, eight minutes after that they saw Sherenko's Oldsmobile in a pull-in. They changed cars, Anna now driving with Sherenko and Kincaid following, and continued south. Ten miles short of Buffalo they stopped at a Chinese restaurant in another line of diners and fast food pull-ins. It was late afternoon Eastern Standard Time, plenty of time to make the evening flight to Newark, but late evening in Europe, and their body clocks were beginning to slow. They parked at the side, chose a table in the corner from which they could observe both the cars and the road, and helped themselves from the buffet.

'When are you phoning your contact?' Sherenko was seated opposite Kincaid. 'When will we know who Vorkov is working to?'

'I'll make it in the morning.'

So what about Yuri Dushkin, Jack old friend? What about the fact that Yuri Dushkin was calling Moscow USA? What about Joshua?

Anna stared at him. 'Something on your mind, Jack?'

'Why should there be anything on my mind?' The reply was too defensive, and obviously so.

Anna's eyes were still focused on him. 'Because there are things you and Nik are keeping to yourselves, but Nik's come clean on one. How he knows Vorkov. So isn't it about time you came clean on at least a part of what else it is that you know?' She held him with her eyes and wouldn't let him go.

'Yuri's telephone calls,' Kincaid said at last. 'Most of the calls were logical: business contacts, hotels, people or organizations. Two weren't.'

'Two different numbers?'

'No, two calls to the same number.'

'Russia, Europe or the UK?'

'Actually it was to the US . . . Actually it was to Moscow.'

Illogical, Anna's eyes still held his. You said the calls were to the US, so what are you talking about?

'Moscow, Idaho,' Kincaid explained. 'Moscow USA.'

He thought he saw the faintest tightening of the muscles and skin round Anna's eyes, the first flicker in the depths of the eyes themselves.

'You've tried it?' Sherenko spoke for the first time. 'You've tried to see who or what it is?'

'No.'

'Why didn't you tell us before?'

'A few years back I was involved with a case which had a connection with Moscow, Idaho. Now Yuri's making a call to there.'

The words were fading into the distance; Anna could no longer hear them. For one moment her mind and her brain were no longer focused on the conversation. For one moment she was at the graveside in St Petersburg, the snow on her shoulders and the letter in her hands.

'Coincidence?' Sherenko asked Kincaid. 'Same number?'

'I don't know. There wasn't a specific telephone number in the first case.' Only the pay phone Joshua had used to call from the airport.

'What was the first case about?' Anna asked the question even though part of her mind was still locked into another world and another time.

'I can't say.'

'Was Yuri Dushkin involved in the first case?' It was Sherenko again, Anna still wrapped in the silence and the cold.

'Not to my knowledge,' Kincaid told him.

'How about whoever's trying to take us out?'

'Until we know who they are I don't know.'

'Are the two connected?'

'I have no idea.'

'But Yuri Dushkin is taking us back there.'

'So it would seem.'

Anna tried to pull herself from the vacuum. 'Excuse me.' She rose, pushed back her chair, and went to the ladies room. Splashed water over her face and stared at herself in the mirror above the basin. She reached into her bag and took out the envelope, read the writing on it and ran her fingers across it, stared at the stamp and the postmark in the top right corner. Not the same Moscow USA, she told herself, there must be several. Hell, she knew there were, because she'd checked on the atlas when the friend had hand-delivered the letter to her.

Twenty minutes out of Buffalo they had flown through a thunderstorm, now the evening was fresh, the sky was clear, and Newark was winding down for the night. Five years ago Joshua came through here – the thought hung in Kincaid's subconscious.

Sherenko and Anna took one cab and Kincaid another, each telling the driver to take them to Penn Station. A 737 climbed into the darkening sky and the first star flickered in the purple.

285

They left Newark, took 1 and 9 north, crossed the Pulaski Highway and dipped through the Holland Tunnel into Manhattan. Penn Station was like Newark – easing down and echoing. When Kincaid arrived Sherenko and Anna were waiting. They took the subway, and checked in to two double rooms at the Ameritania on West 54th.

That night Anna slept fitfully, waking regularly and wide awake at five, perhaps the change in time zones, perhaps the adrenalin of the past hours, perhaps the edge of nerves which had cut across her stomach for the past hours. You all right, Sherenko had asked during the night; had wrapped his arms around her and asked her if there was something she wanted to tell him.

Kincaid woke at four; for the two hours after that he lay on the bed and stared at the ceiling. Perhaps the adrenalin of the past hours, he told himself, perhaps the thought, which he did not try to shake off, that it was coming together. Whatever it was. At seven he showered, dressed, and left the hotel.

Manhattan was coming to life: the first businessmen of the new day and the last hookers from the old. The office was on the second floor, the name of the investigation company was on a plate on the door, and the door was open. A receptionist – late twenties, blonde hair – was at a desk inside, and there were certificates on the walls and doors to offices behind.

'You're open early.' Kincaid was already on automatic.

'You know what they say.' The receptionist wore a pink blouse and her make-up was slightly overdone.

He gave her a sheet of hotel paper, the name of the hotel torn off, with the telephone number in Moscow, Idaho. 'I'd like a listing. I'll wait.' Straightforward job, run it on a CD ROM in thirty seconds, therefore almost not worth bothering with as far as the agency was concerned. He took out his wallet and gave her two one-hundred dollar bills. Five minutes later he had the name and address. Fifteen minutes after that he telephoned another investigation agency from a pay phone at Grand Central station.

'Yeah . . .' He was deliberately more hesitant this time. 'I need a check on a Yevgeni Sobolev, of Moscow, Idaho.' He gave the agency the address. 'Yeah ... he's trying to sell me a franchise and my bank wants to know. Yeah, this evening. Cash.'

He hung up and called the number at Langley.

Miller had been in since seven. 'Jack, how you doing?' He activated the record button of the tape.

'You know me, Ed. You able to find out what I needed?'

'Sorry, Jack. I ran the checks. No trace of anyone called Vorkov. You sure you got the name right?'

'Sure I'm sure.'

'Okay. I'll try again, you know what the system is like; might have missed something. Give me a contact number where I can reach you.'

'Like I said, I'm moving about. Appreciate it if you could run the check again, though. I'll call you later.'

He hung up and took the subway back to the hotel. Sherenko and Anna were at a deli on the corner opposite. Kincaid sat down, and the waiter poured him a beaker of iced water and took his order.

'You want the good news or the bad?' he asked.

The nerves laced through Anna's stomach. Tell them, she had decided; even though it wouldn't be connected. 'Start with the good,' she told Kincaid.

'The person Yuri phoned in Moscow Idaho is a Yevgeni Sobolev.' Kincaid looked at Sherenko. 'Mean anything to you?'

'Nothing.'

'An investigation agency's running a check on him for me. We'll get the details this evening. I've also spoken to the contact at Langley. The bad news is that there's nothing on file for anyone called Vorkov.'

There's something else, Anna began to say; probably not important, almost certainly not connected. Except it's tearing me apart and I have to tell you.

Sherenko's face was bleak. 'Who told you there's nothing on Vorkov?'

'Someone called Miller.'

'Who's Miller?'

Kincaid hesitated. This isn't the sort of thing you give out, he thought; even after you've left the Agency, even after the

287

Cold War is dead and buried. 'Miller's chief of division.' So Miller knows. Miller may not be God Almighty, but Miller's higher than most people ever dream of. 'He's checking again. I'm calling him back.'

The bleakness deepened like winter on Sherenko's face. 'Miller's lying.'

Kincaid stared at him. 'Evidence supporting that statement?' he asked quietly.

'Vorkov was First Directorate. Now he's SVR. Vorkov has been around. Last I knew of him he was a major. There's bound to be a file on him.'

'What about if he wasn't of first-hand interest to us?'

'You mean what if he didn't serve in the United States?'

'Yes.'

'Vorkov did serve in the United States, out of the embassy in DC and out of the United Nations in New York. So Langley is bound to have a file on him, because a file on such a person is routine.'

'How do you know?'

'I know because I worked for him here.'

'Explain,' Anna told Sherenko.

'I can't.'

The waiter brought Kincaid's order and topped up their coffee.

'Anyone else you can go to?' Sherenko asked.

'Yes.' As long as Bram was back from wherever he'd been. 'I'll phone him, arrange to see him. I'll probably be all day. How about you?'

'Boston. I used to have a safe house there. I'll check it out in case we need it.'

So why hadn't she told them, Anna asked herself. Because it wasn't important – she threw the answers back; because there were more important things to resolve; because the letter was her last line of defence – she wasn't sure against what – and she didn't want anyone past it. Herself included.

'One question,' she asked. 'If Nik's right, why should Miller be lying?'

*   *   *

Miller's Lincoln left Langley, turned south on George Washington Parkway, crossed Roosevelt Bridge and eased down Constitution Avenue. Miller, as chief of division, attending the Senate Select Committee on Intelligence. Run of the mill, the sort of thing the Director did every week.

Washington simmered in the late summer heat; the traffic was busy and the crowds queued at the White House and round the base of the Washington Monument. The Lincoln turned into the car lot for senators beneath Senate Hart building, and Miller and his deputy stepped out, took the senators' lift one floor then the connecting security lift to the reception area of the Intelligence Committee, no one outside those with a need-to-know even aware of their presence. Fifty minutes later the session ended. Take the car back, Miller told his deputy, have to do coffee with someone. Collect me in an hour, he instructed the driver.

The Lincoln left. Miller went to the pay phones on the ground floor, called the number in London, walked to Union Station and called the second number.

Sheila Harrington answered on the third ring.

'Going secure,' Miller told her.

'Secure.'

'Kincaid's been in touch again. He's not in Europe, he's in New York.'

'What about Sherenko and the woman?'

'We have to assume they're with him.'

'What else do you suggest we assume?' Harrington's voice was cut glass and cold.

Miller swept the area around him. 'Same as before. That they're trying to find the way in to what's going on through Dushkin. And that they're here in the US because Dushkin is here.'

'Any indication they're on to Sobolev and Moscow yet?'

'No, but perhaps they're not. If they were, Kincaid might have asked for a check on Sobolev as well.'

'But if they're on to Dushkin, then it's only a matter of time.'

'We have to assume that.'

'So what do you suggest?'

Miller went into detail. 'Malenkov might have some additional ideas,' he suggested when he had finished.

'Phone you back in fifteen.' Harrington hung up, and called the number in Moscow.

Miller left the phones, went downstairs to the food hall, and bought himself a coffee. He and Harrington went way back, of course. Berlin in the old days, to be precise. Then London, as they were both going up the ladder. And after London, DC. Not that either of them would make it to the top, Harrington because of what she called the Boys' Room, himself because he was wrong school.

And he and Harrington had both known Malenkov, as you did in this business. Just as Joshua had known Leo Panelli. Same cocktail circuits, same trawling through the foreign diplomats trying to recruit the same people. Even so, when Malenkov had suggested it, both he and Harrington had been suspicious. Not reported it, though. Boys' Room and bankers, he guessed. Plus the fact that Agency salaries weren't as high as outsiders imagined, girlfriends were expensive, and the bills had been mounting like he was taking over the entire Third World debt. Which was the first thing he'd examined, made sure that there was no chance that the mounting debts were a scam to get him over.

And lots of guys were teaming up with what had once been the Evil Empire, even then. As long as it wasn't a set-up. Then the first deal had gone through, no come-backs, and after that the second. Everything planned and no one greedy. Cut-outs built in, so nobody knew the key players, and the money shifted round till it was untraceable – but hell, that's what they all did every day of the week anyways. As long as you didn't let down Uncle Sam, as long as you did nothing to damage the Stars and Stripes. You were careful, of course, no Jag or house or holidays you shouldn't be able to afford. But a few investments here, a few moves there, all open and above board, building the cover for when you left the Agency. And after that nobody would know. Just as long as you didn't betray your country, and Ed Miller would never do that. Even the Joshua mess hadn't been a betrayal.

Fifteen minutes later Harrington called the second number in

Moscow. Malenkov answered on the third ring and they went secure.

'The problem has escalated. Kincaid is in New York. He phoned Ed again. We have to assume Sherenko and Anna Buskova are with him. This is what Ed suggests . . .' She went into detail.

'What about Sobolev?' Malenkov asked as she had asked Miller. 'Did Kincaid mention him? Is there any suggestion whatsoever that Kincaid and Sherenko are on to Moscow?'

'Kincaid didn't ask, and Ed obviously couldn't ask him.' But . . . 'They're getting close. We've missed them twice. It's probable they know Dushkin's business. Kincaid's enquiry about Vorkov suggests they've worked out that whoever was behind the hits on them are the people for whom Dushkin is working, though with any luck they still think it's because of the scams Dushkin is fronting. If they get on to Sobolev, however, if they get on to Moscow USA, then they might start asking something else.'

Might start asking about Joshua.

'Anna Buskova,' she asked.

'What about Anna Buskova?'

'Assuming they find out about Moscow USA, is there any way she can give them the link to the past, is there anything she has or might know which might give them the link to Joshua?'

'No. Anna Buskova thought her father died of a heart attack in Moscow. She didn't even know he'd been in the US, let alone Moscow USA.'

Thank God for small mercies, Harrington thought.

'One other thing,' Malenkov told her. 'Sherenko used to run from a safe house in Boston. He might seek to use it again. I'll get it covered.'

Harrington hung up, called Washington, and updated Miller.

Bloody Joshua, she thought.

The three of them had just started working together. Pulled off a couple of small deals, mainly for Malenkov to show that he could deliver. A picture and a rock, which was why Sobolev had been involved. Sobolev had still been working for the First Chief Directorate. A man had to keep his day job, but he could also make a little on the side.

Then Joshua comes through – Major General Mikhail

Sergeyevich Buskov to be precise, though even now she thought of him by the file name the CIA had given him. Joshua had set up some of the First Directorate's financial scams and Sobolev had been one of his people. Joshua didn't know about the little deal Malenkov and Miller and Harrington had with Sobolev, of course.

But then Joshua does one of his drop-ins on Sobolev. And the next thing they know is that Joshua is on to Leo Panelli, asking for a meet and saying it's an immediate. And Miller thinks Joshua has discovered their little goldmine and is going to blow the whistle on it, so Miller contacts Harrington, because at that stage all calls made by the Langley team handling Joshua are being recorded, because Langley thinks Joshua might be coming over and is not only pulling out all the stops but wrapping them in security like you wouldn't believe. So Miller brings in Harrington – open and above board. And Harrington is in a position to alert Malenkov, who arranges what he has to arrange.

And all the time Joshua doesn't know about their little shenanigans, or if he does it's the last thing on his mind. Because the next day the Gorbachev putsch takes place. And the conventional wisdom after, amongst the handful privileged to know and discuss it, was that Joshua had got wind of the putsch and opposed it. And because he didn't know which of his superiors in Moscow he could trust, Joshua had decided to take it to CIA in the hope that the West could stop it.

But this they didn't know at the time. Malenkov wasn't high enough up the pecking order in those days to know the things Joshua knew. So they had taken Joshua out. And all the time they needn't have done. And if they hadn't they wouldn't be having to deal with Kincaid and Sherenko now.

When Life wanted to be a bitch she made sure she was a bloody First Class Bitch.

Miller had been back at Langley seventy minutes and was attending a budget meeting chaired by the Deputy Director, Operations, when the call came. London chief of station wishes to speak with you urgently, he was informed. He excused himself, returned to his office, and took the call on a secure line.

'Ray, what's running?'

'Ed, we might have a problem. Jack Kincaid and the mafia scare. I just took a call from the Russian *rezident* here. He's just been tipped off by the FSB in Moscow. Kincaid, Sherenko and the woman are no longer in the UK.'

'Any idea where they might be?'

'That's the problem. Seems they're in New York.'

'Christ . . .' Miller swore louder than normal. 'Source of the information?'

'I'm not sure. I asked. Either he didn't know or he wasn't telling.'

'Riverside knows?'

'About to.'

'Anyone else?'

'Special Branch.'

And if the British police know, then the first thing they'll do is cover their backs and pass it down the line to the relevant people in Washington and New York, including the FBI.

'How much lead time we got?' Miller asked.

'I reckon an hour.'

'Thanks, Ray.'

Briefings with desk and security chiefs plus FBI liaison officer, he ordered; meeting with the DDO after the budget session. Everything low-key and routine, though. Nothing to get the DCI involved at Langley, or The Judge at FBI. Because then people might start to ask questions. But play it according to the book, get the Langley liaison officer to deal with his opposite number at FBI, and the Bureau would take over just as Special Branch had appeared to take over in London. And by that time Malenkov would not only have arranged for Vorkov's hoods to be standing by, but everything would have a veil, everything would be covered.

Another time and another reason for the trip and he might have enjoyed the flight to Norfolk, Kincaid thought: the green of Virginia below, the land marked by the battle sites of the Civil War, the blue of the Atlantic to the east, then the sparkling water of Chesapeake Bay and the whites of sails flashing in the sun.

O'Bramsky was waiting, '89 Chevy pick-up and flash of white

hair. Parked away from the airport's normal pick-up point. Bram playing it like he always played it. Kincaid crossed the parking lot, got in, and shook hands.

'Good to see you, Bram.'

'You too, old friend.'

They left the airport and headed east. Kincaid took off his jacket, wound down the window, and enjoyed the fresh air. 'One thing I have to say before we go any further, Bram. I wasn't here, I never called, you never saw me.'

O'Bramsky's eyes flashed blue. 'So what sort of shit are you in this time, Jack?'

'Who said I was in the shit?'

O'Bramsky laughed and turned into the side road leading to the bay. 'How's Mary?' Kincaid asked.

'Mary's fine. She'll be sorry she missed you.'

Mary had always been good. A soldier's wife; knew the rules and accepted them. A spy's wife, knew when she was needed and when she shouldn't be around.

O'Bramsky turned off the side road and along the track. The houses were wood shingle chalet-style, a thin line of dunes behind those on the right, and the sand of the Chesapeake the other side, the salt smell of the sea mixing with the heat of the sun.

'Great place to live, Bram.'

'Shoulda lived here sooner.'

They pulled on to the rough grass in front of the house and went inside. The main room was large and light, the wooden walls relaxing and the chairs around the log stove – unlit at this time of year – were large and comfortable. There was a television set in one corner, a music centre in another, and bookshelves on the wall. Nothing to even hint at Bram's former occupation, Kincaid thought, but that had always been the case. A room off to the side, he assumed; computer on the desk, a few manuals and reference books, but even then nothing connecting him to the Agency.

'Beer?' O'Bramsky asked.

'What you having?'

'Apple juice. Make it myself.'

'Apple juice sounds fine.'

O'Bramsky poured them each a glass from the jug in the freezer, then they kicked off their shoes and walked over the dunes. The beach was almost deserted, someone rigging a catamaran two hundred metres away, no one closer.

The barbecue was by the Hoby, the charcoals glowing. How much time you got, O'Bramsky asked. Not much, Kincaid told him. Assumed so – O'Bramsky threw on the swordfish steaks – got everything going before I left.

'Vorkov,' Kincaid asked. 'First Directorate.'

Business or personal, Bram asked.

Both, Kincaid told him.

O'Bramsky stared at the blue of the water. 'Vorkov, Felix.' The IBM mainframe punched out the information. 'Born Moscow, 1951. Education: School Number Fifteen then Moscow State Institute of International Relations. First came to US on a Fulbright scholarship. Later served with First Chief Directorate in the US, using fronts as radio correspondent, then commercial attaché, both in DC and at the United Nations in New York. Rumoured to have been involved in some wet jobs but nothing was ever proven. Last posting in the US 90/91. Returned to Moscow September 1991.'

'Who was his superior?' Kincaid asked. 'Who did he answer to?'

The man who told the driver to drop him at the bottom of the street in Boston's North End was thirty-two years old and fit-looking.

Shops and cafés on street level, he noted: nothing especially prosperous but everything doing a reasonable trade. Offices above, sometimes apartments. Doors between the shops to access the upper floors. He walked on the left pavement, going up, passed the deli, then the shoe repair shop, passed the doorway between the repair shop and the dress shop next to it.

As a teenager from Kiev, Josef Bukanin had done his compulsory military service, then extended it another seven years including a period with Special Forces. In December 1991, after the dissolution of the Soviet Union, he had found work where many like him had found it, in Bukanin's case for Alexei Kosygin.

In 1993 he had come to the attention of Felix Vorkov, a year after that, and with false papers, he had begun work in the United States as Vorkov's *komandir* in New York.

On the opposite side of the road two women were talking by a pram.

The entrance to the safe house was behind them.

Someone might try to use it – Vorkov had briefed him. Therefore put some people inside to wait. Be careful, though, because two of the targets are pros. Therefore Bukanin passed by, not even looking, just getting his bearings and imprinting the layout of the street on his mind. Stake the place out before he put anyone in; see if there was any movement before he himself moved.

The car was waiting a block up. He slid into the front passenger seat, checked that each of the team had memorized the photographs of the targets, gave them their instructions, then walked back down the street, confirmed the details, and took his position in the coffee bar two up from the corner and some fifty metres from the safe house.

Kincaid and O'Bramsky left the bay and returned to the airport. It was fifty minutes to the flight. They shook hands, then Kincaid went inside, checked in, and looked at the faces around him.

Miller had been with the Deputy Director, Operations, fifteen minutes.

'You're sure about Kincaid's involvement?' the DDO asked.

'No,' Miller told him. 'That's why we're keeping it low key.'

FBI liaison on line two, he was informed. No record of Kincaid, Sherenko or Anna Buskova entering the USA – Palmer, the Langley liaison, updated him from FBI headquarters. The Bureau was assuming that all three were now in-country, therefore were ignoring international flights and concentrating on domestic flights in and out of New York just in case the targets moved round.

The flight board showed twenty minutes to departure. Kincaid confirmed the gate number, bought copies of *Time* and *Newsweek* and drifted through.

Bukanin had been in the café thirty minutes. The street had changed – different cars, different people – though not significantly. By which he meant no target. He checked with the others on the cellphone, each of the conversations veiled. Everything quiet, he was informed, nothing moving back or front. Almost time to do it, he decided. One more check, though, just in case. He left the café, crossed the street, and went to another twenty metres up.

There had been an afternoon during the siege of Leningrad, an old trapper had once told Sherenko: a Russian sniper and a German sniper, two hundred metres apart. Not the ball-shrivelling white and cold of winter, but the heat and almost perpetual light of a northern summer. After six hours the German sniper had changed position, another seven and he changed again. When he changed five hours after that the Russian had shot him. Therefore Sherenko had sat motionless at the table by the window on the second floor, back from the window slightly, yet able to view the street. Not even lifting the coffee he had ordered, the waiter was aware, but fifty dollars was fifty dollars, so what the hell. Man goes into café, Sherenko had noted, which was fine; but man does not leave one café to go immediately to another. Man leaving second café, so what does man do now? Below him Bukanin walked nonchalantly up the street and turned into the doorway leading to the safe house. Bastards – Sherenko counted the seconds and saw the second man go in, then the third. He left the table and exited by the door at the rear.

Anna plugged in the laptop, logged in, and accessed the copies she had made of Yuri Dushkin's Berlin files. Pity Nik and Jack had told her not to leave the room, pity she couldn't slip out and buy some clothes to augment the handful she'd brought from London. Pity she couldn't do something about the storm in her head and the nerves in her stomach.

Whoever had set up Yuri's computer had given him a Borland Paradox system, she remembered from the first time she'd hacked in in London; and a Borland Paradox was a relational database, which opened up a whole scope of opportunities. Two minutes later she was inside. In London there hadn't been time; in London she'd switched to accessing Yuri's telephone records. Now she sat back, punched each keyword into the system in turn, and began to take notes on what the search threw up. Christ – the excitement grew: the organization Yuri worked for was making millions. She pulled up details of the items Dushkin and those he worked for had moved out of Russia over the past months, the people and galleries they used to provide false provenances where necessary, the outlets they used and the profit they made on each item. The items already shipped out and which Dushkin was about to sell or which were in storage waiting for the market on an individual trend to turn up. In the last category she had just made herself twenty million dollars, she thought.

The phone rang.

Three rings, Nik and Jack had told her, then four, then five. Wait for the full code and don't answer if it's anything else. She counted the first rings, then the second, almost picked up the telephone on the fifth ring of the third set and stopped herself. The phone went dead then rang again.

'Anna, it's Nik. Everything okay?'

'Sure.'

'Has Jack been in touch?

She picked up the tension. 'No . . .'

'Stay in the room. If Jack phones, tell him the accommodation had visitors. You have that: the accommodation had visitors.'

Oh Christ . . . the shock hit her. 'Yes, I have that. You okay, Nik?'

'I'm okay. If Jack phones just tell him not to come in the way he went out.'

'Okay.'

'I'll be back in two, three hours.'

'Take care.'

Continental flight for Newark now boarding – Kincaid heard the announcement. At the podium in front of the gate the airline officials began checking the passengers through. He finished *Time* magazine, stood, and left it on the seat.

For God's sake be okay, Nikolai Alexandrovich – Anna sat in front of the computer and told herself to focus. For God's sake spot it, Jack.

The phone rang and she began counting.

'Anna, it's Jack.'

'Listen to me, Jack. Nik phoned. The accommodation he was checking out had visitors. You understand what I'm saying, Jack. The accommodation had visitors. Nik says not to come back the way you went out.'

'I know. You okay, Anna? Nik's okay?'

'Both fine.'

'See you in a couple of hours.' He hung up and called O'Bramsky.

'Bram, I missed the flight. Wonder if you fancied another beer?'

'Pick you up in fifteen.'

So what shit's hit the fan now, O'Bramsky asked thirteen minutes later. Big shit, Kincaid told him. You know a private pilot who can fly me to the Big A; cash, no questions? O'Bramsky laughed and gave him the telephone number. The normal drill, he said, just in case.

The Seneca bucked in the thermals. The pilot banked right, circled, and dropped in. In front of him Kincaid saw the grey of the runway. Commercial fight into Newark and somebody might be waiting for him as the Special Branch tails had been waiting for him in London. Private flight into Teterboro, however, $500 cash and two hours max in a twin-engined, no commercial traffic at the airfield therefore no need for a stake-out, and he was clear.

The cab into Manhattan cost another forty dollars. When Kincaid picked up the second cab fifty-five minutes later, the sports bag he carried contained two Sig Sauers, shoulder holsters, Heckler and Kochs, and what he considered a sufficient amount of ammunition. Legislation was legislation, but old contacts were still worth their weight in gold.

The second cab dropped him three blocks from the hotel. He circled the area twice before entering, checking as best as he could for surveillance vehicles, then used the house phones in the foyer to call Anna's room, ran the code and went upstairs. It was early evening, the sun slanting through the window and the room bathed in yellow. The laptop was on the desk, still running, and Anna was gripping her fingers nervously.

'What happened?' he asked.

'Nik phoned. He didn't say much more than I've already told you. He hasn't phoned since. What about you?'

'Miller said there was no Agency file on Vorkov, Nik said there should have been. My second contact confirmed there was.'

'How far did you get before you realized what that meant?'

'Too far. I was about to board the flight back.'

'And you think the airports in New York might have been watched?'

'Perhaps.' He fetched them each a beer from the minibar.

'You really all right?' he asked.

'Why do you ask?'

'I'm not sure.'

The phone rang. Three times, four, five. Sherenko. Two minutes later he joined them. The sun had shifted slightly, so that it was no longer shining into the room. They sat drinking cold beer from the bottle, Sherenko and Kincaid in the chairs and Anna on the bed.

'The safe house in Boston is staked out.' Sherenko's voice was calm.

'Yours or ours?' Kincaid asked. 'Russian or American?'

'Ours.'

'Official or unofficial?'

'Difficult to say, but I think unofficial. You met your contact?'

'Yes. You were right, there's an Agency file on Vorkov.'

'Who's he answering to?'

'The last intelligence my contact has was five years ago. Vorkov was then working to a Sergei Malenkov. At the time Vorkov was a major in the First Chief Directorate and Malenkov was a full colonel.'

'So Malenkov is the opposition . . .'

'But there are other questions to answer.' It was Anna.

Sherenko nodded in agreement. 'The safe house in Boston. Somebody told them, so who?' He looked to Kincaid.

'The only people who knew we were in the States were my two contacts. Miller, because he could have traced the calls I made to him, and the second. The second was with me until fifteen minutes before I phoned Anna, though it's possible he could have alerted the opposition after my first call to him.'

'Except if that was the case, why weren't they waiting for you in Norfolk?' It was Anna again.

'So Miller,' Sherenko suggested.

Kincaid nodded. 'Miller said there wasn't an Agency file on Vorkov, my second contact said there was and gave me details. So Miller was lying.'

Sherenko looked at him. 'What about the possibility that he genuinely did overlook something? What about the possibility of a glitch in the system?'

'You prepared to believe that under the present circumstances?' Kincaid asked.

'No.'

'Neither am I.'

Consider what you're saying, Anna told them. Explain, Kincaid came back at her. It was like the meeting in the bubble would have been after Joshua made first contact, Kincaid thought; the eagles tight round the conference table and throwing ideas and angles like they were going out of fashion. Except that was five years back.

Anna looked at them both then focused on Kincaid. 'Miller was the only one who knew we were in the United States, therefore Miller was part of the set-up in Boston.'

'Yes,' Kincaid agreed. 'Except the stake-out in Boston was the opposition.' Oh fuck . . . he heard himself groan. 'So Miller and Malenkov.'

'Why Miller and Malenkov?' Anna asked.

'Because of the set-up . . .'

'I mean: why *only* Miller and Malenkov?'

They looked at her.

'Why did you phone from Norfolk? Why did you get a private flight back?'

'Because the tails were waiting for me when I went into London, therefore I thought the tails might be waiting for Nik and I at the airports here.'

'Official tails?'

'Yes.' He understood where she was taking him.

'But Nik says the stake-outs in Boston were unofficial.'

'Okay. Miller goes down the official road, gets Langley involved then the FBI, because the Bureau handles national matters. That way he gets other people looking for us, and by doing that he also gives himself and Malenkov a cover.'

'Apply the Miller theory to London,' Anna told them. 'Whoever set everything up in London was doing the same as Miller seems to be doing now.' She rolled off the bed and switched off the laptop. 'So what now?'

'Check on Malenkov's position now, how important he is and what he's doing. Check on who might have been running the show in London.'

'Who do you check those things with?'

'Gerasimov and Jameson.'

'You trust them?' Anna asked doubtfully.

'No option.'

Kincaid would remain with Anna while he contacted Gerasimov, Sherenko suggested, then he would stay with Anna while Kincaid spoke to Jameson. She didn't need anyone to hold her hand, Anna told them. Kincaid and Sherenko left the hotel, went to the World Trade Center and used the phones in the shopping mall. In Moscow it was the middle of the night, Kincaid was aware. What's going on, Jameson would ask, where the hell are you? Why the hell are you running with Sherenko, because that's the story on the grapevine.

He called Jameson's number.

'Grere, it's Jack. Don't hang up.'

'Jack, where the hell are you? I've been trying to contact you.'

'Listen to me, Grere. I'm clean, Nik Sherenko's clean. So listen to me.'

'I know Nik's clean. I know he wasn't responsible for the ConTex money.'

What the hell do you mean, Kincaid wanted to ask. He glanced through the partition at Sherenko. Time running fast, he reminded himself; traces only took seconds nowadays.

'Grere, you know what happened in London?'

'I heard.'

'I need the name of whoever ran the show there. I'll call you back in fifteen minutes.' He checked how long he had been on. 'What about the ConTex money?' he asked.

'Sherenko's clear on it. We made a mistake. You remember the ConTex VP, Dwyer, why he needed the money, for advance details of an oil and gas licence? Couple of things about Sherenko didn't tie in, so we pressured Dwyer through Cal McIntyre in Houston, and he gave us the names of the people he was dealing with. The gas and oil details he was paying for were correct, but some of the people running it got greedy and tried to get the money twice. Mikhail's boys put the frighteners on them, and they gave us the number in a Swiss bank account. It's now up to ConTex.'

Time to close it, Kincaid knew. 'I'll call you back.'

Ten metres away Sherenko hung up on the call to Gerasimov and they moved quickly away from the phones.

'Malenkov is Foreign Intelligence Service,' Sherenko told him. 'He's now a major-general. Gerasimov doesn't know Vorkov, but the KGB was a large organization and Vorkov was probably too low down the ranks, or in a different department.'

They cleared the shopping mall.

'How was Jameson?' Sherenko asked.

'He'll help. I'm phoning him back. Big Mishka tell you about the ConTex money?'

'Yeah.'

'Jameson said the same.'

They cleared the World Trade Center and separated. Sherenko took the subway, returned to the hotel, and ran the security procedure on the telephone before going to the room. Anna was seated in a chair. The laptop was in front her, the letter was gripped tight in her hands, and her face was white and wet with tears. Sherenko knelt beside her and put his arm round her. What is it, he asked.

The Sobolev material was in a sealed brown envelope at the reception desk of the enquiry agency. Kincaid used the name he had given that morning, paid in cash, and left. It was almost time to phone Jameson again. He found a bar and ordered a beer. Funny how in the past hours he had forgotten about Sobolev. Forgotten about Moscow USA. Forgotten about the ghost on his shoulder.

He opened the envelope and read through the material.

Sobolev was squeaky clean. Sobolev was a university professor and small-time businessman. Sobolev was also a Russian. More correctly, he was a *former* Russian. His green card details were listed in the agency's report. Sobolev had come to the US from the United Kingdom and had taken up residence in Moscow, Idaho, in 1987.

Therefore Sobolev had been in Moscow USA when Joshua had begun his last journey from there. Kincaid felt the ghost settle on his shoulder again and ran through the connections. Dushkin and Sobolev; Dushkin and Malenkov via Vorkov – it was as if he was standing in a field in winter, the fog icy cold and impenetrable around him. Sobolev, Vorkov and Malenkov. And now Miller, tied in to Malenkov, therefore presumably to Vorkov and Dushkin, though neither would know of his existence. But therefore tied in to Sobolev and Moscow USA. The more Kincaid fought to see through the fog the deeper and colder it became. Miller and Malenkov linked to Moscow USA through Dushkin, presumably because of the scams they were running using Dushkin as the front man. Miller and Malenkov linked to Moscow in the present tense. But Miller also linked because of the Joshua affair.

The fog lifted, suddenly and abruptly and the sky was suddenly blue. Except Kincaid was not standing in a field, but in a wilderness, the vast empty icy waste stretching before him to the mountains in the farthest distance, so far and so bleak he could not estimate how far, and no ways to them, no tracks telling him which way to go.

So Miller and Malenkov linked to Moscow USA in the present, Miller in the past, so perhaps Malenkov as well. Even though the fog had lifted Kincaid felt colder, suddenly more isolated. But what about London, because somebody had set up London just as Miller had set up New York and Boston, but that was the weak link, because London might be connected to Moscow USA in the present, but there was no indication whatever of a link in the past.

He left the bar and called Jameson.

'Grere, it's Jack. You have what I want?'

'The London set-up was run by Riverside using Special Branch. The person running it was Sheila Harrington. She's the approximate equivalent of chief of division.'

'You know her?' Kincaid asked.

'I met her a couple of times . . .' Jameson paused. 'What's this all about, Jack; what shit are you getting yourself into now? Because you're heading somewhere none of us want to go back to.'

Jameson was hesitating, Kincaid thought; Jameson was stalling. Christ, Jameson was playing for time and running a trace. Miller and Malenkov and London linked to Moscow USA in the present, a segment of his brain was still thinking; Miller in the past, possibly Malenkov, but no London. Time to move it, his logic told him; time to thank Grere, hang up, and clear the area as fast as he could. Hang in, his instinct countered; run with it, risk it.

'Actually, you've met her as well,' Jameson told him. 'Sheila Harrington rode shotgun for London on the Joshua affair.'

Hang up and bug out, Kincaid's logic and training screamed at him. You've been on the line twenty, thirty seconds. Something he'd missed, his instinct told him, something else that was screaming at him. Move it, his logic ordered him, this isn't the time to think this through; the time to think it through is after you've cleared the area.

'Thanks, Grere,' he said and began to hang up. 'What did you say?' he asked.

'I said you've met Sheila Harrington as well. Sheila Harrington rode shotgun for London on the Joshua affair.'

Oh Christ – the day was still arctic cold and the wilderness was still around him, but the track to the mountains was clear and distinct. 'Explain,' Kincaid asked Jameson.

'Sheila Harrington was involved immediately in case London had an interest. She was also involved after the operation. Sheila Harrington came over to represent London's interest during the enquiry.'

'Thanks, Grere.'

Kincaid hung up, cleared the area, and called O'Bramsky in Norfolk. 'Bram, wondered if you fancied that beer?'

Ten minutes later Kincaid phoned the public number O'Bramsky had given him. O'Bramsky was waiting. 'The Joshua enquiry,' Kincaid came immediately to the point. 'Someone from London was involved. What was his name?'

The IBM mainframe reacted immediately. 'Actually it was a woman.'

'Name?'

'Sheila Harrington.'

But what about Joshua – Kincaid made himself confront the unfaceable. 'The official line was that somewhere along the way Joshua missed the fact that his own people were sitting on him,' he asked O'Bramsky.

'Yes.' Bram snorted. 'Even though that raised more questions than it answered, but everything was washed away by the Gorbachev putsch.'

'No way there could have been a leak from the Agency?'

'No way. The team was tight, everything need-to-know. Security even within the division. People we were asking about Joshua didn't know why we were asking. People handling the security didn't know who they were handling it for. Only three, four of us knew everything.'

'One of you could have phoned out?'

'No way. Except to brief the DCI or the president, no one left the bubble, and all calls made from the bubble were logged. That was the first thing the security people checked, after.'

'So no one, by which I mean no one who knew, made any unlisted calls outside the Agency.'

'Even within the Agency,' O'Bramsky told him.

'Except to London, of course. Except to Riverside.'

O'Bramsky understood what he meant. 'But that was via the London chief of station, so it was official and logged. And not even the London CoS knew what was going down.'

'Then Riverside became involved.'

'In case they had something we could use,' Bram told him.

'By Riverside we mean Harrington?' Kincaid asked for confirmation.

'Yes. After that the CoS was out of the game and the division dealt with Harrington direct.'

'Who dealt with her direct, whose contact was she? Jameson's or yours?'

The IBM mainframe thought through it. 'Actually it was Ed Miller.'

The wilderness was bright and cold around him, and he was halfway to the mountains. 'What about during the enquiry,' Kincaid asked O'Bramsky. 'Wasn't Harrington involved at that stage as well? I remember when I was being interviewed.'

'Yeah, Harrington was present at that stage as well.' There was something in Bram's voice now.

'How do you mean, Bram?'

'Grere and I were on the way out, even by that point. I mean, heads had to roll. Harrington played her game like I'd never seen.'

'What about Miller?'

'Yeah, Miller as well.'

'Thanks, Bram.'

'Jack?'

'Yes?'

'I just thought of something. I said all the calls during the Joshua build-up were made from the bubble.'

'Yes . . .'

'That's not strictly accurate. Couple of times, when Miller talked with Harrington he was in his own office.'

Kincaid reached the mountains. 'Thanks, Bram.' He hung up, walked three blocks, and took a cab to the hotel. Told the driver to drop him two blocks away, went to a liquor store and bought a bottle of Jack Daniels. Checked the hotel for tails, ran the security routine on the telephone, and took the stairs rather than the lift. Stepped into the room, waited as Sherenko locked the door behind him, and sat in the chair under the window.

Sherenko sat in the other chair, Anna on the bed. Anna had been crying. Outside it was dark, the blinds of the room closed. What is it – Kincaid looked at both of them. What's happened? There was a letter on the bed close to Anna. He opened the Jack Daniels.

'Anna was right. There's a third person. Her name is Sheila Harrington. She's Miller's approximate equivalent at Riverside.' He collected three glasses from the bathroom, filled them, passed them round and waited.

'Anna has something to tell us,' Sherenko said softly.

Anna pulled herself upright. 'Originally you and Nik thought you were being targeted because you were investigating Alexei Kosygin. Then the three of us thought we were being targeted because Yuri Dushkin was the way in to whoever was targeting us.'

'Yes.'

'It wasn't Yuri they were afraid of, it was me. At least something to connect me to what they were trying to protect.'

She took a *stogram* of Jack Daniels and picked up the envelope. Opened it and took out the second; opened the second and took the letter inside it, crossed the room and gave the letter to Kincaid. Her face was tight and her hands were shaking, he noticed. The letter was in Russian, the writing strong though with the appearance of being rather hurried. No names, he noted, no clue who wrote it or to whom.

He read it, looked at Anna, and read it again. Anna was standing in front of him. Kincaid folded the letter and gave it back to her. She took the letter, folded it carefully into the inner envelope, and gave it to Kincaid. He took it and examined it. The envelope was blank, no name or address, no stamp. What is it, he thought; what have I missed? He handed it back and waited. Anna folded it, placed it inside the outer envelope, and gave it to him. Kincaid took it and read the name and address on it. American name, Boston address, 32-cent stamp so posted in America. Someone using a cut-out – the automatic part of his brain flicked into gear: letter posted to intermediary and hand-delivered to final destination. He looked up at Anna again and began to give her the envelope, knew that was not what she wanted. He opened the outer envelope again, took out the inner, then the letter inside, then re-read it. I don't see it, Anna; I'm sorry, but I'm still missing it. She held out her hand. He folded the letter into the first envelope, then the first into the second. Looked at the name and address again, looked at the stamp again.

Looked at the postmark across the stamp, felt his body tighten and his entire world drop into the abyss.

I still don't understand – it was in Anna's face, in her eyes; in Sherenko's silence from the other side of the room.

Kincaid took the bottle and re-filled his glass. For one moment he was back in the morgue in Belle Vue, back with Sherenko in the morgue on C'urupy Ulica. Then he was back on the mountain top, the past and the present clear around him no matter which way he looked.

'I was with the Soviet Division of the CIA. On the day in question I was in Miami. Early in the afternoon of that date I was pulled out and flown to New York.' He did not specify what day in question. 'That morning a man calling himself Hemmings had telephoned the Agency's New York office and said he wished to speak to a Leo Panelli. Panelli was on leave in Paris. The caller said he would only talk to Panelli and asked for him to be contacted. He said it was an immediate.' Kincaid glanced at Anna. 'Immediate is an Agency priority classification. There's only one classification above it: war's started and the bombs are falling.'

He turned away from her and was back on the mountain.

'Hemmings said he would call again for a number where he could speak to Panelli, and Panelli was contacted in Paris. No one at this point, except Panelli, knew who Hemmings was, and not even Panelli knew why he was making contact. After he was briefed Panelli cabled Langley. Hemmings, he said, was a private code between himself and a KGB officer whom he had met while both were working the UN.' He glanced again at Anna. 'That wasn't unusual. Certain times, certain situations, each side knows the other. We're all in the same club.

'Panelli also identified Hemmings. Hemmings he said, was known to the Agency and on file at Langley. His code name was Joshua. It was at this point that it went ballistic. All the way up to the White House. When I say White House I mean the President. Joshua was that big.'

He leaned across and handed Sherenko the bottle.

'Joshua speaks to Panelli and says he needs an immediate meeting – always that word immediate, you note. Panelli says he's in Paris but can be East Coast the following morning. The following morning is too late, Joshua says. Then Joshua changes the priority coding. It's not an immediate, he says, it's a flash: war declared and the fingers on the buttons. Or the political equivalent.'

Anna sat mesmerized. What must have been going through Joshua's head – the thoughts ate through her brain. What could be that important that he was in contact with the enemy? Was he afraid, was he thinking of his family?

'Panelli suggests someone meet Joshua in his place. He names me, Joshua agrees and I'm pulled from Miami. Everything is set up: location for the meet, cut-outs before and safe house after. Moscow station ready to lift Joshua's wife and family and get them out of Russia if that's what Joshua wants. Depending, of course, on why he's asking for a meet. Which nobody knows.'

Anna stared at Kincaid and reached for Sherenko's hand. Saw the man Kincaid was calling Joshua, felt with him and heard with him. Was afraid with him and made the journey with him.

'Joshua flies into Newark and begins the cut-outs. I'm waiting for him. I'm informed that he's passed the last cut-out and will be with me in ten minutes.' His voice dropped. 'Joshua doesn't make it.'

What do you mean – Anna wanted to scream. Because it was important, because it was a flash. Joshua had risked everything, so he wouldn't pull out. 'Why didn't he make it?' she asked.

'He was assassinated on the way in.'

The world collapsed around her. The sun disappeared and the room dipped into half-light, shadows folded on shadows. I'm there with you, Anna told Joshua; I'm beside you in that last terrible moment. Did he know – the thoughts came in kaleidoscopes now. What did he think the moment he knew he was going to die? Did he think of the thing that was so important, or did he think of his wife and daughter?

Sherenko's voice echoed in the gloom. 'Why are you telling us this, Jack? How does this connect with Moscow USA? How does it relate to Anna's letter?'

Kincaid stared back. 'You remember I said that Dushkin made two calls to Moscow, Idaho.'

'Yes.'

Kincaid breathed deeply. 'Joshua made his first call from Moscow, Idaho. Actually, from a pay phone at the airport.'

The silence wrapped round them like a shroud. Anna sat tight against Sherenko; her eyes were filled, her face was frozen, and her body was beginning to shake. The letter was in her hand and the words were burnt into her mind.

... *When you receive this it will be over. If I have been able to achieve what I am about to do, then I will tell you; if not, then others might not. If others tell you, judge them, not me, by what they say* ...

Tell me more about Joshua – the kaleidoscope flashed in Anna's mind. 'Why do you think Joshua was in contact with you?' she asked at last.

Kincaid was back in the morgue on C'urupy Ulica, back in the morgue at Belle Vue, back in the restaurant on East 54th and hearing the single shot. 'The first theory was that Joshua was going to defect.' He saw the expression on Anna's face. 'Remember, however, that he told Leo Panelli that it was an immediate. Defections aren't about that, defections are for money or politics. Joshua was about something else.' He saw the relief on Anna's face and in her eyes. 'You remember that Panelli said he could be East Coast by the next morning and that Joshua said that would be too late.'

Anna nodded.

'Something went down that next morning.'

'Big enough to be an immediate?' Anna's voice was thin, hopeful.

'Bigger than that. Big enough to be a flash.'

What was it – Anna's eyes stared at him, pleaded with him.

'The day Joshua contacted Panelli: 18th August 1991.' The date on the postmark of the letter she held in her hand. 'You remember that day. Actually, you remember what happened the next day?'

Anna's mind was too numb to think. 'No,' she told Kincaid.

'Think of what happened the day after, Anna. Think what happened in Russia.'

Oh God – even through the gloom he saw it in her eyes. 'The Gorbachev putsch.'

'Precisely.'

'So what was Joshua doing?' Anna asked.

'I think he had become aware of the putsch, was afraid it signalled an end to the reforms in Russia and a return to the old days, and was trying to stop it. But he couldn't go to his KGB masters, because he couldn't be sure who was involved.'

'Therefore . . .' Anna's voice was almost lost.

. . . What I do, I do because I remember the day you were born and wish that others might know such happiness. What I do, I do because even now I know I have a smile on my face at the memories of our family together, and wish that others might also smile. But that they may smile in freedom and in joy. What I do now, I do because I am a patriot. What I do now I do for Mother Russia . . .

Kincaid's eyes were fixed on her. 'Therefore Joshua contacted the West. Someone he knew he could trust.'

'So Joshua died for his country?'

'I would put it stronger than that. I would say he died trying to save his country. I would say he died trying to save the new Russia he believed in.'

'And who was Joshua?' Anna asked.

'You know who Joshua was.'

She was unable to see him now, the mist was across her eyes and her soul. *I remember you, my father. I remember how you told me stories when I was a child; how you made toys for me when times were hard. How, when times were better but you began to be away a lot, you brought me back little things. But I also remember how you brought them back. Not with show and panache, but gently and kindly, as if the things you brought me were no more yet no less than the wooden toys and dolls you carved for me at the kitchen table. I remember the day you gave me a porcelain horseman, the stallion reared up and its hooves pawing the air. I remember the way you were brought home and the afternoon of your funeral. And now I begin to understand so many things.*

She tore herself from the past and answered her own question. 'Joshua was Major General Mikhail Sergeyevich Buskov, of the First Chief Directorate of the KGB. Joshua was my father.'

The shroud wrapped around them again. They sat in silence, each in his or her own world. The Jack Daniels was almost empty, the thin brown liquid washing in the bottom of the bottle.

'How exactly did my father die?' Anna asked. 'Where, what time? I never knew, you see. They told us he had a heart attack in Moscow, they never said he'd been killed. And we didn't discover that, because they took care of that as well.'

'As I said, he was shot by an assassin.'

'How,' Anna asked. 'Where?'

'The meet was at a restaurant,' Kincaid told her. 'I was waiting for him inside. He was shot as he came in.'

'The moment he entered the restaurant, you mean? His hand on the door? I need to know these things, Jack, I need to know the smallest detail.'

'He stepped from a cab. There were cars parked at the side of the road. He walked between them and on to the pavement. The pavement was three, four metres wide. He cleared the parked cars and began to cross it, then he was assassinated. He didn't know anything.'

'Where was he shot? In the back or the front, I mean; in the head or the body?'

'He was a moving target, so the assassin went for a body shot. A head shot would have been too risky.'

'In the back or the front?'

'The back. He was walking away from the assassin.'

'So whoever killed him never saw his face?'

'No. Whoever killed him was given a time, place and description, and did what he'd been trained to do.'

'Would it have made any difference?'

'How d'you mean?'

'Would it have made a difference if the assassin had seen his face?'

'No.'

Anna drained the glass and placed it on the floor between them, picked it up again and held it tight. Help me, Nikolai Alexandrovich, save me, because you're all I have. Thank God you're here, Nikolai Alexandrovich, thank God you're with me and can hold me; thank God I have you beside me tonight. Why

313

are you staring at me, Nikolai Alexandrovich; why are you not supporting me, why are you not helping me as I journey with my father through the valley of the shadow of death.

'A restaurant in New York, you said?' What's wrong, Nikolai Alexandrovich, why is your face drained white, why do you look as if you've seen death?

'Yes,' Kincaid told her.

'What was the restaurant called?'

'La Famiglia.'

'I'd like you to take me there.'

'Of course.'

Without warning, Sherenko rose, left the room and closed the door behind him. What's wrong, Nikolai Alexandrovich – Anna stared after him. Why are you leaving me when I need you? The elevator was stuck on the sixth floor. Sherenko would have used the stairs anyway. The grey was around him and the hurricane was almost upon him. Sherenko felt its strength. Was back in the safe house in Boston five years ago, staring out of the window. The streets cleared and the city on emergency standby, the news from Russia on CNN and the epicentre of Hurricane Bob whipping up the New England coastline and closing on Boston. The hurricane hit the city. The trees bent double and the clouds swirling in the turbulence, the rain sheeting down and the roofs and cars being torn away. Stay inside, the radio and television had warned. Remain under cover until Hurricane Bob has passed. Sherenko walked down the stairs from the safe house, opened the door, and stepped into the eye of the storm. Left the hotel and walked the streets, left the lights of the streets and walked the alleys, left the alleys and walked in the darkness of his mind. Sometime in the next thirty minutes he passed a man with a placard inviting him to be saved; sometime he stared at the oily grime of the East River; sometime he stopped at a liquor store and bought a bottle of Stolichnaya. Sometime he returned to the hotel room.

The tears streamed down Anna's face and her hair hung over her shoulders.

'Give me two minutes with Anna,' Sherenko asked Kincaid.

Why, Nik – Kincaid wondered. Sure, Nik. But why? Oh

Christ, Nik. Oh my God, Nik, I understand. He stood and began to turn. Went back, bent and kissed Anna on the cheek. Then he turned again and left the room.

Sherenko locked the door and sat down, Anna close to him but opposite him, eyes looking at each other's. You want a drink, Nikolai Alexandrovich – Anna washed the glasses, broke the seal on the cap and poured them each a *stogram*. What's wrong, Nikolai Alexandrovich; what is it that you have to tell me? He stretched his head back and stroked his throat. You look an old man – Anna stared at him. In the past thirty minutes you have aged a lifetime.

'Tell me, Nikolai Alexandrovich.' She held his face in her hands and cradled him to her. 'Tell me what you have to tell me.'

'You know, don't you?'

'Yes, but tell me anyway.'

'I was the assassin. I was the one who killed your father.'

The calm was upon her. 'When did you know?'

'When Jack told us the date of the Joshua assassination.'

'Not before? Not when we first met in Moscow? Not when we made love? Not when you killed for me?'

'No.'

'What about the photographs in my apartment?'

'As Jack said, I never saw your father's face.'

She looked at him, the tears like a veil over her eyes. Then she rose, not speaking, went to the door, walked along the corridor, and knocked on Kincaid's room. You'd better come back, she told him; Nik has something to say to us.

They sat in a circle on the floor.

'August '91.' Sherenko's eyes were held by Anna's. 'La Famiglia on East 54th Street. I was the one who took out Joshua.'

'Details,' Anna told him, kept her eyes on his.

'I was in Boston. The safe house. Vorkov called. Vorkov was my controller, that's how I knew Langley had to have a file on him, even though they wouldn't know the precise details of what he was doing. He instructed me to fly to New York. I took the shuttle down. Vorkov contacted me on schedule and gave me an address and a target. I collected the gun, already zeroed by myself and not touched by anyone else after that, and went to the location. Vorkov gave me the description of the target and the time he was due. Ten minutes before the target arrived Vorkov contacted me to tell me he was on his way.'

'What name were you using?' Anna's voice was arctic. Winters past upon winters future. Winters back to the Creation and forward to the Day of Judgement.

'Daniel Erickson.'

He was running through the streets, Hurricane Bob tearing at him and the rain flooding down on him.

'What did you do after?' Anna asked him.

'I left the KGB.'

The answer was not what she had wanted. What she had wanted was the detail, as Kincaid had given her the detail. 'Why?' she asked.

'Because of the involvement of some of its leaders in the Gorbachev putsch.'

'That's when you turned to drink? That's when your wife and daughter left you? That's when you found the body of your best friend's daughter in the morgue at C'urupy Ulica?'

How did you know that – it was in the slightest turn of the head and the slightest flash in the eyes.

'You told me. The night we walked in Red Square. The night you said there were certain things you would never do again.'

His mind was lost in the hurricane. 'If you say so.'

'So what are you thinking now?' she asked him.

'You want the truth?'

'Yes.'

'The truth is I don't know what I'm thinking.'

'What about you, Jack?' Even though Anna addressed Kincaid her eyes remained riveted on Sherenko.

'Your father turned to the West, and the West betrayed him. I guess I feel a great shame.'

She was still holding Sherenko with her eyes, still held by his. 'Give us thirty minutes, Jack.'

Kincaid rose and left the room.

The tears had stopped now and her face was dry. 'Cry with me, Nikolai Alexandrovich, mourn with me. Make love with me, grieve with me.' She stood and lifted him up, changed her balance slightly, raised her hands and undid his shirt. Changed her balance again and unzipped her dress, stepped out of it, undid her bra and eased it off. Bent slightly, her eyes still looking at him, hooked her fingers in her pants and stepped out of them. She was crying again now, her eyes red and the tears streaming down her face. She reached forward slightly and kissed him on the lips, undressed him, her body shuddering and the tears a veil between his eyes and hers.

An hour later she knocked on Kincaid's door. She was wearing a dressing-gown and her hair was still wet, as if she had just showered. 'Don't ask.' She stepped into the room. 'Don't even try to understand.'

Kincaid held her, wrapped his arms round her. You okay, he asked. I'm okay, she told him. They went back to the other room, sat on the foot of the bed, unscrewed the cap from the bottle, and filled the glasses. Sherenko came out of the bathroom; he was fully dressed and his hair was glistening. Anna passed him the glass.

Do it, Kincaid urged him silently. Say it, Anna pleaded without saying anything.

Sherenko stood to attention and raised the glass. Kincaid and Anna rose and stood to attention facing him, glasses raised. None of them speaking, no clinking of glasses or speeches or toasts. The Russian tradition, the silence for a lost comrade.

Major General Mikhail Sergeyevich Buskov, Sherenko thought. A sword of the Party and a shield of the people. The old KGB motto, except he inserted one word. Mikhail Sergeyevich Buskov, a *true* shield of the people.

Mikhail Sergeyevich Buskov, Anna thought. A beloved father.

Joshua, a patriot, Kincaid thought. That his sacrifice not be in vain.

They drained the glasses and sat down, refilled them and drained them again. Sat in silence, but the silence different this time. So what do you want to do, Anna – it was in the way they looked at her, the way they waited. Because Joshua was your father, and that supersedes anything we might feel.

Anna refilled her glass. 'In London we said that if we don't get them, they get us?' Her voice was cold.

317

'Something like that.'

'In London you also said that we're dead, no matter what happens.'

'Yes.'

'Is that still the case?'

'Yes.'

'Despite the fact that Gerasimov and Jameson have wrapped up the ConTex affair and know you were set up?'

'We're light years from the ConTex money,' Sherenko told her simply. 'We crossed the Rubicon five years ago.'

But still your decision, Anna. Because as we said, Joshua was your father.

Anna stood and walked round the room. Stopped in front of the curtains and looked back at them. 'Nik?'

Sherenko sat forward slightly. 'Recap. Yuri Dushkin is in contact with Sobolev in Moscow USA.'

It was Kincaid who responded. 'Yes.'

'Joshua was also in Moscow USA?'

'Yes.'

'What are the chances that Joshua was also there to see Sobolev?'

'Yevgeni Sobolev is a university professor and small-time businessman. He's also a Russian. An émigré. He spent two years in the UK, then came to America. Every indication therefore is that he was not just allowed to leave Russia, but that everything was planned, that he was KGB. When Joshua was in Moscow USA, or at least on the occasion when we know he was, Sobolev was there. So it would be one hell of a coincidence if Joshua and Sobolev weren't also connected.'

'We have a link between Joshua, Dushkin and Sobolev, and we have another link between Dushkin, Miller, Harrington and Malenkov. So how do these tie together, how do they explain why Miller, Harrington and Malenkov are after us?'

Kincaid was on the mountain top again. 'Try this . . . Miller is Russia desk chief in Soviet Division in '91. Joshua contacts the Agency. Miller, Harrington and Malenkov are already running their little scam, and Miller thinks this is what Joshua wants to tell the Agency about. Miller can't do anything direct, so he does

318

it through Harrington. Harrington in turn contacts Malenkov.'

'So what do we do?' Anna asked.

Kincaid leaned across and took the Stolichnaya. 'We go in through Sobolev.'

The 747 dropped out of the purple above New York. Twenty-five minutes later Vorkov had cleared immigration and customs. The pick-up car was waiting outside. By eleven in the evening he was in the safe house on the East Side, his body clock still on London time and telling him it was four in the morning and he should be asleep. He accepted a coffee and spoke to Malenkov on an encrypted line.

'They know about Moscow, Idaho,' Malenkov told him.

'How?'

'Gerasimov at Omega just asked for the Sobolev file.'

'And you think he's doing it for them?'

'Why else would he?'

'So what do you want me to do about Sobolev?'

'It's already under way. We pulled Sobolev out half an hour ago. By tomorrow morning we'll have a team in Moscow in his place.'

12

The neon seeped through the curtains. Anna lay on the bed and stared at the ceiling. The image drifted across her mind and she fought to recognize it through the fog; saw the face of Joshua and fought to return the image to wherever it had come from. The cold wrapped round her like a cloak of frost; she reached across the bed and felt for Sherenko's hand. The space beside her was empty. She sat up and looked round the room. Kincaid was half-asleep in the armchair by the window, and the bathroom light was on. She heard the shower running then stop, and Sherenko came out. It was three in the morning. I'm afraid, she thought; I'm terrified in a way I could never have imagined, though not in the way I was moments ago. Kincaid rose from the chair, went to the bathroom, and she heard the shower running.

Sherenko sat on the bed and held her. 'You okay?'

'I'm okay.'

Sherenko left the hotel and collected coffee and bagels from an all-night two blocks away. By the time he returned Anna had also showered and dressed. They sat on the chairs and the edge of the bed, and began the briefing; the main ceiling light was off, just the bedside lamp on, and the night outside was still the orange-grey of night over a city.

'We assume that by now Vorkov will be in New York . . .' Kincaid led the discussion. 'We also assume that by now Malenkov, Miller and Harrington will know we know about Sobolev and Moscow USA . . . We assume that Vorkov will have pulled Sobolev out of Moscow and will have a team sitting in his place waiting for us . . .'

Anna felt the image begin to come at her again through the

fog. No time to think of the past, she told herself. No time for her to think of her father, for Sherenko and Kincaid to think of the man they knew as Joshua. Only time to think of the present and the future.

Kincaid took a mouthful of bagel. 'When we're set up, Anna hacks into Sobolev's computer and lets them know where we are. The key moment is when the hit on us goes in. We assume they'll use a sniper, but they might not, so let's run it again . . .' He looked to Sherenko.

'They need to be sure the three of us are together.' Sherenko spoke quietly. 'The first time Anna accesses Sobolev's computer they'll get our location, but they can't be sure all of us will be there. The second time we let them know all three of us are there. At that point they have two options. Either they take us there, at the address, or they wait till we leave and are in the street. Perhaps in a cab or a car . . .'

In the half-gloom on the other side of the room Kincaid nodded. 'They'll take us at the address, that way they assume they're in control. And they'll take us the first moment they think they're in control. The only question is how exactly they'll come at us.'

Sherenko picked up on the point. 'Not through the door. They know me, they know all of us by now, they think they know how we think. So they'll assume there's a possibility we'll have boobytrapped the place as a precaution, even though we don't know they know where we are.' His face was lost in the shadows. I want to see your eyes, Anna thought, I want to see deep into your soul. You don't, Kincaid would have told her.

'So they use a sniper.' Sherenko stood up and changed position, as if he had changed sides and was now the opposition. 'Building opposite ours. I check it out beforehand, as soon as we know the address. I select my position and confirm I have line of vision into the target. Specifically, that I have line of vision to Anna on the computer. Her back will be to me, but that won't concern me. I'll have a minder with me, because the chances are I'll have to use an apartment, therefore I'll need someone to take care of anyone returning while I'm there. I check my way out, probably a fire escape at the rear or the side, because I don't want

321

to go out the front door. I also confirm the arrangements for the pick-up car and the disposal of whatever weapons I choose to use . . .'

Anna shuddered. This is how Nikolai Alexandrovich planned the death of my father; this is how Nikolai Alexandrovich and Jack Kincaid probably planned the deaths of many men. Except that the deaths we are now planning are our own, because only through death is there life.

'Kincaid leaves the location. This is not my concern, though I report it.' Sherenko still spoke as if he was the opposition. 'Kincaid picks up a car which is parked outside, drives off, and a team follows him. We're not sure about Anna Buskova and Sherenko; we consider entering the apartment and taking them, in case they're there, but decide against it. Kincaid goes to Newark airport, as if he's waiting for someone, then leaves the car in Manhattan and returns to the apartment. I see Sherenko arriving and report this back. The team in Moscow USA report that some-one has just started hacking in to Sobolev's computer from the telephone number at the target apartment, so we know Buskova is there. I confirm three figures in the apartment. I confirm two men, plus a woman at the computer. I can take Buskova in one, but what about Kincaid and Sherenko?' He swung slightly, as if between targets. 'One, two, three. I'm good, but not even I can guarantee that. But I must guarantee it, so what do I do . . .'

He locked himself into the darkness for twenty seconds, then re-emerged. His eyes were ringed with black and the muscles of his face were clenched tight.

'I take out Buskova. One shot, no problems. Which still leaves Kincaid and Sherenko, because first shot and they'll hit the floor. But I know they're there, because I've seen or heard them. And even if they've left the room for a moment, they'll come back, because they'll want to get to Buskova, try and help her. So they're in the room. I can't see them, but it doesn't matter. The only thing that does matter is that I know they're in a room to which I have line of vision. Then I take them. Grenades or rockets. I can get one off every three seconds with a launcher. Accuracy at that distance no problem. The launcher small, so no difficulty getting it in . . .'

He changed sides again, was back with Kincaid and Anna. 'And we're all dead. And Malenkov, Miller and Harrington are home and laughing. Vorkov as well, because Vorkov won't be far from the action on this one. Vorkov will be supervising it personally, because his people screwed up in Moscow and missed us in London.'

The coffee from the all-night was cold. He sipped it anyway, then sat down and listened as Kincaid took them to the next stage.

'We assume Miller will involve the FBI as Harrington used Special Branch in London. We assume that the FBI will be sitting on the target location, because if they aren't, Miller and company won't have their cover . . .

'We exit. We assume that when we do, both the Bureau and the opposition will pick us up and follow us . . .' He finished the bagel, rolled the paper in a ball, and threw it in the bin, finished the coffee and threw the beaker in the bin. 'Once the grenades or rockets go in the 911 calls will start. We assume that the first blue and whites will be there within forty seconds, a minute at most. The FBI will inform the PD of their interest in the case, though they won't give too many details. The first patrolman, plus probably the FBI team leader, check out the apartment. Lot of blood, lot of mess.' He paused. 'But no bodies . . .'

'Then Times Square.' Anna's face and voice were almost lost in the dark.

'Then Times Square,' Kincaid confirmed. 'So they know they've got rid of Anna. Now they get rid of Nik and I . . .'

It was thirteen minutes to four, seventy-three minutes till the dead hour; the first grey was streaked into the sky but the city was still asleep. Sherenko and Kincaid left, Anna locking the door after them. The Ford van was parked three blocks away. They accessed and started it without difficulty, and drove to 28th and First. The hospital was quiet. An ambulance eased past, the crew looking tired and drawn; from somewhere in the grey of early dawn came the wail of a police siren. They entered the building, picked up the signs, and followed the corridor, the hospital still quiet and their footsteps making no noise on the floor.

Hope to hell someone's there, Kincaid thought; hope to hell it's an attendant or someone they could bribe or frighten to do what they wanted and keep his mouth shut after, because three bodies known to have been stolen from the city morgue and it would be all over the breakfast bulletins.

They passed a cleaner, bent over a mop, passed an intern, hurrying head down, white coat flapping and eyes bloodshot and tired.

The door was locked, a security pad on the side and a buzzer below it. Kincaid rang the bell and they waited. Thirty seconds later the door opened fractionally and the face looked out at them. The attendant was mid-twenties and Latino, his greens were creased and he looked as if they had woken him. 'Yes . . .' he began to ask. They pushed past him, and closed and locked the door. The last time he had been here was with Joshua, Kincaid suddenly thought; the last time he had been listening for foot-steps in the corridor as the Russians came to take their man home.

He turned to the attendant. 'Three bodies, two male one female, Caucasian. Males six-one and six-two, female five-eight.'

Police, the attendant tried to tell himself. Except they'd forgot-ten to show him their IDs. No one came at this hour, though, especially not in suits. Not even the police. 'You got the names?' he asked. 'You got where they were brought in from?'

It was five in the morning.

'Plus we'll need bags for them.' Kincaid told him.

'You *want* three bodies.' The realization was creased in the attendant's voice. You can't – it was in his eyes, in his body language. Who are you – the fear cut deeper into him. I know about people like you; where I come from people like you come at this hour. Except those they take away aren't dead, though they will soon wish they were, and will be at the end.

Kincaid slid an arm over the attendant's shoulders. '*Dedonde esta, compadre?*' Where are you from, my friend?

'*Bogota*,' the attendant tried to say. '*Colombia. Estoy estudi-ante.*' I'm a student. '*Tengo todo la documentación.*' I have all the right documentation. He was shaking, unable to move Kin-caid's arm from his shoulders.

'Colombia . . .' Kincaid nodded as if he understood. '*Sabe lo*

324

que dicen en Colombia.' You know what they say in Colombia.

'*Que dicen?'* What do they say?

'*Que prefiere, dicen.'* Which do you prefer, they say. '*La plata o el plomo.'* The silver or the lead. The bribe or the bullet.

The morgue was cold around them. Sherenko took out his wallet. 'You married, you got kids?'

'Not married.' The attendant barely heard his own voice. 'One kid.'

'How old?'

'Three.' It was little more than a croak.

Sherenko counted off two hundred one-hundred dollar bills. 'Twenty thousand dollars. Five thousand per body, should help you through school for the next couple of years. Five grand for the kid.' He snapped off another fifty bills. 'Plus five grand for the paperwork which says we were never here.' And you can do that, because some of the bodies in the refrigeration units here in the county morgue at Belle Vue are unclaimed; and after two weeks they pass on to the next stage of their journey – if they believe in such a journey – via a city burial. No mourners and no tears. And no problems. 'Three bodies, two male and one female, Caucasian. Males six-one and six-two, female five-eight. Let's do it.'

As they left Belle Vue the sky to the east was still leaden grey, still no pink of the first dawn. They drove north then east, crossed the East River at the 59th Street bridge and dropped into Queens, stopped at an all-night liquor store, drove on, and passed under the raised section of the metro, which locals called simply *the elevated.* A lot of people lived in Queens, most of them good and honest and God-fearing. A number of people used Queens, however, used its anonymity and its broken buildings and empty warehouses, some of them bad, others like the Bureau for its black bag jobs and its secret locations for undercover cars and operations.

The first pink was like a ghost in the grey. They followed the elevated, cut right and left and picked up the elevated again. On the other side of the East River the lights of Manhattan belonged to another world.

The road was broken by the wheels of heavy lorries. They

eased down the slope to the skeletons of the warehouses at the bottom. The metal-framed windows were broken and open, and the glass in them was smashed. On the left a small fire crackled in a fifty-gallon drum, a circle of derelicts huddled around it, blankets over their shoulders and their eyes black and hollow. Kincaid drove past them, bumped another hundred yards and stopped at the wooden slide door. The lock was broken. Sherenko pushed the door open and heard the rats scuttle in the dark. Kincaid passed him a torch from the glove compartment; Sherenko took it, eased open the wooden door, and stepped inside. The interior was dry and musty, dust on the wooden stairs and cobwebs strung unseen from the ceiling. He went up the stairs, checked the corridors and rooms, picking his way in the beam of the light, and came down again.

'Not what we need,' he told Kincaid.

They drove to the next door. Kincaid waited while Sherenko went inside. The figures were like wraiths around the fire a hundred metres away. Kincaid checked them in the rear mirror, heard the wooden door open again, then saw Sherenko.

'It's good.'

Kincaid opened the rear door of the van. Sherenko pulled one of the body bags on to his shoulder, picked his way up the stairs by the beam of the torch, and came to the first landing. The floorboards were broken and rotting at the ends. Another set of stairs turned back left to the next floor, and a corridor ran in front of him toward the rear of the building. He ignored the corridor and followed the stairs to the second landing. The stairs dog-legged up again, and a second corridor ran to the rear. Sherenko picked his way down it and broke open a door on the right. The room smelt damp. He tipped the body on to the floor and went back for Kincaid and the other two bodies. Then he padlocked the door to the room and secured the sliding wooden door.

Kincaid swung the van in a full turn and bumped back along the ruts. The pink of the new day was stronger in the sky and the eyes of the derelicts were still on them. He stopped the van, got out, pulled out the carrier bag, then walked toward the circle. The men tensed angrily, hands feeling for pieces of wood. Kincaid reached the circle and sat down. The fire in the drum flickered red. He pulled the first bottle of Jack Daniels from the bag, cracked the top, and took a shot, aware of the eyes following his every movement. The fire flickered again. He reached forward and threw wood on, took another shot, sniffed, and passed the bottle to the man on his right. Then he moved the bag, so the shapes around him could hear the bottles inside, nodded at them, returned to the van and drove away.

Anna sat on the foot of the bed and stared at the wall in front of her. The fear crept into her again, the ghost of her father and the trauma she was about to impose upon her mother. Perhaps, one day, she would see her mother again, tell her what she had needed to do. Not for a while though, not till it was over and the flowers had grown on the graves. So why the fear, Anna? Because the fear was not about her father or her mother. It was for Nik.

The fear was illogical, she tried to tell herself. Nik and Jack had everything planned, everything worked out. Nik and Jack were doing what they had to do. She shuddered at the thought of what precisely they were doing and told herself it was time for her to begin planning her part of the operation, time for her to start building in her safeguards.

She crossed the room, sat at the laptop, and logged on. Called up the first number – in India, though the exact geographic location was irrelevant – then called up the second through the first, and the third from the second.

Hack in to Sobolev's computer in Moscow USA, and the first thing the hoods sitting in his place would do would be to check the telephone number from which she was calling. Go in through a number of cut-outs, though, run it via a whole series of computers round the world, make sure the penultimate call was to the phone number in the target apartment, then call Moscow USA from that last number, and Vorkov and Malenkov and Miller and Harrington would think she was calling from that number. And if and when they discovered she wasn't, it would take them hours, if not days, to trace the network back to the number and hotel room she was actually calling from. And by then it would be over and she and Nik and Jack would be dead anyway.

Vorkov was dropped at Newark airport at eight. The night before the *komandir* Bukanin had left two men sitting in the safe house in Boston and flown down on the last shuttle. Vorkov passed through the security and baggage checks, and made his way to Gate 130. Christ, the flight to Moscow would take all day. At least Idaho was East so he was gaining hours. Except if he had to return in a hurry he would be losing them. He bought a copy of the *Herald Tribune*, checked in, and ran through the arrangements.

Sobolev was tucked away and the West Coast team were already in his place. Sherenko and Kincaid, and probably Buskova, were on to Sobolev, and were probably on the way to Moscow. Be funny if they were on the same flight. He realized he had glanced around, and laughed at himself.

The cellphone rang.

'Yes.'

'Someone has just called Mack,' Bukanin informed him. Mack was the agreed code for Sobolev and the team sitting in his place. 'It might be them. Mack's voice mail was running but the caller rang off without leaving a message.'

'Any other calls?'

'No.'

'Where was it made from?'

'Manhattan. A pay phone at the Javits Center.'

Vorkov drew the air between his teeth. Sherenko and Kincaid running a first check on Sobolev. 'Keep me informed.' He saw that the flight had been delayed twenty-five minutes, and moaned quietly.

Getting close to you, Nik. You always were good, probably the best. You made it out in Moscow and London, but you're not going to make it out of Moscow USA. Business not personal, you understand, Nik. Just as it had been in Moscow and London, except on both those occasions you and Kincaid survived.

So why are you and Kincaid calling Sobolev? Assuming it was you who made the call, but everything pointed to it. Someone calling locally, a friend for example, and they might not leave a message on the voice mail; someone calling from New York was more likely to. So at least the call confirmed that Gerasimov's request for Sobolev's file had been for Sherenko. Interesting that they were calling from New York, therefore at least one of them was still in New York. Except why should Sherenko and/or Kincaid be phoning from New York if they knew Sobolev was in Moscow?

The cellphone rang. 'They've been in touch again,' Bukanin told him. 'The World Trade Center this time.'

The flight was beginning to board.

'Keep in touch,' Vorkov told him. He sat down, waited for the queue to shorten, and sifted through the options.

Sherenko and Kincaid knew about Sobolev, but they didn't know he knew. So why should they be phoning? Okay, they could be checking whether or not Sobolev was in the house, which was fine because he already had the house covered. But if they were checking whether or not Sobolev was at home, then why from New York?

Other factors, Vorkov told himself, other considerations. Backgrounds on Sherenko and Kincaid, try to work out from their past how they might be playing it now. Nothing there, nothing which would tell him what they were playing and how they were playing it. Background on Anna Buskova, he told himself. Last shot, but he was out of others. He joined the queue and shuffled forward. Anna Buskova was a computer specialist, Buskova had a Masters from MIT and ran her own computer company in Russia.

Christ that was it – it hit him. That's what Sherenko and Kincaid could do, because that's how they must have discovered Sobolev's phone number. Use Buskova to access Sobolev's computer, find out what they needed to find out about him, before they closed in on him. Just as they must have accessed Yuri Dushkin's to get the information which led them to Sobolev. All Sherenko and Kincaid needed to do at this stage, therefore, was sit on Buskova's shoulder and see what she came up with. So at this stage they wouldn't go anywhere near Moscow USA, because there was no need, never had been. Because Sobolev wasn't the end, Sobolev was only the means to whatever and whoever the end was.

Business problems – he smiled at the ticket clerk; have to cancel his flight. Tell the driver to pick me up, he ordered Bukanin.

The apartment which Sherenko and Kincaid selected and Anna Buskova rented was on the fifth floor of a modern block on East 79th, four blocks from the river. East 79th at this point sloped downwards, west to east; its pavements were wide, with shops and occasional restaurants or coffee houses. The block itself was on the north side, facing south. Entrance was through a marbled foyer, the concierge's desk always staffed, and the underground parking lot was accessed internally by a private elevator, and protected by an electronically operated security grille. The apartment itself comprised a sitting-room, kitchen, and two bedrooms. The furnishings were modern, even esoteric, and the blinds on the windows could be slatted to allow differing degrees of light – and therefore vision – in.

The blocks on the other side of the street were older. The building immediately opposite was an end block, separated from the next down by an alleyway leading to more blocks behind. Both ends of the alleyway, on 79th and 78th, were secured by wrought iron gates, with fire escapes at the side and rear of the building, their metalwork zigzagging down the exterior walls and ending ten feet above the ground.

At ten-thirty Anna and Sherenko left and took a cab to the World Trade Center, returning shortly after one, Sherenko driving the Buick. In ninety minutes of the preceding two hours they had purchased a laptop, modem and cassette recorder from a cut-price store off Times Square, the relevant software from another store, straightforward items from a theatrical shop, a set of clothes for Anna from Macey's, and three cellphones from an office supply store off 28th. The remaining thirty minutes of the two hours the three of them had spent in the hotel with the cassette recorder.

At this time of day the street was busy with cars, though not pedestrians. Sherenko swung a U-turn and parked the Buick in front of the block. The remote control for the barrier to the underground parking lot was on the dashboard. He placed it in his pocket, locked the car, then they went inside, and took the elevator to the fifth floor.

Anna unpacked the laptop, placed it on the desk in the sitting-room, set it up, and plugged in the modem. Sherenko watched her, then went to the window and stared across the street at the block on the other side. Anna crossed the floor and stood beside him. The knot tightened in her stomach and she felt the fear again. 'Which one?' she asked.

'Sixth floor, immediately opposite. Perfect angle and line of vision.'

What are you thinking, she wanted to ask; what do you normally think at this sort of moment? Do you feel anything, or are you as cold and detached as you seem to be? Do you feel fear as I now feel fear? The phone rang, and the voice mail cut in and invited the caller to leave a message. 'Five minutes out,' Kincaid informed them from a pay phone. Sherenko lifted the receiver. 'On our way.'

They checked the cellphones, put one in Anna's bag, and began to leave.

'Your ring,' Sherenko reminded her.

Anna nodded and eased it from her finger. The ring was gold, the inscription on the inside. She played with it, held it for the last time. 'My father gave it to me.' It was somewhere between an explanation and a plea.

Sherenko took it from her. 'It's okay, he'd understand.' He slipped his arms round her.

'Are we going to make it, Nikolai Alexandrovich?'

'Of course we're going to make it, Anna Mikhailovna.'

'Don't want to leave you, Nik; don't want to do it.'

They left the apartment, took the elevator to the foyer, and stepped into the street. Kincaid was parked in a station wagon two blocks up.

'See you,' Anna told him.

'Yeah, see you.'

'See you, Nik.'

'Yeah, be seeing you.'

She turned away from them and walked up 79th toward

331

Second. Keep walking, she told herself; don't look back; don't betray your weakness. The void engulfed her; she felt lost and alone, understood the fear which had swept over her before and which swept over her again now. She was standing by her father's grave five years before, except it was not five years ago and not the grave of her father. It was later that evening, and the grave was of Nikolai Sherenko. She stopped at the lights and glanced back. Sherenko was standing at the car, looking at her. She thanked him for the simple action and waved goodbye.

Sherenko opened the passenger door of the station wagon and Kincaid slid away, picked up the approach to the 59th Street bridge, and dropped into Queens; picked up the route they had taken in the grey hours of the morning and threaded their way toward the urban wasteland of the warehouses. The area was deserted; they bumped past the drum around which the derelicts had huddled, stopped a hundred metres on, and confirmed that no one was watching them. Sherenko took the flashlight, left the car, unlocked the warehouse door, and checked inside. Knelt down and examined the dust he had brushed across the dry wood of the rickety stairs. No one had been there since his last visit. He went back outside. The warehouse area was still quiet. Kincaid unlocked the rear lift-up door of the station wagon and they pulled the roll of carpet from the back, carried it inside, and checked again that no one was observing them. Kincaid pulled the sports bag out, gave it to Sherenko, slid back into the driver's seat, and pulled away. Sherenko carried the bag upstairs, picking his way with the flashlight.

The bodies were still in the room off the corridor to the rear; as he opened the door a rat scuttled past him. He jerked involuntarily, put the sports bag down, and unzipped the first body bag. In the beam of the flashlight the face seemed grey and waxen. Male face. Himself, he decided grimly. He unzipped the second bag and shone the flashlight on to the face. Male again. Kincaid. He pulled the third bag to the door, picked up the sports bag again, and turned right along the corridor. Ten metres on, the corridor opened into a large storage area, wooden pillars supporting the ceiling and the floor covered with a thick layer of dust, broken crates scattered along the walls, and a second doorway off it in the far corner to the right. Welcome to the killing room, he thought.

He opened the bag and shone the flashlight on the contents. In the silence he heard the grating sound as the door on to the street was opened then closed. He switched off the flashlight and padded silently to the landing, heard the soft sound of footsteps on the bare wood then saw the first glimmer against the dark of the walls.

'Nik' – he heard Kincaid's voice.

'Next floor.' He shone the flashlight down the well of the stairs. Fifteen seconds later Kincaid loomed like a ghost. 'Everything okay?' Sherenko asked.

'Fine.' Kincaid's voice echoed slightly in the emptiness. 'So tell me.'

Sherenko led Kincaid through: the corridor, the room to the right and the killing area at the end. 'When we come in tonight, you take the lead. We leave the flashlights inside the main door, on the right, pick them up as we enter. They'll be right behind us, so we cover each other, place some crates on the first landing to roll down the stairs and slow them down, give us time to get in position up here.' He showed Kincaid the room on the right where he had left the bodies, then they went through to the killing room. In the shafts of torchlight the room seemed bleak and unforgiving. Sherenko directed the beam across the floor. 'We place more crates here so they have to follow a set path. You're in front, remember; you take your position through the door on the far right.' He shone the flashlight at the door, then indicated another position against the far wall of the killing room. 'They see two shapes, here and here. Trip wire across here; I'll leave it loose when we leave now. You tighten it as you come through, you should have just enough time. I take my position in the room off the corridor where we've stored the bodies. You make enough noise to distract them, make them think I've gone through into the main room. They follow what they think is me, see the shapes and assume it's us trying to hide. They probably begin shooting then move forward and hit the trip wire. We don't use too much explosives for the first charge. As soon as the charge goes, we both come out, get them in our cross-fire.'

He swung the flashlight around the killing room. 'The angles of fire are good, we won't hit each other. When it's over we position our two bodies and activate the second charge.' He took off the ring he wore on the second finger of his right hand and gave it to Kincaid. 'You deal with the bodies, I'll set up here.'

Forty minutes later they turned down East 79th and pulled on to the ramp leading to the parking lot beneath the apartment block. Sherenko pressed the remote control he had taken from the Buick and the security grille lifted. They drove beneath it and it came down again. The service elevator was on the right, just past a bend. Kincaid stopped beside it, unlocked the rear door, then he and Sherenko pulled the carpet roll out and laid it on the ground. There was a smell of gasoline in the air. Sherenko called the elevator while Kincaid found the space for the apartment and parked. The elevator doors opened. They carried the roll in, stood one end of the carpet on the floor, leaned the other against the side, and pressed the button for the fifth. The elevator rose silently and the doors slid open. There was no one in the corridor. Sherenko held the doors open while Kincaid unlocked the apartment, then they carried the roll across into the sitting-room, laid it against the right hand wall, and locked the door.

The blinds were closed. They opened them, rearranged the furniture, and checked the line of vision with the apartments one floor up on the opposite side of the street.

Anna waited in the hotel room. The knot was tight in her stomach and the nerves cut through her like knives. Her cellphone rang and she picked it up immediately.

'You okay?' Sherenko asked on the second cellphone.

'I'm fine.'

'We're ready. Good luck.'

'Going in now.' Anna swung in the chair, ran through the cut-outs till she was going through the laptop she had set up in the apartment on East 79th, and entered the number in Moscow USA. 'I'm running,' she told Sherenko.

'Take care.' He ended the call and left the apartment.

Vorkov paced the study and waited. The safe house was quiet, a clock ticking in the kitchen and the boys watching a replay of a

Yankees game in the sitting-room, the sound turned down and no one really interested. Everyone just passing time. Always the same in holding positions, those with military service might have told the others. Please God and Marx and the Angel Gabriel may I be right, Vorkov prayed. Please may the action be going down here, in Manhattan, and not on the other side of the continent in Moscow USA.

It was two in the afternoon, Eastern Standard Time. In Moscow Russia it would be late evening; in Moscow Russia the sun would be setting over Red Square, the domes of St Basil's would be sparkling against the electric blue of the evening sky, and the first lights would be twinkling in the Kremlin. In Moscow USA . . .

He left the study, went to the kitchen, poured himself another coffee, drifted into the sitting-room and nodded at the boys. It was four hours since the second call to Moscow USA from the World Trade Center, and two since he had last updated Malenkov.

The telephone rang. 'Yes.' Bukanin did not identify himself. He listened, saw Vorkov's eyes tight on him, shook his head and put the phone down. 'The boys from Boston just reporting that they've arrived at La Guardia and are on their way in.' He placed the handset back on the base unit. The ringing was immediate.

'Yes.'

'It's Mack.' The team leader in Moscow USA on a cellphone. 'Someone's just started hacking in to the man's computer.'

Bukanin cupped his hand over the mouthpiece, nodded at Vorkov, and reached for a sheet of paper. Behind him the boys switched off the Yankees game.

'They're having problems,' the team leader in Moscow USA informed Bukanin. 'Mack obviously has a good security system. They've just exited . . . We're tracing the number now . . . Got it.'

Bukanin wrote down the number, handed the sheet to Vorkov, and remained on the phone. Vorkov in turn handed it to the man already booting up the Pentium in the corner of the study. Nine seconds later the name and address appeared on the screen.

'Manhattan,' Vorkov told Bukanin. 'Apartment on East 79th.'

'We have it,' Bukanin told the team leader in Moscow. 'Good work.'

Vorkov went to the kitchen, closed the door, and called Malenkov.

'Going secure.'

'Secure.'

Vorkov gave Malenkov the address. Bukanin and a four-man team using two cars to run a first recce, they agreed, check out the location and possible sites near it. Everything softly, softly: nothing which might give the opposition the slightest warning.

And in the meantime Malenkov would alert Miller. Through Harrington, of course, which was the normal procedure, and without Vorkov knowing the details. And in an hour, two hours, depending on what Bukanin reported back, Malenkov would set it up so that Miller could arrange for the FBI to stake out the apartment, just as Harrington had engineered the Special Branch veil in London.

Kincaid crossed to the window and looked out. The blinds were tilted down, so that he could observe the street below but could not be observed by anyone in the apartments opposite. He stood a metre back and focused on that section of the street and the pavement opposite which he could see. 'Running,' he told Sherenko on the cellphone.

'Understood.' Sherenko entered the restaurant and settled at the table. The restaurant was on the other side of the street, so that he could observe the section of pavement not visible to Kincaid in the apartment. The changes to his appearance had been small but significant: the usual cheek padders and moustache, stylish spectacles and subtle alterations to his hair colour and style.

It was thirty minutes since Anna had hacked into Sobolev's computer, twenty-nine minutes since she had come out, probably twenty-eight since the opposition had the address on 79th. So the opposition should be showing soon. Not in force, yet. Just one man eyeballing the area and assessing the target location.

He smiled at the waitress and asked for coffee.

Bukanin left the cars on the other side of Second Avenue and walked down 79th, keeping to the right pavement. The target location was on the left – his observations were automatic, no turn of the head, nothing to suggest he was even remotely interested. Modern block, fifth floor, blinds on windows and expensive-looking entrance hall to the block. Outer glass door, which was open, then inner door which was locked, with a security combination lock, phone system on the left to contact the apartments direct and ask them to open the door, or to speak to the concierge desk inside. And at the concierge desk they'd check the apartment to confirm you were expected.

He switched his attention to the side of the street opposite the target.

The buildings were older, and the one immediately opposite the target was an end block, an alleyway between it and the next. Access was through an archway to a central open area, separate stairs off it he supposed, but protected by an iron gate with a combination lock. The alleyway had gates at either end, which were no problem, and there were fire escapes at the side and, he assumed, the rear.

Everything fine, everything looking good.

'White male, aged early thirties,' Sherenko informed Kincaid on the cellphone.

'Six-two, light grey suit, black shoes, medium-length black hair.'

'He's left the area,' he updated Kincaid. 'He's a Red Sox fan.'

'Understood.'

The Red Sox were the Boston baseball team. Therefore the man Sherenko had eyeballed was one of those who had staked out the safe house in Boston.

Bukanin returned to the cars. 'Time to do it,' he told the man in the rear seat. Kaspov was the team's *chernomeshochnik*, its black bag man. 'Checking out the location opposite,' Bukanin informed Vorkov. 'I might need a telephone number.'

'Standing by.'

They left the cars.

'He's back,' Sherenko informed Kincaid. 'Our man plus one other.'

Kincaid picked them up as they crossed the road from his left. 'Got them.'

Bukanin turned off the street and under the archway to the courtyard at the centre of the building opposite the apartment. At this time of day both the passageway and the courtyard itself were empty. The *chernomeshochnik* cleared the lock on the gate to the courtyard in eight seconds. Bukanin turned up the second flight of stairs to the right, began counting the floors, and came to the sixth. The passageway ran both to his right and his left. The prime point for surveillance on the target apartment was between windows nine and twelve from the end of the block. Three windows per apartment, he guessed. He called Vorkov on the cellphone and gave him the number of the fourth door. Thirty seconds later Vorkov told him the telephone number of the apartment. Bukanin punched the number, let it ring for twenty seconds in case someone was at home, then nodded at the *chernomeshochnik*. Fourteen seconds later they were inside.

The apartment was small: a kitchenette/dining area to the right, a television in the corner, a bedroom to the left and a small shower room between. It was well-decorated and neat. There were blinds at the windows, pulled up at the moment, and the windows overlooked the target location forty metres away. One single female occupant judging by the items in the shower room and bedroom, therefore no problems.

Bukanin confirmed there was no indication of their entry, then they left, checked the fire escapes and the alleyway at the side and rear of the block, exited the location individually, returned to the cars, left the occupants of one car to continue surveillance on the target location, and drove back to the safe house. Vorkov was waiting. They fetched fresh coffee from the kitchen, then closed themselves off in the study.

'I assume we take all three out at the same time,' Bukanin asked.

'Agreed.'

Bukanin sipped his coffee. 'In that case parameters first. We need the three together, but we don't know when or where that might be: in the apartment, in a motor, on the street. We can't plan for the latter two, but we can for the apartment.'

Vorkov nodded again. 'How can we be sure all three will be in the apartment?'

Bukanin had already thought it through. 'The woman is the computer expert. We'll know she's there when someone hacks into Sobolev's computer. We'll know all three are there by audio and visual surveillance from across the street, laser surveillance in case the blinds are closed.'

'Options for the apartment?' Vorkov asked.

'There are two. An assault squad goes in the apartment, or I take them from across the road.'

'Break down a frontal assault.'

'The building has the obvious security measures on the main entrance, which wouldn't necessarily present any problems, plus there's access through the service elevator to the parking lot below the block. There's a security grille to the parking lot, but again that wouldn't be a problem. The problem is that even though the targets shouldn't be expecting us, they might have taken precautions.'

'Such as?'

'Boobytrapped the door.'

Plus the FBI, Vorkov didn't say. 'Break down the second option,' he told Bukanin.

'A sniper shot from across the street. The position is available and could be made secure. There are fire escapes at the side and rear, plus access to the street at the rear for the exfil.'

'What about the fact that there are three of them?'

'You mean how many rounds can I get off and be sure I take them all? That's only the first consideration. The second, and assuming I go for the hacker first, is that immediately I hit one, the other two will drop out of sight.'

'So?'

'I do what the mafia would do in Moscow. Take the hacker out with the rifle, then the other two out with grenades or rockets. Easy and accurate from a launcher. No problems.'

'Why not take them all out with grenades?'

'Because we might have to wait too long for all three of them to be in one room at the same time. We can hold the apartment opposite for as long as we want, of course, but the longer we're there, the longer we're exposing ourselves. So we need to take them fast. The obvious moment is when the woman is on the computer. If the other two aren't in the target room and we use a grenade on her, they may not go into the room, even to try to save her, because they'll know another grenade might go in. Use a rifle to take her, however, and there's no reason for them not to go in. More than that. Take her with a rifle shot and we entice them into the room, because they'll want to help her and think they can. They'll go in in a certain way, of course. They'll cover themselves, won't let us have vision of them. But with grenades it won't make a difference.'

'So we use the rifle shot to take out Buskova, then we use Buskova as bait to take out Sherenko and Kincaid.'

'Precisely.'

Vorkov smiled his agreement. 'Arrange it. Two teams covering the place in the meantime in case they move.' He waited for Bukanin to leave the room then used the secure phone to contact Malenkov. 'It's arranged.' He went into detail. 'Everything will be in place within the hour.'

He hung up, locked himself into his thoughts, and called Bukanin back in. 'Everything running?' he asked.

'The boys will be in place in five minutes.'

'Good.' There was the first hint of hesitation in the voice.

'Anything wrong?' Bukanin asked.

'No.'

'But?'

Vorkov swung in the chair and stared at the ceiling, then swung back again and looked at Bukanin. 'It's almost too easy.'

'Moving in two minutes,' Kincaid told Sherenko on the cellphone.

'Standing by,' Sherenko informed him from the café across the street.

'Coming out now.' Kincaid left the apartment, crossed the pavement, unlocked the Buick Sherenko had parked earlier, and drove away. Behind him the Oldsmobile dropped into place. 'You got one,' Sherenko informed him.

The knock on the door was urgent. 'Kincaid's gone walkabout.' Bukanin updated Vorkov. 'He left the block two minutes ago and has driven away in a motor which was parked outside. One team is following him, the second is still on 79th.'

'What about the others?'

'The team's not sure; nobody's seen Sherenko or Anna Buskova yet.'

'You think those two might be in the apartment?'

'It's possible.'

'So why not take them now?'

'Same reason as before, plus they've probably got a code, so Kincaid won't go back in until he's confirmed with the others that everything's okay. And we need all three of them.'

The Holland Tunnel was busy, the late afternoon traffic already streaming from Manhattan. Kincaid waited patiently then took the Pulaski Skyway south. 'At Newark airport,' the tails informed Vorkov. 'Seems to be waiting for someone.' Who was Kincaid waiting for, Vorkov wondered, what the hell was Kincaid playing at? 'Leaving Newark,' the eyes informed him. 'Heading north on 1 and 9. Pulaski Skyway and Holland Tunnel. Manhattan.'

The alleyway was behind a block of shops and restaurants three minutes from Times Square, fire escapes down the backs of the buildings, rear doors heavily locked, emergency exits with DO NOT OBSTRUCT signs on them, and limited parking along one side. Kincaid reversed into a space close to one of the emergency exits, locked the Buick, and left the alley.

So what was Kincaid playing at, Vorkov wondered again. Who had he been waiting for at Newark? Leave the Buick which Kincaid had dropped or stake it out – he ran through the options. Place an explosive charge on it in case Sherenko, Kincaid and Buskova were ever in it together, or assume they were using it as back-up and use that fact against them, put a tracking device on it in case the teams ever lost them.

Tracking device, he decided.

It was fifteen minutes since Kincaid had parked the Buick. The alleyway was deserted. The man who approached the car was inconspicuous and his movements were casual, as if he belonged. He checked behind him, unlocked the trunk, slid the device inside and connected it to the wire of the offside rear light. Run a tracking device off its own battery and it lasted three hours, run it off a wire leading to the car battery and it ran for ever.

The window at the side of the door thirty metres from the Buick was too small to climb through; metal bars crossed over it anyway, and it was grimed with dirt. One small circle in the grime where the glass had been cleaned. Sherenko watched the man who had planted the tracking device leave, gave him ten minutes, then cleared the area.

Ed Miller was in conference when the Langley liaison with the FBI telephoned the division. He left the meeting and took the call in his own office.

'What do you have for me?'

'The Bureau have just got an intelligence update from the FSB in Moscow, through the Bureau's legat in London. The intelligence quotes unnamed sources, though the Bureau presumes wire-taps, and gives a Manhattan telephone number for the suspects Kincaid and Sherenko. The number is listed to an apartment on East 79th. The intelligence has been passed to New York FBI. A Special Operations Group has been assigned and is about to be briefed.'

Miller sat back. 'Good work. Tell everyone I appreciate it.'

Three minutes later the briefing began at the FBI New York headquarters on the top floors of the tall slim building at 26 Federal Plaza. Each Special Operations Squad comprised three teams, and each team ran with a minimum of four agents and an optimum of seven. That evening the team code-named Blue, which the supervisor assigned to an immediate surveillance role, consisted of six agents, four male and two female.

Blue team would mount one four-hour session to begin to establish some pattern – the procedure was routine: don't commit too much up front too soon; put too much in too early, and you risked letting the opposition know you were on to them before you knew what they did and how they did it. Therefore one agent would be positioned in a television van in the underground parking lot servicing the apartment and the others would be strung in cars in the area, the team leader flip flopping the eye, changing the front man, regularly. Priority rankings already defined, of course: what they should do if the targets left the location, what they should if the targets split, what they should do if the targets met another party. But everything low-key at this stage, though at least they could pull the details off the airports.

The sun was going down and the windows tinted orange in the glow. Sherenko and Kincaid sat in the bedroom, not talking. In the block on the other side of the street the *chernomeschochnik* slid effortlessly into the apartment and was joined by Bukanin, plus the minder who would deal with the owner should he or she return. In the hotel room Anna paced the floor and prayed that they would telephone soon.

'Update,' Vorkov requested. 'No movement,' Bukanin told him. 'No one in the sitting-room and the blinds to the other rooms are pulled shut. Kincaid's been back an hour and Sherenko thirty minutes. No audio pick-up from the laser directed at the window of the sitting-room.'

'Everything quiet,' the FBI eye reported to his team leader. The team were on a separate secure radio channel and able to communicate with each other, though only the team leader was in contact with the supervisor in Federal Plaza.

The sun was gone and the light was beginning to fade. Sherenko left the bedroom, went through the hallway, into the corridor outside the apartment, and called Anna on the cellphone.

'We're about to do it. You okay?'

'Sure I'm okay.'

'One minute,' he told her and went back inside.

Bukanin picked up the first movement, the two men crossing the room opposite, then the blinds slanted shut again. Sherenko and Kincaid pulled the body from the kitchen and positioned it on the chair so that it was facing the computer and with its back to the window. Kincaid went outside, called the service elevator to the underground parking lot, and confirmed it was working. Sherenko activated the cassette recorder he and Anna had worked on in the hotel that morning.

'Ready?' The *chernomeschochnik*, the black bag man, heard the first male voice. Audio pick-up, he told Bukanin.

'Ready,' he heard the female voice.

'Do it.'

The blinds of the target apartment half-opened. Bukanin saw a male figure walking back across the sitting-room, a second male disappearing from his vision, and the female hunched over what he assumed was a computer, her head and shoulders clear and her back to him.

In the hotel room Anna tapped the number of the first cut-out and began the sequence, ran the other cut-outs and came to the number of the target apartment on East 79th, keyed in the number of the farmhouse in the rolling hills to the south of Moscow USA, activated the code-cracker, and slid easily through Sobolev's firewalls.

'Somebody's hacking in,' the Moscow team leader informed Vorkov.

'Hacking in now,' Vorkov passed the information to Bukanin.

'Female target in vision.' Bukanin told him.

'In your time.'

Bukanin reached to his right. The RAI weighed 5.67 kilos and measured 160 cms. The round normally fired from it was a 7.62x51 standard NATO issue, though Bukanin had changed the barrel and bolt head to accommodate a Research Armaments Industries' 8.58x71 special. The grenade launcher was on the floor and already loaded.

Sherenko and Kincaid left the apartment, jammed the door of the service elevator open with a chair and waited in the corridor. Please may it work, Anna prayed; please may Nik and Jack be okay.

How's it going – the *chernomeschochnik* picked up the male voice in the conversation from the target location.

I'm in – he heard Anna's voice.

What about the security – a second male voice.

No problems.

'Three of them present,' he informed Bukanin. 'Female, two males.'

The woman's back filled the cross-wires, the RAI cradled easily against Bukanin's shoulder, and his breathing was controlled and rhythmic.

What are you getting – the technician picked up Sherenko's question.

Christ – he heard the excitement in Anna's voice. *The bastards.*

'They're in,' he informed Bukanin. 'They're on to something.'

'Still three?' Bukanin asked.

'Still three.'

Bukanin breathed out gently, breathed in, and squeezed the trigger. Knew he had hit the moment he did so and did not even bother to check. Placed the RAI in the bag and picked up the grenade launcher.

What the hell was that, the FBI eye in the street thought.

The woman was slumped forward over her computer. Bukanin aimed the grenade launcher and began counting. One ... Sherenko and Kincaid would be fighting out of the shock. Two ... Sherenko in particular would be assessing the situation, because that was his background and his training. Three ... Sherenko and Kincaid would be reacting. Not needing to speak to each other because both were pros. Sherenko and Kincaid would be on the floor now, making their decisions. Four ... Sherenko and Kincaid would be crawling across the floor to the woman.

He squeezed the trigger. The first grenade screeched across the street, shattered the glass of the apartment window, tore through the flimsy plastic of the blinds, and entered the sitting-room. Bukanin loaded the second. Half a second later the first grenade detonated. In the corridor outside the apartment Sherenko and Kincaid ducked instinctively and began timing.

'Christ,' the FBI eye whispered in his radio. 'Oh Jesus Christ!'

'What?' the team leader asked.

'First grenade,' the surveillance team half a block from the apartment told Vorkov. 'Looks good.'

Bukanin squeezed the trigger and the second grenade screeched across the street and exploded in the apartment, the third immediately after. Should be it, Sherenko told Kincaid; three seconds between each.

'Two more,' the surveillance team informed Vorkov.

'Fuck . . .' The eye's voice was louder, more excited. His gun was in his hand. 'Oh fucking hell. They're attacking it. They're fucking attacking it.'

'Calm it,' the FBI team leader told him. 'Calm it and tell me what's happening.' Move it, he ordered his driver.

'There's been an explosion in the target apartment.' The agent's voice was suddenly calm. 'One explosion, followed by two more. Source is unclear.'

Bukanin slid the launcher into the bag and pulled up the zip. The *chernomeschochnik* was already at the door. Clear, the minder told them from the corridor. They left the apartment and walked quickly to the rear of the building. In the emergency switchboard of the New York Police Department the first 911 call was received.

Eighteen seconds since the last grenade – Sherenko counted, then nodded at Kincaid. Might be a come-on, but there was no time to waste if it wasn't.

They checked that the door of the elevator was jammed open and went back into the apartment, went through the hallway and into the sitting-room. The computer was smashed and sparking, the furniture and walls were ripped by the grenade fragments, and the body was draped over the desk like a torn doll. The blue dress Anna had bought that afternoon was shredded by metal, the blood already over it, and the entry hole in the head was undetectable in the mess of blood, hair and bone. Kincaid crossed the room and lifted the body off the computer. The face was destroyed by the exit of the round, the white of the torso was visible through the gashes in the dress, and the gold of Anna's ring glittered in the red of the blood. Kincaid took the weight of the shoulders and slid the body round. Sherenko stooped and took the feet, then they lifted it off the chair. Somewhere in the block Sherenko heard someone screaming; somewhere outside he heard the first sirens.

At the rear of the apartment opposite Bukanin and the other two slid unnoticed into the yard and out of the gate on to the street at the far side.

'Explosion at target location,' the FBI team leader informed Federal Plaza. 'Source unclear.' The driver slid to a halt one block up. The team leader left the car and hurried down the street, and the first police car screeched past him.

Kincaid and Sherenko carried the body into the elevator, pulled the chair inside, and pressed the button for the parking basement.

'Am entering the block to investigate,' the team leader informed his supervisor.

'Explosion at target location,' the FBI supervisor informed his ASAC. 'Recommend we send another team and request aerial surveillance just in case.'

On East 78th Bukanin and his team slid into the pick-up car and the car slid quietly away, a second car removing the RAI sniper rifle and the grenade launcher from the area.

The supervisor in the FBI command centre hit the switch for the video phone to his opposite number in the NYPD building across the street. 'Lou, this is John. The incident on 79th. We have an interest in it. We have teams staking out what seems to be the address.' But keep it quiet, between you and us. And no indication what interest, not even to the police attending the scene, no suggestion of a stake-out, because the press would be monitoring the police radio traffic.

'Police arriving at scene,' the surveillance team updated Vorkov.

'Clear of the area,' Bukanin informed Vorkov. He sat back, relaxed, and told the driver to pull in.

The elevator opened. Sherenko ran for the Chevrolet and Kincaid carried the body out, his left arm round the waist and his right hand holding the body's right arm round his shoulder. Sherenko started the engine, accelerated past the TV service van parked in the corner, and braked by the elevator, jumped out, opened the rear left door, and helped Kincaid lift the body inside. Kincaid slid in beside it. Sherenko shut the door, ran to the driver's seat, slid the Chevrolet into drive, and accelerated round the corner to the ramp. The security grille was down. He pressed the remote control, slid under the grille as it rose, and turned left down 79th. To his right the first police car screamed to a halt in front of the apartment.

Patrolman Leroy L. Mathers and his partner left their blue and white and ran up the steps. The concierge saw them and unlocked the door. The lights above the elevators indicated that one was on the seventh floor and one on the sixth; there was no indication of a service elevator to the parking basement. Mathers turned right and ran up the stairs, suddenly aware someone was running behind him. In the distance he heard the wail of a fire engine. He passed the third floor and came to the fourth, slowed slightly, worked out what to do, and cleared the next set to the fifth, his breathing hard but rhythmic.

'Fifth floor,' he reported in on the radio. He drew his 9mm, turned, expected his partner, and saw a man in civilian clothes, 9mm also drawn. FBI, the man flashed his identity. What the hell is this, Leroy Mathers wondered; why the hell did he get here first? 'Am accompanied by an FBI agent,' he told control.

'Am approaching apartment with NYPD,' the FBI team leader told Federal Plaza.

They rounded the corner to the hallway of the fifth floor. The doors of the apartments were shut. Second along, Mathers calculated; nothing in the hallway or on the floor, he noted. He edged forward, the FBI man at his side, came to the door, and stood to the right, the FBI man to the left. 'Police,' Mathers shouted. 'Open the door.' There was no reply. In the quiet later that evening he would realize that he hadn't expected any. He looked at the man on the other side of the door, aimed, and shot three rounds into the area of the lock, jerked back, waited for a response, nodded at the FBI man to cover him, kicked the door open, and went in.

Christ, he thought.

The room reeked of carnage. Shattered furniture and walls, everything torn apart. Computer smashed and sparking, blood and destruction and more blood, but no bodies. Every sign of carnage, every sign that at least one person had been killed or seriously injured, but no bodies.

'Target address destroyed by what appears to be a grenade or rocket attack,' the FBI team leader informed his supervisor. 'Evidence of death or injury, but no bodies.'

'Confirm that message,' the supervisor requested.

'Target apartment destro—'

'Two targets have exited premises.' He heard the radio message from the eye in the TV service van in the parking basement. 'Two males, carrying a female. Female appears badly injured.' He gave the team leader the colour and numberplate details of the Chevrolet.

Fuck, the FBI man swore. 'Target apartment empty,' he informed the rest of the team. 'Suspect car leaving premises, three targets on board.' He gave them the description and plate details. 'Follow but do not intercept. Back-up being requested.'

'Something's wrong,' the surveillance team half a block up informed Vorkov. 'Other surveillance in area, looks like FBI. Car has just left location and the others are following it.'

Chert, Vorkov swore. So what the hell was going down?

'Are they our targets?' he asked calmly.

'Not sure,' the stake-out reported back.

'How many are there in the target car?'

'Again not sure, but it looks like two in the front and one in the rear.'

Chert, Vorkov swore again. Too easy, he remembered he had told Bukanin. He distanced himself from the urgency of the surveillance leader's voice and thought it through. 'Pursue and update,' he ordered the team. 'Confirm you have two phones.'

The surveillance team were already pulling away. 'Confirmed.'

'Use this phone to communicate with me. Use the other to communicate with our man.' He didn't use Bukanin's name. His mind was cold and calm. He made himself think it through for another five seconds then called Bukanin.

'You're aware what has happened?' he asked.

'Yes,' Bukanin told him.

'You remember I said it was too easy?'

'Yes.'

'It still is. The apartment was a set-up, but the set-up isn't over yet. Be careful.'

Bastards, Bukanin thought. Understood, he told Vorkov.

'Got them.' The FBI team leader heard the voice of the eye on 78th. 'Just passed me heading south down York Avenue.'

'Target vehicle heading south on York,' he informed his supervisor, and ran for the elevator.

'We have a tail,' Sherenko informed Kincaid. 'Fine,' Kincaid told him and called Anna on the cellphone.

The hotel room was like a morgue. Wrong analogy, Anna was aware. The cellphone rang.

'It's Jack, you okay?'

'I'm okay. What about you? What about Nik?'

'We're clear. It happened as we anticipated. We're on to the next stage. Stay where you are.'

Thanks for the last words, Sherenko thought.

Can't stay here – the nerves pumped through Anna; can't seal myself off in this tomb while Nik and Jack are on the street. She pulled on the wig, pulled on the dress she had bought at Macey's, pulled on the tinted glasses. Nothing special, she thought, Nik would pick her out. But in a crowd ... She picked up her bag, made sure her money, her false passport and her father's letter were inside it, left the hotel and waved down a cab.

'Target car turning west on 77th,' the FBI agent in the lead tail car reported. No point running the switches now, no point trying to hide they were there. The target car had seen them and was trying to lose them.

Bukanin answered the cellphone on the first ring. 'Our friends seem to be going for a drive,' Vorkov told him. 'Tails are sitting on them, Penkovski and his team are sitting on the tails. Penkovski will communicate with you on this line. Keep the other clear for me.'

Change places, Bukanin told the driver. The other cellphone rang. 'Where are you?' he asked Penkovski.

'Back on 79th heading west.'

A hundred metres in front of him the lights changed to amber. Sherenko accelerated through and the lights changed to red. Fuck, the FBI driver swore softly and pressed his foot to the floor. *Chert* – Penkovski followed him through. 'Just crossed Third,' he told Bukanin.

'We have target,' the surveillance helicopter told the lead FBI car. 'Back-up on way,' the supervisor informed the team leader. 'Recommend actuate Command Post,' he told his ASAC. The command post was the FBI nerve centre on the 26th floor of the building on Federal Plaza, state of the art communications and surveillance, including computerized video facilities to blow up street maps, even individual addresses, on the silver screen in front of the half-crescent of desks.

Time to be on the street, Vorkov understood; time to oversee it all personally. Because Sherenko was setting it all up for one last stunt. Which would be good, which would be deadly. But think it through in advance, work out what Sherenko was planning, then turn it against him. Joining you, he informed Bukanin. Move it, he told his driver.

'Back on 79th and heading west,' the surveillance helicopter informed the FBI teams. 'West through Central Park on 79th Traverse Road.' So where the fuck are they going – the team leader tried to second guess the targets, tried to work out how he could best deploy his teams. 'At Central Park West,' Penkovski informed Bukanin and Vorkov. Command post in operation and SWAT teams on way, Federal Plaza informed the team leader.

The light had gone, dusk closed in. Anna paid the cab driver and hurried towards Times Square.

Sherenko checked the rear view mirror. 'Still with us,' he told Kincaid. 'Should have a chopper up by now. How you doing?'

Kincaid grabbed the seat as Sherenko skidded left. 'Thirty seconds.'

Target turning south down Central Park West, the surveillance helicopter informed the teams and the Command Post. Target on Broadway at 59th and moving south toward Times Square, Penkovski updated Bukanin and Vorkov.

'Ready,' Kincaid told Sherenko.

'Almost there.'

The traffic was round them, the lights in front on them flicking to red, and Times Square beyond. Summer night, queues at the cut-price theatre ticket booths and neon hoardings flashing on the sides of buildings. 'Stand by,' Sherenko warned Kincaid.

'Target at Times Square,' the helicopter observer reported. 'Lotta traffic,' the pilot cursed. For Chrissake don't lose him, the FBI man in the lead tail car prayed.

'Now,' Sherenko told Kincaid. He cut through the space between two cars and jumped the lights. Drove into the clear space in the centre and jammed on the brakes, leapt from the car and opened the rear door for Kincaid. Kincaid activated the switch and slid out. 'Get clear' – they were running, shouting. 'Car on fire. Clear the area.'

Anna saw the Chevrolet stop, saw them running from it.

'Target stopped in Times Square,' the surveillance helicopter reported. 'Two suspects running from it.' Get clear – Kincaid and Sherenko were still running, still shouting. The lead FBI car crashed left, on to the pavement, and accelerated through. To their left an NYPD patrol car screeched to a halt, lights flashing and sirens screaming. 'Where the hell are the targets?' the lead FBI eye almost shouted. 'I see their car, I don't seem them any more.' The woman who was his partner was at his side, running past him, her badge held high in her left hand and the 9mm in her right. 'FBI,' she shouted at the patrolman.

Anna was on the edge of the crowd. Sherenko and Kincaid ran past her. Nobody chasing them – she felt the relief; nobody running after them or trying to stop them. She followed them with her eyes then looked back at the car.

The first orange glinted in the rear seat of the Chevrolet.

'Christ,' someone shouted. 'Fire.'

'Cool it,' the FBI team leader told the eyes. 'Update on targets,' he requested.

The first flames licked over the seats and began to spread through the Chevrolet.

'They've dumped the car in Times Square,' Penkovski informed Vorkov, the man beside him updating Bukanin simultaneously. 'We can't get through, I don't know what's happening. Christ . . .' His voice rose a little. 'The car's on fire.'

'You see anyone leaving the car?' the FBI eye asked. 'Two men running away,' she was told. 'Which way?' she asked. She turned to run, her partner beside her. Oh God, they both heard the scream: there's someone in the car. Oh God, there's a woman in the car.

They turned and looked at the Chevrolet. The flames were fanning up the doors and along the ceiling, the red and yellow spreading into the front seat. Eating their way toward the engine at the front and the gas tank at the rear, and licking round the shape of the woman in the rear seat.

Priorities – the same instinct, the same training, flashed

through both their minds. Get everyone back, the male agent told the patrolmen, clear the area. The woman was already running for the car, 9mm tucked into its holster. Just make it, she thought. Perhaps it was her training, perhaps because the figure in the rear seat of the car was a woman like herself. Got to get her out, got to save her.

'Still part of the set-up,' Vorkov told Bukanin. So think it through, work out what Sherenko and Kincaid are doing now and what the bastards are going to do next. The Buick in the alleyway three blocks away, he remembered. Of course. Got you, you bastards. Except the Buick was also part of the set-up. Have to go for it, though, have to let Sherenko lead them all to the killing zone. He pulled the briefcase from the rear seat and opened it. The 486 notebook was fitted neatly inside. He opened the lid, booted up the computer and keyed in the track programme. The street map of Manhattan flicked on to the silver grey of the screen. 'This number is now off-limits, repeat, off-limits,' he told the tail car on the first cellphone, then he called Bukanin on the second and asked his location.

'54th at Avenue of the Americas and standing off.' Bukanin pulled into the kerb and waited.

'Update you in two minutes,' Vorkov informed him. He closed the call to Bukanin and used the first phone to dial into the number of the tracking device in the trunk of the Buick. A police car screamed past him, followed by another. The screen flickered slightly then the cursor flipped on in the alleyway where the Buick was parked.

Just make it, the FBI woman told herself. She was at the door of the car, trying to pull it open, the flames shooting red and the heat suddenly searing. Don't do it, Anna almost screamed at her; it's not me inside, the woman you're trying to save died days ago. Can't let you risk your life trying to save me, can't let you die for me. She broke from the crowd and began to run. The FBI woman felt the hands on her shoulders and her partner dragged her away. The flames were consuming the blue dress of the figure in the seat, the head appearing to turn and the eyes appearing to stare in anguish at her. Then the face was lost in the red and the gas tank ignited.

I'm dead therefore I can live, Anna thought; now it was only Nik and Jack who had to die.

'Stand by,' Vorkov told Bukanin. The cursor on the map on the screen of the laptop began to move. 'We're in business,' he updated Bukanin. 'On 46th at Fifth and heading east. They're in the motor they dropped this afternoon.' His driver pulled away. 'Turning left up Lexington.' They closed to two hundred metres of the target, Bukanin and the other cars closing on them. 'Still heading north up Lexington. Be aware it's still a set-up.'

'You sure you know the way?' Kincaid asked.

'Try me,' Sherenko told him.

They slowed at a set of lights and pulled forward slowly, eased to the inside lane and turned right at the next set, jumped two more sets and picked up the run into the 59th Street bridge. The East River was suddenly below them and the iron struts of the bridge whipped across the night sky above them. They left the bridge and dropped into Queens, Manhattan behind them and the streets suddenly different, the neon more garish and the pavements emptier.

Vorkov told his driver to slow, and waved Bukanin past him. 'Keep this line open,' he told Bukanin. Don't do anything unless I tell you.'

Sherenko passed under the elevated, a train clattering above them. Turned right then left and followed the street alongside the elevated. He drove faster now, whipping the Buick tighter against the kerbs and running the lights. The next set loomed in front of him. He swung right, down an alleyway, slid the Buick right again then left. The tails now close behind him. No pretence any more, no cover.

The East River glimmered on their right, and the lights of Manhattan on the far side were another world away, another lifetime. The outlines of the warehouses were in front of them, coming up fast. They passed through one gate, hanging loose on its hinges, through a second, a small fire sparkling in an oil drum in the gloom and the shapes of the derelicts silhouetted against it. Sherenko spun right and gained ten metres, the first of the tail cars now fifteen seconds behind, swung right again and accel-

354

erated down the alleyway, the warehouses blocking out the sky on either side.

Got them – Vorkov's driver saw the fence in front. Dead end.

Vorkov saw the two figures run from the Buick, saw Sherenko and Kincaid disappear through a broken doorway into the warehouse on the right. Saw Bukanin's car slam against the Buick. 'Let the boys go after them,' he ordered Bukanin. 'You and I wait.'

Sherenko and Kincaid pushed the door of the warehouse open and ran inside. Sherenko pulled the door shut and jammed a crate against it. Kincaid picked up the flashlights on the right of the door and gave one to Sherenko, gave him one of the Hecklers. Shone the flashlight up the wooden stairs and ran up them two at a time, Sherenko close behind him. Below them they heard the staccato burst, then the first of Bukanin's team bulldozed their way in. Sherenko was on the first landing, Kincaid in front, already running up the flight to the next. Sherenko fired two short bursts down the stairs, ducked round the corner as the bursts were returned, heard the silence then the footsteps coming up, and pushed the crate he had positioned on the landing down the stairs, followed it with another burst and ran up the next flight.

Penkovski ran outside, grabbed a flashlight from the pursuit car, and ran back in. Kincaid reached the next landing, picked his way along the corridor which ran off it in the beam of the flashlight, passed the room where they had stored the bodies, and stepped into the killing room at the end. There was another burst of firing from behind and below him. Christ, not much time; Christ, less time than he and Nik had planned. He told himself to focus and shone the flashlight on the floor of the room. In the beam of the flashlight he saw the glint of the trip wire. In front of him he saw the two figures behind the crates against the front wall. There was another burst behind him. He shut himself off from it, stepped over the wire, tightened it, then picked his way through the killing room and took his position in the doorway in the far right corner. Felt on the floor for the length of cord which ran from his hiding place to the crate behind which the two bodies were semi-concealed. Wait till the bastards were almost in the killing room, Sherenko had said; pull the cord, dislodge the crate slightly, and the bastard's attention would be attracted toward it. Christ where was it – his fingers felt in the dark; Christ he couldn't find it. He held the Heckler in his left hand and felt in the black with his right.

Sherenko pushed another crate down the stairs, fired another burst, exposed himself momentarily, saw the flash of light from below, sent another crate tumbling down, cleared the second landing and ran for the corridor leading to the killing room. Christ it was tight; Christ may the bastards fall for it. Christ may he have the time to get to the room on the right before they reached the top of the stairs.

In the gloom behind him Vorkov saw the fire in the oil drum burning bright against the black. In the building above him he heard the sound of footsteps running on wood, the echo of something slamming down stairs, the short staccato sound of weapons firing, then more running. Bukanin was coiled beside him. 'Sherenko's not here by accident.' Vorkov pulled the Uzi from the car. 'He's set it up.' So ... Bukanin's eyes asked. 'So let the boys deal with it. If they do, fine. If not, then we go in after Sherenko and Kincaid think they've won and have relaxed.'

Penkovski cleared the first landing and turned up the next flight of stairs. The boys were at the bend to the next. From above he heard the sound of feet running. Away from the front and towards the back, he thought. He cleared the corner and fired two bursts, ducked back and waited for the response. Go, he told the boys; shone the flashlight up the stairs, allowed three of the boys to go first and followed close behind them, picking their way with the flashlight, two more boys behind him.

Sherenko turned into the room on the right of the corridor, closed the door, tried to control his breathing, and changed magazines. Kincaid crouched behind the doorway on the far right of the killing room and scrabbled in the dark for the cord. Christ can't find it. Christ, have to find it. No noise from the killing room and the bastards might turn right into the room where Nik was hiding. Christ, where is it? Can't put on the flashlight, because that might tell the bastards where he was in the doorway. His fingers touched the cord.

The first gunman hit the second landing, saw the corridor in front of him and the next flight of stairs round the turn to his left. He dropped into a crouch, fired one burst down the corridor, moved left, and fired a second burst up the stairs. No sound – he listened carefully; no one running. The other two lead gunmen joined him, Penkovski close behind and taking cover against the wall of the landing, and the other tensed on the stairs. Sherenko held his breath. Do it, he whispered silently to Kincaid. ·

The gunmen heard the sound. Somewhere in the black at the end of the corridor leading away from them toward the rear of the building. Penkovski held the flashlight away from his body, swung the beam down the corridor, and gave the lead gunmen enough light. The gunman fired one burst and dropped back behind the wall. No response. Penkovski moved slightly and redirected the beam. The two gunmen on the stairs went past him, down the corridor, firing continuously. Penkovski followed, more gunmen behind him. Door on right, he noted automatically. He turned to tell the gunman behind him to check it out.

Kincaid pulled the cord again and Penkovski heard the sound. Turned away from the door and directed the beam into the room at the end of the corridor. Part of the light was cut out by the men in front, part of it reached like a finger to the wall at the rear. In the split second before the men in front of him opened fire he saw the two shapes. The noise around him was deafening. In that part of the beam which penetrated to the far wall he saw the figures more clearly, saw the moment they began to tumble. No return fire – his reaction was automatic; no problems. The lead gunmen ran into the room, the first still firing then dropping and the second firing over his head while the first changed mags, Penkovski and the others close behind. Christ the room was a mess, Christ there was only one narrow way through. The second gunmen stopped firing, the first stood and moved forward. One pace, two. Still no return fire. Three paces. His right foot broke the trip wire.

Vorkov heard the explosion. 'Bastard.' He turned to Bukanin. Set-up, his face said, except now Sherenko thinks he's won. '*Vpered*.' Let's do it. He entered the building, Bukanin in front of him and the rats scuttling in panic.

Sherenko stepped from the room on the right. Held the flashlight in his left hand, high in the air and away from his body, the Heckler in his right. The dust rolled down the corridor, from inside the killing room he heard the sounds of men screaming. He leaned forward in the combat position and eased his finger on the trigger. In the doorway on the far right Kincaid stepped one pace forward and opened fire.

Vorkov and Bukanin trod carefully. Up one flight of stairs, the wood rickety and giving way, first landing, then another set leading up. From above, and to the rear of the building, came the sounds of execution.

Sherenko stopped firing, changed magazines, and listened. Waited three seconds until the firing from Kincaid's position also stopped. A last death rattle echoed in the killing room, then the silence fell like a shroud. He edged forward, Heckler still in the combat position and finger on trigger.

'You all right, Jack?' he asked.

'All right, Nik.'

Vorkov heard the voice. In front of him Bukanin froze. Vorkov gave it three seconds then touched Bukanin on the back and told him to continue. Their footsteps were silent in the dust. They cleared the first flight of stairs from the landing, turned the corner, and edged their way silently up the second.

Sherenko allowed the Heckler to drop slightly. One more thing to do, one more explosion, plus the fire, so that the two bodies from Belle Vue could only be identified as himself and Kincaid, by the ring one wore and the remnants of a watch round the wrist of the other. Then he and Jack were dead. He relaxed a little more, changed magazines automatically but allowed the Heckler to swing to his side.

The dust was beginning to clear. Kincaid stepped from the doorway into the killing room. Change mags – it was as if he heard Sherenko's voice in the range in Moscow. No need, he told himself; everything done, everything over. That's the time you change mags – it was if he and Sherenko were back in the range, the young bloods looking at them and telling them they were too old for it. The dust cleared a little more. Left hand to mag, eject empty mag. Left hand in left coat pocket because that's where you keep spare mags. The beam from Sherenko's flashlight picked out the details of the carnage in the room. One of the bodies was also holding a flashlight, the beam pointing up toward the ceiling. Kincaid stepped forward cautiously. One of the crates creaked, the position of the body changed slightly, and the beam from the flashlight it was holding flickered from the ceiling toward the doorway to the corridor. The dust behind Sherenko was settling, Sherenko silhouetted against it.

'Nik, down.' It was somewhere between a shout and a command.

Kincaid's left hand was still in his coat pocket. In one fluid extended movement he pulled out the spare mag, snapped it in, brought the Heckler into the combat position, and squeezed the trigger. Hope to Christ Nik reacts – it was in his subconscious; hope he understands and reacts quickly enough.

Sherenko dropped, rolled forward and left, and turned. Heckler coming out and firing into the dark and the dust behind him. Two figures, Jack's round passing above him where his head and body had been. Figures behind him with fingers pressing triggers as Jack had shouted. His finger was still on the trigger, Jack's on his, and the fire unremitting, the figures falling so he was in Jack's line of fire, then Jack stopping, clearing the bodies in the killing room and changing mags again, standing over him as he changed mags and keeping up the fire power.

The silence descended again. Sherenko rose, picked up the flashlight, and shone the beam on the faces.

'Who?' Kincaid asked.

'Red Sox and Vorkov.' He straightened. 'Thanks, Jack.'

'No problems.'

Personal, Nik, not business.

Sherenko pulled the bodies into the killing room. 'So we're dead. So let's finish it.'

Round the fire a hundred metres away the derelicts heard the explosion. They turned, stared for a handful of seconds at the flames licking into the night sky from the warehouse, then shrugged their shoulders, reached for the Jack Daniels, and turned back in on themselves again.

OMEGA
the ending

The first snow of the new winter was sprinkled on Berlin's Kurfürstendamm, the Christmas lights hung in the shops, and the square in front of the Europa Centre was packed with stalls, as it always was at this time of year. The smell of candy floss and chestnuts drifted in the air, and the sound of barrel organs and children's laughter rose into the dark of the late afternoon sky.

Yuri Dushkin bought himself a plastic beaker of glühwein and watched a juggler.

So it was almost over; the last run coming in from Russia tomorrow, then the secret faces who ran the organization had decided there should be no more. Perhaps the death of Vorkov in New York, perhaps other reasons. Not that it concerned Yuri Dushkin. In this world things began and things ended. Alpha and Omega. Besides, he had enough contacts to continue in his own way, enough items already in the pipeline. And the last shipment alone was worth around twenty million dollars. So life was good. He laughed at a monkey dancing on a barrel organ and bought another glühwein.

Malenkov lay spreadeagled on the bed. The incense drifted above him, or perhaps it was the shapes of the two women; the candles flickered around him and the champagne seeped gently into the cells of his brain. Malenkov groaned as they worked on him, moved around and against and over him. Sometimes touching him, stroking him; sometimes, if they saw it exhilarated him, each other. Malenkov had always liked threesomes. Either way. It didn't matter.

The last run into Berlin tomorrow. Pity, but everything had to end. Time to pull out, time to be careful. At least for a while. His body was oiled and his mind was slipping into another level of pleasure. One of the women was taking him in her mouth, the second doing something to the first and the first writhing slightly. He laughed and reached for the champagne, drank some and poured some over himself, over the women, he wasn't sure. The first woman's tongue was almost penetrating him, the second woman moving round the bed. He felt the cold round his ankles and his wrists, and the exhilaration as his body was stretched and the handcuffs clipped on to the posts of the bed.

The room was suddenly silent, suddenly empty. He turned his head and saw the other woman. She was dressed in black. Not one of those who had worked him so deliciously. He saw only half her face, her features lost in shadow. Saw the liquid glint in the candlelight as she tested the syringe, his mind suddenly clear, suddenly aware. 'What are you doing . . .' he heard his own voice.

Miller accepted another malt and laughed at the latest of a long round of shooting jokes his host was telling. The shoot that afternoon had gone well and the drinks after, in the most English of English pubs, had gone even better. The beaters had been allowed to join them, their wives serving the food. The Land-Rovers were parked outside, the dogs sprawled in the backs, their tongues lapping, and the guns securely locked away.

Last run into Berlin tomorrow. Good call to end it. The mistake most people made was not knowing when to call it a day, when to cut one's losses and get out. Not that there were losses, of course. Christ, no.

His bladder was full. Miller laughed an excuse and went to the gents. The door was locked. He pushed open the emergency exit next to it and stepped into the cold of the night. The sky was clear, glistening with stars but no moon. He undid his trousers and leaned against one of the Land-Rovers. 'Hello, Ed . . .' he heard the voice.

Sheila Harrington gunned the 900 and thought back to the college reunion she had just left, thought forward to what the rest of the night, the rest of the week, might bring. The road was clear and the stars were bright above her. Pity about New York, but in a way New York had decided them. Time to close down for a while, time to play another game. Lots to play with now, of course. The country road was deserted, she opened the sun roof and felt the wind whip round her. In the headlights she saw the Alvis slewed into the ditch on the right. Don't stop, she told herself, partly instinct, partly training. The Alvis had been parked at the hotel where the reunion had been held – she remembered seeing it, remembered the man who had waved to some of the other girls as if he knew them. Now she saw him again. Old and white-haired. Not waving her down to help him. Bent over the Alvis and trying to push the vintage motor back on to the road. She pulled in front and wound down the window. 'You'll never get it out,' she told him. 'There's a garage up the road, you can phone from there.'

'Thank you,' he told her and slid into the passenger seat beside her.

'Saw you earlier,' she began to say.

Yuri Dushkin allowed his mind to drift, allowed himself to enjoy the champagne. The last run would come in tonight; tomorrow he would organize its unloading and the day after he would fly to Zurich, confirm the provenances he had arranged for those items needing such attention, confirm with New York the anticipated sale price of the rock he had delivered in August. The music centre played Queen and the champagne bottle was half empty to his right. Dushkin thought he heard a noise and began to turn, realized he could not have done because the door was locked and began to turn back. Turned anyway, for no logical reason.

'You . . .' he could hardly speak the words. 'They said you were dead . . .'

'Hello, Yuri . . .' she greeted him. Behind her he saw the other two shadows. 'The last run . . . Change of plan. Just for this one. Temporary change of ownership . . .'

For some reason unexplained to the public, Red Square had remained closed that day, barricades blocking the entrances and guards turning away those who sought access, so that the snow across the cobbles was pure and unbroken.

The two men were wrapped against the cold. One was tall, big build, and the other was equally tall but slimmer. They walked with their hands dug deep into the pockets of their overcoats, their collars turned up.

The barrier was in front of them, the guards sheltering to their right. The first man – the bigger of the two – moved the barrier aside and they walked through, their footsteps the only break in the white of the snow.

'So what happened?' Gerasimov asked.

'What do you think happened?' Jameson was noncommittal.

They walked on, Lenin's mausoleum on their right and the lights of the GUM department store on their left.

'The bodies themselves were unidentifiable of course . . .' Jameson dug his hands deeper into the warmth of the coat pockets. 'Identification of Anna by a ring her father gave her. Sherenko by an Alpha ring. Kincaid by an inscription on a watch.' What remained of the rings and watch, because little remained of anything. In the car in Times Square or the warehouse in Queens.

'But they're dead . . .' Gerasimov.

'Is that a question or a statement?' Jameson.

'Whichever way you want to take it.'

'They were dead anyway, of course. No matter what happened.'

They walked on, the snow clear in front of them and their footprints in a line behind them.

'Strange about Malenkov and Miller and Harrington,' Gerasimov suggested.

'Why strange?'

'Heart attack, gun accident and road traffic accident.'

'All in the same night.' Jameson laughed.

Saviour's Gate was to their right, and the wind cut from the north, whipping the snow into small flurries round them. They came to St Basil's, walked through the small garden and sat on the covered steps on the right.

'Interesting thing happened the other day.' Gerasimov took

the Lagavulin from the pocket of his overcoat and broke the seal. 'Actually, it's happened more than once.' He unscrewed the top, took a *stogram*, and breathed deeply as the heat seared his throat. 'Alpha men, or their wives or widows. Veterans from the first Afghan op.' You know the story, he didn't need to say. The guys go in, do the job, then the Kremlin says screw you, you're on your own. No way back. No acknowledgements, no pensions. 'Anyway, I've been getting phone calls from them.' He took another *stogram* and passed the bottle to Jameson.

'Why?'

'They were phoning to say thanks.'

The woman's feet and body and face were cold, but not as cold as they would be when the winter really set in. Most of the others had already left, but it was when you were alone that you sometimes stood a chance of making a last sale.

Love you, my husband, will fight for you till the day I die. Know that if you could you would work, that if you could you would stand here in my place. But you can't. Not since you were a young man. Such a young man, such a lover. Then you went to Afghanistan, and that was the end. So today I stand at the metro station at Tverskaya, as I stand every day. Today, even in the cold, I try to keep my shoulders straight and some semblance of pride in my face, even though the world passes me by. Today, as every day, I wear your medals and your lapel badge, in the hope that someone might remember what you fought for, yet in the knowledge that in the world today no one cares. Please God may I last this winter, because if I do not no one will care for you. Please God that when we go, you go before me, because if I go first there will be no one to look after you.

Her fingers were stiff with cold. She placed the cassettes in the plastic bag, tucked the tray under her arm, and hurried down the steps and into the passageway to the station. A student was playing a violin, the music haunting and painful. She went down the escalator and stood waiting. The digital clock at the end of the platform showed that the last train had passed through forty-eight seconds before. She held the plastic bag tight – some-one might put their hand in, someone might steal her precious cassettes. Soup tonight, my husband, because that is all we can afford. The train came and she stood aside, allowed those on the train to get off first. A man and a woman passed her – she was only half aware of them, not even half aware. Well-dressed, so not pickpockets. The man bumped into her – just enough to disturb her balance. Sorry – the woman held her arm and apologized to her. Okay – she smiled back. Expected the man and woman to step on with her but they were no longer there.

The doors closed and the train jerked on, stopping, the compartment emptying till she was almost alone. Oh Christ – the fear hit her. The man behind her when the couple had bumped into her ... Her bag and her precious cassettes ... She tried to control the panic and opened the neck of the bag. Looked inside, saw the cassettes, and felt the flood of relief.

She saw the envelope.

Brown and thick.

Not my envelope – it was as if she was talking to herself, talking to her husband. I didn't put it there; it wasn't there when I left the room we call home this morning. Wasn't there when I laid out the cassettes on my tray, or when I packed them into the bag after I had finished trying to sell them tonight.

Her fingers were trembling. She reached down into the bag and held the envelope, saw the way it was sealed, saw the plastic band around it.

She took the envelope out and saw the words on it.

Na Pamyat ob Afghanistane. For the memory of Afghanistan. Why, she thought. What did it mean?

Her fingers were still trembling. She took off the band and opened the envelope. Inside, in pristine new-issue notes, were two hundred and fifty thousand United States dollars.

Kara's Game

Gordon Stevens

'A blockbuster . . . a lesson in political reality'
Guardian

Once, behind the lines in Bosnia, she saved the lives of two
SAS soldiers. And they made Kara a promise. 'We will
never forget. Anything you want, you have. Anything you
need, you get.'

Now the tables are turned. Kara's in the West – Paris,
Amsterdam, London. And she's dangerous. Now the
powers-that-be call her a terrorist.

Now the SAS have been sent to kill her.

So what about their promise?

'A cracking thriller with all the pace and tension and
authenticity of *The Day of the Jackal*'   *Publishing News*

'Luminescent . . . Anger and compassion shine through
the characters'   *Daily Telegraph*

ISBN 0 00 649781 0

Kennedy's Ghost

Gordon Stevens

A nerve-shredding thriller of kidnap,
conspiracy and assassination

Former SAS man Dave Haslam is hired to negotiate the
release of a top banker being held to ransom in Italy. In
America, Deputy Director Brettlaw of the CIA has dark
reasons of his own to fear for the banker's safety, while
charismatic politician Jack Donaghue is striding ever
closer to the White House ... and the deepest secret of the
Camelot years.

Haslam, Brettlaw, Donaghue: three men on a collision
course, on a switchback ride of intrigue and suspense, on
the shocking trail of *Kennedy's Ghost*.

'Gordon Stevens is a first-rate thriller writer, all action,
plot and tension'   *Today*

ISBN 0 00 649002 6

Provo

Gordon Stevens

Two women. One war. No rules.

Catcher is the codename of Cathy Nolan, working under-cover for MI5 in Northern Ireland, fighting against not only a major IRA threat, but also the internal politics of her own side.

Sleeper is the perfect assassin, put in place years ago, unknown even to the top-ranking members of the Provisionals' Army Council.

PinMan is the target of this, the ultimate coup. Now there is no way of stopping the mission.

Provo is the novel that redefines the modern thriller. From Whitehall to Belfast, Hereford to South Armagh, it is an adrenaline-pumping, white-knuckle ride behind the head-lines to a land of danger and betrayal.

'Hugely enjoyable and gripping tale . . . with a refreshingly non-partisan approach'   *Time Out*

ISBN 0 00 647632 5

Peace on Earth

Gordon Stevens

Collision course . . .

A young Palestinian born to live in a holy land, almost certainly to die in an act of violence.

An Israeli family, finally allowed to put a lifetime of persecution in Russia behind them, flying to a future full of hope.

An SAS officer, his years of training counting down to minutes of heartstopping action.

Destiny will bring them together in the terrifying drama of a hijack that will mesmerize the world.

Unbearable tension, powerful emotion, chillingly authentic detail make *Peace on Earth* one of the most stunningly brilliant novels of recent times.

'An explosive novel packed with emotion, insight and action'
CLIVE CUSSLER

ISBN 0 00 647315 6

The Heart of Danger

Gerald Seymour

'Unmissable' *The Times*

In a wrecked Croat village, a mass grave is uncovered and the mutilated body of a young Englishwoman, Dorrie Mowat, is exhumed.

Her mother, who loathed Dorrie in life, becomes obsessed by the need to find out about her death. But with civil war tearing apart the former Yugoslavia, none of the authorities there or in Britain are interested in a 'minor' war crime.

So she turns to Bill Penn, private investigator, MI5 reject. For him this looks like a quick trip to safe Zagreb, the writing of a useless report and a good fee at the end of it. But once there he finds himself drawn inexorably towards the killing ground behind the lines, to find the truth of the young woman's death and, perhaps, the truth of himself.

Penn's search for evidence that could, one day, convict a war criminal in a court of law becomes an epic journey into a merciless war where the odds are stacked high against him.

'It's impossible to find fault with this book, which builds relentlessly to its climax. It has an intense feeling of authenticity and it's well written'

NICHOLAS FLEMING, *Spectator*

'Vivid stuff. I write a fortnight after finishing the book and some of the scenes of pursuit and mindless cruelty still return to me' DOUGLAS HURD, *Daily Telegraph*

ISBN 0 00 649033 6

Charity
Len Deighton

The stunning conclusion to the Bernard Samson trilogy,
Faith, *Hope* and *Charity*

Bernard continues to chip away at the mystery of his
sister-in-law Tessa Kosinski's death in Berlin on the
crucial night when his wife Fiona was brought out of the
East. Fighting to uncover the truth, he must also confront
the key relationships in his own life: Fiona is still far
from stable now that she has returned to work, and their
children remain in the clutches of his wealthy and mani-
pulative father-in-law. Meanwhile, Werner Volkmann,
Bernard's friend since childhood, is reluctant to get
involved in Bernard's crusade.

A wonderful depiction both of covert operations and office
politics, *Charity* is packed with action, incident and
intrigue, bringing to a triumphant conclusion a series of
ten novels that represents one of the great achievements of
modern English fiction.

'Here is the master of espionage writing at his brilliant best
… an authentic, compelling read'   *Mail on Sunday*

'Deighton's prose is tough, clean and compelling … story-
telling of this high quality will never go out of fashion'
                                        Sunday Express

ISBN 0 00 647900 6

Under Siege

Stephen Coonts

'Brilliant, exciting and highly provocative. An impressive tour de force'   TOM CLANCY

In a stunning explosion of terror, America's worst nightmares come true when Colombian suicide squads hit the streets of Washington. They have gone to war and will destroy everything and everybody in their path.

With its power and communications systems blown apart, the city is plunged into turmoil. In the Pentagon, Captain Jake Grafton and the Joint Chiefs of Staff face the most deadly challenge ever to threaten America.

But while confusion and chaos rule the streets, a ruthless hunter, serving an unknown master, has his own catastrophic mission. He will not rest until he has wiped out the whole cabinet, starting with the President himself . . .

'Nobody does it better than Stephen Coonts. He's unsurpassed at creating a story that bristles with intrigue, excitement and surprise'   CLIVE CUSSLER

'A terrific novel . . . a hell of a story. Coonts gives the idea some special twists and tells it with pulse-racing excitement'   *New York Daily News*

ISBN 0 00 647062 9